CAT &
MOUSE

Also by M.J. Arlidge

CAT &
MOUSE

M.J. Arlidge

ORION

First published in Great Britain in 2022 by Orion Fiction,
an imprint of The Orion Publishing Group Ltd.,
Carmelite House, 50 Victoria Embankment
London EC4Y 0DZ

An Hachette UK Company

1 3 5 7 9 10 8 6 4 2

A CIP catalogue record for this book is
available from the British Library.

ISBN (Hardback) 978 1 409 18850 6
ISBN (Trade Paperback) 978 1 409 18851 3
ISBN (eBook) 978 1 409 18853 7

Typeset at The Spartan Press Ltd,
Lymington, Hants

Printed and bound in Great Britain by Clays Ltd,
Elcograf S.p.A.

www.orionbooks.co.uk

Day One

Chapter 1

Martha White stirred, rolling onto her side and clutching her pillow. She'd been caught in a strange netherworld between sleep and wakefulness, her uneasy rest punctured by nightmares of missed connections and lost children, but a noise downstairs had brought her back to reality. Often she was aggravated by Greg's return – trainers tossed off noisily in the hall, fridge door slammed shut – but tonight she was glad of the disturbance. She always slept better when she knew her husband was home.

Settling back down, Martha buried her face in the soft cotton, breathing in the washing powder scent, praying that sleep – *proper sleep* – would claim her. She was bone-tired, the customary round of chores and childcare having sapped her last vestiges of energy. Given the chance now she would sleep for a thousand years, happily embracing the oblivion of the night, waking refreshed and revitalized, ready to be the mum she always hoped she *could* be. But this was not an option, of course. She would be up at the crack of dawn, so the best she could hope for was a few hours of decent rest before duty called.

Happily, Greg was not lingering tonight. Sometimes when he returned from training, adrenaline coursing through him, he'd loiter downstairs, snacking, watching TV, catching up on emails. But already she could hear him locking the front door and switching off the hall lights, a sound that always reduced Martha's anxiety levels, signalling the true beginning of the night. Grateful, Martha felt a pulse of love surge through her. Despite their occasional differences, she and Greg *were* a good team – kind, caring and always thoughtful towards one another. She knew they were lucky to have found each other, luckier still to have been blessed with a happy, healthy child. There was so much misery, disappointment and anger out there in the world – they were the fortunate ones.

Sleep was fast claiming Martha and it was with a lazy tug that she hauled over Greg's side of the duvet, revealing a welcoming patch of pressed white sheet. How nice it would be to drift off in his arms. How nice to be at peace, if only for a few precious hours. Martha's body felt heavy, her consciousness dimmed, barely registering the gentle closing of the bedroom door, then Greg's measured tread towards the bed. But she felt the mattress sag as he climbed in beside her and she gently slid her bottom towards him, waiting for his bulk to envelop her. Did life get any better than this?

To her surprise, however, nothing happened. Martha was so nearly asleep now, lost to all-consuming fatigue, yet still she registered the lack of contact, the absence of Greg's muscular body next to hers. Why was he holding off? What was he *doing*? And now through her groggy confusion, Martha realized something. The mattress was sagging more than usual tonight, an unexpectedly heavy weight pushing down on it, her body sliding inexorably towards her companion. And, even as confusion consumed her, Martha noticed something else – a smell. An unfamiliar aroma, musky and intense, like a man's aftershave ...

Martha's eyes snapped open, her heart pounding. Panicking, she tried to turn, to cry out. But before she could so, a hand clamped down forcefully over her lips, stifling her scream.

4

Chapter 2

A piercing shriek rent the air, then rubber bit tarmac and the bike sprang forwards, roaring away from the scene of the crime. Within seconds, the impounded boat was just a speck in Detective Inspector Helen Grace's mirrors, her Kawasaki Ninja propelling her away from Southampton Docks. It had been a successful night, but now she wanted to be away.

It was a bitterly cold January night and fog shrouded Millbrook Road, as Helen powered along the dual carriageway. Within seconds, she found herself at the Teboura Way round-about and, swinging right, she changed direction, doubling back on herself and heading fast towards the city centre through the suffocating mist. In one sense, these conditions were comforting – in the fog you could be anonymous, secretive, concealed. But in another way, they were alarming, as it was impossible to tell who might be lurking within the dank, cloying shroud.

Helen kept low over her handlebars, her eyes searching for – *anticipating* – danger. She made it to Winchester Road without incident and before long was bearing down on the heart of this complex, damaged city. Now a number of options opened up to her, an assortment of routes back to her flat, the selection of which seemed fraught with peril. Helen always chose at random, having only one rule – that she never used the same route on successive days. Perhaps she was being overcautious, but she was not prepared to take any chances – not when she had a death sentence hanging over her.

Helen was celebrated at Southampton Central for bringing her cases to a successful conclusion, but her last investigation had ended badly. Yes, she had brought a killing spree to an end, unravelling the mystery that lay behind a series of baffling murders, but the perpetrator had escaped, vowing to revenge himself on Helen by sending an anonymous killer her way at a moment of *his* choosing. It had been four months since Alex Blythe's chilling threat, four months during which Helen had hardly slept.

Helen knew that she was running scared, jumping at shadows, but it was impossible not to be fearful when you considered how far Blythe's reach extended. A psychiatrist and addiction counsellor, Blythe had compromising material on scores of local people – husbands, wives, mothers, fathers who had confessed all to him, believing that their sins, their obsessions, their addictions would remain confidential. Blythe had chosen to use this information against them, coercing his patients into killing for his pleasure and, though his reign of terror was at an end, there was one more murder he intended to execute.

Keeping alert for fellow bikers, for vehicles pulling alongside her, Helen swung suddenly across the traffic, nipping ahead of a dawdling car to dart down Bentham Street. Her journey home was always like this – fitful, erratic, improvised. If she couldn't predict her route home, then hopefully neither could a potential assassin. It was exhausting, living one's life in permanent expectation of violent death, but Helen could see no other way. For even if her logical self urged her not to see phantoms in the shadows, her animal side remained forever alert, regarding even the narcotics officers at tonight's port raid with suspicion, anyone she couldn't personally vouch for now a source of concern. Given Helen's chequered past, the list of bona fide allies was very short, hence her constant state of alert.

She was now on Firth Street, bearing down on her flat. Part of her longed to be back there, within those familiar walls, but another part of her was tempted to keep going – to drive along the coastal road or even north to the M25, where she could weave in and out of the traffic, forever one step ahead of her destiny. It was foolish, but these days she never felt safer than when she was roaring along the open road. It was, she reasoned, harder to hit a moving target.

One day perhaps it would be over. Maybe the National Crime Agency or Interpol would get a fix on Blythe, finally bringing her persecutor to book. But in the meantime, her paranoia, her suspicion, continued to run rampant, her nightmare seemingly without end.

Chapter 3

Martha kept her eyes shut, praying for her ordeal to be over.

Her attacker had ordered her to lie face down on the bed and Martha hadn't dared resist, even when he stuffed a dirty rag in her mouth and wrenched her arms backwards, binding her wrists together. Seconds after this, she'd felt his fingers seek out hers and for a disorienting moment, she'd thought he was trying to hold her hand. But then she felt a sharp tug on her wedding band and realized the nature of his intentions. Her engagement ring soon followed, both yanked without ceremony from her protesting flesh, before her assailant relented, rising and moving away.

Momentarily, Martha was too shocked to react, but confusion and alarm now turned to anger. This was *her* house, *her* bedroom, those were *her* rings – treasured keepsakes that spoke of her commitment to Greg, but which also conjured up precious memories of their engagement in Hawaii and wedding in Beaulieu. How dare he snatch her rings away as if they were mere baubles, chunks of metal and stone to be sold for cold, hard cash. What kind of low-life was he? Even now, she could hear the intruder rifling through her jewellery box, helping himself to a lifetime of gifts and purchases, not to mention the heirlooms she'd inherited from her mother, before her untimely death.

8

Keep it together, Martha. Keep it together.

The words sprang to her mind, unbidden, but welcome. Yes, half of her wanted to scream, to yank at her ties, to thrash out her outrage, but her wiser half counselled caution, reminding her what was at stake. Images of Bailey suddenly filled her thoughts and Martha's outrage immediately vanished, replaced instead with concern for her baby girl. As long as both she and her daughter were unharmed at the end of this awful attack, what did it matter if she lost a few valuables? She felt foolish now for caring about things which could be replaced, maybe even recovered. It was flesh and blood that counted.

She had to keep quiet and sit it out. To do as she was told, then wait, helpless but relieved, for Greg to come home. As she thought this, anger bullied its way into her thoughts – why *wasn't* Greg here to protect them? – but she quickly shrugged off these fruitless accusations. This wasn't his fault. The only person to blame here was the violent intruder now stalking her home.

Her attacker had finished ransacking the dresser and once more all was quiet. Martha didn't dare look, hardly dared to breathe, waiting for the thief to leave the room and pad away down the corridor. She strained her ears to take in his departure, but to her alarm, he now headed back to the bed, climbing onto the mattress. Instinctively, Martha pulled her knees up, clamping them together. Terror mastered her – she felt breathless and dizzy, even as tears filled her eyes. Was his grim theft just the opening insult, the first part of a sickening violation of her life and happiness? Suddenly, Martha knew she had to move and she lurched sideways, attempting to throw herself off the bed. She had barely shifted her body, however, before a heavy hand clapped her on the back, forcing her down. Still Martha bucked, desperately trying to free herself, but her attacker's hold was unyielding, the weight of his arm flattening her. Any moment now she expected to feel his coarse hands on her, tearing at her clothes, her skin, but to her surprise nothing happened. It was as if he was just sitting there, staring at her. She could feel his eyes boring into her, as they lay on the bed together like an odd couple...

And now suddenly, with total clarity, Martha knew *exactly* what was happening. Knew that the situation was far worse than she had initially imagined. This was the reckoning. What the events of the last two years had been building inexorably towards. Now Martha *did* open her eyes, craning around to see her attacker, determined to beg for her life, despite the awful, choking rag in her mouth. But once more she was pushed back down, her nemesis unwilling to face her.

Desperately, Martha's eyes scanned the room, searching for some means of salvation. Her gaze was drawn to the mirror on the wardrobe door, which provided her with a partial view of her tormentor. He was swathed in shadow, sinister and indistinct, but even so she knew it was him, knew what he had come for. And now, as if in answer to this sickening realization, she noticed him move, raising something above his head. Fixing her eyes on the mirror, Martha tried to work out what it was, peering through the near darkness, as her heart pulsed with terror. And now, finally, she saw it – the blade of a hatchet catching the light sneaking in from the landing.

Martha froze, then with a sudden burst of energy, she screamed, screamed for all she was worth, even as the damp cloth slid down her windpipe. It was painful, muffled and ultimately fruitless – before her muted scream had ended, her attacker struck, bringing the axe down hard on the back of her head.

Chapter 4

Nothing stirred, nothing moved. Outside, the unforgiving wind could be heard, rattling the windows and shaking the letterboxes. But inside, the house was quiet as the grave.

Turning the lights off, Detective Sergeant Charlie Brooks headed upstairs, taking care to avoid the seventh step which always protested loudly, keen not to disturb her slumbering children. Jessica and Orla were a handful at the best of times, but had been particularly trying tonight, bickering, crying, answering back, leaving Charlie utterly exhausted by the time they finally went to sleep. She'd been supposed to read with Jessica tonight, the elder of her two, but couldn't face it, instead adding a fictitious entry to her reading record and opting for a glass of wine instead. The crisp Sauvignon Blanc had been refreshing, but hadn't dispelled the knot of tension in her stomach. It would take more than alcohol to do that.

Cresting the stairs, Charlie slid across the landing into the master bedroom. Her hand moved instinctively towards the light switch, but then she pulled it back. She didn't want its harsh glare tonight, illuminating the neat, empty bed, so opted instead for the comfort of darkness. Increasingly Charlie preferred it this way, often getting undressed in the gloom, preferring not to draw attention to her post-baby figure, which had once been trim and lithe, but now felt lumpen and unattractive. At first, she'd done this to conceal her form from long-term partner Steve, but now she did it as much for herself, though this scarcely made her feel any better.

Sipping her wine, Charlie sat down on the bed, pulling her phone from her pocket. She scrolled through her recent calls, then, after a moment's hesitation pressed CALL. Immediately she felt the knot in her stomach tighten. She knew she was being silly, a little crazy even, but she wanted to talk to him, to be reassured by his smooth, gentle voice. But with dull predictability, voicemail clicked in.

'Hi, this is Steve. Leave a message!'

Charlie hung up, tossing the phone onto the bed. Another night spent alone, another night wondering where he was. Every time she asked, he blamed work, saying he'd been kept late at the body shop, but where was all this work coming from, this sudden flurry of vehicle repairs? What was so pressing that he had to spend night after night away from home? It made her angry, it made her resentful. But more than that it made her scared. It was their anniversary soon – an event Steve normally made a big deal of – but this year he'd hardly said a word about it. It was as if he was no longer interested, as if he no longer *cared*.

Rising, Charlie crossed to the window, tugging the curtains aside. The wind had dropped now and the darkened street was lifeless and cold, as if frozen in time. She longed for some activity to distract her – a couple snuggling as they hurried along, a dog walker braving the elements, even Steve scurrying back home – but there was nothing, no movement at all. Charlie felt a wave of emotion rise within her, distress cloaked in panic, and she tried to clamp it back down. She must not be paranoid, not let her anxiety run away with her. Instead, she should gather herself, do something productive – there was plenty of casework to catch up on and numerous domestic duties outstanding – yet despite her best intentions, she found she couldn't move. She was gripped by insecurity, by fear, and though she knew she was torturing herself, she remained stock-still, staring out into the night, lost in the darkness.

Chapter 5

He paused on the threshold, looking back into the room. Martha White's lifeless body lay on the bed, hidden in the gloom. From a distance, you'd think she was slumbering, dead to the world. But the blood spatters on the wall, which were now creeping their way earthwards, staining the wallpaper an obscene crimson, gave the lie to that fantasy.

A woman's cardigan hung on a chair by the door and he paused now, wiping the axe blade on the fabric, watching with fascination as the wool sucked up the viscous liquid. Satisfied that the blade was clean, he turned and moved away down the corridor. The carpet was rich and yielding, the sound of his tread consumed by the thick pile, yet to him each step sounded like a hammer blow, alerting the world to his crime. His brain was pulsing, his heart pounding. Having done the deed, he now just wanted to get the hell out.

He hurried towards the staircase, but even as he did so an ear-splitting cry rang out. It was so sudden, so unexpected that he jumped out of his skin, before spinning to face his accuser. But there was no one in the corridor, no one near the scene of his crime and to his surprise, he now realized that the noise was coming from the bedroom across the landing. His instant reaction was to turn and run, but so piercing was the noise that instead he pushed open the door and hurried inside, determined to confront his accuser.

As he did so, he realized how addled his thinking had become. In the gentle light of a rotating mobile, a baby girl was illuminated, hollering for all she was worth. Crossing quickly to the cot, the intruder stared down at the unhappy infant. He wasn't sure what he'd been expecting, but his sudden appearance only distressed her further, the baby's face screwing up in alarm. The sheer force of her crying, the savage volume of her cries took him aback. Is it possible she *knew*? That somehow she'd sensed her mother's death and was determined to raise the alarm, trumpeting her outrage in the hope that good folk would now descend on her killer? Surely there could be no other explanation for the superhuman decibels that she dragged from her tiny lungs? Was she accusing him? *Shaming* him?

He had to make her stop. Even putting aside his paranoia, it was possible her persistent crying would alert passersby or excite the interest of neighbours. Even as he thought this, he heard a noise outside. Was it someone opening the garden gate? Coming to investigate? Turning to face the infant, he knew she had to be silenced, that he could not make his escape with this persistent alarm ringing out. Gripping the handle of the hatchet, he stared at the baby girl, willing her to cease crying, but her little face was puce with distress, beyond consolation. There would be no stopping her... unless *he* stopped her.

This had never been his intention, she was the innocent in all this, but suddenly he felt as if he had no choice, as if life, fate, karma was driving him towards this grievous act. Slowly, he raised the axe, willing himself to be bold, to screw down his courage. Looking away from the scrunched-up face, he counted down from three.

Three, two, one...

Letting out a curse, he brought the axe down.

But as he did so, he caught himself, stopping the blade in mid-air. Something had captured his attention. And now, in spite of himself, he let out a laugh, a long belly laugh. It was so obvious, so bloody obvious – why hadn't he thought of it before? Lying next to the baby's sticky mouth, half concealed under her chubby cheek, was a dummy. A bright yellow dummy. This was what she'd been craving, its absence the cause of her sudden distress.

Lowering the axe, he picked up the dummy, placing it gently in her mouth. Immediately, the howling ceased, the baby sucking contentedly on the rubber teat. Even more amazingly, within seconds, the little girl was asleep, her distress forgotten. Peace reigned, the silence broken only by the gentle music of the spinning mobile.

Shocked, but relieved, the intruder turned on his heel and hurried out of the room, leaving the unwitting baby girl to her slumber.

Chapter 6

Helen moved fast up the silent stairwell, her gaze searching the dark corners, the gloomy doorways. But the home straight presented no dangers tonight – she was quite alone.

Mounting the top-floor landing, Helen hurried to her front door. Swiftly, she slid a key into the upper deadlock, then the lower one, before moving on to the latch key. Moments later, she was inside, the steel door bolted and secured behind her. Routine now kicked in and, baton drawn, she moved cautiously from room to room, satisfying herself that no intruders lay in wait. Helen was exhausted, out on her feet, and part of her was tempted to throw herself down on the bed and pass out, but fear drove her on. Leaving the bedroom, she returned to the kitchen, snapping open her laptop to scroll through the footage from her security cameras. The door cam revealed little, save for her neighbour's excursion to Tesco Metro and the in-flat cameras less still. Her home was secure.

'The temperature will be an icy three degrees tonight and the wind chill factor will make it feel considerably colder...'

Helen liked to have the radio on in the evenings, a voice to penetrate the all-consuming quiet of her flat, and as the weather report continued, she crossed to the living room, throwing herself down on the sofa. Tugging off her boots and socks, she let her head fall back onto the soft fabric, closing her eyes. Images of the night's work filled her thoughts – the protesting ship's captain and crew, the aggressive search team, a huge haul of cocaine found in a secret compartment under the transom – but she pushed them away. She needed to escape from her duties, her daily life, to embrace something outside of herself, something mundane, ordinary and safe.

'So, if you are heading out tomorrow, I'd dig out a hat and gloves and if you've got a nice woolly scarf, I'd throw that on too ...'

The gentle Hampshire lilt of the reporter's voice added to the cosiness of this image, and Helen longed to lose herself in fantasies of winter fun, but her mind wouldn't let her rest, intent on playing its usual grim game of word association. Mention of the scarf made Helen think of necks and suddenly her thoughts were drawn to Alex Blythe, standing in her flat, in her *bedroom*, slowly ringing the life out of his poor pet. Blythe had left his spaniel on her bed as a parting gift, even as he called Helen to make his final, awful threat. The import of his chilling message was bad enough, but the knowledge that he had delivered it whilst standing in *her* home struck deep. He had been here, sitting on her bed, calm and collected, amused by his omnipotence.

Blythe hadn't been seen since – not a single sighting in over five months – but his presence lingered. Helen had reinforced the flat's defences, installed top of the range security equipment, but this hadn't made her feel any better. A vendetta had been declared, one Helen felt sure the psychiatrist would make good on, in person or by proxy. Which is why even when she was home at night, safely locked away from a dark, dangerous world, Helen couldn't rest. Isolated, lonely, she was never truly alone these days, the spectre of Alex Blythe forever on her shoulder.

Chapter 7

He slid the key into the lock and turned it gently. Sighing softly, the door relented and he hurried inside, keen to be out of the cold. His running gear was expensive and efficient, trapping the heat generated by his exercise, but the wind was cold tonight, its bite sharp.

Closing the door behind him, Greg White slipped off his trainers. They were still damp and he knew that he would get it in the neck if he left wet footprints all over the hall floor. Removing his clinging socks, he hung them on the nearest radiator, then padded into the kitchen. The lights were off and he left them like that, keen not to disturb his slumbering family. Their newly fitted kitchen was still visible, however, the moonlight streaming in through the roof lights, illuminating quartz, steel and oak. Greg knew it was pathetic to covet inanimate objects, but the sight of their kitchen, which had been designed to wow visitors, never failed to thrill him.

Why not, mate? You've earned it, he thought to himself happily, crossing to the fridge and pulling the door open.

A chilled bottle of water awaited inside and he snatched it up, pouring himself a large glass. One gulp, two, three, he sucked the icy liquid in until he could hold his breath no more, lowering the glass and drinking in the air instead. Man, he felt better than ever tonight – energized, adrenalized, alive. Why did he not do this more often? It was such a refreshing alternative to the rigors of work and the endless demands of their delightful but demanding baby girl. Replacing the bottle in the fridge, Greg slid across the tiled floor, keen to be upstairs. Martha had not been sleeping well, had complained as much this morning, and the sooner he was in bed the better. He was tempted to head to the very top of the house, to use the guest room, but he knew Martha wouldn't stand for this. However tired they were, however ground down by parenthood, there was no question of separate beds. Martha's parents' fractured marriage made her very sensitive on that point.

Mounting the stairs, Greg hurried towards the bedroom, pausing only to peek into Bailey's bedroom. To his relief, she was sound asleep, sucking contentedly on her dummy. Greg knew people had differing views on the use of pacifiers, but God, how it had improved their lives. Whoever had invented them deserved a knighthood, along with the clever people who thought up swaddling blankets and Calpol.

Retreating, he moved on, padding as quietly as he could to the bedroom. He hesitated on the threshold, intrigued to see if Martha was asleep or not. Occasionally she conked out, but if she hadn't managed to, she was often to be found tossing and turning in the darkness, occasionally offering a terse comment about his late return. Happily, all seemed quiet within, the still form of Martha just visible in the gloom, so teasing the handle down, he crept inside, closing the door gently behind him.

Day Two

Chapter 8

DC Japhet Wilson hopped from foot to foot, casting accusing glances at the Whites' front door, now decorated with yellow-and-black police tape. He was only a week into his new job at Southampton Central and, though he'd known he'd have to confront some challenging situations, he hadn't been expecting *this*.

The police operator had fielded the call just before midnight. A panic-stricken husband begging for help, trying to put into words the scene of horror he had just discovered.

'My wife... she's... she's been attacked... There's blood everywhere, oh my God... Come quickly. Please just *come*...'

Japhet was glad he'd never manned the phones during his career – how did these people remain calm, collected and dispassionate when confronted by such distress? – but better that perhaps than having to deal with the grim reality. Uniform had secured the house in St Denys by the time he arrived, giving him fair warning of what he was about to discover, but still the sight of that poor woman took his breath away.

Nauseous, Japhet tugged a packet of cigarettes from his pocket. He was still the senior officer on site, had been for hours, witnessing the sickly grey dawn break over this blighted house, but he could probably get away with a crafty smoke before the boss arrived. Yet, as he put the cigarette to his lips, bile suddenly rose in his throat. Thinking better of it, he replaced the cigarette in its packet. He'd enjoy one later, when he felt normal again. Whenever that would be.

He was due to finish his shift soon, had said he'd call his mother when he was done, but that would have to wait. No one would be clocking off today. Even when he *did* finally talk to her, what news would he send back to Walthamstow? There was no question of giving her the full details of this incident – she would be sick with worry, convinced Southampton was a hotbed of murder and depravity – but she'd know that he was distressed, so he'd have to give her something. The question was what.

He was still mulling on this when he heard a motorbike screech to a halt. Without looking up, he instinctively straightened, turning to face DI Grace. She was the reason he'd joined the Major Incident Team, impressed by her courage, leadership and dynamism. Even now she was tugging off her helmet and bearing down on him, eager for news.

'What have we got?' she asked, getting straight to the point.

'Female Caucasian, thirty-two years old. Martha White, wife of Greg White and mother to a six-month-old, Bailey.'

Helen Grace said nothing, grim-faced.

'We believe she was killed sometime after 7 p.m. last night. The husband found her just before midnight.'

'What about the child?'

'She's fine, though we believe she *was* in the house when the incident took place.'

'Jesus Christ...'

Wilson nodded; that was exactly how he'd reacted when told of the baby's narrow escape.

'Who's had access so far?'

'Just uniform. They've established a common approach path,

taped off the significant areas. Oh, and Jim Grieves is in there. He's in the bedroom now.'

Nodding, Grace turned to leave, then paused, turning back to her latest recruit.

'Do you want to come with me? You might learn something.'

'Better stay here, ma'am. We've already had a few rubber-neckers. Don't want them contaminating the scene ...'

A ghost of a smile seemed to pass across Grace's face, before she replied:

'Right you are.'

She departed, picking her way carefully towards the front door. Wilson watched her go, knowing his dedication hadn't fooled her for a second. She knew by the look on his face, his body language, why he wanted to remain outside. He always tried to be dispassionate, to do the job without emotion or fear, but he couldn't muster his normal composure today. He didn't feel professional. He didn't feel in control. In truth, he felt sick as a dog.

Chapter 9

She was immediately struck by the silence. Stepping inside the well-appointed house, Helen noted the family photos, the neatly stacked baby toys, the pile of letters on the hall table – this was clearly a busy family home, full of hustle and bustle, but today it was deathly quiet, as if everyone present was holding their breath.

Holding their breath for what? For something to happen? Well, something *had* happened, something unexpected and shocking. Helen only had the outline details so far, but she could tell from DC Wilson's haunted expression that she was walking into a horror show. *That* she was prepared for, she had attended countless scenes of butchery over the years, no, it was the lifelessness of the house that set her nerves jangling today. It was the kind of sombre quiet usually reserved for funerals.

Sticking carefully to the common approach path, Helen made her way to the first floor. A familiar face, PC Frank Cottesloe, stood guard on the landing and he nodded towards a door at the far end of the corridor as she approached.

'You'll find laughing boy in there ...'

Helen returned the nod, hurrying past. She wanted to get this over with now, to ascertain the hard facts and start the investigation into this gruesome crime. Even so, she slowed momentarily as she passed a door on her right, peering inside to see a spacious nursery. Helen was momentarily thrown back to her own childhood – you could have fitted their entire flat into this little child's room – then was yanked back to the present, the eerie atmosphere of the vacant nursery making Helen feel crushingly sad. What an awful start in life for the poor kid.

Pulling herself together, Helen carried on, reaching the end of the corridor and teasing open the bedroom door. Stepping inside, she found the burly form of Southampton Central's chief pathologist looming over the marital bed, engrossed in some close quarters examination. Beneath him, on the blood-soaked mattress, lay the brutalized body of a young woman. Face down on the bed, Helen couldn't divine what she looked like – what her colouring, complexion or expression was – but she had a clear view of the inside of her skull. The back of her head had been split open, revealing brain, sinew and muscle, and there appeared to be several further gashes on her upper back and shoulders. Above her, on the wallpaper, on a canvas portrait of her family, were numerous streaks of dried blood, a testament to the frenzied nature of the attack.

'No, I don't think much of their taste in decoration either.'

The pathologist straightened up, his tone as dry as a bone.

'Jim...'

Her rebuke was good-natured, but he waved it away anyway, too long in the tooth to countenance criticism.

'As you'll have gauged, this was an extremely violent attack,' Grieves continued, unabashed. 'The victim had a rag forced into her mouth, her hands were bound with elasticated cord, then she was struck four times with a bladed implement. Could be a garden tool, but I'd say it was probably a small axe or hatchet of some kind.'

Helen winced.

'First blow did the damage, square to the back of the head, fracturing the skull. Death would have been pretty much instantaneous, so I'm guessing the blows that followed – one to the right shoulder, two to the upper back – were probably just the result of adrenaline or someone enjoying themselves.'

It seemed an odd way to describe this vicious attack, but Helen let it go.

'The spatter patterns on the wall are consistent with the blows, so the blood wasn't placed there deliberately. This was an in-and-out job, brutal but efficient.'

'So, no other injuries of note? No signs of sexual assault? Or torture?'

'Nothing obvious. Nor any defensive injuries on her hands or arms, so it's safe to say she was subdued before she was attacked.'

The thought made Helen's blood run cold – was Martha surprised by her attacker as she slept?

'That said,' Grieves continued, 'the marks on her fourth finger suggest her rings were recently taken off, which might provide some clue as to motive.'

Helen was already scanning the rest of the room, her eyes latching onto the empty jewellery box that lay upside down on the disordered dresser. Had Martha's attacker fumbled in the darkness for his spoils, upsetting perfume bottles and keepsakes as he did so? If so, was it worth it? Was any amount of material gain worth *this*?

'If I were you, I'd have a scout around the garden shed, talk to the husband, see if there are any tools missing, if the elasticated cord belonged to them. Might help you decide whether this was opportunistic or professional...'

Helen seriously hoped it was the former, but as yet there was no way of knowing.

'Any signs of the attacker? Hairs, fibres?'

'Not so far,' Grieves replied. 'I can't see any scratching around the victim's mouth where the rag was applied and the elasticated cord seems to be clean as a whistle. Also, you'll note that the killer found time to wipe his blade on her cardigan, just where you're standing…'

Helen took a step away from the chair, noticing now the dull smear of brownish red on the white woollen cardigan.

'…which suggests that he was in control throughout, measured and precise, despite the excessive violence,' Helen added, concluding Grieves's thought.

This time it was Grieves's turn to nod, as he responded:

'Brutal and assured. Not two adjectives you generally want together.'

Even as he spoke, Helen's gaze was drawn to the blood-spattered canvas above the bed. It was a studio shot of Martha White and her husband sitting cross-legged on the floor, their baby girl between them. Both parents were beaming, flush with the joy of their new arrival and even baby Bailey appeared to be smiling, gummy and toothless, her mother's hand supporting her, as the infant twinkled at the camera. Once more Helen felt a sharp stab of sorrow for the little girl, barely a year old, who would never feel that support, that love, again. Helen knew these photos were often contrived and that it was possible dark secrets lurked within the private lives of this happy trio, yet it was impossible not to read the love, excitement and optimism in their faces, a testament to a family who had lived, loved, then been violently ripped apart.

Chapter 10

A noise made him look up, snapping him out of his reverie. Greg White had been lost in thought – bleak, horrible thoughts – before a squeal from Bailey suddenly brought him to his senses. Disoriented, confused, he turned to discover that he'd been disturbed by a squeak of excitement. His little girl was enjoying herself.

It seemed impossible given the horrific events of the night, but there was no denying it. She was propped up on the carpet, staring at the TV, gurgling and smiling at the antics of JoJo and GranGran. It was at once intensely moving – to see that happiness *was* still possible – yet also deeply jarring. The contradiction cut deep, the realization that Bailey had no idea of the disaster that had befallen her family, of the bitter loss they had endured. In time, when she was capable of understanding, he would have to explain to her what had happened, but the thought made him feel sick. What words could he find to express such horror? How could he explain it to *her* when none of it felt real to *him*?

He was in shock, he knew that, still not really processing what had happened. Once he'd given his statement to the police, he'd fled to his parents' house in Shirley, collapsing into their arms, even as Bailey slept, oblivious in her car seat. They both had journeys to go on – he from dull shock to anger to grief and perhaps eventually to acceptance, she from happiness to loss. It would be a slow, painful process and for both a bewildering one. Though in full command of the facts, he couldn't make sense of Martha's horrific death and Bailey would be similarly helpless. She wouldn't be able to verbalize her feelings for years to come, but there was no question that she *would* miss her mother's presence in the interim. That she'd yearn for her touch, for her kisses and tenderness. What would she make of her mum's sudden absence? Would she cry? Would she protest? Or would she just move on, finding comfort in her father's arms or those of her grandparents, who'd always doted on her and who'd now be an ever-present feature of her life.

It suddenly occurred to Greg that Bailey might not even remember Martha. Obviously he would show her photos and do everything he could to keep her memory alive, but would Bailey truly remember her mother's smell, her touch, her presence? It was awful to think that she might just simply... forget.

He by contrast would never forget. As soon as he'd entered the room, he'd sensed that something was wrong, even before he'd flicked on the bedside light to reveal that scene of carnage. He had stumbled backwards at first, landing in a heap on the landing outside, unable to take in the blood-soaked sheets, the brutalized body on the bed. *Their* bed, the marital bed, where they had laughed, cried, fought, made up and loved. Where they had conceived their baby girl. It was the crucible of their marriage, their family, a place of so much joy, happiness and emotion, yet in the end it had proved to be the site of their undoing, a place of violence, horror and pain. He had run from it, run as fast as he could to scoop up his baby girl and sprint to the phone, yet he knew that the image of desolation would stay with him forever, burned in bloody detail on his brain.

He would never be free of it, it would haunt his waking

thoughts and nightmares for years to come. He'd had it all – a lovely wife, a beautiful daughter, a big house, a successful business – but it was all worthless now, stained by another man's evil. He would never see his lovely Martha again, never thrill to have such a wonderful lady in his life, nor would he ever set foot again in the house that had once been his pride and joy.

Chapter 11

'Front door was locked from the inside, according to the husband. So it looks like our man gained access from the rear, ma'am...'

Thanking PC Cottesloe, Helen descended the stairs. Her timing was spot on, for as she reached the hallway, a familiar face appeared, stepping cautiously into the house, whilst pocketing her warrant card.

'Morning, Charlie.'

Her old friend looked up, startled, before managing a half smile.

'This is a nasty one, so if you've just had breakfast, I'd give it a moment,' Helen continued. 'Jim Grieves will be done shortly, then it's all yours...'

Helen's words seemed to depress Charlie even further, the latter managing a resigned shrug. Her deputy appeared tired this morning, her usual sparkle absent.

'If you're OK to scout around upstairs,' Helen added briskly, 'I'd like to check out the point of entry.'

'Sure thing,' Charlie replied, slipping on latex gloves and heading towards the stairs.

Helen watched her go, intrigued, then turned and followed the marked path through the kitchen towards the utility room.

Something was clearly up with her comrade in arms – Charlie had been distant and uncommunicative of late – but whatever it was would have to wait. Helen had work to do.

The small utility room was deserted, the photographer already having been and gone and Helen took her time to examine her surroundings. It was a modern, well-appointed space with a washer dryer, lacquered storage cupboards and an old-fashioned pully maid hanging from the ceiling. A pile of clean laundry hung on the wooden slats – pants, socks, T-shirts and a host of brightly coloured Babygros – but Helen turned away from those, not wanting emotion to distract her from the job in hand.

Crossing the tiled floor, she came to a halt by the door, which gave onto a narrow side passage. It was modern in style, a huge slab of reinforced glass with a tasteful aluminium frame. Just in front of the door on the inside was an inlaid mat, on which the lock mechanism lay, buckled and redundant. Already Helen was doing the calculations – the house was at the end of the street, meaning an intruder in the side passage wouldn't have been visible to any other house. The glass pane in the door meant the intruder could see in clearly, ensuring the coast was clear, and the solid matting would have deadened the sound of the falling lock. The question now was, how it had been removed.

Stepping out into the side passage, Helen turned back to examine the frame. And now she had her answer. Something large and flat – an axe blade perhaps? – had been forced between the edge of the door and the door frame just above the lock, then worked back and forth, the pressure increasing with each motion, buckling the frame, until eventually something had to give. That something had been the lock, popping obligingly onto the floor. How long had it taken the intruder to gain access? Two minutes? Less?

Moving away, Helen was intrigued to spot a security camera

in the side access, pointing directly down at the doorway. It looked modern and operational, a little red light glowing on the face of the machine. For a brief moment, Helen's spirits rose, but as she moved closer, she noticed that the lens had been spray-painted black.

Swearing under her breath, Helen continued on to the garden. It was a large, manicured space, a vast lawn flanked by a stone path leading to the rear. On the back wall of the house hung a large security light, its sensor keeping a watchful eye on the lawn and borders. But a loose trailing wire below it served as further evidence of the intruder's caution. If it had illuminated him on the way to the house, he'd made sure it wouldn't do so again on the way back.

Suppressing her rising anxiety, Helen moved swiftly down the path, searching for signs of damaged foliage or footprints in the soil. Finding nothing, she soon found herself at the garden shed. If the intruder was an opportunistic attacker it was probable that he had stolen his weapon here, but the padlock was firmly in place and the windows locked, further evidence that Martha's attacker had come prepared.

Pressing on, Helen found herself by the back gate, guarded now by a uniformed officer. Beyond it, a rear access passage ran the length of the street. It was no doubt convenient for residents, but also a security nightmare, offering unfettered public access to the rear gates of these high-end properties. Leaning down, Helen was not surprised to see that the gate had been forced open, the broken padlock lying on the floor below.

Retreating, Helen returned towards the house. The narrative of Martha White's murder was slowly taking shape and even as she approached the shed, Helen noticed something else, another small detail in the grizzly story of trespass and violence. A large bush flanked the garden path and approaching it from a different angle, Helen noted that some of the lower branches had been recently broken, the inner flesh of the snapped branches still a vivid white. Dropping to her hands and knees, Helen made out a partial footprint, pressed into the moist soil, rainwater still visible within it.

Inwardly, Helen shivered, knowing exactly what this meant. Having gained access to the garden, Martha's attacker had hurried to this bush, using it as cover perhaps as he surveyed the house. There he had lingered, swathed in the darkness, his mind pulsing with violence, looking up at the quiet suburban residence, watching and waiting for his moment to strike.

Chapter 12

'I spy, with my little eye, something beginning with "H"...'

Emilia Garanita couldn't suppress a smile, as she looked down at Helen Grace from her vantage point.

'Hopeless? Hapless? Hilarious?'

The journalist chuckled, amused by her own wordplay, watching with naked enjoyment as the veteran police officer walked slowly up the garden path. Even from this distance, Emilia could see that Grace looked troubled.

'What's worrying you, Helen? What have you found?'

Shifting her position, Emilia tried to get a better angle, hoping to see Grace's expression more clearly. This was no easy feat, the experienced reporter perched precariously in the upper branches of a tree which stood on the street adjacent to the Whites' property, affording a decent if partial view of their large garden. Emilia knew she would cut a comic figure if discovered, but she'd had no choice. The neighbours had told her she wasn't welcome on the street and with no other properties looking onto the crime scene, she'd had to improvise. It had been the devil's own job getting up here, but once safely in the upper branches, the journalist could linger, concealed in the shadows of the tree's mighty arms.

'What's going on, Helen? Tell Auntie Emilia...'

Her eyes remained glued to the police officer, who stood stock-still, examining the path edge and flower beds. Since DS Joseph Hudson's sudden fall from grace, Emilia had lost her main source of insider information and, without a willing stooge within the Major Incident Team, she'd had to gather what scraps she could from less senior sources. She had cultivated one of the desk sergeants, a garrulous new officer called Jack Sumner who liked a drink or three, who had told her of a serious night-time incident at a detached house in Belmont Road, in the St Denys area of the city. More than that he couldn't tell her, but Emilia had been doing this long enough to guess some of the details. CID, pathology and forensics were all present, and in force, meaning this was clearly a serious crime, presumably murder. The owner of the house, Greg White, had been spotted earlier this morning leaving the house with a baby in tow, but there was no sign of his wife Martha. Presumably she lay somewhere in the house, though the circumstances of her demise remained shrouded in mystery for now. As Greg White had not been arrested and, given Grace's careful investigation of the back gate and garden path, it was safe to assume that the house had been visited by an intruder. A burglar? A rapist? Angry relative? Spurned lover? Time would tell, but Emilia longed to know.

Her legs were beginning to ache, permanently tensed to keep herself upright, so she shifted position. As she did so, her left foot slipped slightly and she had to grasp a nearby branch to save herself from falling, snapping it as she did so. Steadying herself, Emilia looked down into the garden and was surprised to find Helen Grace looking in her direction. Shielding her eyes from the winter sun, the Inspector seemed alarmed, startled even, clearly fearful that she was being watched. Emilia stayed completely still, holding her breath and happily a few seconds later, Grace turned away, continuing her inspection of the garden.

Settling back down, Emilia resumed her stakeout, mentally scrolling through the possible circumstances of Martha White's death, all the while keeping a firm eye on her old nemesis. So often in their relationship Helen Grace had had the upper hand, but today Emilia was in the ascendancy, watching the troubled officer from her high vantage point, undetected, unsuspected and totally in control.

Chapter 13

Charlie hovered over the empty cot, trying to calm her breathing. She'd felt anxious from the moment she awoke this morning and being in the bereaved baby's nursery was not helping her state of mind. Gripping the rail, Charlie closed her eyes, inhaling and exhaling methodically, trying to muster some semblance of professionalism.

'Come on, Charlie, keep it together...'

Easy to say, less easy to do. She'd had a poor night's sleep, disturbed by Steve's late return, then been further discomfited by Helen's early call, asking her to attend a major incident. She'd hoped to spend some time with Steve and the girls this morning, but instead had hauled her weary bones to an address in St Denys, only to be confronted there by a scene of indescribable horror. A young mum butchered – there was no other word for it – *butchered* in her own bed.

Charlie had lingered in that awful room for as long as she could bear, before retreating here. Grieves, Meredith Walker and the others would provide the hard intel from the physical crime scene, it was her job to investigate the surrounding rooms, and she was profoundly glad of it. She felt nauseous and dizzy already, feelings only exacerbated by exposure to the corpse across the corridor, so she was glad to have something else to concentrate on.

She'd investigated the landing and two of the rooms that led off it. These, a guest bedroom and a spacious study, appeared untouched, so her search had led her to the nursery. Wooden letters were fixed to the door, spelling out the name Bailey in gentle pastels, and inside the room was just as tasteful. Newly decorated with elegant blinds and furnishings, stuffed full of soft toys, cushions and family photos, the room was dominated by the large wooden cot. Charlie stood by it now, thinking not of the crime scene itself, but of the cot's occupant – a little girl whose life had just taken a savage and unexpected turn.

The tiny bed lay empty, save for the baby's blanket and a toy monkey that lay on its back next to a yellow dummy. The whole room seemed undisturbed and Charlie was about to turn away when she spotted something. In the corner of the cot, half hidden by the scrunched-up blanket, was a small red dot. Teasing the soft fabric aside, Charlie's suspicions were confirmed – the mattress was stained with a single drop of blood. It was fresh, a rich crimson colour, neither smeared nor smudged. In fact, it was a perfect circle, as of course it would be, if dropped from above.

Charlie gripped the rail tighter. *He had come in here.* Whoever had murdered Martha White had come into the nursery, weapon in hand, standing over the crib to peer down at the sleeping babe. She felt light-headed, choked with emotion at the thought of a brutal killer ranged above the helpless child. What had gone through his mind? Had he been tempted to harm the baby too? It didn't bear thinking about, yet couldn't be ignored, as there might be valuable forensic evidence within the cot itself. Rattled, but determined, Charlie called out to Meredith – the whole room would have to be dusted and swept, the contents of the cot bagged and labelled. It felt good to be doing something useful, sending a spike of much needed adrenaline coursing through Charlie. Perhaps her discovery might help them progress the case. Perhaps it might even help them unmask Martha White's killer. And at the very least it would help keep Charlie's mind off what had happened here last night, how close one tiny girl had come to disaster.

Chapter 14

Killing the engine, Helen kicked out the stand, then dismounted. Pulling her helmet off, she scanned the street quickly, checking for approaching pedestrians or vehicles, but the suburban street was quiet and unthreatening. It was mid-morning and Leith Avenue, nestling in the heart of sleepy Shirley, was at peace.

Crossing the road, Helen made for number thirty-two. Gerald and Anne White, Greg's parents, had lived at this address for over forty years and it was here that their son had sought sanctuary. This interview was not one Helen was looking forward to – you never knew how people would react to such a traumatic event – but she knew she couldn't avoid this conversation if she was to make sense of this baffling crime.

The gate squeaked noisily, heralding her arrival, so Helen didn't waste time, striding purposefully towards the front door. Raising her hand, she was about to rap on it when suddenly her pocket started vibrating. Quickly, she retrieved her phone, checking the caller ID. Immediately, her heart sank – it was Chief Superintendent Alan Peters.

'Good morning, sir,' Helen answered, in as bright a tone as she could muster. 'What can I do for you?'

It was a question Helen had asked herself many times since

the conclusion of her last major investigation, given the tension that continued to plague their relationship.

'I'd like an update on the Belmont Road murder,' came the brief response.

Just wanted to check up on me, Helen thought to herself. Her maverick style of policing and her ill-judged relationship with former colleague DS Hudson had permanently soured her relationship with the station chief and now Peters kept a watchful eye on her. This angered Helen more than she could say. She was the innocent party in the whole sorry affair – hence why she was still in post, whilst Hudson had been kicked out of the Force and was even now facing criminal charges for misuse of public office – but she knew that if she wanted to keep her job, she would have to play nice.

'I've done a preliminary tour of the property. It looks like an intruder gained access to the house late last night, murdering Martha White and making off with some valuable items of jewellery...'

'Bloody hell. Didn't they have any security?'

'Her attacker took care of that whilst gaining entry. He was very methodical and measured, which suggests he's either a professional or someone who was highly motivated to kill.'

'You keep saying he,' Peters responded calmly. 'Are you sure it's a man?'

'Not one hundred per cent, but the size of a partial footprint found in the garden points that way, as does the violence of the attack. The killer blow was struck with considerable force, splitting the victim's skull wide open.'

That shut him up. Helen seized advantage of this lacuna to try and make good her escape.

'I'm just about to interview the husband – obviously I'll report back anything significant.'

'Be sure you do. Given the affluence of the victim and the nature of the attack, we can be sure this is going to be a very high-profile story.'

Helen suppressed her desire to reply that Peters was stating the bloody obvious. When the victim of a violent crime was photogenic, rich and white, the story always had top billing in the press, other 'less marketable' victims shunted further down the batting order. It made Helen's blood boil, but it was unquestionably true, meaning Peters would be on her back constantly from now on.

'So I want to be across everything,' Peters continued, confirming her fears. 'And I want this investigation done *by the book.*'

Helen didn't need reminding. After the unhappy conclusion of the Blythe case, Peters had read her the riot act, promising her that from now on the slightest misstep, the tiniest procedural error on her part, would result in dire penalties, perhaps even dismissal. Helen was dancing on a tightrope, one Peters was prepared to shake at any given opportunity. Indeed, Helen sensed he would enjoy doing so, finally ridding Southampton Central of a known troublemaker.

'Absolutely, sir. I'll call you later with an update.'

She rang off, pleased to be rid of his insidious presence. Angry and frustrated, Helen rapped on the door. Never had she felt so beleaguered as she started a major investigation. Last night's brutal crime was bad enough, but Peters' constant questioning of her, and the looming threat of a shadowy assassin, shredded her nerves, making Helen feel as if she was under siege. It was dispiriting and upsetting, sapping her energy and resolve. But as she heard cautious footsteps approaching the door, Helen knew she had to swallow down her emotion and focus on the needs of the White family. They were suffering and it was her duty to be professional, to deliver justice for them. There was no question of being weak, distracted or selfish.

She had a killer to catch.

Chapter 15

'This was *him.*'

The words flew from his mouth, harsh and bitter. Greg White paced the floor of the living room, gesturing to Helen as if she should know what he was talking about. Helen took him in – the pallid expression, the dark rings, his shaking hands – this was a man on the edge of a breakdown. He looked exhausted, yet couldn't stop moving – anger, desperation and adrenaline powering his restless movement.

'Who are you referring to, Greg?'

'Him,' he repeated impatiently. 'Andrew Berman.'

'Why do you say that?'

'Because he's made her life a misery for the last two years. You *know* he has...'

Helen knew exactly who he was referring to. She'd run a check on Martha White's name before biking to Shirley, intrigued to discover that the victim had recently suffered a campaign of harassment and intimidation at the hands of a former work colleague, but she was wary of getting ahead of herself. Martha's personal history *did* suggest an obvious suspect, but she'd need more details before she could form any meaningful conclusions.

'Tell me more,' she replied calmly. 'We have the basic facts on file, of course, but I'd rather hear about it directly from you.'

Her request seemed to take the wind out of his sails, White crumpling onto the sofa, cupping his face in his hands. For a moment, Helen thought he was going to break down, but when he removed his hands, Helen could see that his features were set and angry.

'Martha ... Martha used to work for an accountancy firm, one of the big ones, before she quit to help me with the business.'

'You run a chain of nurseries across Southampton, right?'

'Yes, have done for several years now. I'm CEO, Martha's CFO, we're a tight ship, but prior that she worked for Anderson's.'

'On Dorset Street?'

Greg nodded, but for a moment said nothing, lost in thought. Eventually, he continued, his voice bleak.

'She and this guy Berman had a one-night stand, after a drunken work do. She immediately regretted it – the guy was a creep – and she made it very clear that she'd no interest in any kind of romantic relationship with him. But Berman wouldn't have that, felt that they had some kind of special connection, so he started harassing her, trying to woo her. When she told him it wasn't going to happen, it got nasty.'

'Meaning?'

'He started spreading rumours about her, blackening her name. He had sex toys sent to her office in her name, trying to make out that she was some kind of slut...'

His voice wavered, raw distress tempering his fury.

'What happened then?'

'Well, she complained *obviously*. The company tried to wriggle out of it, but over time Berman's behaviour became so objection-able that they were forced to conduct an internal investigation. In the end they threw the book at him – he was suspended, then fired when things didn't improve. He was a bloody outcast.'

'But that didn't resolve things?'

White looked up her, his expression cynical and jaundiced.

'His life had gone to shit and he blamed Martha for it. He confronted her in the street, turned up at her flat. Later on, after we'd got together, he even turned up at our engagement party with an armful of fucking lilies. He was a *nutter*.'

'Presumably you applied for a restraining order?'

'And we got one. For all the good it did. He still turned up at the house, which is why we had the cameras and lights put in. That seemed to do the trick for a while, but he turned up again a couple of weeks ago, accosting her in town. We'd thought we were past all that, that we could lead a normal life...'

And now he did break, sobbing bitterly into his hands. Helen let his distress pour out, biding her time before asking her next question.

'Did you see him near your property last night?'

White shook his head slowly.

'And Martha? Did she flag any specific concerns or worries yesterday?'

Another shake of the head.

'I see. And can you give me a sense of *your* movements last night?'

Now the sobbing ceased, Greg White looking up sharply.

'I was out training, like I am every Tuesday night. I'm supposed to be doing the London Marathon in February, raising money for our children's charity.'

'Alone?'

'Yes, I couldn't find any other bugger who wants to run twenty plus miles, three times a week.'

'And where were you running last night?'

'The Common. Takes me ten minutes to run there, I do twenty circuits, then I run home.'

'What time was this?'

49

'I ... I left the house around seven. Got back just before midnight.'

Helen was about to follow this up when White suddenly continued, the words tumbling from him.

'I didn't want to train nights. Of course I didn't, but we were so busy with work, and with Bailey around, there wasn't any other time to do it...'

Once more, his distress assailed him, tears running his cheeks. If his anguish at not being home to protect his family was faked, he was certainly an accomplished actor – the bereaved husband looked desperate, gaunt, haunted.

'OK, I'm going to send a family liaison officer to help guide you through the process. In time we will need you to make a formal statement, testifying to those timings, so if there's anything that can back up your account of your whereabouts – mobile phone, witnesses, cameras, whatever – that would be helpful.'

White didn't react at all, staring down at the floor.

'Mr White, did you hear what—'

'I heard you all right,' he interrupted, looking back up at her. 'And I'll do whatever I need to do, but I'm telling you that it's a waste of time. I had nothing to do with this...'

His eyes bore into Helen's, as he concluded:

'This was *him*.'

Chapter 16

'Police haven't confirmed the name of the victim, but the property belongs to long-term Southampton residents, Gregory and Martha White, local entrepreneurs who run the highly successful Banana Tree nurseries. Mr White and his daughter were seen in the Shirley area of the city earlier this morning, leading to speculation that his wife Martha was the victim of a violent attack...'

He stood stock-still, drinking in the words. The newsreader was so pompous, her words so measured, like she was talking down to a kindergarten class. Why could she not say it more directly, more decisively? The bitch was dead, that's all there was to it.

Still the newsreader bleated on, but her words were drowned out by noises from upstairs, footsteps pounding the creaky floorboards. Were his parents also listening to the news story, working themselves up into a frenzy? He wouldn't put it past them to march down here, demanding explanations, but he couldn't sanction that, not today. Crossing the floor quickly, Andrew Berman locked the door, flicking the lights off for good measure, before returning to his decrepit desk. Teasing the volume down, he prayed that they would be fooled, that they would think he was still out and leave him in peace to enjoy this precious moment. He had waited too long for this to have it spoiled by *them*.

How he loathed them. Their disappointment, their distress, their *judgement*. Ever since he could remember, they had belittled him, their anguish at having a fuck-up as an only child all too apparent. Well, screw them. Soon he would be rid of them too, free at last, and how sweet would life be then?

Snapping out of his reverie, Berman returned his attention to the news. Now it was the turn of the on-site reporter, bagging vox pop interviews with the terrified residents of St Denys. He couldn't help but laugh at their suburban delusions, the idea that a smart neighbourhood, expensive locks and a couple of security cameras could protect you. How ignorant, how blind they were, hoping against hope that wealth could shield them from a just retribution. All these morons would get what was coming to them in the end. The world was a nasty, thankless place and the sooner you accepted that, the better. He knew that from bitter experience.

The newscaster was back, moving the conversation on to other stories, but Berman didn't want it to end. He wanted to dwell in this special place. Thoughts flooded his mind – Martha's hot, panting body beneath him, the sweet ecstasy of their souls entwined, but also her vile accusations afterwards, the slander she'd meted out, her subsequent, open-legged promiscuity, her lies, lies, lies ... No doubt there would be all sorts of eulogies now, glowing tributes to a wonderful wife and mother, served up over the ensuing days, but the simple truth was that Martha White had deserved to die; in fact, she'd had it coming for years and her murder was his final victory.

And yet ... for all that he willed himself to savour this moment, something was missing. He was working hard to feel elated, free, drunk on his triumph, but it wasn't working. It felt bogus, forced even. But how could that be? This was what he wanted, *all* he wanted. He'd sacrificed so much, suffered so much just to get to this point, so why did his victory taste so sour? Fury, frustration, disbelief rose up in him now, but there was no denying it. The woman he'd loved, then loathed, was dead.

But still he felt no better.

Chapter 17

Helen hurried from the neat suburban house, deep in thought. They would have to corroborate Greg White's movements last night in case he was trying to conceal his own wrongdoing, some moment of madness or a terrible schism in their marriage, but on the face of it he seemed an unlikely suspect. Andrew Berman looked a much better bet – it was he that Helen wanted to talk to now.

Reaching the end of the path, she tugged open the gate, and checking the road was clear, hurried across to her bike. As she did so, however, a battered red Corsa swung into the street, driving too fast along the quiet residential road, before screeching to a halt next to her. Seconds later, Emilia Garanita emerged, a wolfish smile on her face.

'Good morning, Helen. How are you?'

'All the better for seeing you, Emilia, but unfortunately I can't stop.'

'I'm not surprised. That brutal murder in St Denys, it's a bad business…'

Helen suspected the journalist was chancing her arm, fishing for confirmation of her suspicions, so kept her counsel.

'Cat got your tongue? Oh well, I'll just have to ask Greg,

then. I assume you're here because he's sought sanctuary with his parents…'

She checked the notes on her phone.

'Gerald and Anne White, according to the electoral roll. I was going to beard them now, but you could save me the bother and just tell me what we're looking at here.'

'As if you won't knock on their door the moment I'm gone…'

Emilia laughed at Helen's accusation, as if this was all a jolly game. Anger immediately flared in Helen – how dare the journalist treat this case so flippantly, when a young mum had been savagely murdered – and though she knew she should just walk away, this time she didn't.

'You really are a ghoul, aren't you?'

'I'm sorry?'

To Helen's surprise, Emilia looked shocked, even a little hurt.

'I wonder if you have any conscience at all, any understanding of what these poor people are going through.'

'There's no need to be catty, Helen,' Emilia replied, recovering her spark. 'It's nothing personal.'

'Except it is to these people,' Helen fired back, gesturing to the Whites' house. 'It couldn't *be* more personal.'

'It's a public interest story. If there's a madman, or madwoman, on the loose in suburban Southampton—'

'Oh, spare me,' Helen interrupted. 'This isn't about the public, it's about you. About your career, your profile, your macabre interest in other people's suffering.'

Helen knew she'd said too much already, but suddenly couldn't stop.

'Don't you ever get tired of it, Emilia? Tired of twisting the knife, of turning the screw when people are at their most vulnerable?'

'And what about you?' the journalist retorted. 'Don't you ever get tired of chasing your tail? Of failing to protect the citizens of this city? Of coming off second best?'

For a minute, Helen was speechless, rocked by the journalist's barefaced cheek and Emilia was quick to take advantage.

'How is Alex Blythe by the way? Any sign of him yet?'

Helen said nothing, the mere mention of the psychiatrist's name provoking a physical reaction in her. She was tempted to slap her adversary, to wipe that smug smile off her damaged face, but she knew this row was of *her* making, so instead she turned her back on Garanita, heading fast towards her Kawasaki.

'Don't be a stranger, Helen.'

Garanita's words were drowned out by the roar of Helen's bike as she sped away. Helen had been very tempted to tell her where to go, but as she glimpsed the journalist cross the road in her side mirrors, she was reminded that her adversary had the upper hand here. A brutal murder and a grieving, well-to-do family made for a sensational story. The media would be all over it, the pressure for an arrest huge, which meant only one thing.

Helen had to act *fast*.

Chapter 18

Charlie kept her speed high, bullying the cars out of her way. The siren was off, but the lights were flashing, anxious motorists spotting them and making way. She manoeuvred the car skillfully, using bus lanes and cut-throughs to burn towards Berman's registered address in St Mary's. Speed was of the essence now.

She'd been on her way back to Southampton Central when Helen had called her with an update. On hearing her news, Charlie had immediately changed course, diverting towards the east of the city. She was closer to Berman's home, could make it there in under ten minutes and, though Helen wouldn't be far behind, Charlie was keen to get this unhinged young man in custody as soon as possible.

En route, she had called DC Ellie McAndrew and Charlie was pleased to see her dark blue Audi pulling up as she brought her own vehicle to a halt in Chapel Road. Killing the engine, she climbed out, joining her colleague on the pavement in front of number thirty-four.

'You head to the rear. Cover the back entrance...'

'Sure thing.'

The experienced officer headed off without another word. Charlie gave her thirty seconds' head start, then turned her attention to the tired terraced house in front of her. Noting that the lower ground floor had its own front door – a lodger? Tenant? Berman himself? – she stepped forward to ring the doorbell. Seconds later, a pale middle-aged woman opened the door.

'DS Charlene Brooks. May I come in?'

'What's this all about? What's our Andrew supposed to have *done*?'

Nina Berman dogged Charlie's steps, her anxiety bubbling over.

'We just need to ask him a couple of questions,' Charlie replied, moving fast down the stairs to the basement.

'About what?'

'A serious incident which occurred last night.'

The formal nature of Charlie's response silenced the anguished mother. Charlie could tell Nina was already scrolling through a list of possible misdemeanours he'd committed, but she knew she had to keep her focused.

'What time did you say he got back last night?'

'I can't say for sure. Around 3 a.m., I think...'

'And what frame of mind was he in when he went out? Did he seem agitated? Distressed? Angry?'

Charlie saw her reaction, knew she had hit a nerve.

'Mrs Berman?'

'Well, he... he was angry, and upset, I suppose. His father and I, well, we'd told him that we wanted him to move out, that we didn't feel it was good for any of us, him staying here.'

'And he didn't take kindly to that?'

Berman's mother shook her head, tears filling her eyes.

'Have you seen him since then? Last night? This morning?'

'No, but I know he's home. I heard him moving around earlier, plus he had the radio on...'

Straining, Charlie could just make out the local station playing inside. Rapping on the door, she called out:

'Andrew? This is DS Charlene Brooks, Hampshire Police. Can you open up, please?'

No movement from within, so Charlie rapped again.

'We've officers front and back, so let's do this the easy way, shall we?'

Still nothing. Charlie turned to Nina, who looked horrified by the notion that her house was surrounded, but ignoring her distress, demanded:

'Would you mind?'

Shaken out of her stupor, Nina Berman leaned forward, unlocking the door, allowing Charlie to slip inside.

Closing the door behind her, Charlie took in the flat. The first thing that struck her was the smell. Pungent, festering, unpleasant. A strange combination of mildew, unwashed clothes and rotting food. The contrast with the tired but pristine interior upstairs was striking. Nina and her husband clearly didn't venture down here, or weren't allowed to.

Charlie pulled her baton from her belt. If Berman had lost all connection with reality, then there was no question of taking any chances. Tiptoeing forward, she poked her head into the front room. The remains of a takeaway sat on top of a pile of magazines, a pair of flies circling it lazily. On the table nearby, an old portable radio was playing.

Stepping into the room quickly, Charlie checked behind the door, then moved across the room to peer behind the sofa. Finding nothing, she moved on to the kitchenette, but this too was empty, save for the army of ants dancing around the bin. Continuing her search, she darted into the bathroom nearby, then on to the bedroom to the rear.

A short corridor led to the bedroom and Charlie moved fast down this now, keen to end this game of hide and seek. The door was closed and Charlie carefully teased the handle down. Then, without warning, she flung it open. She tensed herself, ready for the suspect to burst forth, but there was no movement from within. Cautiously, Charlie stepped into the room, scanning the poky space for an approaching assailant. But everything was quiet within, the room bare, save for a few possessions lying abandoned on the untidy bed.

Charlie craned down, peering under the bed. Straightening, she noticed the wardrobe. Everything else was unkempt and messy, the chest of drawers sprawling open, but the door of wardrobe was firmly closed. If Berman was in here, then this was his only remaining hiding place. Taking another breath, Charlie stepped forward and wrenched the door open.

'Charlie?'

She jumped out of her skin, turning away from the empty wardrobe to find DC McAndrew peering through the open window.

'Back gate was unlocked and this window was open, so ...'

She didn't need to say any more – they were too late.

Frustrated, Charlie turned away. As she did so, her eye fell on the belongings that lay on the bed. In the middle of the rumpled duvet was a plastic bag, which appeared to contain jewellery and clothing, but it wasn't this that grabbed her attention. Instead, her eyes were drawn to a photograph propped up next to the bag. It showed a youthful Berman with his arm around the shoulders of an elegant young woman. It had been taken at a works do, revellers visible in the background drinking in the sunshine, but this happy scene was marred by what had been done to the photo since its capture. Berman's face was still intact, beaming happily at the camera, but the attractive woman next to him, who looked very much like a young Martha White, had had her eyes gouged out.

Chapter 19

Helen roared along the road, the speedometer nudging seventy miles per hour. She was driving too fast, but her sole focus now was in getting their prime suspect in cuffs as quickly as possible. The longer the press believed an axe-wielding maniac was on the loose in Southampton, the worse things would be for everyone.

Tapping her Bluetooth, she dialled Charlie's number. Almost immediately, her old friend's voice came through inside her helmet:

'This is Charlie Brooks, please leave me a message.'

Helen clicked off, annoyed. Why had everyone suddenly gone radio silent? What had happened at the Berman house? Was there some kind of problem? Lowering her eyes to her phone, Helen flicked through to DC McAndrew's number, then tapped 'dial', before raising her eyes to the road once more. As she did so, her heart froze. A pedestrian had appeared from nowhere, stepping out directly in front of her. Instantly, Helen tugged at her brakes, her bike bucking, before skidding dangerously across the gravelly surface of the road. She was heading directly towards the startled man, any second now she would smash into him, sending him spiralling through the air...

Acting on instinct, Helen risked everything, tugging on the throttle and yanking the handlebars around. To her immense relief, the tyres bit the road and the bike lurched to the left, just missing the startled pedestrian, who cried out as Helen roared past. The danger was not over yet, however, Helen's front tyre colliding hard with the kerb, throwing her forward. For a moment, Helen was airborne, helpless, then gravity prevailed and she crashed back down onto her seat, squeezing the brakes and planting her right foot down, angling her ride back onto the road once more.

Swearing loudly, Helen shot a look behind her, but the startled pedestrian had already disappeared. Relieved, Helen drove on, dropping her speed slightly, and offering up a silent prayer that the gods had been looking out for her today. Gathering herself, she angled a glance at her Contacts list once more, but even as she did so her phone started ringing.

'Charlie? What have you got for me?'

'It's a no show, I'm afraid. Berman was here, but we must have just missed him.'

'Talk to the parents, find out if he has any obvious boltholes. In the meantime, circulate a description to uniform. I want every beat copper looking for him. Do we have a photo of him, something we can use?'

'Sure. He's quite distinctive-looking. Six foot and lanky with it, tight curly brown hair.'

'Any idea what's he wearing?'

'Apparently, he always wears the same thing. Faded jeans and a light grey hoodie, under a black leather jacket with a Mötley Crüe logo on the back. I'll draw up a proper description—'

But Helen had tuned out, her mind racing back to her near collision moments earlier – with a young man dressed *exactly* as Charlie had described.

'Sorry, Charlie, I'm going to have cut you off,' Helen interrupted breathlessly. 'I think I've just seen our man.'

Chapter 20

His heart was thumping, sweat rolling down his face, but there could be no question of stopping. His breathing was laboured and he had a savage stitch, but Andrew Berman was well aware that the next ten minutes would decide everything, so ignoring his discomfort, he upped his pace, powering along the pavement.

There was no question they were after him. Moments after he'd slipped out the back gate, he'd spotted them – two unmarked police cars speeding down the street towards Chapel Road. Lights flashing, but sirens off, they were obviously intent on a surprise raid. And he didn't need telling which address they were heading for.

He hadn't lingered, darting up the narrow lane and onto Evans Street. He was making good progress, putting a lot of distance between himself and home, but he must have let his attention wander for a second because suddenly he had found himself staring down the headlights of a speeding bike. Whether it was a psyched-up petrol head or an impatient courier, he had no idea, but one thing was certain – the biker was about to take him out, the roaring machine screeching inexorably towards him. It seemed impossible, unfair, that he should escape the police's attentions, only to be struck down by a random biker, yet wouldn't that just be his luck? A shitty end to a shitty life.

Then, suddenly, inexplicably, he was spared, the bike changing course and rearing up onto the pavement before speeding away. Terrified, but relieved, he had let loose a litany of vile curses, then realizing the culprit was long gone, gathered himself. If he was going to get away from this dump of a city, he had to stay focused and calm.

This was easier said than done. He had to keep moving at all costs, but his lungs burned and his legs felt like lead. Why when it mattered most did he feel so listless? Was it fear? Panic? Guilt? Urging himself on, he stalked along the busy pavement, bundling aggrieved pedestrians aside. He cared nothing for anyone else now, only about his own momentum. Finally, after years of pain, misery and despair, he was getting out. Momentarily, he felt elated at this thought and his heart swelled further as he spotted the railway sign up ahead. He was so close now, one final push and he would be free.

But even as his spirits soared, his legs finding renewed energy, he noticed something. A noise. An angry, throaty roar behind him. He craned round, before letting out a sudden expletive. The maniac biker was back, speeding once more in his direction. It didn't make any sense. What possible interest could he have in him, unless...?

It was a police officer. There could be no other explanation for it. He'd been spotted.

His heart was in his mouth. How had they got on to his scent so quickly? Turning away from his pursuer, Berman ran, sprinting across the busy Western Esplanade without looking. Normally, such a move would be suicidal, the traffic roaring along this major artery, but somehow he made it to the other side unscathed. Better still, the traffic lights had turned green behind him, the line of cars lurching forward aggressively, temporarily halting the biker's progress.

This was it, then, his chance to get away. Tearing into the station, he cast a wild eye at the departures board, then across at the clock. The next train to London left in two minutes. Could he make it? Already he could hear doors closing, whistles being blown. If he hesitated, all would be lost, so summoning his last reserves of energy, he sprinted forward, vaulting the ticket barriers and haring away down the empty platform.

Chapter 21

It was a straight race now. One Helen was in danger of losing.

As soon as she'd clocked the fugitive heading west, Helen had had an idea where Berman was headed, and when he dived recklessly across the Esplanade, it was all but confirmed. It wasn't a particularly sophisticated escape plan, but it might prove effective. They hadn't had enough time to post officers at the train station and, once on board, Berman would have numerous opportunities to descend at minor stations before they could scramble officers to intercept him.

Helen gunned the throttle, waiting for a gap in the traffic, but still the cars roared past, bumper to bumper in their eagerness to escape the city centre.

'Come on, come on...'

Suddenly, she spotted a gap in the flow and yanked the throttle, only for a van to divert unexpectedly into the inside lane, clipping her front wheel as she braked to arrest her progress. Horn blaring, the van sped on, accompanied by Helen's curses, but now finally she caught a break. The traffic lights changed and with reluctance the cars ground to a halt. Seizing this opportunity, Helen tore at the throttle and her bike leaped forward, racing across the tarmac towards Southampton Central train station.

Moments later, Helen was skidding to a halt by the entrance, vaulting off her bike and landing elegantly on the pavement. Startled travellers looked up, but Helen didn't linger, sprinting through the main doors. Scanning the entrance foyer, Helen quickly realized that Berman was not loitering here, so she powered on, hopping up, onto and over the ticket barrier, to the evident surprise of the guard.

'Hey, where do you think you're going?'

His words faded away, as Helen raced on. Her feet pounded the floor as she sought her quarry, moving fast towards the only train currently in the station. If Berman was anywhere, he would be here. The clock on the digital display signalled that the train was due to depart – would Helen have to go carriage to carriage on a moving train to hunt him down? Spilling onto the platform, Helen's eye was drawn first to an irate commuter aghast at having arrived too late to board, then further up the platform to a skinny man in jeans, hoodie and black leather jacket hammering maniacally at the button on the door. He had also arrived too late, the door refusing to yield.

Already Helen was bearing down on him, upping her pace as she raced along the platform. Now Berman looked up, Helen clocking a pale, sweaty face turning a shade paler. Once more he hammered on the door, then promptly gave up, scouting around desperately for another method of escape. But there was nothing – no other trains, no stairs, no lifts – Helen breathing a huge sigh of relief as she approached the trapped suspect.

Her relief was premature, however, for now the terrified young man did something she *hadn't* been expecting. With no other course left open to him, he jumped off the adjacent platform, hitting the ground hard, before pulling himself to his feet and racing away down the open track.

Chapter 22

For a second, Helen couldn't believe what she was seeing. Such a stunt was suicidal, but it was a measure of Berman's desperation to escape, meaning Helen had no choice but to follow. Brushing aside the protests of the approaching station manager, she jumped off the platform and gave chase.

The suspect was a hundred yards ahead, so Helen kept to the track, springing from one sleeper to the next. Berman was fast and desperate, but Helen felt sure she could close the gap. Bounding forward, her hands clawed the air, propelling her towards the scrabbling fugitive. She fixed her eyes on him, pleased to see him stumbling and sliding as panic took hold, but even as she scented victory, she came unstuck.

Concentrating on her quarry, she'd failed to spot a missing sleeper and she lost her balance now, skidding forward and connecting with the next plank of wood. Now she was plunging forwards, throwing out her hands to break her fall. They connected sharply with the stones, causing Helen to cry out, even as her knees slammed into the next sleeper. The pain was incredible, shooting up her legs to her spine, but somehow she found herself scrambling to her feet. Now she was limping forward, then lolloping into a rhythm and finally running, swallowing down her agony to remain in the hunt.

Up ahead, the fleeing figure had turned his head, hoping perhaps that his pursuer was immobilized. Even at this distance, Helen could see his anguish as Berman realized the pursuit wasn't over. Turning, he raced on, but once more Helen was gaining on him – and this time she was determined to bring him down.

Luck was not on her side, however. The suspect was fifty feet from the mouth of the main tunnel, a dark, yawning hole beckoning him into the darkness. Once hidden within the gloom, Berman could ambush her in the darkness, attempt to escape via one of the service hatches or skulk in the shadows before doubling back. Helen knew she had to get to Berman before he made it there and redoubled her efforts, determined to bring him in before they both got killed. Even as she thought this, however, the wires above the track fizzed into life. A train was coming.

Berman seemed unaware of this, fear seeming to give him a second wind. Speeding up, the lithe figure made it to the tunnel moments before Helen, racing inside. His pursuer was not far behind, however, and as Helen pushed into the gloom, she was pleased to see that Berman had opted not to hide, continuing his headlong sprint. She felt certain the end was nigh, so she upped her pace, her footsteps echoing menacingly around the arched brick interior. This seemed to alarm Berman – she saw him cast a desperate look back, stumble, then plunge to the ground. He cried out in pain, then struggled back to his feet, but he must have injured himself because it was clear he wouldn't be able to keep going. The race was over.

Helen slowed, breathing out heavily, as she dropped from a sprint to a jog. As she did so, however, the tracks started humming and looking up, Helen saw lights in the tunnel ahead.

The train from London was approaching fast and they only had seconds to save themselves.

'Andrew?'

No reaction. Could he hear her above the noise of the on-coming train?

'Andrew, you have to move ...'

Still the train kept coming, yet the fugitive refused to budge. Swearing, Helen picked up her speed. Could she get to him in time? If he could just shift himself off the track, then they would be both be—

Now she saw him move, stumbling upwards. Her heart leaped ... then immediately plummeted. Berman had only risen to his knees and remained there. She was only thirty feet from him and to her horror, Helen saw him reach out his hands to the oncoming train, inviting oblivion. As Helen lunged towards him, the lights of the train dazzling her, she saw him cry out in excitement, revelling in the imminent kiss of the train. They were both moments from disaster, but as Helen flew through the air, she caught hold of Berman's arm, wrenching him sideways. Off balance, he tumbled off the track, rolling twice before falling into Helen's arms, as the train roared past, its horn blaring.

Chapter 23

She opened her mouth and let out an earsplitting scream. She was distraught, desperate and nothing – or nobody – could appease her.

Greg White held his baby close, desperate to soothe her, but incapable of stopping this torrent of unhappiness. Bailey's face was a deep pink and her cheeks stained with tears, a sight which all but broke his heart. Desperate to stem her crying, he looked anxiously towards the kitchen, where his mother was struggling to prepare a bottle of formula milk.

'Please, Mum, she needs feeding…'

'Give me a chance, will you?' his mum snapped, her voice quivering. 'I'm out of practice…'

Giving up, Greg marched towards the kitchen. He should have done it himself, had done it thousands of times whilst managing their first nursery in Bitterne Park. It was foolish to have entrusted the task to his mother, who always panicked when the heat was on. Happily, however, his urgency seemed finally to cut through and his mother appeared in the doorway, proudly shaking the full bottle.

Taking it gratefully, Greg perched on the sofa, cradling Bailey in the crook of his arm as he held the rubber teat to her lips. To his annoyance, she pushed it away, protesting, but he persisted and now, to his enormous relief, she took it in her mouth, sucking greedily. For a few precious moments, peace reigned, his heartbeat slowly returning to normal. But the respite was brief, however, as once more his baby girl pulled away from the bottle, complaining bitterly.

'Did you warm it up?' he asked, turning to his mother.

'Yes!' she insisted. 'I put it in the machine, just like you said ...'

Trying to block out Bailey's crying, Greg turned the bottle upside down, depositing a few drops onto his wrist. To his dismay, his mother was right, the milk was the perfect temperature.

'Come on, Bailey Boo, let's try again,' he said soothingly.

But this time his daughter didn't even pretend to play ball. She turned her head away, as he tried to place, then force, the teat into her mouth. She was having none of it, looking to the heavens and letting out another bone-shaking cry. And now the fight went out of him, Greg dropping the bottle to the floor and hanging his head. He knew what Bailey wanted, what she *needed*. Her mother's milk, her mother's skin, her mother's love.

Suddenly, he felt an explosion of grief within him, as the true awfulness of their tragedy made itself felt. It was just him and his little girl now and he felt profoundly unfit for the task. He was lost, floundering in a sea of grief, horror and fury.

Dropping his head to his chest, he wept bitterly, father and child crying in unison.

Chapter 24

It was perfect.

Leaning back in her chair, Emilia surveyed the double-page spread. She'd known she'd get the front page, but this was the real prize, a centrefold masterpiece of emotion, tragedy and alarmism. Emilia was not prone to modesty – she knew she was good at her job – but even by her high standards, this was a corker.

Her phone pinged, alerting her of an incoming notification, but she ignored it, keeping her eyes glued to the screen. The paper only had generic pictures of the bereaved family so far – something she would have to rectify soon – but what they had spoke volumes. Martha White had been a regular poster on Insta and Facebook, someone who appeared keen to share her good fortune with the wider world. Next to a company photo of the happy couple posing outside a Banana Tree nursery, there was a selection of personal snaps – beatific shots of mother and baby, Greg and Martha on exotic foreign holidays, the three of them frolicking in their spacious garden. These images trumpeted success, wealth, happiness – but the latter had been suddenly snatched away in the most unexpected fashion.

People like this didn't die at the hands of a murderous assailant. They were wealthy, white, middle-class success stories, shielded from the darkness of the world in their expensive suburban homes. Well, that myth had been well and truly shattered last night and Emilia knew that across Southampton, scared citizens would be checking their doors and windows. Was Martha White the victim of an aggravated burglary? A sex attacker? Or did the crime have a personal angle? The motive remained opaque, but Emilia was happy to leave the details vague – her readers' imaginations would do the rest, stoking the fire further.

The beaming photos were flanked by Emilia's artful prose, half of which focused on the disturbing circumstances of the killing, the other half on the people left behind. This was the real juice and Emilia had gone to town, tugging at her readers' heartstrings, as she conjured up an image of a broken, confused husband, clinging to his baby whilst trying to come to terms with the fact that Martha White, beloved wife and mother, was gone. Nothing moved people as much as a vulnerable widower, so despite the fact that Greg had told Emilia to piss off in no uncertain terms a few hours earlier, she was careful to offer a sympathetic picture of him, inviting others to share his pain. She could only imagine the response this would provoke on social media – the poor man would be overwhelmed with love.

Rising, Emilia clicked 'send'. There was plenty more to be wrung from this story, but she'd done enough for now. Better to let the initial shock sink in tonight, before riding the horse again harder tomorrow. Now she needed to go home and take control of her unruly band of siblings. Usually, she went to this task with alacrity, enjoying bossing them around and picking at their faults, but tonight she felt bored by the prospect, annoyed by the predictability of their messiness and misdemeanours. She was therefore pleased to see that the notification on her phone was not some mindless spam, but the offer of a date.

Emilia had signed up to Bumble three weeks ago, after several months of depressing disappointment on a rival app. For her new profile, she had opted for undiluted honesty, showing her handsome but damaged face full on, under the legend 'I am what I am'. Better this than be coy and have to endure her date's disappointment in person. So far this approach had yielded a few conversations that had led nowhere, but here was a message from Sam, a marine engineer whom she'd exchanged a few messages with, asking her if she fancied meeting up for a drink tonight.

In spite of her natural cynicism, Emilia felt a rush of optimism and excitement. It'd been ages since she'd dated properly and she liked the look of him. Smiling to herself, she snatched up her bag and hurried across the newsroom, mentally scrolling through a list of possible locations to meet her handsome date, all thoughts of Greg White's awful tragedy long forgotten.

Chapter 25

Helen was back at Southampton Central, marching towards the incident room, when her phone started buzzing. She answered it without hesitation.

'Helen Grace.'

There was a tiny pause at the other end, then a familiar voice replied:

'Helen, it's Joseph.'

Helen shuddered to a halt. The door to the incident room was just in front of her, but she remained where she was, disbelieving.

'You shouldn't be calling me,' she hissed. 'We've said all we need to say to each oth—'

'Just two minutes of your time, that's all I ask.'

Helen was tempted to hang up – her former lover had no claim on her time – but she resisted, deciding that it was better to engage briefly and decisively, rather than deliberately frustrating him.

'Let me be clear,' she replied tersely. 'There can be no communication between us. You are no longer a member of this Force and, more to the point, you are facing criminal charges. If you stand trial, I will be called as a witness for the prosecution.'

'That's why I'm calling you. To throw myself on your mercy.'

This brought Helen up short. She had been expecting abuse, not capitulation.

'I know I treated you badly,' Hudson continued softly. 'That I let you down...'

'That's the understatement of the year.'

'And I'm sorry for that, Helen. I really am. Believe me, not a day goes by when I don't regret my actions.'

'Too little, too late, Joseph. Now if you'll excuse me, I'm in the middle of a major—'

'Call off the dogs.'

For a moment, Helen wasn't sure she'd heard right.

'I'm sorry?'

'Tell them you made a mistake, that you can't testify. Do this for me and I promise you'll never hear from me again.'

There was a hint of desperation in his tone, but Helen was not inclined to be merciful.

'You tried to *destroy* me, Joseph. You lied, you schemed, you turned my team against me. Moreover, everything you're charged with, *you're guilty of*. Conduct unbecoming, misuse of public office – why on earth wouldn't I testify?'

'Because you'll kill me if you do.'

'You're being overdramatic.'

'I can't go to prison, Helen. I just can't...'

There was real desperation, real fear in his voice now.

'Think about it. A copper in jail, mixing with all the low-lifes I helped put there. Do you think they'll pass up an opportunity to settle the score? I won't last five minutes.'

'You'll be protected.'

'Bullshit, they'll throw me to the wolves and they'll enjoy doing it. The screws won't intervene to save a "bent" copper, of course they won't.'

'You should have thought of that before you got into bed with Garanita, before you betrayed your vocation—'

'Please, Helen. I'm begging you. Despise me if you want, blacken my name, laugh about me, but please don't do this. You've been in prison, you know what it's like, spare me that at least. I was a good officer once, I *did* want to serve you, to learn from you. Please remember that now and do me this one last act of kindness.'

In spite of herself, Helen hesitated. She wanted Hudson convicted, sent down for his crimes, but she was still a human being, capable of guilt, regret, even pity.

'Come on, Helen. Show me you're capable of mercy, that there's still *some* goodness in your heart...'

Anger had crept into his tone now and that decided it for Helen.

'I'm sorry, Joseph, I can't help you. Don't call me again.'

With that, she hung up, marching purposefully into the incident room.

Chapter 26

'The victim's name is Martha White, thirty-two years old, wife of Greg White, mother to six-month-old Bailey.'

Helen paused to take in the faces surrounding her. Since Joseph Hudson's fall from grace, Helen had shaken up the team, removing the dead wood and bringing in DC Wilson from the Met. She was pleased to see him and two other loyalists, DC Malik and Charlie Brooks, in the front row, drinking in her words.

'She was confronted, subdued, then murdered last night. This is what we've got so far in terms of crime scene photos…'

She pinned the grim pictures onto the murder board.

'She was bound and gagged, then killed. Elasticated cord was used to bind her hands. You can see here that it's been secured in a tight, figure-of-eight knot. There are no prints or DNA on the cable and it'll be hard to work out where it was bought, as you can get them from any number of home stores. Ditto the rag that was forced into her mouth, though it did have engine oil on it, so could have come from a workshop or factory or perhaps a domestic garage.'

Helen noticed one of the younger members of the team pull a face – clearly distressed by the idea of a filthy rag being forced into the victim's mouth – and she understood why. Being surprised like that in the middle of the night must have been utterly terrifying.

'You've had the basics from Jim Grieves. Martha's attacker used a hatchet or small axe of some kind. One blow to kill, then three more followed. Hard to say if this was overexuberance or a deliberate attempt to mutilate the victim post-mortem – we'll need to keep an open mind on that. What *is* interesting is that the blade seems to have been well used – the imprint of the victim's wounds shows that there's a chip on the axe head, a tiny part missing. So this was either something that the perpetrator owned or obtained from a second-hand store or tool auction. Let's not waste time chasing down recently purchased axes.'

The team nodded, a couple of the newer ones making notes, as Helen continued:

'First important question is time of death. Where are we at with that?'

Predictably it was DC Malik who spoke up first.

'Been looking at Martha's comms history. Last message sent was via WhatsApp at 22.04 last night, thanking a fellow mum for some hand-me-downs: *Thanks for the bundle, hun. You're a star. Mx.*'

The words hung in the air, mundane and tragic.

'After that, no communication of any kind. Her phone was on silent when the forensics guys recovered it, so perhaps she went to bed around that time? I'm guessing she was likely to be up early with Bailey...'

'Makes sense. So, Greg White claims he returned home at midnight, having been training on Southampton Common.'

'Imagine that, ladies,' Charlie interjected ruefully. 'Being able to train on the Common after dark with no fear for your personal safety...'

'Indeed,' Helen replied with feeling, echoing the sentiments of many present. 'Do we have any evidence to corroborate White's account of his movements?'

'Seems to check out, guv,' DC Wilson replied, keen to make an impression. 'Got CCTV of him entering the common shortly after 19.10 and leaving around 23.50. Plus, a publican saw him run past the Eagle pub at the end of his road, just before midnight, so...'

'OK, double check those timings, please. Triangulate his phone, see if he has a Fitbit, Strava, anything that can help pinpoint his movements and location last night,' she replied, before turning to DC Wilson's colleagues, 'but I want the rest of you to focus your fire elsewhere. It's possible Greg White might have arranged to have someone murder his wife, for life insurance or personal reasons, and we need to be alive to that possibility, but honestly, I can't see him being involved. They appear to be a happy, successful family and I'm not sure I buy him setting some murderous thug on his wife, especially whilst his baby was in the house.'

'Is the fact that they were visibly successful important?'

Now it was Charlie's turn to intervene, picking up on Helen's thread.

'Martha White wasn't shy of displaying her wealth and good fortune online,' she continued. 'It's not just the foreign holidays and big house – it's the jewellery, watches, iPads that always seem to be in shot. If I was a burglar, I'd be targeting people like the Whites.'

'Have there been any recent burglaries with a similar MO?'

'I'm still waiting for a call back from the burglary squad,' Charlie replied, 'but I know there were a couple of high-value jobs last week, cameras ripped out, homes raided and so on.'

'Were the owners at home when the burglary took place?'

'Not sure yet,' Charlie conceded, 'but I'd like to look into it in more detail, maybe even look further back, because whoever conducted the raids last week was methodical and professional. They knew what they were doing, both in terms of victim selection and the job itself.'

'Sounds plausible,' Helen replied cautiously, 'so you should run with it. But I'm not completely convinced an experienced raider would target a security-rich house like the Whites', when it was obvious someone was at home. The car was in the drive, the lights would have been on until at least ten p.m.'

'Plus, why the extreme level of violence?'

This from DC Reid. He was still trying to work his way back into Helen's good books, having been a close ally of Joseph Hudson's in the past.

'The intruder had Martha White tied up and gagged – why did he need to butcher her like that?' he continued.

'She might have seen her attacker, been able to identify him?' Charlie offered.

'Potentially, but I'm inclined to agree with DC Reid on this one,' Helen replied. 'This was a savage, unrestrained attack, not an attempt to silence anyone. And look at the items that were taken – jewellery, keepsakes, family heirlooms and, perhaps most importantly of all, her wedding ring, pulled from her finger either during the attack or post-mortem. *All* these articles were precious to Martha, they meant something, and appear to have been targeted specifically, whilst iPads, laptops and other valuables were left behind. This attack feels personal to me. Which brings us to Andrew Berman, who was apprehended earlier today trying to leave the city.'

Helen avoided mentioning her role in Berman's capture, but she could tell that some of the younger members of the team were impressed by her heroism.

'He's being printed and processed now, so let's pull together what we've got on him. DC Jennings?'

Jennings, a flame-haired young man with a keen brain, recently recruited from Devon and Cornwall Police, took a step forward.

'Pretty much everything Mr White said about Andrew Berman was true. He *was* fired from Anderson's eighteen months ago because of his inappropriate behaviour towards Martha White. Started innocently enough with flowers and chocolates being delivered to her office, but Martha White later testified that during this time, personal items of hers were going missing – gym gear, jewellery, photos and so on. After she rejected Berman, following their one night stand, Martha started receiving deliveries from Ann Summers at work – dildos, whips, furry handcuffs and so forth. On and on it went, until Berman was hauled up and fired. Soon after that, he had to give up his flat and return home…'

'Which didn't exactly please his parents,' Charlie added wryly.

'After that things got really weird – bunches of lilies delivered to Martha's engagement party, to the maternity suite where she gave birth to Bailey.'

'For God's sake…' DC Malik muttered.

'There were also three or four instances where Berman actually confronted Martha White,' Jennings continued. 'Outside Pret a Manger in the Westquay, outside the Banana Tree nursery on Falmouth Road and a couple of times near their home on Belmont Road. All this *despite* having received a restraining order six months ago.'

'Good work, thank you,' Helen responded, pleased by the thoroughness of his response. 'We've drawn a blank on triangulation, as Berman appears to have left his phone at home last night, but we've managed to get a rough idea of his movements from street cams and have some decent witness testimony concerning his movements, but *ideally* we need to place him at the Whites' property. So far we've only got circumstantial evidence putting him at the scene, so I want us to double our presence in the neighbourhood, knocking on doors, stopping shoppers, dog walkers, students, anyone who might have seen him in the area between the hours of 9.30 and 11 p.m. Perhaps forensics will help us out, but if we draw a blank there, we're going to need some very solid witness statements.'

'So are we saying it's him? That *he's* our man?'

This from DC Malik, who seemed suddenly energized. Rising, Helen replied:

'That's what I intend to find out.'

Chapter 27

'Can you take me through your movements last night? Minute by minute, from 8 p.m. onwards, and please don't leave anything out.'

Andrew Berman refused to meet Helen's gaze. Battered and bruised from their tussle in the tunnel, he seemed distant and detached, wishing himself elsewhere. In a different room, a different situation, a different life. Darting an exasperated look at Charlie, Helen continued:

'I'll remind you that you are the prime suspect in a murder enquiry, so I'd suggest you co-operate. Let me start you off, see if I can prod your memory. Your mother told us you left the house around 8 p.m. Is that correct?'

Berman made an odd whistling noise and shook his head, as if dismissing the very notion, but offered nothing concrete by way of response.

'The landlady of the Lamb and Flag...'

Helen made a show of checking her notes.

'...A Mrs Vivienne Armitage remembers serving you three pints of lager between your arrival around quarter past eight and your departure just after 9.30. She remembers it clearly, as you were fairly drunk when you arrived and became increasingly obnoxious to her other customers during your stay. Which means, incidentally, that we have a whole host of witnesses, plus the pub CCTV, of course ...'

'So I went for a drink. What of it?'

Berman stared at his dirty fingernails, picking at them absently, but Helen was pleased she'd managed to get a response at last.

'Can you tell me what you were wearing?'

'What?'

Berman looked up, confused.

'Your clothes? What were you wearing last night?'

'Don't know, don't pay much attention to that kind of stuff.'

'You were wearing dark blue jeans, a black T-shirt and a dark brown trench coat.'

'Why ask if you already know the answer?'

'Because we need you to confirm it,' Charlie replied, stepping into the fray.

'Well, I'm not denying it,' Berman spat back. 'Happy now?'

Now it was Charlie's turn to angle a glance towards her colleague. There was something dismissive, even cocky in Berman's tone, which was encouraging. He was starting to relax into the interview, enjoying the skirmish, which is usually when suspects made mistakes.

'After that we lose sight of you, until 11 p.m., when you turn up at the Cube Bar in Bitterne Park,' Charlie continued. 'What were you doing in the interim?'

'Sorry?' Berman replied, feigning confusion.

'Where were you between 9.30 p.m. and 11 p.m.?' Helen interjected, losing patience.

'Walking around, I don't remember ...'

'Did you go to Martha White's house?'

'Of course not, I'm not allowed to, *remember* ...'

'It would have been on your route to Bitterne Park. By my

reckoning it would only take half an hour, forty minutes tops, to walk from the Lamb and Flag to the Cube Bar, so what were you doing the rest of the time?'

'Beats me, I was pretty pissed by then.'

'Why was that, Andrew?' Helen persisted. 'Working yourself up to something, were you? A bit of Dutch courage?'

'I'd had a bad day, that was all,' Berman responded drily, his distaste for Helen clear.

'That's a bit of an understatement,' Charlie responded, taking up the reins. 'Your parents had just told you to pack your bags, hadn't they? They wanted rid of you.'

Both police officers saw a reaction, a flash of anger.

'That's right,' he eventually responded. 'Washing their hands of me, their only child...'

'Not without good cause, by the sounds of it,' Charlie persisted. 'Your mum said you'd made their lives hell. Always drunk, aggressive, argumentative. Always leaching off them, unable to hold down a job. And as for the state of that basement flat, it wasn't fit for an animal...'

To their surprise, Berman laughed, long and bitter.

'You sound just like my mother. You got kids?'

Charlie shrugged, not willing to go there.

'Well, I pity the poor bastards. No one rubs salt in the wound quite like your mother.'

'Is that why you were so agitated last night?' Helen queried. 'Your family had turned their back on you. You had nowhere to go, no job, no money, no friends...'

The suspect didn't deny it, glaring at his inquisitor.

'Any normal person might hold their hands up at that point,' Helen continued. 'Acknowledge that *maybe* they were to blame, but I don't think you're made that way, are you, Andrew? I think you blamed *her*. Blamed Martha White for all your misfortunes.'

'It starts and ends with her. I don't see how you can read it any other way,' he replied tartly.

'What do you mean by that? "Ends" with her?'

Berman looked away, ducking the question, but Helen wasn't going to be deflected.

'I think you blamed Martha White for ruining your entire life. You *used* to have a career, you *used* to have friends, a family that loved you. I think in your mind if Martha hadn't rejected you, if she'd returned your feelings, then things could have been very different. But she didn't. She spurned you, married another guy, had a kid with him and did everything in her power to ensure that she'd never have to lay eyes on you again.'

The suspect remained silent, returning his attention to his fingernails.

'I'm showing the suspect a photograph that was retrieved from his basement flat earlier today. Could you tell me what it is, Andrew?'

Berman cast a dismissive look down at the photo, but couldn't help reacting to the sight of his former love with her eyes scratched out.

'No? Let me help you then. It's a photo of you and Martha White, taken at a work do. She's smiling, happy... except her eyes have been scratched out. Why did you do that, Andrew? Why did you deface this picture?'

'If she couldn't see, then why would she need eyes?'

'Couldn't see what?' Helen queried quickly. 'That you were meant to be together? That you were the man for her?'

'You wouldn't understand.'

'Try me.'

But once more, Berman kept his counsel.

'We also discovered several other items in your flat,' Charlie added. 'Items we believe belonged to Martha White.'

She slid another clear evidence bag onto the table.

'Necklaces, earrings, a gym card, items of clothing, even underwear...'

Another flash of anger, as if Berman was annoyed that Charlie now possessed these treasured keepsakes.

'Why did you take them, Andrew? What did they *mean* to you? Did they give you a thrill? An erotic charge? Or were they gifts in your head? Tokens of love?'

Scenting sarcasm, Berman looked up sharply.

'She *had* feelings for me, all right? Told me that herself.'

'For one night, maybe...' Charlie responded, pouring cold water on his protests. 'But those feelings didn't last, did they? She wanted to move on...'

'But you didn't,' Helen overlapped. 'Which is why we are where we are. She rejected you, pushed you away, but the more she did so, the more you wanted her.'

'You don't know what you're talking about.'

'You loved Martha, but you also loathed her. She was your *everything*, but your obsession with her destroyed *everything*. You know what I think happened last night? I think the last pillar of your life gave way. Your beleaguered family, who'd tried to turn a blind eye to your erratic behaviour, your grim fascination, your criminal behaviour, finally pulled the rug from under you. You had nothing left – and nothing left to lose. Angry, drunk, desperate, you went to Martha's house, forced your way in and took revenge on the woman who'd destroyed your life.'

Berman was shaking his head, but Helen continued:

'And after that, you ran. Ran to escape punishment for your dreadful crime.'

'I ran because I knew you'd try to pin it on me!'

'And even when you *were* cornered,' Helen continued, ignoring his interruption, 'you tried to avoid having to face up to what you'd done. In fact, you'd happily have killed yourself if I hadn't intervened.'

'More fool you.'

For once the sarcasm had gone. Berman sounded like he really meant it, bitterly regretting the fact that he was still alive.

'That would have been the easy way out, wouldn't it?' Helen continued. 'But life doesn't always work out that way and now you have to answer for your actions.'

'Ask me then. Ask me if I killed her,' Berman countered forcefully.

'Did you?'

Berman paused, then lowered his neck to be close to the recording device.

'No. I. Didn't.'

'So where's your coat?'

Berman appeared startled by Helen's question, wrong-footed by the change of subject.

'You were wearing a brown trench coat when you left the Lamb and Flag at 9.30, but when you arrived at the Cube Bar at 11, you didn't have it anymore, despite the fact that it was absolutely freezing last night. What happened to it?'

And now for the first time, Berman looked rattled.

'I'm showing the suspect a CCTV still from the Cube Bar, which clearly shows the suspect arriving at around 11 p.m., wearing only—'

'I don't remember,' Berman interrupted.

'I'm sorry.'

'I was wasted last night, all right? I'd had half a bottle of vodka before I left the house, more beers at the Lamb and Flag, I was all over the shop. Maybe I left it somewhere, gave it to someone...'

'Who?'

'I don't know.'

'Well, that's very convenient, Andrew, but I don't buy it.'

'It's the truth.'

'Bullshit. I think you went out in your trench coat, carrying the axe inside, then once you'd got up the courage, you murdered Martha White, before disposing of the coat and the axe. Then you headed to Bitterne Park to drink away your guilt or celebrate your bravery. Which one was it, Andrew?'

'Piss off.'

'If I'm wrong, tell me where the coat is. Tell me why you were wandering around on the coldest night of the year, wearing only a T-shirt. I'm curious to know. Why would you dump that nice warm coat? Was it because Martha White's blood was on it?'

Berman was agitated, his hands gripping the side of the table.

'Got it all worked out, haven't you?' he hissed. 'I'm the bad guy and she's the angel.'

'I didn't say that.'

'You're just like those bitches on the panel, sitting there, judging me, belittling me, painting me as the aggressor, the troublemaker, the bloody stalker, for fuck's sake. Destroying my career. And for what? Some hurt feelings? A woman in denial? Well, listen to me, you sad little dyke. Say what you like, do what you like, but you're not going to pin this one on me.'

His eyes sought out Helen's, as he concluded:

'I didn't do it.'

Chapter 28

It was fascinating to watch her in action, but it gave him no pleasure. In fact, everything about Helen Grace made him feel deeply uncomfortable.

Chief Superintendent Alan Peters stood behind the two-way mirror, watching the interrogation. The suspect looked a mess and was clearly rattled by the persistent, forensic questioning, but somehow Peters' gaze never seemed to linger on him, his attention focused on the principal inquisitor instead.

It had always been like this – Helen Grace had a way of commanding your attention. Peters realized now that this was in her DNA – her desire to be at the heart of things, orchestrating events, controlling the narrative, making sure that it was *she* who was front and centre. Initially, Peters had been prepared to accept this. Though he bridled at the endless commendations and newspaper inches Grace commanded, he couldn't argue with the fact that she got results. Latterly, however, he had become increasingly troubled by her self-absorption, her desire to be the heroine, realizing that her behaviour was actually pathological – hence her incessant rule-breaking and risk-taking, which not only endangered her own life, but that of her colleagues, too, not to mention the good reputation of Southampton Central.

Ever since this thought first landed, Peters hadn't been able to think of much else. Helen Grace was the most decorated CID officer the station had ever had, but she was also its greatest liability, having been officially censured multiple times for her erratic, impulsive behaviour, which had cost both money and lives over the years. Her conscience seemed impervious to these stains on her character, to the blood on her hands, but Peters was not so thick-skinned. He knew what other senior officers said about Southampton Central, that it was out of control, run by a renegade, that it was Grace, not he, who was in charge. The thought made his blood boil, not least because there was an element of truth to their jibes.

She had grown too big – in every sense. Too powerful, too indulged, too convinced of her opinion, running the Major Incident Team as her own personal fiefdom. She had scant regard for him, though she played the game, of course, curtseying when necessary, but he knew she bridled at his attempts to check her power and influence. Perhaps this state of affairs, this low-level war could have rumbled on interminably, but recent events had exacerbated the situation, raising the stakes significantly.

Despite what she might say, Grace was in a bad way. Alex Blythe had left his mark on her, the experienced detective more secretive, guarded and paranoid than ever. Nobody seemed to be able to get close to her anymore, not even her old comrade-in-arms DS Brooks, and though Grace was trying to act as though it was business as usual, Peters knew something was badly wrong.

He regretted now having offered her a reprieve, following her disastrous clandestine relationship with Joseph Hudson, at the conclusion of the Blythe case. He could have had her head then, but such was the collective relief that Blythe's killing spree was at an end, that he'd decided against pushing it through. He had issued her with a stern warning instead, declaring that another misstep would result in her suspension or worse, but to him this warning now seemed weak, a capitulation to her superior reputation and popularity. Now, with another major investigation ongoing, it was too late to do anything. How he rued his cowardice, his indecision. Yes, he carried on as normal, dispensing his duties efficiently and professionally, but his thoughts were forever drawn to her, convinced that the next time Grace messed up – as she surely *would* – that she might take *him* down with her.

Watching her through the glass, Peters was struck once again by her remorselessness, her ferocity, her focus. For her there was no middle ground; it was death or glory. Others might find this thrilling – her team holding this battle-scarred warrior in awe – but to him it smacked of danger, an impending threat. For one thing couldn't be denied about Grace. Whether it be in her personal or professional life, whenever she went for something, when she *fully* committed to it, carnage usually followed.

Chapter 29

'When are you going to get it into your thick skull? *I'm* the innocent party here.'

Andrew Berman launched the words at Helen, spittle flying through the air.

'Even though you subjected Martha White to a campaign of harassment lasting *nearly two years*. You made her life hell,' Helen retorted.

'Oh sure, she was really suffering, with the big house, the rich husband ...'

'You accosted her outside a mother-and-baby group, for God's sake. Scared the life out of her. You followed her from her place of work, turned up at the family home.'

'She started this, not me. She came onto me—'

'But you finished it, didn't you? Like you said earlier ...'

'Don't twist my words.'

'What shoe size are you, Andrew?'

'What?'

'You heard me.'

Helen stared directly at him, determined not to be messed around any longer.

'Size nine.'

'Thought so.'

She let Berman squirm in his seat for a moment before continuing:

'A partial footprint from a size nine trainer was found in the Whites' garden this morning. An Adidas trainer, same brand as you wear. The soil had been freshly laid, the footprint recent for sure and I'm betting that if we compare the soil from the soles of your shoes with that from the garden—'

'OK, I went there, but I didn't do anything, all right?'

Helen raised an eyebrow, but didn't respond, watching Berman's agitated body language with interest.

'Just to be clear then,' Charlie intoned, 'you went to Martha's White's house on Belmont Road last night?'

'Yes,' was the muttered response.

'And?'

'And nothing. I don't know what I was thinking really, I just… just wanted to scare her, freak her out a bit. So I climbed the back fence, went into the garden, but then the security light came on, I think…'

'You think?'

'No, it did. The light came on, so I thought better of it, went on my way. I was stupid to have gone there…'

'So…' Helen stepped in, choosing her words carefully. 'Drunk, embittered, you gained access to Martha White's garden, intent on terrorizing her. But then suddenly you had a moment of clarity, of self-possession, and quietly retreated?'

'Believe what you like, I'm telling you the truth.'

'I'm amazed that you can be so precise, so definite, when you can't remember where you dumped the coat you were wearing, or the jewellery you stole—'

'I didn't steal any jewellery—'

'Or the axe that you were carrying. Tell me, why did you choose to use an axe? Was it to make a point, to terrify your victim? Or was it just something you could lay your hands on without arousing suspicion?'

'What are you *talking* about, woman? Do you think we'd have an axe hanging around the house?' Berman countered. 'My dad's an accountant, for God's sake, my mum's a teacher, we don't have tools like that...'

'But you did work at the refuse and recycling centre on Alma Road recently, didn't you?'

Once again, Berman looked unnerved, Helen's diversion catching him by surprise. Consulting her notes, she continued:

'You only lasted three weeks, which is a bit of a record apparently. One of my colleagues spoke to the manager earlier, says he showed you the door because you were thieving, taking things from the site that didn't belong to you.'

'You don't want to believe that old drunk, he had it in for me from day one...'

'Now, according to him, much of your time was spent breaking up furniture and other household items, using sledgehammers, mallets, hatchets and so forth. Well-worn, sturdy tools, fit for purpose. Would have been easy to slip one into your coat at the end of a shift. Not much CCTV on site, hard to prove it was *you* that stole it...'

'You've got it all worked out. All neatly tied up with a bow.'

'I wouldn't say that, we're still working on some of the minor details, but I do know that you've lied to me repeatedly during this interview—'

'Go to hell...'

'I also know that you had motive, means and opportunity. You've admitted you gained access to their property, that you blamed Martha White for all your misfortune and that you wished her harm. You can't give me a satisfactory account of your movements last night, nor can you account for your missing coat, which must have been stained with blood, following your brutal attack on the woman you had come to loathe. But...'

Helen paused to gather her breath, then continued in a softer tone.

'...I know that you are not a bad man, Andrew. You're not a psychopath, or a common-or-garden killer. You *do* have humanity, goodness, in you. You could have harmed Martha's baby last night, but you didn't. You spared her, which says a lot. I know what happened was the conclusion of two years of emotional and psychological anguish, a terrible aberration committed when you felt at your very lowest. I understand that, which is why I'm not judging you. It will make a difference to your sentence, of course it will. You were clearly not in your right mind last night... but I do need to hear it from you. I need you to tell me exactly what happened. Only then can we make this *right*.'

It was a gamble, but Helen was hopeful it might work. If she appealed to Berman's sense that he'd been wronged, that somehow this situation was not of his making, then she might be able to unlock his defences. She watched their prime suspect closely as he leaned back in his chair, raising his gaze to the heavens.

'I can't deny I haven't thought about it,' he replied eventually. 'Haven't fantasized about taking that bitch out. I'd enjoy seeing the look on her stupid pretty face, the realization that she *could* have had me but didn't and now has to pay the price... I'd have loved that. But you know what, however much I hated her, however pissed and angry I was, I'm certain of one thing. I couldn't do it. I *didn't* do it. And everything you've said today is just... words. Because I wasn't in that house last night and *you* can't put me there.'

As he spoke, he leaned in towards Helen, challenging her directly.

'What do you say to that, *Helen?*'

She regarded him coolly, just about concealing her distaste, before responding:

'I say you've pretty much talked your way to a murder charge, *Andrew*. And when we get the corroboratory evidence – which we *will* – I will take great pleasure in charging you myself. Martha, Greg and Bailey White deserve justice.'

She rose, towering over him.

'And I intend to see they get it.'

Chapter 30

Her eyes flicked up, keen and suspicious, sizing up the approaching intruder.

'We don't open for another hour, mate. You're too early…'

DC Wilson smiled, trying to put the young bartender at her ease, as he raised his warrant card for inspection.

'It's all right, I'm not after a drink. But I would like to ask you a couple of questions.'

'I'm flat out here and the manager doesn't pay me for chatting.'

She'd already dropped her gaze, uneasy at the prospect of official enquiries. Wilson could guess why – the Cube Bar promised much from the outside, but in reality was a down-at-heel dive in a forgotten part of the city. Who knew how much low-level criminality went on within these tired walls?

'Don't stress, it's nothing to worry about. I'm just wondering if you recognize this guy?'

He offered her a recent photo of Andrew Berman, who scowled at the camera. Instantly, he saw a flash of recognition, but once again caution was her watchword.

'What's he done?'

'Just answer the question, please. You were working here last night, right?'

'Sure,' she conceded, unnerved by his apparent knowledge of her whereabouts.

'Did you serve him?'

'*Several times...*' she replied ruefully. 'Though I didn't want to. I would have thrown him out as soon as he arrived, but the manager told me not to refuse good money, so...'

'What was it about him that troubled you? Was he drunk? Aggressive?'

'*And some,*' the young woman replied with conviction. 'Right from the off, I could see he was trouble. He barged into someone on his way over, spilled a load of drinks, but just carries on as if nothing had happened. Plus he looked bloody weird – tatty jeans and an old metallers T-shirt – as if he'd found his way here by accident.'

'So he's not a regular?'

'I'd never seen him before and I work most shifts...'

'What happened after that?'

'Well, he manages to pour himself onto a stool and stays there for the next two hours, just drinking. And he's not fucking about – Scotch all the way.'

'And he had the money for these drinks?'

'At first. But after a couple of hours the money ran out. So, then, he asked if he could get credit, and when I told him where to go, he offered me this watch. Looked flashy, expensive, but what the hell do I know? Anyway, I told him it was time to move on, which he didn't like at all. Started acting up, calling me names, so I told him I'd get security on him. Well, that didn't faze him either, his blood was up, so I threatened to call the cops and that shut him up.'

'What time would you say this was, roughly?'

She thought for a moment, picking at one of her nails, before replying:

'Around 2 a.m., I think.'

'And what happened after that?'

'Nothing.'

Wilson was surprised by her response, expecting some kind of scene.

'Meaning?'

'Meaning he just sat there, staring into the distance. That was what freaked me out really. The rest of it I'm used to – the aggro, the drunkenness. This was something else. He just sat by himself until closing time, totally still, totally quiet. Couple of times I met his gaze, trying to see if there were any signs of life, but there was nothing. I've never seen anyone look so …'

She thought for a moment, before adding:

'…so empty, so broken. At the end of the night, I had to physically shake him to snap him out of it.'

'And then?'

'Then he left. Just got up and walked out, but something was wrong. He hardly registered what was going on around him and was *so* pale. To be honest, he looked like he'd seen a ghost.'

Thanking her, DC Wilson took her details, then left, content that he had all he needed. It was only circumstantial, but it fitted the narrative of events they had established thus far – of a young man at a crisis point in his sorry life, driven to a dire, desperate act in his anger and despair. Wilson was pleased to have something to offer DI Grace – some strong first-hand testimony regarding Berman's mood and behaviour – but the interview had also left him feeling unnerved, disquieted by the image the young bartender had conjured up of a hollow, tarnished creature, whose life had been soured by a dark, unforgiving love. Wilson had only recently got engaged, to a woman he'd doted on for over five years now. Was it possible that Andrew Berman once felt the same way about Martha White, as he did about his lovely Juliet? The thought made him shiver, the notion that something pure and life-affirming could become so corrupt, so violent, so evil.

Pulling his collar up around him to ward off the cold, Japhet Wilson hurried to his car. After a difficult day, he wanted to be back home, with the love of his life, to remind himself that despite all the darkness and despair out there, there was still goodness in the world.

Chapter 31

Her eyes ran over his pleasingly muscular physique. Sam Teller, a marine engineer recently moved to Southampton, looked good in his profile picture, but even better in the flesh. Moreover, he seemed gentle, even a little shy, embarrassed by the confident, carnal gaze Emilia fixed upon him.

'So, you're a journalist, right?'

Unlike most men she'd dated, Sam didn't seem keen to talk about himself, appearing much more interested in her life.

'*Southampton Evening News*. Been there for over ten years, barring a brief flirtation with the capital.'

'Didn't like the big city?'

'It was more that it didn't like me,' she replied quickly, glossing over her failed attempts to establish herself as a London journalist. 'But I'm cool with that. I like being a regional journalist, easier to be a big fish in a smaller pond...'

'So you're well known here?' he asked, with genuine interest.

'You could say that,' Emilia teased, dropping her eyes to the table.

'Go on,' her date coaxed in response.

Smiling, Emilia tossed back her hair, before continuing.

'So I report crime. Which means that I get to spend time with, and write about, a lot of wicked people.'

'Real-life crims?'

'And the rest. I've broken bread with serial killers, rapists, arsonists. Even got kidnapped once.'

'You're kidding me?!'

'Don't worry, I got out of it OK, no harm done. As you can see...'

She gestured to the historic scarring on her face.

'...I'm something of a survivor.'

The handsome young man paused, surveying her face, before replying:

'I was going to ask about that, but I wasn't sure if you'd mind...'

'Oh, I'm comfortable talking about it. In fact, it's quite an interesting tale...' she said, smiling wryly. 'But it's a long story and kind of personal, so why don't you fetch me another drink and then I'll tell you *all* about it.'

'Sure thing. Same again?'

'Roger that, but easy on the tonic this time.'

Sam hurried to the bar. Emilia watched him go, running an approving eye over his tight ass, amused by how well their date was going. He was young, handsome, considerate, keen, intelligent... so normally there would be a catch. A girlfriend still on the scene, an obsessive personality or, worst of all, a tourist, someone just interested in bagging an unusual – should that be damaged? – catch. But this time she could detect no such bear trap – he appeared to be the genuine article. Perhaps her up-front approach to dating was working.

Relaxed, happy, Emilia let her eyes drift away from Sam to take in the other revellers in this cheerful, city centre pub. Whenever she was out, she loved to drink in the lives of others, speculating from afar about their situations, their personalities, their jobs. Part of her job was about reading people and she loved to imagine what celebrations or crises, possibilities or disasters occupied those around her. The pub was busy tonight and there were rich pickings to be had, her gaze stealing over a couple of vastly differing age, locked in earnest conversation. Was this a date? Or were they father and daughter? Moving on, she spotted two young men together, teasing each other playfully. Friends? Brothers? Lovers? She moved on to her next target, a middle-aged man drinking alone, but now her jolly game ground to a halt, her playful mood dissipated by the shock of recognition.

It was Joseph Hudson. Sitting at the bar alone, halfway through a pint. Immediately, Emilia lowered her gaze and turned away, pretending to scroll on her phone. She was not by nature one to back down from a challenge, but she suddenly felt tense and uneasy, as if she'd been caught out. For over a year, the former Detective Sergeant had been her mole in Southampton Central, giving her unfettered access to Grace's investigations and the inner working of the Major Incident Team – until Professional Standards had got wise to his transgression. As part of their investigation into his wrongdoing, their officers had collared Emilia in her office, demanding details of her interaction with Hudson. Backed into a corner, Emilia had had no choice but to throw him to the wolves, giving them everything she had, in an attempt to avoid prosecution herself. Her ruse had worked, but Hudson's life was now in tatters and there could be no doubt that he partly blamed *her* for his downfall.

She kept her gaze pointed resolutely down, cursing her choice of venue. What were the odds that the pair of them would end up here together, barely twenty feet from one another? What would happen if he spotted her? Would he make a scene? Abuse her? Attack her even? It didn't seem possible, it didn't seem fair, that this wretched soul should put in an appearance when her date was going so well. What did life have against her that it would send her Hudson tonight?

She counted to ten, then glanced towards him. Happily, Hudson seemed utterly unaware of her existence, staring forlornly into his near-empty glass as if searching for answers. And now, as her fear and alarm subsided a little, she noticed how terrible he looked. Yes, he was wearing a suit, and still possessed some of the chiselled good looks that had once appealed to Helen Grace, but he looked to have aged massively, seeming greyer and thinner than before. More than that he seemed stooped, having lost his impressive carriage and bearing. He looked beaten.

And now, in spite of herself, Emilia felt a stab of pity. He looked shocking, a man in abject despair, and though she fought hard against this conclusion, it was impossible to deny that she *was* partly to blame for his current situation, having blackmailed him into getting into bed with her. But wasn't that how the game worked? How it had always worked?

'There you go. I got you a double and you can pour the tonic yourself...'

Emilia snapped out of it, as Sam sat down. Chancing another look at Hudson, she snatched up the gin, downing the generous measure in one go.

'Actually, I've had a change of heart. It's getting busy in here and I've got much more interesting drinks at home, so why don't we go there?'

Grabbing her bag, she held out her hand to him. For a second he seemed shocked by her brazen suggestion, but then he relented, stretching out his hand to meet hers. Relieved, Emilia led him forcibly from the bar, happy to be away, never once looking back at the husk of a man she was leaving behind.

Chapter 32

'First thing in the morning, we need search teams scouring the area.'

Charlie nodded, but said nothing in response. Following their interview with Berman, Helen and her deputy had returned to the incident room, which was now deserted, the clock having crept round to ten o'clock. The pair stood by the murder board, Helen jabbing a map of Southampton, her index finger zeroing in on the St Denys district of the city.

'My guess is Berman will continue to deny involvement, meaning we have to place him in the house and/or recover the discarded coat and axe. Soon as we have those, we've got him.'

'Where do you want to start?' Charlie responded, sounding as tired as she looked.

'Well, the local search has turned up nothing, so let's go wider. To get to Bitterne Park from the Whites' house, Berman's quickest route would be via the A3035.'

'That's pretty public, isn't it? Lots of traffic, possible witnesses ...'

'True, but going via Kent Road would have been an incredibly roundabout route, and I think he'd want to get away from the scene as fast as possible.'

'Which would take him over Cobden Bridge,' Charlie offered.

'Exactly. If you're looking to dump something, it's as good a place as any. He could wrap the axe in the coat, toss it into the river or there are plenty of good hiding places below the bridge, on the banks of the river.'

'So if we get a team to do a walk through from the Whites' to the A3035, but focus most of our efforts in and around the river?'

'My thoughts exactly,' Helen returned with a smile.

Charlie smiled back at her old friend, but somehow it didn't reach her eyes.

'Are you OK, Charlie?' Helen asked, deciding that bluntness was best. 'You seem a bit distracted.'

'It's nothing,' Charlie replied, dropping her gaze. 'Kids were up in the night, that's all.'

'You get off home then,' Helen replied warmly, deciding not to push it. 'We've a 7 a.m. start tomorrow...'

Pulling a face, Charlie picked up her bag and departed. Helen watched her retreat, more concerned than ever. Something *was* wrong, that much was evident, but what it was Helen couldn't say. She'd hoped that after Hudson's dismissal and Charlie's return to work, things would pick up again, that the MIT would feel like a happy, functioning unit. And whilst morale *had* improved, Charlie had not been her old self. In days gone by, she and Helen had been peas in a pod, professionally and personally, working the mean streets by day and supporting and confiding in each other by night. Helen was godmother to Charlie's two lovely girls and had spent many happy nights at their family home, including a couple of memorable Christmases. Throughout that time, Charlie had been warm, affectionate, open and honest. But not now.

Was there some problem at home? Some issue with the kids? Or did the problem lie within the walls of Southampton Central? Previously Charlie had returned from maternity leave with relief and zeal – she was a police officer who loved her job and considered it her calling. But her energy, her enthusiasm, had waned of late, leaving Helen wondering if she *regretted* returning to work this time. Was it possible that she was fed up of being a working mum, of forever juggling plates? Or was it the job itself which troubled her? Ground down by the never-ending carousel of violence, criminality and anguish? It was a thought that unnerved Helen deeply. What would she do if her rock and support through the last decade decided she'd had enough? Was it possible Charlie was considering quitting? Or was Helen being paranoid, letting her imagination run away with her?

Helen was lost in these disquieting thoughts when a sudden buzzing made her look up. Seeing her phone vibrating on the desk, she snatched it up.

'Meredith, what can I do for you?'

'Sorry to disturb you late in the day,' her chief forensics officer replied. 'But I thought you'd want to hear this.'

'Go on,' Helen replied, intrigued.

'Well, we've just been doing some work on the dummy recovered from the nursery and we've got a useable print off it.'

'And?'

'And it's Andrew Berman's.'

Helen didn't respond, a broad smile spreading over her face. Despite Berman's denials, despite his insistence that he had never set foot in Martha White's house, they now had positive evidence to the contrary.

Thanking Meredith, Helen rang off, snatching up her keys and heading for the door. It had been a tough day, but at the eleventh hour things were finally looking up and it was with a spring in her step that Helen flicked off the lights and marched away down the corridor.

Chapter 33

Walking up the front path, Charlie paused as she approached the front door. She had been half dreading, half anticipating this moment all day.

Having had to run out the house first thing, she had exchanged only a few words with the kids and fewer still with Steve. And whilst she was looking forward to seeing the girls, it was her partner, the love of her life, that she really wanted to spend time with tonight. They had become ships that passed in the night of late, their lives running on different timetables, with the result that communication was sparse and there seemed, to Charlie at least, to be a growing distance between them. She hoped and believed that Steve wasn't the type to stray, but two of her closest girlfriends were already dealing with the fallout from messy affairs and, in all honesty, how well could you know another human being?

Slipping her key in the lock, Charlie resolved to be positive, happy and communicative tonight. To try and banish her doubts and fears and have a nice, relaxed evening with Steve. Perhaps that was all they needed. A glass of wine, a mooch on the sofa, a good chat. She wouldn't be accusatory, she wouldn't judge, but she would nevertheless ask about his work, find out what was keeping him at the garage late and thus put her mind at rest.

Who knows, perhaps if the girls were sound asleep, they might even have an early night. It was ages since Charlie had taken Steve to bed and she missed his touch.

The door slid open and she stepped inside. Shutting out the night, she suddenly felt her spirits rise. It was warm and cosy in their little house and the comforting aroma of lasagne crept out of the kitchen, greeting her. Suddenly she felt foolish to have been so melodramatic about things when there was nothing tangibly wrong. Now was not the time for imagining problems, now was the time for pasta, Barolo and a little downtime. Encouragingly, the house seemed quiet, the girls hopefully fast asleep upstairs.

Smiling, Charlie strode into the kitchen, slinging her bag down on the chair. But as she did so, her heart tumbled into her boots. Standing by the sink, arm deep in washing up, was Steve's mother, Pam. Turning, the septuagenarian smiled broadly at her daughter-in-law.

'Evening, Charlene. How was your day?' she asked, beaming.

'Fine, thanks,' Charlie responded dully. 'Where's Steve?'

'Oh, he's had to work late again, so he asked me to field the kids. No need to worry, they were good as gold. They've eaten, bathed and are now sleeping like angels. Really, they couldn't have been sweeter to deal with.'

She announced this as if confident that it would fill Charlie with pride, happiness, even gratitude. But in reality, Charlie just wanted to cry.

Chapter 34

Helen sped along the road, relaxed, content and in control. In her world, there were very few easy wins, few straightforward cases, but tonight she felt confident and assured, hopeful that justice would soon be delivered for Martha White. Normally, she raced home, keen to be inside her sanctuary, but tonight she took her time, determined not to run scared, to take in the sights and sounds of the night, whilst nevertheless keeping a weather eye on those around her. It was possible to remain alert and vigilant, without assuming that every passing car or idling pedestrian had murder in mind.

Dropping her speed to thirty miles per hour, she drank in the night-time carnival of Southampton at play. A group of exuberant football fans were trying to climb a lamppost, a pair of loved-up teenagers giving them a wide berth as they hurried down the street. Further along, there were joggers, dog walkers and the obligatory hipster on his electric scooter. Helen thought she detected an appreciative glance as the young man clocked her ride, but she didn't linger to find out. Tonight was about looking forwards, not back.

Five minutes later, she was rolling up the street to her block of flats. Already she was projecting ahead to a relaxing evening. A bit of yoga to wind down perhaps, some home-made Thai curry and then her guilty pleasure – a few episodes of *Brooklyn Nine-Nine*. She knew it was daft, but she was never happier than when settled on her sofa, letting the easy laughs wash over her.

Approaching the ramp to the car park, she swung her bike round and began to descend. As she did so, the steel grille that barred access to the underground car park juddered into life, recognizing her approach. With practised ease, she glided underneath it, her helmet just missing the lip of the grille. Pulling into her reserved space, she killed the engine and flicked out the stand, before dismounting quickly, stowing her helmet under the seat. Relaxed, content, Helen made her way quickly across the rough concrete towards the stairs, keen to be back in the sanctuary of her flat.

The car park was deathly quiet, save for the low buzz of the strip lighting. Usually, Helen found this lifeless silence depressing – emblematic somehow of her isolated, occasionally lonely existence – but of late she'd taken comfort in the stillness and safety it promised. Tonight, however, something was different. Helen couldn't put her finger on why this was, but as she crossed the dirty floor towards the stairwell, there was no denying that the atmosphere felt ... odd. She had a knot in her stomach and couldn't shrug off the nagging sense that she wasn't alone, that she was perhaps even being watched.

Slowing her pace, Helen scanned the basement, searching for a potential assailant. Cautiously, she moved from vehicle to vehicle, darting anxious looks between them, but there was nobody lying in wait. Was she imagining the danger? Letting her fears run away with her? She was tempted to make a dive for the stairs, to run from her anxiety and paranoia, yet she remained rooted to the spot, trying to penetrate the shadows in the gloomy space. Instinct told her that something wasn't right, that there *was* another presence here, malign and threatening.

'Hello?'

Helen's voice echoed off the walls, eliciting no response.

'I know you're down here, so why don't you step out and face me?'

As she issued her challenge, her eyes swept over the surrounding cars. She had already done a brief circuit around them, finding no one. Was it possible someone lurked *beneath* them? Surely not, it would be near impossible to fit underneath and would hardly be the best position from which to mount an ambush. Where then? The only other hiding place would be behind one of the large concrete pillars that propped up the ceiling. There were four of these substantial blocks and Helen padded towards the nearest one now. It would be possible to lurk behind these stanchions, concealed from view when Helen entered the building and parked up. If someone *was* lying in wait for her, surely *this* was the place.

She'd made rapid progress, was only a few feet from the pillar, so paused to ready herself. And now in the deathly silence, she heard it. Faint, but instantly recognizable, the sound of someone breathing. She had been right, there *was* an intruder down here.

How best to defend herself? Any element of surprise was now gone – on both sides – but perhaps if she made the first move, she could seize the initiative. Sliding out her baton, she extended it quietly, then took a step forward.

Instantly, he bolted. Helen jumped out of her skin as the dark figure burst out of his hiding place, readying herself to repulse an attack, but her would-be assailant was heading not towards her, but *away*, towards the exit ramp. Without thinking, Helen gave chase. He was moving fast, desperate to make it under the security grille that was now descending, but Helen covered the first few yards with lightning speed. Her prey tried to respond, upping his speed, but Helen lunged forwards, clawing at him.

For a moment, she thought she had him, her gloved fingers gripping his flailing left arm, but with a desperate wrench, the man pulled free. Unbalanced, Helen stumbled, one knee kissing the concrete, before she righted herself and charged on.

The grille continued its steady descent, but there was no guarantee it would cut off the fugitive's escape, so Helen raised her pace once more. The fleeing figure was only yards from safety now, but Helen knew she could take him. A well-timed rugby tackle would bring him to the ground, where she felt confident of disabling him. Timing would be everything, however – she would have to launch herself at just the right moment – and she braced herself, preparing to spring forward.

She sensed it before she saw it. A slight slowing in his pace, the sudden movement of his shoulder ... then he struck, her assailant spinning to face her. Feeling the danger, Helen jerked back, as a flash of silver, a long steel blade, missed her throat by an inch. Skidding to a halt, Helen braced herself for another blow, but to her dismay, her attacker now pivoted, rolling under the falling grille. Helen reacted, but too late, the metal shutter reaching the ground before she could follow suit. She crashed into it, prompting her assailant to dart a quick, fearful look at her. She saw a flash of fair hair, a sweaty unshaven face, then the intruder was gone, sprinting away up the ramp.

Desperate, Helen hit the manual override, but she knew it was too late. The grille was aged and slow – her attacker would be long gone by the time she made it up the ramp. Slamming the shutter, Helen roared out her frustration, but her anguished cry provided no relief. Her nerves were jangling, her brain on fire, her whole body reacting to the crushing realization that Alex Blythe had finally made good on his threat.

Someone – some faceless assassin – had penetrated her building tonight, lying in wait in this shadowy space, intent on stabbing her in the back. The thought of bleeding out on the cold, oil-smeared floor made Helen shudder and a sickening feeling of dread now took hold of her. Suddenly all her precautions seemed hopeless, doomed to fail, for how could she possibly hope to evade the attentions of a committed and desperate assassin? There was no point denying it – she was living on borrowed time. Death was stalking her, waiting for an opportune moment to strike.

The only question was when.

Chapter 35

She tugged at the handle, but the door wouldn't budge. Satisfied, Emilia moved away from the rear of the house, pausing to check the kitchen window, before heading into the small lounge. The catch on the large casement window here was not fully pushed in, so Emilia rammed it home, then applied the lock. Better safe than sorry.

Exiting the lounge, Emilia continued her tour, checking the front door before heading upstairs. She was well aware of the irony of these security checks, but as the only grown-up in this busy, chaotic household, she wasn't going to take any chances. Still, it amused her to think that all over the city tonight, anxious residents were enacting a similar ritual, keen to keep dark forces at bay because of her words. Her articles in tonight's *Evening News* had certainly hit their mark, the paper's Twitter feed exploding with anxious questions, fearful speculation and dozens of sightings of suspicious figures loitering in residential areas. Normally at peace with the world, the good folk of Southampton were running scared tonight, seeing killers in every shadow.

The story would grow and grow, Emilia felt sure of that. Grace's team apparently had somebody in custody, but even if they had managed to arrest the perpetrator, the impact of Martha White's savage murder would be felt for weeks to come.

According to her source at the mortuary, the weapon used was an axe – a fact Emilia intended to reveal to the general public tomorrow. That would set the cat amongst the pigeons, as would other elements of this shocking crime – the youth, affluence and beauty of the victim, the potential danger to the slumbering baby, the frenzied nature of the attack. Yet for all this, what really struck home with local residents was the terrifying notion of home invasion, of someone stealing into your house when you were fast asleep. All notions of safety, security and comfort evaporated with the idea of a ski-masked man (why avoid clichés?) padding across the carpeted floor, hungry for violence and bloodshed. It was an image which, once implanted in your mind, was hard to shift and Emilia was no exception, despite her professional detachment and complicity as progenitor of this panic. She loved and was frustrated by her siblings in equal measure, but she certainly didn't want any harm to befall them. So whilst there was a mad axe man on the loose, she would take no chances.

Reaching the top landing, she tried the last window, then descended to her bedroom once more. Teasing open the door, she saw Sam, propped up in her bed, his nakedness covered by her bulky duvet. He looked relaxed, happy and wide awake, which pleased her greatly as she was more than ready for Round Two. And if their first bout of love-making had been anything to go by, a lot of fun lay in store. Smiling to herself, Emilia stepped inside the room, closing the door behind her, shutting out the night.

Day Three

Chapter 36

The lighter sparked in his hands, then a strong flame sprang to life, dancing in the cold breeze. Leaning into it, Japhet Wilson lit his cigarette, feeling the warmth of the blaze on his cheek. For a moment, he lingered, enjoying the sensation – this flame was the sole source of heat and light on this bitterly cold January morning.

It was one of those dull winter dawns that sap the soul – grey, brooding and lifeless. It had been a struggle to haul himself out of his bed this morning, to leave his beloved fiancée behind, but duty called, hence why he now found himself on Cobden Bridge, surrounded by uniformed officers and the suited search team. They were just waiting for an official 'go' from DI Grace, allowing Wilson a few minutes to enjoy a cheeky cigarette. He'd promised Juliet that he'd already quit – and he *was* trying to limit himself to a few a day – but in truth his addiction to nicotine was too strong, the result of too many early starts like this and endless days waiting, waiting, waiting for something to happen. He was embarrassed by his deceit, his trickery, but wasn't ready to go cold turkey yet, hence why he always kept a packet in the glove compartment of his car, hidden discreetly behind a torch.

'Got one of those for me?'

He turned sharply, annoyed to have been surprised by his boss's approach. Helen Grace was virtually on top of him, appearing as if by magic from the mist that hung over the Itchen river.

'Of course, guv.'

In his eagerness, he fumbled with the packet, self-conscious and thick-fingered. He expected Grace to smile at his clumsiness, but this morning her expression remained curiously blank and opaque.

'Here you are.'

She took the cigarette from him, accepting the light he offered her, before drawing deeply on it. Turning away from him, she exhaled the smoke, long and slow, casting an eye over the other officers. Dropping his cigarette to the floor, Wilson extinguished it, but remained silent, awaiting orders. To his surprise, however, Grace said nothing, staring dully at the assembled masses. The silence lingered – grew – before finally Wilson felt compelled to speak.

'So we've got a team at the White property and I think we're all good to go here.'

Still nothing from Grace.

'The crews are suited and booted. We thought we'd start on the east bank and work south, as the canal path is more shaded there, better possible site for disposal. If that yields nothing, we'll try north, before crossing to the western bank. ETA for the dive crew is an hour. They'll hit the water as soon as they arrive, following a similar search pattern to the main team...'

Wilson was keen to sound professional, decisive, an officer willing and happy to shoulder responsibility. It was pathetic, really, how keen he was to impress her, how nervous he felt around the mythic DI Grace, yet he couldn't help himself. This was a big move for him, a stepping-stone to greater things perhaps, and he desperately wanted her respect and patronage. But to his disappointment, she seemed hardly to have heard him.

'I want community officers on the bridge and both banks, please,' she said quietly, turning slowly to him. 'Stopping anyone who might have been in the vicinity that night.'

'Of course, I'll get onto it right away.'

She nodded, moving away, then paused, returning to him once more.

'And you're all right? Fitting in OK?'

The question took him by surprise and for a moment he couldn't think what to say.

'Er, yes, of course. Loving every minute of it.'

He died quietly inside, the preppy exuberance of his enthusiasm utterly at odds with the sickly grey dawn and the brutal case they were investigating. He half expected Grace to laugh at him or at the very least muster a sardonic smile, but instead she just nodded absently, as if his response was what she'd been expecting.

'That's good. Carry on then...'

She darted a brief glance at him, then hurried away to her bike, deep in thought. Wilson stood rooted to the spot, confused by the exchange. He knew his commanding officer had a lot on her mind, following the conclusion of the Blythe case, but of late she seemed to have had a burst of renewed energy and drive, the product perhaps of a couple of successful investigations. Today, however, she seemed all at sea, distracted and unhappy. Had something happened? If so, would he ever get to hear about it? Or would he remain forever on the outside looking in?

He had gambled a lot coming here, leaving a perfectly good job in London, dragging Juliet away from her family to set up home in a new city – now he prayed he'd made the right call. On paper it'd seemed a no-brainer, a chance to work with the most successful MIT unit in the country, to learn from its celebrated leader, but today he wasn't so sure. Grace was a living legend – fearless, indomitable, a one-woman powerhouse – but today she seemed a shadow of herself, unhappy, troubled, her pallid countenance perfectly matching the anaemic weather.

In truth, he had never seen anyone look so haunted as Helen Grace did today.

Chapter 37

Nicholas Martin stared venomously at the bathroom mirror, disgusted by the figure in front of him. He had long despised himself, but today his loathing had reached new heights. Once he had been a commanding presence – a handsome, charismatic teacher – but no longer. The man who met his eye was a mockery of all he'd once been.

Rubbing his unshaven chin, Nicholas turned on the tap. Cupping the scalding hot water, he threw it on his face, revelling in the body shock, the life and energy the pain brought him. Lathering up, he worked the shaving foam into his stubble, then picked up the razor. But the blade shook in his hand, beating out the rhythm of his panic. Suddenly he was back there, Helen Grace pursuing him across the unforgiving concrete, her footsteps pounding in his ears. He had thought of nothing else during the long sleepless night. How close he had come to discovery. How close he had come to *disaster*.

'Don't be too long in there, I've got to shower and run...'

Siobhan passed by the open doorway, unaware of the terror that gripped him. Grunting a response, Nicholas closed the door, ashamed of his petrified torpor. He raised his hand once more, but still his body refused to obey. Questions pulsed round his brain. What would he have done if Grace had caught him?

What would he have said? How would he have attempted to explain away his failed ambush?

It was a small miracle he'd escaped, the juddering security grille separating him from his pursuer with exquisite timing. There was no place for self-congratulation amidst his relief, however – he had failed, failed utterly. Berating himself for his ineptitude, Nicholas had raced home, determined to abandon his crazy scheme, to put the whole venture behind him, regardless of the consequences to himself.

But life was not that simple of course and his determination to be strong, to stand up to his persecutor wavered as he lay, sleepless and rigid, next to his beautiful slumbering wife. Later, when Izzy had stumbled into their room, on the edge of a nightmare, his resolution weakened still further, reminded of all he stood to lose as he tucked his beloved toddler back into bed. This was a prison of his own making, one from which it would be nigh on impossible to escape.

On cue, his phone now started ringing. Number withheld. His heart sank and his first instinct was to reject the call, turn the phone off... but he knew this would be a mistake. Turning the taps up louder, he moved further into the room.

'Yes?' he whispered into the receiver. 'What do you want?'

'You know what I want, Nicholas.'

Blythe's voice was sardonic and cold, as always. How Nicholas hated him, how he regretted ever having sought him out, unwittingly walking straight into his web.

'And I must say, I'm getting a little impatient.'

'I'm on it, all right?' he protested. 'I was at her building last night.'

'Do you think I don't know that? What the hell went wrong? You ran away from the place as if you were on fire.'

'The opportunity didn't present itself, that's all. I have to pick the right time to do this...'

'You've had time – *weeks* – to do the one, simple thing I asked of you,' Blythe snapped back. 'I have told you – on numerous occasions – exactly where she'd be and when she'd be there. I've given her to you on a plate and still you hesitate. If you can't do it, or won't do it, just say the word, because there are others who would willingly take your pl—'

'Look, I've said I'll do it and I will...'

'I hope so, Nicholas. Because it would be a terrible shame if I was to have to share those video clips with Siobhan and the kids. All those lovely young schoolgirls in the showers—'

'Enough, OK? We've been through this.'

He tried to sound angry, decisive, but Blythe ignored him.

'What would your mum and dad say, if they realized what their golden boy had been up to? Bit embarrassing for the family, I'd say, with your dad a headmaster and all...'

'You've made your point.'

'Then it's time for you to make *yours,*' Blythe fired back. 'Do it and do it *soon*, or face the consequences.'

The line went dead, Nicholas Martin dropping the phone to the floor. All resolve, all energy, all hope seemed to drain from him, Blythe's insidious voice rendering him powerless. He realized now that he still had the razor in his hand and part of him was tempted to drive it into his wrists, his throat, whatever – anything to end his pointless, tainted existence. But Siobhan's impatient pacing outside the room and the distant sound of his kids shrieking in the background rendered that an impossibility. There was no way he could abandon them, nor any way in which he could endure being exposed and humiliated in their presence. It seemed crazy, but there was only one solution, one possible way to escape impending disaster.

Helen Grace had to die.

Chapter 38

Was it possible? Was he really being followed?

Greg White upped his pace, urging himself not to start imagining things. He hadn't slept a wink, felt totally wired – it was no wonder his brain was misfiring. Despite the sickening tragedy that had befallen them, the sudden, impossible violence that had destroyed their happy family, he mustn't start believing that danger lurked in every passing face.

Pulling his coat up around the sling, he leaned down to kiss Bailey's head. She hardly responded, happily staring out at the carousel of sights and sounds on Southampton Common. He had come here almost by instinct, his feet treading their familiar path to the huge expanse of green at the heart of the city. He hadn't planned it; it had been an impulse decision, grabbing his little girl from the arms of his protesting mother, wrapping her up and sliding her into the sling, before heading out into the cold. He knew it was cruel, that he was being unfair, but he couldn't handle his mother's low simpering, her strained face, her visible grief. His parents' world had been as horrifically shaken as his by the events of the last two days, he knew that, but he had no head space for their distress. He needed oxygen, freedom, some sense that life went on as normal, despite their awful loss.

Casting around him, he tried to engage with the innocent

scene in front of him. A dog chasing a ball, a mother and daughter walking arm in arm, a teacher leading a phalanx of schoolchildren across the grass. Abruptly, he turned away from them, doubling back on himself, their youthful laughter, their happiness seeming to mock him, reminding him of all he had lost. As he did so, however, he noticed a young woman check her stride, as if wary of getting too close. Even now, she hesitated, uncertain whether to proceed or feign interest in something else.

He *was* being followed, there was no question about it now. And even as this strange thought landed, he realized why. It was her, that unpleasant journalist who'd turned up at his parents' house yesterday, asking all sorts of hurtful questions. Garanito? Garanita? Had she been lying in wait for him this morning, intent on stalking him, of inflicting more misery? Suddenly, he found himself marching towards her, fire in his blood.

'What the fuck do you think you're doing?'

He was onto her in a flash.

'I'm out with my daughter, for God's sake,' he continued, enraged.

'I just wanted to see how you were getting on, Greg? How are you coping?'

He was lost for words, her concern so false, so unconvincing.

'How do you think we're bloody doing?' he spat back. 'Now piss off before I call—'

'I just wanted to ask you a couple of questions—'

'NO!'

The word erupted from his mouth, causing heads to turn. To his surprise, he was in the journalist's face, jabbing a finger at her.

'You leave me and my family alone. You understand?'

'Not a good time for questions. How about a photo, then?'

For a moment, he was lost for words, rendered speechless by her total lack of shame or embarrassment. And as he stood there, poleaxed and impotent, the journalist tugged a camera from inside her jacket and raised it to her eye.

'What are you doing?' he demanded.

Snap, snap, snap.

'Get away from us, you fucking vulture ...'

But it was too late. He had walked into her trap and she had exactly what she wanted, a photo of father and child, the former looking haggard, desperate, even slightly crazed.

'You print a picture of my daughter and I'll sue the crap out of you ...'

But he knew his threat had no teeth. Even now the journalist was backing off, tucking her camera back into her jacket, content, triumphant.

'You look after yourself, Greg. And if you ever want to talk, give your side of the story, you know where I am ...'

Turning, he hurried in the opposite direction, desperate to be rid of her presence. What kind of nightmare was this? Was it not enough that he'd lost his darling wife? Was he to be endlessly tortured too? Ceaselessly reminded of his own loss and the wider world's vicarious *enjoyment* of it? It was awful, just too awful, so cradling his baby, he broke into a run, desperate to be away from this terrible encounter, fleeing a fate that he knew would forever pursue him.

Chapter 39

If he was feeling the pressure, he didn't show it. Andrew Berman, less hungover and more assured than yesterday, leaned back in his chair, surveying Helen with hostile amusement. He clearly intended to dead-bat any insinuation of guilt, to laugh off her attempts to entrap him, but Helen was not in a mood to be frustrated. She wanted his guilt established and the case concluded as swiftly as possible.

'You said yesterday that you gained access to Martha White's garden on the night of her death. Could you talk me through what happened next?'

Berman eyed the recording device, before responding:

'We've been through this.'

'Details, Andrew. I want details.'

'I climbed over the fence, made my way to the shed.'

'Then?'

'Then I started walking down the path, which is when the security light came on. I wasn't sure what to do at first, so I just... took cover.'

'Where?'

'There was a bush close by, so I just kind of climbed into that, waited for the light to go off...'

'Where *exactly* was this bush?'

'On the left-hand side of the path, about fifty yards or so from the house.'

Helen made a note, then continued:

'Then what?'

'Then I got the hell out there. I'd no idea if her husband was around or not, so...'

'But you *knew* he wouldn't be there. He was never there on Tuesday evenings—'

'Bullshit. I don't know what they get up to, how they live their lives.'

'Except you do, don't you, Andrew? Hence why you ambushed Martha when she was at the shops, when she was out with her daughter, not to mention those times at the hospital, at her engagement party.'

'Those were stunts. This was just a spur-of-the moment thing—'

'Except that you'd come prepared, *armed*...'

'No, it wasn't like that. I'd had a skinful of beer, was feeling shitty about everything, but that was it—'

'You forced the back door, didn't you? With an axe that you'd stolen from work.'

'No.'

'I've got three search teams out looking for that axe right now. Not to mention an underwater unit combing the riverbed. We will find the axe, your coat, and trust me we will be able to link them to you, to the murder scene. Blood's much harder to get off than people think—'

'I didn't kill her.'

'Once again, Andrew. And this time with more conviction.'

'*I didn't.* I've never set foot in that bloody house.'

'So why did we find your prints there?'

For a moment he paused, thrown, before resuming his attack.

'Oh no, you're not pulling that shit with me. If you've got proof that I was there, show it to me.'

Helen was happy to oblige.

'I'm showing the suspect a copy of a forensic report, issued last night by Meredith Walker, chief forensics officer for Hampshire Police. It reveals that a fingerprint matching that of the suspect was found on a dummy in the cot belonging to Bailey White – a dummy retrieved from the crime scene just hours after Martha White was murdered.'

Berman looked thunderstruck.

'Tell me, did the baby start crying at some point? Were you worried she would alert Martha to your presence? Or did she start acting up *after* the murder, hindering your escape?'

'I don't know what you're talking about.'

It was a spirited defence, but he looked flustered.

'You *were* in that house on the ninth. You murdered Martha, then you pacified Bailey, then you left. That is what happened, right?'

'No, I've told you—'

'So how come your print is on it, then?'

'It must have been from when I met her in the street . . .'

'*Met* her?'

Helen's scorn was withering.

'Jumped her, ambushed her, call it what you will. That's the only possible explanation.'

'This is desperate, Andrew.'

'No, no, it's the truth. She'd just come out of a mother and baby group. I waited until the other mums had gone, then I approached her. The kid dropped the dummy whilst we were talking, so I picked it up, gave it back to her. Martha didn't like that, didn't like it one bit. Told me to stay away from her, her family.'

'Except you didn't, did you?'

'That's why my print's on the dummy, don't you see?'

'No, I *don't* see. All I see is a man trying to wriggle off the hook.'

'It's not like that.'

But the fight seemed to have gone out of him now.

'Look, we've spoken to the staff at the Cube Bar,' Helen persisted. 'We know what state you were in that night, how far gone you were. You'd crossed the line, hadn't you? You finally acted on your fantasies, repaid Martha in full for all the slights and betrayals. I bet you were in shock, weren't you? More than that, I bet killing her didn't make you feel any better, did it? In fact, it made you feel worse, because, deep down, you still loved her.'

Berman stared at the table, saying nothing.

'But here's the thing – how you feel is irrelevant. What concerns me is the feelings of Greg and Bailey White, his parents, their family and friends. What concerns me is getting justice for an innocent woman. So deny it all you want, but I will see you pay for your crime.'

'But I haven't done anything, I've told you!'

His outburst was shrill, impassioned, but Helen ignored it.

'It's only a matter of time now. We *will* find the murder weapon, we *will* place you in that house, we *will* prove that you killed Martha White. Trust me, Andrew...'

She glared at him, her anger clear.

'...this is the end of the line.'

Chapter 40

He charged along the road, keeping up a fierce pace. His shift started in less than five minutes and he'd already been late twice this week. One more misdemeanour and he'd be shown the door and where would that leave him? Having to beg his sister for a bed? Or worse still, having to return home, tail between his legs? It didn't bear thinking about.

Sweaty, breathless, Harry Coulter stole a look at his watch.

'Shit...'

It was worse than he thought. He had precisely two minutes to get to work if he wanted to avoid his boss's ire. Instinctively, he broke into a trot, but as he did so, his tequila headache punched through. When would he ever learn? He'd deliberately asked for an extra shift this morning, desperate to raise money for a deposit, so why had he gone out with the boys last night? Pushing through the pain, he soldiered on, moving fast across Cobden Bridge. In two minutes' time, he'd be suited and booted and on the job and then everything would be fine – as long as nobody spoke too loudly to him or asked him to do anything complicated.

Cresting the bridge, he now spotted an obstacle in his path, however.

'What the hell?'

How many cats had he kicked to deserve this? There were uniformed police officers at the far end of the bridge stopping passersby. There'd probably been a mugging or something, but whatever it was, he didn't have time for it. Slowing his pace, he sized up his options, waiting for a moment until all the officers were busy in conversation ... then he went for it.

Steaming forward, Harry made for a gap in the human traffic. If he could just slip pass unnoticed, then he might still make it on site on time. All he had to do is keep his head down and keep moving.

'Sir?'

He registered the sound, knew it was aimed at him, but kept moving. What were they going to do, arrest him?

'Sir?'

Louder this time, but still he didn't turn around, didn't acknowledge the summons in the slightest. He was nearly there, just a few yards more ...

But now disaster struck. A burly policeman stepped in front of him, holding up his hand for him to stop. Stymied, Harry had no option but to play ball, feigning surprise.

'Sorry, I was miles away ...'

'No problem. We're just appealing for witnesses, so I was wondering if I could have two minutes of your time?'

Two minutes Harry didn't have.

'Sure, what do you want to know?'

'Just wondering if you might have been in this area between 10 p.m. and 11 p.m. on the night of January ninth?'

Harry's heart sank further. Of course he had been, he'd been here every night this week. But should he own up to it?

Sensing his hesitation, the officer continued:

'If so, did you happen to notice this gentleman in the vicinity?'

Happily, Harry took the print-out from him. Once he'd

confirmed that he didn't know the guy, then he'd be free to race around the corner, this time armed with a good excuse for his tardiness. He lowered his eyes to the photo, then froze. Because he *did* recognize the guy.

In fact, he'd seen him on this very bridge two nights ago.

Chapter 41

Helen was so immersed in her thoughts, so blind to her surroundings, that she nearly crashed headlong into Charlie. The experienced DS was carrying an armful of files, heading fast down the corridor in the opposite direction, managing to grind to a halt just before a possible collision. As she did so, however, one of the files slid from her grasp, falling to the floor and scattering its contents on the tired carpet.

'My fault, let me ...'

Helen bent down easily, scooping up the errant papers and sliding them back into the file. Rising, she handed them back to Charlie, who managed a weary smile. Helen was shocked by her demeanour. You couldn't conceal Charlie's good looks, but her skin this morning was *so* pale and dark rings hung beneath her bloodshot eyes.

'You all right, Charlie? You look like you've had a big night ...'

'I wish,' she replied softly.

'What's up, then?' Helen continued, lowering her voice. 'Sorry to be blunt, but you look like shit ...'

It was meant as a joke, but to Helen's horror, she saw her old friend well up, emotion ambushing her. Shocked, Helen slipped her arm through Charlie's.

'Right, you, come with me.'

And with that, she marched her straight out of the fire exit and into the smoker's yard.

Five minutes later, they were settled in this abandoned corner of Southampton Central, Charlie nursing a cup of tea, whilst Helen drew on a cigarette.

'You *are* kidding?'

Charlie's face suggested she wasn't.

'But this is *Steve* we're talking about…' Helen persisted. 'He loves you to bits.'

'I thought he did…'

'Of course he does. I'm sorry, Charlie, I just can't see it…'

Charlie seemed somewhat mollified by Helen's certainty, yet was still unsettled and distracted.

'Is this what's been eating away at you, lately? Why you've been so unhappy?'

Charlie shrugged a 'yes', looking embarrassed. To Helen's shame, she actually felt pleased by Charlie's response, having been fearful that it was the job – even Helen herself – that was the problem. If it was only Charlie's paranoia, then surely she could deal with that?

'Has he said or done anything to make you think he's been playing away?'

'Nothing concrete,' Charlie conceded. 'But he's very secretive, hardly ever home at nights, always making excuses for where he's been and… and we just don't seem to spend any time together anymore.'

'But isn't that normal, when you've got two little ones and you're both working?'

Helen knew she was out of her depth here, having no knowledge of normal, functioning relationships, but she persisted.

'This is the tough bit, right? A phase that you just have to push through?'

'Maybe... it's just... it's just an instinct, you know,' Charlie replied ruefully. 'A sense that something's not right. We've been together nearly ten years now and maybe... I don't know... maybe the spark just goes out of things after a while. Not from my end, but maybe from his...'

'Really? How would that even be possible? You're gorgeous.'

'I wish. I'm a useless old lump, who's no use to anyone. I'm not spending proper time with Steve or with the kids and I'm hardly tearing up trees at work—'

'No, no, no. I'm not having that.'

Helen stepped forward, grasping Charlie by the shoulders affectionately.

'You are an amazing wife, mother, friend and copper. Never anything less than that, do you understand me?'

Charlie nodded, but didn't look like she meant it.

'But I can see you're worried and you need to deal with it. Which means talking to Steve. Pull in some favours, pack the kids off to your mother-in-law and spend a proper evening with him. Tell him how you're feeling, how you've been worried—'

'He hates that kind of chat.'

'I'm not worried about him, I'm worried about *you*,' Helen countered warmly, but firmly. 'I don't know much about these things, but I do know that if you don't face up to your fears, if you don't lance the boil, then your anxiety, your unhappiness will only grow. Talk to him, Charlie, please. And trust me, everything will be fine.'

Finally, Helen's words seemed to be sinking in. Charlie appeared buoyed by her pep talk, the colour returning to her cheeks, and was on the point of answering Helen in the affirmative, when suddenly they were disturbed. The door to the yard swung open and to Helen's surprise, DC Jennings's ruddy face appeared, breathless and urgent.

'Sorry to disturb you, guv. But we've got a witness sighting.'

Chapter 42

'Tell me exactly what you saw.'

The young man eyed Helen warily. They were standing by the riverbank, in the shadows of Cobden Bridge, under the watchful eye of the telephone engineer's boss, whom DC Wilson was trying to distract.

'This isn't about you, so there's no need to worry,' Helen reassured him. 'We just need to know about your encounter that night.'

The witness seemed to take comfort from Helen's words, finally finding his voice.

'So I was doing some cabling work at a junction box in the lee of the bridge, right?'

Helen nodded encouragingly.

'We have to do it late at night, because of the footfall round here. My shift was 9 p.m. until 2 a.m.'

'I see.'

'Anyway, I was about an hour or so into my shift, when this guy turns up...'

Coulter gestured to the flyer on which Berman's face was emblazoned.

'You're *sure* it was him?'

'Totally. He was there long enough, plus we spoke a bit...'

'You *spoke* to him?' Helen replied, surprised.

'Well, I wouldn't normally. The boss likes us to keep our heads down,' Coulter replied defensively. 'But he seemed in such a bad way that I thought I better had...'

'What sort of state *was* he in?'

'He just kind of looked... lost. He must have stood on that bridge for half an hour or more, just staring at the water. To be honest, he was weirding me out, I wasn't sure *what* he was up to. But then he took off his coat, climbed up onto the bridge wall, like he was going to jump or something...'

'And then?'

'Well, then I dropped what I was doing and went up there, tried to talk to him...'

'And did he respond?'

'Not really. He clocked me, but he was crazy drunk, all over the place. I asked him if he was OK, if there was anyone I could call, but he mumbled something and headed off.'

'In which direction?'

'That way,' Coulter said, gesturing. 'Towards Bitterne Park.'

'And the coat?' Helen pressed. 'Did he take it with him?'

'No. He walked off without it, despite the fact that it was bollock freezing. I called after him, but he never heard me.'

'So where is it now?'

'I picked it up, in case he came back for it. It's still in the cabin, if you want to take a look at it,' he offered helpfully.

Helen's heart was sinking, but she persevered.

'And what time did all this take place? Exactly, please...'

'Like I said, he appeared around ten o'clock.'

'You're absolutely sure of that? This is really important.'

'Yeah, definitely, I heard the bells from St Stephen's.'

'And he was on the bridge for...?'

'At least half an hour or so. Probably left around 10.35 or 10.40.

I texted my boss shortly afterwards, asking what I should do. I can show you the message if you like...'

Helen nodded, but her mind was already elsewhere. She had been convinced they had found the perpetrator of this brutal crime, but as the witness continued his testimony, scrolling happily through this phone, one thing was abundantly clear.

Andrew Berman could *not* have killed Martha White.

Chapter 43

'You're sure he didn't do it?'

Chief Superintendent Peters made no attempt to hide his surprise, nor his displeasure. Nevertheless, Helen refused to break eye contact, refused to be intimidated.

'As sure as we can be at this stage. The timings pretty much make it impossible, plus we've recovered the coat Berman was wearing that night. There's no sign of blood on it, or any other obvious forensic evidence linking it to the crime scene.'

'What about the fingerprint on the dummy?'

'He's got an explanation for that, one which *does* tally with what we know about his interaction with the victim in the period before her death.'

'Which leaves us with *what*? A partial footprint which he also seems able to explain away…'

'That's about the size of it,' Helen conceded, taking it on the chin. 'I think Berman was there that night, but my gut instinct says he's telling the truth. He went to her house, thought better of it, then headed to Bitterne Park. Everything we know about that night suggests Berman was in a pretty deep funk and the testimony from Harry Coulter backs this up – I think Berman was potentially suicidal, probably more interested in taking his own life than Martha White's.'

Peters exhaled theatrically, crossing to the window. A heavy silence filled the room for a moment, before he finally spoke:

'So we're no further on.'

'I wouldn't say that, but it's true that we need to re-evaluate the evidence, our list of suspects—'

'Are you going to tell the press that, or shall I?' Peters interrupted brusquely. 'They're already having a field day with this one. Garanita's got half the city convinced there's a psychopath on the loose.'

'I'll deal with her.'

'I wish you would. Because she's making us look like a bloody laughing stock.'

By us, he meant him.

'I'm sure, given a bit more time, that we'll make concrete progress,' Helen reassured him. 'This is a very unusual crime and I'm confiden—'

'Are you up to this, Helen?'

The question was so unexpected, so outrageous, that for a moment Helen wasn't sure how to respond.

'Because if you've any doubts about your ability to do the job, I'd rather you told me now.'

'I'm fine, sir. Never better.'

'It would be perfectly understandable...' Peters continued, 'if you felt weighed down, distracted, beleaguered even by the events of the past few months—'

'If you're referring to Alex Blythe, I can deal with it,' Helen countered, sounding more certain than she felt. 'I've faced down worse than him.'

'But to have that hanging over you, it can't help but sap your morale, your energy, your resolve. So if you *did* feel that you needed to step aside, if only temporarily—'

'That won't be necessary.'

'Perhaps even seek professional help.'

'I've said I'm *fine.*'

She meant to sound decisive and in command, but there was a bluntness, an acidity in her tone that Peters couldn't miss.

'The team is working well, we've got a good unit now, we're *making progress.*'

Peters didn't look like he believed her. Or didn't *want* to believe her.

'To be honest, sir, what really "saps morale" is having one's role, one's ability, one's state of mind questioned, for no good reason.'

It was a concerted pushback, a blatant challenge to her superior and the twisted narrative of her fading powers. One he appeared happy to sidestep.

'That's not what this is about. I'm simply asking the question, so we can do what's right for everyone—'

'With the greatest of respect, it's *exactly* what you're doing. And it is deeply, deeply unhelpful.'

For once, Peters didn't have an easy comeback, shocked by the vehemence of her response. Helen knew she was stepping way over the line, but her blood was up now and she couldn't stop the words tumbling from her.

'I know that you don't like me, that you doubt me ...'

'Come on now, Helen. Don't be like th—'

'But I would remind you that we have a killer to catch. And every second spent justifying myself to you is time wasted, time that could be better spent hunting him down. You ask me if I'm OK, whether I'm up to the task, what I need to bring this case to a successful conclusion. Well, I'll tell you what I need ...'

She glared at him, eyes blazing.

'I need to be left alone to do my job.'

Chapter 44

'Right, gather round, everyone…'

Helen's voice boomed across the incident room, her anger, her outrage raising the volume higher than was strictly necessary. The team seemed to pick up on her frustration, rising from their desks and hurrying over.

'So in case you haven't heard,' Helen continued, wasting no time in getting to the point, 'it looks like we're going to have to release Andrew Berman. Timings, forensics and his general state of mind suggest that he is *not* our perpetrator.'

A few groans escaped from the team, their disappointment clear.

'So we go back to square one, review every piece of evidence, every whisper, every half-sighting, every possible theory or testimony we might have entertained. Berman seemed like a good fit, but perhaps we let that blind us to other credible suspects. Let's look again at the husband, family, friends, former partners, ex-colleagues, disgruntled employees from their nurseries, anyone…'

She was about to say 'who had an axe to grind', but thought better of it.

'…who might have had a grudge against Martha White. Also, let's check out anyone who was working in the house or garden in the last six months, anyone who might have clocked the layout of the house, where the valuables were kept. Do they have a cleaner? A regular handyman? A gardener? I want every possible avenue explored.'

'I'd like to take the lead on the burglary angle,' Charlie offered, her voice full of purpose and determination. 'I know the violence seems excessive in this case, but it was also a very professional job, no slip-ups, no forensic evidence, plus there has been a clear rise in the rate and severity of home invasions recently. I don't think our guy is an amateur, I think he's an experienced, well-seasoned burglar.'

Her conviction had a visible effect on the team – a rise in interest and energy – and Helen was profoundly grateful for her intervention.

'Absolutely,' Helen confirmed. 'Pull in whoever you need to help. Let's see if we can find a pattern, a similar MO, anything that can give us a bead on the perpetrator. OK, let's get to it, nothing left uninterrogated, no stone unturned...'

The team didn't need telling twice, hurrying away to renew their investigations. Helen knew they had a long road ahead of them, that the hunt would be arduous and complex, but in truth she envied them. Sometimes leadership was about delivering the very worst news, and doing it personally, but it was not a role she enjoyed. Her colleagues faced a stiff challenge rooting out a vicious and secretive killer, yet she longed to be part of the chase. Better that than having to inflict fresh pain, fresh misery on a grieving family. There was no avoiding it, however, so scooping up her bag, Helen headed for the door.

It was time to tell Greg White that his wife's killer was still at large.

Chapter 45

She stared at his handsome face, oddly moved by the anguish that distorted his features. Usually, Emilia managed to keep a safe, professional distance from her subjects, but there was something about the rawness of Greg White's grief, his anger, his desperation that cut through to her. He may have verbally abused her in the roundest terms – twice now – but there was something in the force of his emotion, his devastation, that still struck home. He genuinely looked as if the bottom of his world had just fallen out.

Happily, the force of his grief had found its way into her writing, her prose particularly powerful today. She had cut it fine – she would need to file her copy imminently if they were going to hit the stands – but the effort, the time spent crafting her narrative of loss and desolation, had been worth it. It was a punchy, vivid portrait of a man assailed by terrible tragedy that Emilia was convinced would move her loyal readers to tears. Would the effect of her article have been as pronounced without the striking photo of White which flanked it – red-eyed, dishevelled, unhinged? Probably not, but as it was she who had obtained the photo, this didn't matter. Her stakeout, her pursuit of the tragic widower had been worth it; once more she was ahead of the pack. Another very good day's work.

Running one final spell check, Emilia was about to press 'send' when her phone buzzed next to her. Scooping it up, she saw that she had a new Snapchat message. She scanned it quickly – BERMAN RELEASED. NO CHARGES BROUGHT – barely taking in its import. Her finger was still hovering over the 'send' key, but now she withdrew it, her mind whirling. She had deliberately been light on the detail in terms of the arrested suspect, keeping her powder dry until she knew more. But now a change of strategy was required. If Berman had been released, it meant Grace's team had *nothing*. This could be used against them, more evidence of their failure in the face of a clear and present danger, but better still, it meant the killer was still out there. A killer who might strike again at any time.

Smiling at her relentless good fortune, Emilia dialled the sub-editor's number.

'Paul, hold the front page, will you? I think we might need a new headline.'

Chapter 46

'Mum, there's no need to keep calling. I've told you, everything's fine...'

Ethan was trying not to sound annoyed, but his patience was wearing thin. It was the third time his mother had called in as many hours.

'You've eaten?'

'*Yes...*' he insisted.

'And you've got your stuff ready for school, have you? Remember you've got football training tomorrow, so—'

'Mum, I'm sixteen, I think I can get my own kit together.'

'Boots are in the hall, the rest is on racks in the utility room...'

Ethan mouthed an expletive to the empty room, as his mother continued her monologue.

'...and your boot bag is in the cupboard under the stairs. I'll try not to be too late, but I've got three waitresses off and the place will fall apart if I don't stay...'

'Like I said, everything's under control—'

'And what about schoolwork? Have you finished your German?'

'I was just putting the final umlaut on it now,' Ethan lied, looking at the blank screen in front of him. 'So if it's all right with you, I'll sign off.'

'Well, if you're sure ...'

She clearly wasn't sure, wanting to mollycoddle him further, but he'd had enough. Sometimes being an only child sucked.

'Totally. See you later.'

He hung up before she could interject, exhaling heavily as he did so. Why hadn't his parents had another kid, two even? Something to take the pressure, the endless attention, off him? Shaking his head, he shut his laptop and moved away. His German assignment wasn't due until Friday and, honestly, he didn't feel like working tonight.

Exiting his room, he paused on the landing, pondering his next move. Should he head upstairs to the den, watch a movie on the new 65-inch? Call some friends? Perhaps even smoke a little out of one of the conveniently placed Velux windows? Or should he head downstairs for a little quality time with the PS5? He could hook up with Randall, see if he fancied a little *Call of Duty*?

Drumming his fingers on the polished wooden bannister, Ethan smiled to himself, enjoying the novelty of choice, the seemingly endless leisure time that now spread out before him. His dad was visiting Gran, his mum was stuck at the restaurant, meaning there was no one here to marshal his time, to thwart his desires, to get in his way. If only life were always like this – tonight he had the whole house to himself.

Chapter 47

From his hiding place in the garden, he had a perfect view of the property.

It was a modern design, all steel and glass, meaning he could see the downstairs extension clearly. The fancy kitchen, the expensive dining table, the hanging chair that looked out onto the garden – the whole place had been designed to be admired, and he was glad of it.

Better still, there were no security lights, no hidden cameras. True, he'd had to scale a couple of fences to get here, tiptoeing across neighbours' gardens, but once here he could loiter amidst the dense foliage, unseen. He had been crouching in the darkness for over twenty minutes and his legs were beginning to cramp up. He ached to move, to get the job done, but caution held him back. There could be no question of going too soon, of getting this *wrong*.

Once more he scanned the neighbouring properties, searching for signs of life in the back rooms. But there were no lights on, no movement within, it was all pleasingly, boringly quiet, as he knew it would be. Cocking an ear, he listened carefully for any warning signs, any nasty surprises – a dog alerted to his presence, a car pulling up unexpectedly on the front drive – but the street was deathly quiet.

Returning his attention to the house, his gaze settled on the sliding glass doors that led onto the garden. And now, finally, he spotted movement. The teenager – Ethan – had entered the kitchen, flicking on the lights, the extension lit up like a Christmas tree. Now he could see *everything*, every detail of the opulent finish, every device casually tossed aside, even the wilting flowers on the kitchen island that should have been binned several days ago. He smiled to himself as he watched the boy going about his business. There was something deeply enjoyable about climbing inside another person's existence, living their lives with them, especially when the subject had no idea they were being observed. It made him feel powerful, invulnerable, even slightly mischievous – imagine how the boy would react if he sprinted down the garden now, slamming his hands against the glass. The idiot teenager would probably drop dead from fright, which might be a blessing.

The boy was opening the fridge now, pulling a bottle of juice from inside and filling a glass. He seemed relaxed, happy, tossing the bottle back inside the fridge and closing the appliance with a hefty slam, before departing once more. Omitting to turn the lights off, which burned pointlessly and expensively, the boy left the kitchen, heading first into the hall, before darting left into the front living room. He knew from earlier visits that this would be the last he'd see of the teenager. The boy was work-shy and predictable, spending as much time as he could gaming. Chances are he was set for the night now, leaving the way open for an unimpeded approach from the rear.

The stage was set. It was now only a question of when. Should he delay a little further? Or should he act? It was a tantalizing dilemma, which excited *and* worried him, adrenaline competing with his jangling nerves. There would be no second chances if he messed this up, no escaping the just punishment that awaited him. So he continued to linger, drinking in the quiet house from his hiding place in the shadows, primed and ready to kill.

Chapter 48

'No, you've got it wrong. It was him. I *know* it was him...'

What had Helen been expecting? Understanding? Forbearance? Greg White was a picture of confusion and rage – perhaps rightly so.

'He's admitted he was at the house, that he went there expressly to target Martha—'

'That's not quite what he said—'

'Don't split hairs with me,' White barked back. 'You haven't lived through this nightmare, you haven't seen his obsession first hand. That man lives only to hate my wife. It's bloody obvious that he... he...'

He couldn't bring himself to articulate Martha's terrible fate, grief robbing him of his energy, even his breath.

'I understand all that, I really do,' Helen countered. 'I know what it's like to live under the shadow of a threat like that...'

Despite his fury, Helen saw a flash of curiosity in Greg White's eyes, but she was not prepared to indulge him.

'But the evidence all points against his guilt and, honestly, I don't think he's got it in him. I've spent time in his company and, yes, he's full of anger, and bile, and frustration, but most of it is really directed at himself. He's a fuck-up, a loser and, OK, he's prone to the odd stunt at a hospital or a baby class, but I'm not sure he has violence in him. He's a loner and a fantasist, not a killer.'

Still Greg White shook his head, Helen's words not fully landing yet.

'But it *has* to be him. He's the only person who's ever, ever had a bad word to say about Martha. Everyone loved her, I mean *really* loved her...'

Tears filled his eyes now, aching loss diluting his anger.

'I mean, if it wasn't Berman, who would... who would want to do something like that? It doesn't make any sense...'

She could feel White losing his mooring. In the immediate aftermath of his wife's death, he had clung to his rage, his hatred of Berman, keeping other more difficult emotions in check. Now his world seemed to be shifting on its axis, as raw, unadulterated shock took hold. Helen had seen it many times before, that awful moment when someone realized there was real, inexplicable evil out there, and she moved quickly to take him in hand.

'Greg, I understand your confusion and, yes, it's true, there are many questions about Martha's death that still need to be answered, but we are just at the start of the process and trust me, we will get to the truth. I have my whole team working on this, exploring every angle, every possible motive – we *will* find out what happened that night.'

The widower said nothing, absently picking up one of Bailey's toys and turning it over in his hands. He looked shattered, unable to process the catastrophe that had befallen him.

'We may need to talk to you again, to establish context and background, and in time we'll need to talk to friends and family members, too, in order to get a fuller picture of Martha's life. The process may seem a little bit intrusive, but believe me it's absolutely vital.'

Helen had half expected White to push back, but he remained silent.

'We'll also obviously be liaising with our colleagues in the burglary unit, as well as running the rule over recent incidents nationwide involving extreme violence to see if—'

'What are you saying?' White blurted out, jerking his head up. 'That what happened was nothing to do with us, with Martha, that it was *random*?'

This seemed to appall him even more than the prospect of Berman's involvement.

'I wouldn't say random,' Helen countered gently, 'but it may be that the identity of the victim was not important, that it was the potential material gain or indeed the act itself that drove the crime—'

'Somebody did this *for kicks*?'

The anger was back, punching through his confusion.

'No, but it may be the product of some kind of compulsion, someone in the throes of a deep psychological and emotional crisis. Honestly, though, we just don't know yet, this is purely speculation at this stage—'

'So this person is a madman? Or a serial killer?'

Helen's attempt to shut down the conversation had come too late. Already she could see this interview slipping away from her and she cursed herself for her clumsiness.

'Absolutely not, there's probably a very simple, if distressing, explanation for wha—'

'Does that mean he'll strike again then? That Martha was just … just the first?'

He had gone white as a sheet.

'There's no evidence to suggest that, so don't go—'

'What the hell are you doing *here*? You should be out looking for this guy. What on earth are you doing talking to me, when right now someone could be—'

'Please, Greg, calm down,' Helen intervened. 'You're working yourself up into a state when there's really no need.'

'Get out.'

His demand cut through her attempts to appease him. She had moved towards the desolate widower in order to comfort him, but to her surprise, he now advanced upon her.

'You get out of this house and you do your job.'

Taking another step closer, he took hold of Helen's collar, pulling her face to his.

'You find out who did this to her.'

She could feel his breath on her face and braced herself for more, but as suddenly as he'd advanced on her, he now retreated, marching angrily from the room, slamming the door behind him. Helen watched him go, chastened. She had come here expecting distress and anger, but had reaped much more than she'd bargained for. His aggression had surprised her, the whole interview spinning wildly out of control, but in truth she had no one to blame but herself, thanks to her calamitous handling of the situation. She hadn't been hoping for much tonight, but in truth it had gone far worse than she could have possibly expected.

Chapter 49

So far everything had gone according to plan. He had reached the sliding doors undetected, making his way silently across the pristine lawn, but *this* was the point of maximum danger. If ever he was going to be discovered, his shadowy form clearly visible through the floor-to-ceiling glass panels, it was *now*.

Dropping to his knees, he crouched down by the doors, removing a screwdriver from his pocket. Now his fingers sought out the lip of the door, half shrouded in shadow beneath him. A moment's pause, a second's consideration as he found the sweet spot, then he pressed the screwdriver head down hard on the junction of door and track.

Bang!

He jumped out of his skin, nearly losing hold of the screwdriver. Casting wildly around him, he sought the source of this sudden noise. Had he broken something? Dropped something? Had the glass cracked? Surely not, he had been so careful...

And now a burst of conversation from next door resolved the mystery, a middle-aged man complaining as he dumped cans and bottles into the recycling bin. Seconds later, the back door slammed shut and all was quiet once more. Darting a look into the illuminated extension, the intruder checked that the coast remained clear, then resumed his patient work. Finding his place once more, he increased his pressure on the screwdriver head. At first, the door resisted, the aluminium frame repelling him, but upping the power still further, he was pleased to feel it find purchase between frame and track. Taking a breath, he counted down from three, then wrenched the screwdriver up with all his might. Nothing, so he tried again. Still nothing, but on the third heave, the whole sliding door lifted slightly, allowing him to press forward, easing it up and off its track. There was nothing holding it in place anymore, so keeping a tight hold on it, he rose quickly, sliding it gently to the left. The slow swish, swish of its movement was thrilling, the room opening up to him.

Slipping his screwdriver into his pocket, he paused now to remove the hatchet from his bag, then slowly, quietly, padded his way across the wooden floor.

Chapter 50

She strode forward purposefully, determined not to give into her growing anxiety, but each step seemed heavy and laboured, as if her body was warning her not to proceed. But Charlie had come too far to back down now and, remembering Helen's words, she held her nerve, reaching the body shop and yanking the door open.

McCarthy's Autos had been Steve's home from home for over five years and during that time Charlie had been a regular visitor, hence her lack of ceremony now, even though it was well after hours. Although she knew nothing about cars and was not a fan of manual labour herself, she nevertheless always enjoyed her visits. There was something slightly magical about the closed, confessional space, the tight-knit body of men poring over complicated engines and mechanical anomalies, as they tried to diagnose and remedy the problems of their loyal customers. It was a fun, friendly space and at the warm, beating heart of it, as always, was Graeme McCarthy, Steve's affable boss.

'Good evening, my dear,' the portly fifty-year-old greeted her, as he straightened up. 'No robbers to catch tonight?'

'All safely behind bars,' she returned, smiling.

Casting her eye over the dimly lit interior, she sought out Steve's familiar bulk. His mother was trying to get the children to bed, affording her the opportunity to talk to him, to lance the boil of her paranoia once and for all.

'Steve out back?' she asked, running a finger over the dusty work bench.

Graeme seemed amused by the question.

'Oh, you know Steve. Always on his break when there's work to be done...'

Charlie smiled and said nothing, expecting him to call for his employee, no doubt adding some retrograde joke about the presence of his ball and chain. But to her surprise, he remained silent, looking at her quizzically, before adding:

'So was it just a chat you're after, love? Because I really do need to get this finished and back to base, or there'll be hell to pay, trust me...'

'Sorry, I just wanted a word with Steve,' Charlie insisted, suddenly feeling foolish and flustered.

Another moment of blank incomprehension from Graeme, as if he was the victim of a joke that he was somehow excluded from.

'Must be some crossed wires, I'm afraid,' he responded eventually. 'Steve left a couple of hours ago...'

Charlie's heart sank, even as she heard herself say:

'My mistake. I thought he was working late all this week.'

And now a crease of concern formed on her companion's face. He hesitated, as if thinking what best to say, then added:

'I'm sorry, Charlie, but no, he's... he's clocked off on time every night this week. Do you want me to call him? See if I can raise him?'

He was scrabbling to be helpful, fearful that he'd somehow put his foot in it, or upset her in some way, but Charlie cut him off.

'No problem, I'll call him on the way home.'

She already turned away, unwilling to let him see the tears forming in her eyes. He called after her, bidding her goodnight, but she just raised her hand, unable to speak, as she marched swiftly out the door, shutting it firmly behind her.

It had been a mistake to come here.

Chapter 51

There were only thirty seconds left. It was now or never.

Keeping one eye on the clock at the top left of the screen, Ethan Westlake returned his attention to the battlefield, a blizzard of tie fighters and X-wings doing battle over the frozen wastes of Hoth. As ever he was piloting the Millennium Falcon, the unmistakable symbol of the Resistance's fight against the evil empire of the Second Republic. This had its downsides, as he was a bigger target than the other craft, but its compensations too. His firepower was significantly greater and he was using it to good effect, blasting Darth Vader and his crew to the far side of the galaxy. His fingers moved feverishly, working against the clock to destroy the enemy fleet. He was totally involved in his mission, constantly reacting to the scream of an incoming combatant. Lasers flew, engines roared, machinery exploded, the CGI sky onscreen a spectacular whirl of colour, movement and excitement – and Ethan was enjoying every minute of it.

He cast another glance at the onscreen timer. Only ten seconds to go. For a moment, the sky seemed bereft of targets, then from nowhere a tie fighter shot past, strafing him with laser fire. Immediately, he gave chase, swooping after it in a dizzying dive. Down, down, down they roared, the tie fighter swinging wildly this way, then that, trying to avoid the fire that roared from his front cannons. But Ethan stayed glued to him, his eyes locked onto the sight that seemed to be forever just behind the fleeing craft.

'Come on, come on ...'

Five seconds to go. It all rested on this final kill. And now, at last, his sight locked onto the fleeing craft's tail fire.

'I have you now ...' he chuckled, stabbing the missile launch button.

The enemy fighter erupted in a ball of flames, just as the clock hit zero. Mission accomplished. Happy, energized, Ethan sat back in his chair, pulling the headset from his tousled hair and running his fingers through it. If his folks were here, they would have already intervened, telling him not to put his gaming chair so close to the screen, not to spend so much time hunched over his controller, but their absence meant all things were possible, so without hesitation he hit the restart button. He had done well on that last go, but this time he would do even better.

But as Ethan readied himself to begin another round of destruction, he noticed something reflected in the screen in front of him. A large, dark shape, which seemed to be looming over him. Pausing the game, he stared at it, confused and intrigued. And now it began to become clear, it wasn't a shape, it was a figure, an actual person. Even as he registered this, shock replacing his confusion, he picked out the man's features – the dark hood, the broad shoulders, the prominent nose and thin mouth. Ethan froze, dropping the console to the floor, paralyzed by fear. There was somebody in the room. Somebody who was standing directly behind him.

Terrified, Ethan watched in horror as the figure now lurched forwards, descending upon him. He tried to cry out, his mouth open in a desperate, silent 'O', but a gloved hand clamped down hard on his mouth. Now he was tumbling from his gaming chair, driven earthwards by the sheer weight of the intruder, the ground rushing up to meet him.

Then his head hit the wooden floorboards and everything went black.

Chapter 52

Up, up, up she went, mounting the stairs three at a time. In days gone by, Helen would have saved herself the effort, taking the lift from the basement to her top-floor flat. But now she preferred to use the stairs, liking their openness, their easy visibility, the choice of escape route they offered, should danger rear its head. The lift now seemed like a trap, a cage, even a coffin, beckoning her in, only to snap its doors shut. If someone managed to get in there with her, how could she possibly defend herself? No, she preferred the cavernous shaft of the flat's main stairwell now, enjoying her nightly sprint to the top.

After a difficult day, she had been keen to be back home, but still her anxiety mounted the closer she got. Her heart had been in her mouth as she entered the basement car park and she'd completed several circuits of it, satisfying herself that there was no danger to her, before parking up and dismounting. She'd then hurried to the stairwell and, seeing that the coast was clear, tore up them. Now cresting the penultimate landing, Helen didn't relent, powering on up. As she did so, she slammed the light switch, keen to illuminate the final stretch. But even as her fist hit the button, there was a loud pop and she was plunged back into darkness.

'Shit…'

The bulb had gone, rendering the landing above shadowy and menacing. But was this by accident or design? Helen remained rooted to the spot, halfway between the previous landing and her own, her eyes trying to penetrate to the gloom, straining her ears for any sign of movement. Would she hear her assassin's measured tread? His heavy breathing once more?

No, there was nothing. No signs of life at all. So, moving cautiously, she proceeded, measuring each step carefully to make no noise, holding her baton in one hand and a can of pepper spray in the other. These days she was always prepared for danger.

One step, two, three. Her eyes were becoming used to the semi-darkness now, the sickly yellow tint of the street lighting creeping in through the frosted window, affording her a partial view of her surroundings, as she constantly checked ahead and behind her. She knew she was probably being paranoid, but any change to the normal routine, however trivial, inevitably set her nerves jangling. Perhaps it was just a bulb blowing. But maybe it was her assassin stacking the odds in his favour, disorienting her before his attack. Until she was sure, she would proceed with the utmost caution, unwilling to give Blythe the sick triumph he craved.

Reaching the top landing, she scanned the dark corners of the landing, the doorway to the adjacent flat, before darting another quick look behind her. Everything remained quiet and still, so now she turned her attention to her own flat. Mercifully, her doorway was also deserted, so she hurried over to it now, unbolting the door as fast as she could, before slipping inside.

Leaning against the cold steel, she took a moment to catch her breath. She was jumpy as hell tonight, breathless and tense, in danger of having a panic attack. Exhaling long and slow, she tried to regain her composure and, as the seconds passed, the fear and adrenaline started to dissipate. Now she resumed her usual routine, checking each room in turn, reassuring herself that she was alone, before returning to the living room. Even here, however, a nasty surprise awaited, her phone suddenly coming to life in her hand, making her jump. Worse still, on inspection she recognized the number.

Hudson.

She couldn't believe it. Of all the people to be calling her now, when she felt at her most beleaguered and besieged, it was bloody Joseph Hudson. Angrily rejecting the call, she blocked his number. She had no time for his anxiety, his desolation, his despair. In truth, she had no time for *him* anymore and wondered why she ever had. Dumping her phone on the table, she walked over to the terrace windows, flinging them open and breathing in the cold night air. She longed to be refreshed, renewed, calmed by the biting winter wind, which even now raced over the Solent, whipping the defenseless city beyond, but she felt no relief, no respite. It seemed to Helen now that wherever she went, she was pursued by those who had come before – Hudson, Blythe, and Marianne, to name but a few. They would never leave her alone, never relent, persistently dogging her heels.

Tonight, more than ever, Helen felt thoroughly alone, with only the ghosts of the past for company.

Chapter 53

She looked so pale, so vulnerable, that he couldn't resist, reaching out to the screen and resting his finger on her troubled face. It was a moment of communion between the fugitive and the hunted, Alex Blythe having to live by his wits just as much as Helen Grace did now, but it was also a statement of intent. Helen was so small and insignificant on his laptop screen that he could blot her out completely with his finger. Something he *longed* to do.

His nemesis had suffered much in the last few weeks – when *was* the last time he saw Helen smile? – but her ordeal couldn't possibly compare to his. Six months ago he'd had a thriving practice, scores of desperate, addicted patients and all manner of opportunities for exploiting them. He had extorted money and sex and when he'd tired of that, had forced them to kill. In truth, he'd had the perfect life – he was rich, single, powerful and utterly in control of his life and dozens of others. He'd delighted in his reach, his authority, his anonymity and then in one swift stroke, Helen Grace had destroyed everything. Yes, he'd managed to evade capture, but along the way he'd had to destroy his files, flee his home and – worst of all – abandon his schemes. So much more blood could have been spilled, so many more lives ruined, but now, holed up in an anonymous French hotel with ever-diminishing resources, he'd had to scale back his ambitions. Now there was only one life he was interested in taking.

Helen Grace was still on her balcony, staring bleakly out into the night, unaware that she was looking directly towards his camera. Before he'd gained access to her flat on the day of his flight, he'd paid a visit to the office block opposite. Thanks to the ongoing economic repercussions of Covid, it was deserted and lifeless and he'd had both liberty and time to secure a good vantage point for two cameras – one pointing directly at Helen's flat, the other covering the street below. This allowed him the occasional close-up of his adversary – and there was no denying he *enjoyed* these moments of communion – but the cameras served a more prosaic purpose, allowing Blythe to track Grace's movements. Along with the camera he'd secured to a CCTV bank near Southampton Central, they provided him with eyes on Helen, both at home and work, meaning she was seldom truly alone. Though she didn't realize it, Blythe was forever shadowing her, like a bird of prey poised to strike.

And strike he would. He would not have the satisfaction of delivering the blow himself, but still her murder would bring him intense relief, even joy. No one had ever checked him before, ever frustrated him, and he burned to revenge himself upon her. Content as he was with the current situation – Nicholas Martin would *surely* act soon and act decisively – he nevertheless found it impossible to relax, to quieten his nagging anxiety. He hardly slept, hardly ate, his thoughts forever turning on his perilous situation. Despite his best efforts to change his appearance and conceal his current location, there was always the small chance that Interpol would catch up with him, that he might somehow give himself away. It was a thought that kept him awake at nights, for once he was in custody, his power would evaporate, liberating Nicholas Martin from his clutches, ensuring Helen Grace's survival.

That could not be allowed to happen. Tomorrow morning he would contact Nicholas again, giving him an ultimatum, perhaps sending him a little clip of the incriminating video footage as a prompt, urging him to fulfill his mission. Together they had complete control of the situation, the spy and his assassin patiently plotting the veteran police officer's death, and now was the time to make use of their advantage. The preparations had been lengthy and exacting, the planning precise, all that was wanting now was the coup de grace, the final destruction of his enemy. Blythe had little control over where it would happen – he would have to allow Martin to choose the exact timing and location – but secretly he hoped that the deed would be done in Helen's flat, in her living room, in full view of his camera.

For, it would be sweet indeed to know that Helen Grace was dead, but sweeter still to *watch* her die.

Chapter 54

With a friendly wave, Richard Westlake walked away down the garden path, breathing a sigh of relief as he did so. His mother had been more aggravating than usual tonight, delaying his departure considerably, peppering him with questions, many of which he'd already answered. He loved her, of course he did, but she was increasingly hard work and increasingly ungrateful with it, despite everything he'd done for her.

'Call you tomorrow...' he shouted, opening the gate and hurrying off to his car.

He vaguely heard her reply, but in truth he'd had enough and was keen to be home. He hoped things would be calm there – Vicky had been all of a twitter tonight, having had to pitch in at the restaurant unexpectedly, sending him endless messages urging him not to be back late, as if somehow *he* was to blame for Ethan being home alone. It was ridiculous; she knew this was his regular night with his mother – if anyone was at fault, it was *her*, spending far too much time trying to keep the restaurant on track, a restaurant which doggedly refused to be profitable. And why was she worried anyway? The boy was sixteen years old and though not the sharpest tool in the box, could be trusted not to burn the house down. But it was a mother's preserve to worry, as Vicky frequently reminded him.

Flinging the car door open, Richard tossed his jacket onto the passenger seat, then settled in behind the wheel. As he did so, his phone's jaunty ring tone trilled out, announcing that his wife was trying to contact him. For a brief, petulant moment, he considered not answering it, but then mastered himself, calmly accepting the call.

But there was nothing calm about the voice that greeted him. It was shrill, anguished, incomprehensible. In fact, it sounded nothing like Vicky, sending tremors of alarm pulsing through him.

'What is it, Vicks? What's up?'

A long, desperate howl was her only response.

'What the hell's happened? Are you OK, love?'

'It's...'

She couldn't speak between anguished sobs, unable to form the words.

'It's Ethan...'

And now she broke completely, howling out her pain. The noise cut straight through Richard, chilling him to the bone. He was tempted to end the call, to stop the terrible noise, but whatever had happened, he *had* to know now. So he let his wife keen and groan, even as he fired up the engine and roared away from the quiet housing estate.

Day Four

Chapter 55

She sat still, savouring the moment. The coffee was strong and bitter, the pancakes sweet and comforting, but the best part of this very pleasant breakfast was that she hadn't lifted a finger to prepare it. Usually, Emilia was first up and thus it fell to her to ensure that her siblings were fed. They were too old to be mollycoddled in this way, but she was sure that some of them would simply forget to eat, unless she chivvied them to do so.

Normally her morning routine was to check her email, news feeds and social media, shower and dress and then spend two quick minutes throwing bowls, cereal packets and juice cartons onto the kitchen table, before sprinting from the house, a piece of toast balanced on her coffee. Today, however, things had been different, Sam insisting on making breakfast, meaning that by the time she'd dried her hair, a pile of steaming pancakes was waiting for her, alongside thick Arabica coffee to wash them down.

'Fancy another one?'

For a minute, Emilia was tempted to give a lowbrow, carnal response, but as some of her siblings were present, drawn to the kitchen by the sweet smells, she thought better of it.

'I've already had two...'

'So? Eat them while they're hot, that's what I say...'

'A girl has to watch her figure,' Emilia returned coyly.

Sam immediately shot her a look, clearly feeling she had nothing to worry about in that department. Leaning forward, she forked another pancake on her plate.

'Maybe just one more, then I really must be going...'

It was true, she should already have set off for work. But the novelty of being waited on was so pleasant that somehow she couldn't bring herself to move.

'So what have you got on today?' Sam enquired, rejoining the family troupe at the table.

'Just the usual, following up on the White case. Shouldn't be too arduous. You?'

'Couple of client meetings this morning,' he replied. 'Then a webinar this afternoon. But I'm free later, if you fancy meeting up? There's a really nice Italian place near me that I think you'd like...'

A knowing look passed between Joao and Luciana, two of the younger members of the family, clearly enjoying having one of their sister's gentlemen friends at the breakfast table.

'I'll have to check my calendar,' Emilia teased. 'I'm a woman in demand...'

Once more, Sam pulled a face, in a good-natured display of disappointment.

'But I'm sure I'll be able to squeeze you in,' she added quickly, surprised at herself. 'Especially if you keep up this sort of service...'

'We aim to please,' Sam answered happily, before tucking into his pancakes, wresting the maple syrup off Joao.

For a moment, Emilia just stared at him, lost in thought. It was a strange thing to think, but she couldn't deny how *right* it felt having Sam here. She had only known him a day or so, yet somehow his presence was entirely natural and everyone seemed buoyed by his happy nature, his optimism, his energy. Normally such a situation would have sent Emilia scurrying for well-worn excuses, claiming she couldn't possibly consider a committed relationship given her work schedule, but that was not the case this morning. There was a part of her that felt it was all happening too quickly – that this guy was too good to be true – but another part of her that felt strangely blessed.

Her phone chirruped gently next to her, disturbing her thoughts. Looking down at the screen, she was tempted to dismiss the alert, even turn her phone off, but the unregistered text number intrigued her. Picking up her Samsung, she read the brief message:

Serious police incident in Freemantle. Grace on scene.

She heard her chair scraping back, before she realized she was rising. Sam looked up, surprised, perhaps even a little disappointed.

'Sorry, lover boy,' she smiled. 'Gotta run.'

'But you haven't finished your breakfast...'

'Duty calls. But don't worry I'm sure there'll be other opportunities. Call you later?'

Sam nodded happily, bestowing a winning smile on her, before turning his attention to doling out the remaining pancakes. Again, Emilia paused, drinking in the idyllic scene one last time. Soon she would have her work head on, facing whatever unpleasantness lay in store in Freemantle with her usual professional detachment, but she knew that whatever the world threw at her, she would meet it with a spring in her step.

Today was going to be a good day.

Chapter 56

Nodding at the sombre constable, Charlie raised the tape and ducked underneath, before heading up the path. Her expression was one of studied professionalism, of purpose, but in truth she didn't want to be here. She'd barely slept a wink last night, her anxiety and distress magnified by Steve's decision to sleep in the spare room, following his late return, and it was as much as she could do to put one foot in front of the other. Lack of sleep was playing havoc with her mind, her emotions, she knew that, yet she couldn't shake the feeling that some kind of crisis was fast approaching. It was a feeling of dread, there was no other way of putting it, a feeling strengthened now as she approached the impressive suburban villa, which was already the site of frenzied police activity, despite the early hour.

Swallowing her discomfort, Charlie took a breath and stepped inside, navigating the busy hallway. Immediately, she spotted Helen, who stood grim-faced in the front lounge, taking in the crime scene. Charlie hurried to join her, slowing her pace somewhat as the corpse came into view. She knew what to expect, had got the two-line summary on the way over, but still the sight of a teenage boy lying face down on the ground was chilling.

'It's the same guy,' Helen said quietly, without looking up.

Charlie nodded, bending down to examine the trussed figure.

'The victim's face down, rag in his mouth. Hands securely tied, fatal wound to the back of the head, plus there's significant evidence of post-mortem laceration...'

There were three ugly wounds on the back of his head, plus four deep gashes on the shoulders and upper back, the poor boy's body lying in a pool of his own blood.

'Jim will have the last word on it,' Helen continued, 'but from my brief examination of the wounds, I'd say it's definitely the same weapon. Similar imprint as previously, suggesting a slightly damaged blade...'

'So this is murder number two...'

It didn't need saying and Charlie immediately regretted it, Helen looking up sharply, as if her deputy's tone was off. Quickly, she changed the subject.

'Any idea how he gained access?'

'Sliding doors that lead onto the garden,' Helen returned, nodding towards the rear of the property. 'Lifted off the rail, then opened. Would have been smooth, silent, almost easy...'

'A professional job then,' Charlie replied soberly.

'Probably – the doors certainly didn't pose much of a problem. That said, there's no security lights or cameras, so this was an easier target than the Whites'...'

'Except that there's no obvious way to access the garden. The house is slap bang in the middle of the street and if the side passage hasn't been used, then he would presumably have had to cross at least two or three other plots...'

'I've got Meredith and her team out there now. There's lots of thick foliage, perhaps some clothing or hair got snagged...'

It was clearly said more in hope than expectation. The perpetrator had so far been very cautious, very professional, not disposed to clumsy errors.

'What do we know about the victim? The family?' Charlie asked, moving the conversation on.

'Richard and Victoria Westlake own the property. The victim is their teenage son, Ethan.'

Charlie felt a stab of sorrow. To lose a child, especially in these circumstances, was beyond horrific.

'He's a property developer, she runs a restaurant in town. She was there last night, discovered her son's body on her return just after eleven o'clock...'

Charlie winced, her heart breaking for the poor woman. How could one ever process, let alone deal with, a sight like that?

'They're at a neighbour's place now. We should go and talk to them in a minute.'

Charlie assented dutifully, though wasn't sure she really had the stomach for it.

'Not sure we'll get much out of the wife, she had to be sedated. But the dad might give us something, although he's obviously in a state of shock...'

There was a brief, contemplative silence, before Charlie asked the most pressing, most difficult question.

'What do you think this is all about? Do you think it *is* aggravated burglary?'

'That might be part of it. DC Jennings says the jewellery boxes have been emptied, the master bedroom turned over. Could get away with items worth thousands from a place like this if you knew your stuff, plus it's very portable, of course. But I don't think that's the real motivation.'

'You think the financial gain is secondary to the act of violence itself?'

'I think it's part of the overall act of *violation*. We know that there's an overlap between housebreakers and rapists – perhaps this comes from a similar place. You break into someone's home, butcher the sole inhabitant, steal personal items that have sentimental value. It must be the feeling of power, of intrusion, of control, that's driving the perpetrator. Why else would he break in when it's *obvious* someone's home?'

It was a sobering thought, but Charlie's mind was already racing onto the next question.

'Do you think he *knows* then? Knows that his victim is home alone? Normally there'd be three people living here, but tonight it was just a teenage boy, alone, unsuspecting...'

Charlie could see by the expression on Helen's face that her mind had been turning on this very point. Watching her boss closely, she half expected her to offer up a cogent theory as to the whys and wherefores of that particular line of enquiry, but instead Helen simply looked up at her and replied:

'That's what we need to find out.'

With that, she departed, picking her way from the crime scene. It was a silent summons to begin the next phase of their work, but Charlie lingered for a moment. She didn't feel ready, didn't feel strong enough to face Ethan's shattered parents, but there was no ducking it.

She and Helen had an appointment with despair.

Chapter 57

Slipping on a pair of leather gloves, Nicholas Martin delved into his toolbox, lifting off the top tray to reveal the Wilkinson's bag which contained the knife. When he'd bought it a week ago, he'd been stressed beyond belief, yet full of purpose. As awful as his situation was, he had a plan. It wasn't particularly sophisticated, but he hoped Grace's brutal stabbing would be blamed on an old collar of hers, someone from Southampton's underbelly exacting revenge on its most celebrated crime fighter. As long as he got away, as long as he managed to dump the knife, then it was still possible that he would emerge from this nightmare unscathed.

But planning was one thing, execution another. He had bottled his first attempt in the car park, the shock of discovery mingling with the sudden conviction that he couldn't best Grace face to face, forcing him to flee. After that, he'd been tempted to abandon his desperate scheme, but Blythe's phone call had put paid to that fond notion. The time for hesitation was over. If he didn't do it today, his persecutor would make good on his threat.

Slipping the bag into his briefcase, Martin secured the lock, then turned, darting out of the shed. Without pausing to shut the door, he strode up the path towards the side access. He just had to keep moving now, any hesitation would be his undoing, his courage sure to fail him. He would head to work, calling them en route to say he was sick, before putting his plan into action. If all went well, he would be home tonight, free and clear, his soul forsaken, but his future assured.

'Nicholas?'

He looked up, startled, as Siobhan emerged from the back of the house. He was at the mouth of the side passage but paused now, turning back to her.

'Now that's not very friendly. Sneaking off without saying goodbye...'

'Sorry, love, just running late. Got to talk to Adams before assembly.'

'I won't keep you then...'

Crossing to him, she slipped her arms round his neck, pulling him into a clinch. The feel of her warm, loving lips on his was enough to undo him, to make him to confess all and throw himself on her mercy, but somehow he held firm, releasing himself from her grip gently, only to find her smiling mischievously.

'But I just wanted to say that the kids will be at Mum's for tea tonight, so if you could get off early, I could show you how much I really love you...'

She leaned into him again, slipping her tongue into his mouth, before turning on her heel and departing, winking at him over her shoulder. He watched her go, torn between desire and shame, desperate to follow her, yet powerless to move. And then as suddenly as she'd appeared, she was gone, disappearing back into the house.

Nicholas remained where he was, staring after her, wanting to drink in the perfume that still hung in the air, the feel of her touch on his skin. This was partly out of love, a fascination with this gorgeous woman, but partly out of pure, unadulterated fear. For, although he tried to be optimistic, to tell himself that his best-laid plans would see him free and clear, he was nevertheless gripped by an unspoken anxiety, that things might go wrong today, that he might be apprehended or even injured. That he would never see his darling Siobhan again.

Chapter 58

'I can't believe he's gone…'

Richard Westlake hung his head, the image of desolation. He appeared to lack the energy to raise himself, to face a world that had proved itself to be callous and cruel.

'He was *everything* to us. Everything we did in life was for him.'

The words tumbled from the bereaved father, emotion strangling his voice, rendering each utterance thick with sadness and despair. Helen watched him closely, moved by the strength of his emotion, yet grateful that Westlake was able to find his voice. There was no question of talking to his wife yet – deranged with grief, sickened by her horrific discovery, Victoria Westlake was half-comatose in the bedroom upstairs, under the influence of a strong sedative. There would be time to talk to her later; for now Helen had to get as much information as possible from Ethan's devastated dad.

'I'm sure he knew that, Richard. I'm sure he felt your love every day…'

'Except when he most needed it,' came the terse, bitter reply.

'You must try not to think like that,' Helen counselled. 'I know it's tempting to reproach yourself, but had you been there, you might also have been hurt, and where would that have left Vicky? None of this is your fault, trust me.'

Westlake didn't react, absently wiping away a tear that crawled down his nose.

'What's important now,' Charlie added kindly, 'what you *can* do, is help us find out who did this, help us bring them to justice.'

This seemed to cut through, Richard Westlake darting a look at Charlie, as if seeing her for the first time.

'To do that, we need a clear picture of your timings last night. Can you tell us when you left the house, where you went, when you got back...?'

'I was visiting my mother at the new Grange Park estate,' he replied slowly. 'It's one of our developments, and I recently got her a nice bungalow there. She's a bit up and down these days and this meant she'd be close to us. I was visiting her, like I always do on a Thursday—'

'So this was a regular commitment?' Helen interrupted.

'Yes. Every Thursday we spend the evening together. I cook her a bit of tea, we watch *EastEnders*, whatever else is on. She's not terribly mobile and doesn't have many visitors, so...'

'Are the timings roughly similar each week?'

Westlake nodded absently.

'I head over early evening, around seven, whenever I can get away from work. And I'm usually home sometime after eleven. She's always been a bit of a night owl, which doesn't please Vicky...'

'And your wife was at the restaurant?' Charlie asked, consulting her notebook. 'Albertine's on Jarrow Street?'

'Yeah, she had three staff go down out of the blue, so had to help out. Normally she's home around eight on Thursdays, to sort out tea for Ethan...'

He stumbled briefly at the mention of his son's name, then pressed on:

'...to make sure he's done his homework, get his stuff ready for college. By rights, she should have been there too last night.'

There was no tone of recrimination here, rather a sudden sense of horror that his wife might also have been harmed. Helen stepped in quickly, determined to keep the conversation on track.

'How long have you been visiting your mother at Grange Park?'

'A couple of months or so.'

'Have you ever missed a Thursday visit?'

'No.'

Helen nodded, casting a meaningful look at Charlie, before continuing:

'And during those two months, your wife was regularly at home on a Thursday night? No other calls on her time, occasional nights out or whatever...?'

'Not really. She might have been called into the restaurant on one other occasion during that time, but she tended to socialize at the beginning of the week or at the weekend, as she always liked one of us to be at home for Ethan...'

He petered out, emotional, his own words tripping him up.

'So last night, you left your mother's house at what time?'

A long pause, then with a sigh, the grieving father replied:

'Just before eleven. I was on the way to my car when Vicky rang. You can check my phone records if you want the exact timings... I think I made it home in no more than five minutes, which is when we called you lot.'

'OK, that's very helpful, thank you. We will need to talk to your wife in due course and potentially your mother too. Do you think she'd be up to that?'

'Probably. Mum does get confused at times and God knows how she'll deal with this, she *doted* on that boy ... but yes, I think she could handle a brief conversation.'

'Great, my colleague DC Malik will be in touch to arrange a time. In the meantime, if there's anything you need to ask me, day or night, just call.'

Helen handed her card to him and he took it from her. Rising, Helen was about to make her excuses, when Westlake suddenly spoke once more.

'Is it *him?*'

'Sorry?' Helen queried.

'The guy who murdered that poor woman in St Denys. Is this him?'

'It's too early to say for sure ...' Helen replied cautiously, 'but it's a strong possibility. I can't say any more than—'

'*Why?* Why would someone do something like this?'

Helen darted a look at Charlie, before returning her gaze to him. This was the six-million-dollar question – one she couldn't answer.

'Again, we're not sure yet. Items of value were taken, but whether that's the principal motive—'

'Someone did this for *money?*' Westlake interrupted. 'Killed my beautiful boy for ...'

And now, finally, he broke, dropping his face to his hands and sobbing. Helen said nothing, letting his grief flow, her thoughts turning on his question. Such brutality for such meagre gains was a truly horrific thought, but part of Helen hoped Westlake might be right, that it *was* mere greed driving these gruesome attacks. Because another part of her – the greater part – feared that actually the motive for these crimes was something much, much worse.

Chapter 59

'What on earth are they saying, Greg? That Martha was killed by ... by some kind of serial killer?'

His mother's haggard face looked up at him, fearful and pale. Greg desperately wanted to reassure her, to dismiss her fears, if only to buy him some respite from her questioning, but he was powerless to offer any comfort.

'I don't know any more than you, Mum.'

'You heard what they said on the radio, that this was the second attack,' she fired back.

'It's just speculation, you know what the media are like.'

He said it, but he didn't believe it. Last night, he had been aghast at the prospect of a killer on the loose. And last night, Martha's killer had made good on that threat. Greg was sure the two crimes were connected, but he wasn't going to stoke his mother's anxiety by confirming this. She looked fit to blow as it was.

'I don't know how you can be so laidback about it,' she countered sharply. 'If what they're saying is true.'

Her attack was relentless, panic and horror fuelling her demands for information, reassurance and solace. But her accusation provoked only anger and outrage – she of all people knew how much he had loved Martha, how devastated he was by her sudden death. How could she accuse him of being uninterested? It was obscene.

'I just think there's no point jumping to conclusions, not when we have other things to focus on...' he replied tersely, gesturing towards his father, who was patiently walking Bailey around the garden. 'We have to do our job, let the police do theirs.'

In truth, if DI Grace were in front of him now, he'd be in her face, demanding answers. But he wasn't going to tell her that. Angry, confused and disoriented as he was, he knew he had to be the grown-up in the room if he was to stop his mother having a nervous breakdown.

'Well, I say we give it another couple of hours, then you should ring Southampton Central,' she rejoined, unabashed.

'Mum...'

'It's not fair us being left in the dark like this. Not when the world and his wife seem to know the facts already...'

As she rattled out her grievance, his phone started to ring. Scooping it up, Greg took in the caller ID.

'Is that them?'

The phone number was familiar – it was the incident room at Southampton Central.

'Yes.'

'Well, put it on speaker, then...'

'No.'

The word shot out of his mouth, harsh and final.

'*I* will deal with this.'

Without waiting for a response, Greg headed into the hallway, answering the call.

'Morning, Mr White. It's DC Wilson here. Is now a good time to talk?'

'Sure.'

The word felt entirely inappropriate in his mouth, given what he was about to be told. Was there a good time to have your worst fears confirmed?

'It was really just to follow up on our previous conversation about your movements on the night of the ninth of January.'

'I'm not sure I follow...' Greg murmured, completely wrong-footed.

'Well, it's my job to do the belt-and-braces on everyone's movements that night and I did mention previously that it would be useful if you could bring in your Fitbit, so we could confirm your—'

'You can't be serious. You're calling me about *that*?'

Silence on the other end.

'A child was *murdered* last night. By the same man who killed Martha. And you're calling me about a bloody Fitbit?!'

He was shouting down the phone now, but didn't care.

'As yet, there's no confirmed link between last night's incident and the attack on your wife—' DC Wilson continued, sounding rattled.

'No, don't you dare fob me off. I want answers, I want *the truth*. You owe us that much,' Greg fired back.

'And when there's anything concrete to pass on, I'm sure DI Grace will be in touch. In the meantime—'

'You people really are unbelievable, you know that? There's some kind of madman stalking Southampton and *I'm* a suspect?'

His mother had appeared in the doorway, looking more alarmed than ever. He was tempted to tell her where to go, but turned away, reserving all his venom for DC Wilson.

'Shame on you. Shame on you for keeping us in the dark, for treating us like law-breakers.'

'It's not like that at all, Mr White. We're just trying to eliminate people from our—'

'Oh, go to hell.'

Greg hung up, gripping the phone tightly, his whole body shaking with anger.

'What's happened, Greg? What on earth are they saying now?'

He turned back to his mother, but for once was lost for words. Having braced himself for the awful truth, he had been both confused and enraged by Wilson's ridiculous request, his last vestiges of self-control deserting him. His mother desperately wanted reassurance that the world wasn't a dark, wicked place, but he could provide no such solace, no explanation for what had befallen them. Nor could he fully process the notion that a killer was at large in Southampton, perhaps even now planning his next outrage. No, he had no comfort, no moorings at all in a world which today seemed to offer far more questions than answers.

Chapter 60

'Any confirmed sightings at Grange Park?'

Helen's team had been dispersed to several locations throughout the city, questioning potential witnesses, gathering and sifting information, but now it was time to pool their knowledge, to probe the evidence and see if they could make any sense of these baffling crimes, hence why they were now crowded around her in the incident room once more.

'Obviously I haven't been able to speak to Mr Westlake's mother yet,' DC Malik responded promptly. 'But I have got a couple of concrete sightings. The housing estate's only half occupied – still quite a few units to sell – but I dug up two home-owners who confirmed that Mr Westlake was there last night. They differ on the timings by five minutes or so, but basically they back up his story that he was there from 7 p.m. to 11 p.m. There's traffic cameras on the main road nearby, so we should be able to confirm his movements easily enough.'

'Good work. And Mrs Westlake?' Helen responded, turning to DC Reid.

'She was at Albertine's from 5.30 p.m. until quarter to eleven. Two waiters and three kitchen staff attest to that. Would have taken her five to ten minutes to get back to Freemantle from there, which tallies with her first call to her husband.'

'Also, a neighbour confirmed Mr Westlake roared up just after 11 p.m., knocking over the bins which were out for collection,' DC Wilson added. 'Which fits with him dialling 999 at six minutes past eleven.'

'OK, so unless they are shape-shifters or time-travellers we can rule them out as perpetrators, though obviously we'll have to bear in mind that there may be reasons why they might have played a part in the victim's death, wittingly or unwittingly. What do we know about Ethan Westlake?'

Now it was DC McAndrew's turn to contribute.

'Sixteen years old, only son of Richard and Victoria Westlake. Attends Sherringham Boys' School in Upper Shirley, a private secondary school. Did passingly well in his GCSEs but from the school website it seems as though he was more of a sportsman – football, hockey, athletics. I've had a very brief look through his call and message history – he doesn't seem to have a boyfriend or girlfriend, but it's early days in our search.'

'And what do we know about his movements?'

'He had hockey practice after school, returning home around 5 p.m. After that, it's a bit of a blank. We know he had at least three conversations with his mother during that time, but the calls were short and her accompanying text messages suggest they were mostly talking about practicalities, things that needed doing before school tomorrow.'

'So his mother was nervous about him being alone?' Helen queried.

'Possibly, but the vibe I'm getting is that was just her way, she liked to fuss.'

'Anything else on his movements?'

'Not really, though the lights to the front lounge were definitely on last evening, a couple of people noticed that when they were putting their bins out. It's not uncommon apparently, as that's where the PS5 is…'

A few smiles from older members of the team, a brief moment of levity in what had been a difficult morning for all.

'So, Meredith and her team are on site at the moment, but let's recap on what we know so far,' Helen said, turning to the murder board and tapping the photos of Ethan Westlake's brutalized corpse. 'Sometime between 7 p.m. and 11 p.m., the victim was subdued and killed. I'm assuming he was gaming at the time, as the game was still up on screen when officers arrived and his chair upturned. His hands were tied behind his back with elasticated cord and a rag shoved into his mouth. The knot used was clearly secure, but it looks different to the one used to bind Martha White's wrists, not that I'm an expert. Double check this with Meredith once she's done her first sweep, please…'

She gestured at DC Wilson, who nodded eagerly.

'Once secured, the killer either set off in search of valuables, before returning for the kill, or completed the kill before heading upstairs to remove jewellery, watches and so forth. Either way, when it came to the actual murder, excessive force was used, with three nasty wounds to the back of the head and a further four blows to the shoulders and upper back. The question for us is whether the choice of victim was important, the killer having some special hatred towards him, a desire to mutilate, even eviscerate them. Or whether the victim is unimportant, even selected at random – the act itself, and the charge the perpetrator derives from it, being the main driver. What do we know about these two families? Any friendship, connections, overlap, however tenuous…'

To Helen's intense disappointment, no one spoke.

'Anything at all?'

'Nothing obvious,' Charlie answered. 'They live in different parts of the city, work in different industries and crucially are at very different stages in their lives, so there's no obvious overlap in terms of NCT classes, schools and so on. The Whites' life revolved around babies, both professionally and personally and, in terms of leisure time, they were very devoted to exercise. The Westlakes were more focused on their careers, Ethan's schooling and, when they weren't working, they seemed to prioritize pleasure over exercise.'

'I've had a look at their contacts, Facebook posts and so on,' DC Malik added. 'Can't see any mutual friends or shared groups that they belong to, other than generic Southampton ones that have thousands of casual followers.'

There was a brief, heavy silence, before DC Jennings spoke up, trying to inject some energy and optimism.

'Talking of Facebook, one thing that does possibly link them is that they were both very visible on social media. Banana Tree nurseries is obviously well known to local people and we've already established that Martha White wasn't backward in displaying her good fortune for the world to see. Ditto the Westlakes. The husband's construction firm trades on building homes for families, with lots of adverts to that effect on local Facebook groups, full-page ads in the *Southampton Evening News* and so on. He makes a big play of the family side of things and Vicky Westlake does, too, bigging up their son's achievements, awards that she and her husband have won professionally, as well as extensively detailing their foreign holidays, busy social life, new cars and so on. I wouldn't say either family was shy in trumpeting their material wealth...'

'But they're hardly alone in that,' Helen countered. 'Scan through the Insta and Facebook posts from residents in the well-off areas of Southampton and you'll find scores of images blatantly inviting burglars to take an interest, so what makes these two families special?'

Another telling silence, before DC Reid finally ventured:

'Is it that the perpetrator knew that someone would be home alone? If the victims revealed their regular routine through social media posts and so on, the perpetrator might have known when to target the house, when there would only be one occupant—'

'Except that Victoria Westlake should have been at home last night,' DC McAndrew intervened. 'So, he would have had to be watching the family's movements very closely to know that this night of all nights she'd be away. We've no evidence at all so far of anyone staking out the property or stalking Victoria Westlake, despite there being a lot of cameras on that street, so ...'

'Are we saying they were selected at random, then?'

DC Malik looked like she didn't want to ask the question, but felt compelled to.

'I think we have to consider that a very real possibility,' Helen answered calmly. 'There's no obvious connection between the families, other than their demonstrable wealth, so why them? We ... I presumed that Martha White's murder was personally motivated, given the levels of violence employed *and* the fact that her wedding ring was deliberately removed during the attack, but now I'm wondering if these attacks are entirely *impersonal*. There's no correlation in the type of jewellery taken from the two crime scenes, and no obvious overlap in the age/gender profile of the deceased. So maybe it's *the act itself* that's significant, not the identity of the victims.'

'Someone with a visceral hatred of the rich perhaps?' DC Reid offered.

'Possibly, but more likely someone with a taste, a *compulsion*, to dominate, subdue and destroy. It's not just the extremity of the violence, it's the sequencing of the attack. Very cautious and precise to begin with – gaining entry, subduing the victim, murdering them – but, after that, frenzied and unrestrained. According to Jim Grieves, the lacerations to the shoulders and backs occurred *after* both victims were already dead, which might suggest the attacker taking some kind of pleasure from destroying the victim's corpse post-mortem.'

'Could it be some kind of ritual, then? Occult, even?' DC Jennings asked, blanching.

'I don't see any evidence of that,' Helen replied evenly. 'Unless we're all missing something—'

'There is one possibility I've turned up ...'

Charlie spoke with evident caution, but nevertheless all eyes now turned to her.

'I've been liaising with the burglary squad, who've confirmed that there has been a significant rise in aggravated burglaries in the last twelve months, up nearly 50 per cent year on year. The burglaries come in waves and the timing is quite unpredictable, but the trend seems to suggest that there *is* a perpetrator at large. Someone who is skilled and professional, always accessing properties from the rear or the side, using a screwdriver or blade to force doors and windows open. A couple of the early incidents were on unoccupied houses, but the more recent ones have included violent attacks on home-owners. The perpetrator chooses carefully – young women, the elderly, people with disabilities—'

'What level of violence?' Helen asked, suppressing her disgust.

'Extremely high. He uses tools to break in – hammers, blades, crowbars – then employs them on his victims. A retired businessman had his cheek, nose and jaw broken back in October, barely survived. Also, in the same month a luxury car salesman had both kneecaps shattered with a hammer, despite having complied with his attacker's demands.'

'And you're thinking escalation? The violence spiralling?' Helen quizzed her.

'It's got to be a possibility, given the items taken. The perpetrator was only interested in portable stuff – jewellery, watches, rings and so on – which obviously fits with the MO here, but interestingly none of the items taken have ever been recovered.'

'None at all?' Helen reacted, surprised.

'Nothing,' Charlie replied, shaking her head. 'Normally you'd expect some of them to turn up in pawn shops, markets, jewellery outlets, but nothing with this guy. It's like they've vanished into thin air.'

'Or he's kept them.'

Helen was only saying what they were all thinking. Once more, silence filled the room, before Charlie finally continued:

'What if they're trophies? What if their value is not financial, but emotional or psychological? Killing the home's occupant, taking items that are important to them. Maybe you're right, maybe it's the violation of someone's home, the permanent desecration of these rich folk and their good fortune that's the real motive here.'

'Keeping hold of the trophies would allow him to relive the moment of violation again, at his leisure,' DC McAndrew agreed. 'Keeping the feeling, the thrill alive, perhaps even encouraging him to offend again.'

A couple of the team looked sick, but conversely Helen felt a shiver of excitement.

'How definitively can these attacks be linked? Over the last year, say…'

'They think they can link over a dozen. The MO could fit with ours, given the mode of entry and the care taken, so I think it's definitely worth a look…'

'And correlation in terms of location?' asked DC McAndrew.

'Only rich neighbourhoods,' Charlie replied.

'And what about the timing of them?'

This time Charlie paused before answering, now appearing less surefooted.

'Well, that's the tricky part. There's no obvious rhyme or reason to the attacks. They come in waves, two, three, even four incidents in the space of fortnight, then nothing for months. Then another burst of burglaries. Then nothing. And so on. I've had a good look at it and, honestly, I can't make head or tail of it.'

'Perhaps he's just being cautious,' Jennings offered. 'Filling his boots, then backing off when the heat becomes too great, when the community's on its guard.'

'I don't buy it,' Helen responded. 'If he's getting an emotional, psychological, even sexual charge from these violations, he wouldn't be able to just turn it off like that.'

'What about if he's travelling around the country, committing offences elsewhere?'

Charlie was already nodding, liking this line of thought.

'So he's a truck driver? Or itinerant worker?'

'Or part of the travelling community?' DC Reid added ruefully, holding up his hands in mock apology. 'I know it's not very PC to say it, but you know what happens when the fairground comes to town...'

As these thoughts settled, the team seemed to turn back to Helen, as if seeking guidance.

'Charlie, do you have the name of the businessman who was attacked by this guy?'

'Roger Morton, lives in Poole. I've got a mobile number for him.'

'Good, I'll talk to him. In the meantime, DS Brooks is in charge, she'll assign you your duties. I want half of you staying on the Westlake case, the rest following this new line of enquiry. I want you to look for overlaps with current cases and any patterns, details that might explain the stop/start nature of these offences. Right, everyone, get to it ...'

The team were already on their toes, as Helen grabbed her phone and keys.

'...and nobody goes home until we've got something,' she added pointedly, masking the tension she felt inside. 'We need some *progress*.'

Chapter 61

'Get out of here right now or I'm calling the police.'

The woman's tone was strident, thick with emotion. Emilia wasn't sure if she was about to explode or cry, possibly both. Leaning forward, she clocked the sales rep's badge.

'Come on now, Karly. There's no need to be like that. I simply want to ask you a few questions.'

'I've got nothing to say to the likes of you.'

Emilia suppressed a smile, her combatant's moral indignation glancing off her. She was too long in the tooth to be shamed by this middle-aged pudding.

'Look, I understand that you're upset, but this case is very much in the public interest, as there are real concerns now for people's safety in this city—'

'This "case" is my boss's son,' her emotive companion shot back. 'A beautiful, sweet-natured boy, who never did any harm to anyone.'

'Tell me more, he sounds like a lovely kid.'

For a moment, the sales rep was almost fooled, foxed into sharing private memories of the tragic boy, but she caught herself just in time.

'Get out of here, you … scum.'

'You're going to have to talk at some point, the press will be all over this,' Emilia warned. 'So why not say your piece now and get it over with?'

But Karly had rounded her desk and grasped Emilia forcefully by the arm, marching her to the door of the neat sales office.

'You get out,' she repeated, her volume rising with each word. 'And don't come back!'

Emilia found herself jettisoned onto the pavement beyond. Turning, she was about to state her case once again, but the door slammed in her face. Seconds later, the CLOSED sign was in place and the blinds dropped, concealing the interior.

Shrugging off her disappointment, Emilia headed back to her car, her mind turning on her next move. The boy's family had gone to ground, his school had rejected all requests for information and loyal Karly had shut the door in her face. Perhaps other colleagues of Richard Westlake might be more forthcoming, or perhaps one of the waiting staff at Albertine's could be 'encouraged' to provide some useful background about the bereaved family. But if all else failed, she could just cull the necessary from Westlake's social media feeds – they were both *very* busy in that department.

Thanking her lucky stars for the convenient short cuts of modern journalism, Emilia paused by her car, turning back to the take in the Grange Park show home. As she did so, she couldn't suppress a smile, the dark irony of the advertising hoarding too much to resist. Richard Westlake, flanked by his family, was front and centre, promising to 'Build the perfect home for you'. He beamed out at the viewer, confident, happy, successful, prompting Emilia to wonder about the motive for these sudden attacks. She had assumed there might be some personal motive behind these killings, or that they were just aggravated burglaries gone badly wrong. But now, looking up at Richard Westlake's handsome, smug face, she wondered if there might be a more pointed, more sinister psychology at play here. Was someone deliberately targeting these high-profile, successful couples simply because of their good fortune? Was there a rage, a jealousy, even a violent hatred of these rich self-starters? If so, then the implications of this were exhilarating and terrifying in equal measure. If a shadowy figure really *did* want to attack the visibly wealthy, then he would have plenty of targets in this prosperous city. It would just be a case of picking who to target and when to strike. It would be a catastrophe. An outrage. No, much more than that, it would be a bloodbath.

Chapter 62

'Who is it?'

The disembodied voice sounded tinny and hollow through the intercom.

'It's DI Grace, Hampshire Police. We spoke earlier...'

'Show me your ID,' came the brief, barked response.

Helen obliged, holding up her warrant card to the camera. Moments later, the intercom buzzed loudly and, pushing open the heavy door, Helen disappeared inside.

Roger Morton sat in his armchair, staring at her like a frightened owl. He had not offered his visitor a cup of tea, a word of greeting or encouragement of any kind. In fact, he seemed keen to be rid of her.

'As I said, I'm sorry to intrude on you at such short notice,' Helen said, keeping up her friendly patter. 'But I need to ask you a couple of questions about the break-in you suffered three months back? It's related to a current investigation which appears to have some connec—'

'So, when you need me, you come running, but when *I* want answers, I get the silent treatment.'

Morton had found his voice, his tone bitter and hostile.

'I'm sorry if you feel that way. It's a separate team that's dealing with your case—'

'Isn't it always?' he interrupted caustically.

'But if I can expedite your case in any way, throw some light upon what happened, then obviously I'll do so. It's in everyone's interests that this dangerous individual is brought to book.'

Morton couldn't argue with that one, retreating into angry silence.

'Obviously I don't want to upset you by stirring up distressing memories, but if you could walk me through what happened that night...'

He looked appalled at the request, so Helen added quickly:

'I wouldn't be asking unless it was genuinely a matter of life and death.'

Her evident sincerity, the urgency of her request, seemed to give him pause for thought.

'Please, Roger, anything you can give me...'

There was a long silence, then the old man sighed, a sigh that seemed to incorporate a world of suffering.

'It was late October, the twenty-sixth,' he wheezed. 'Miriam was away visiting her sister, so it was just me. I was getting ready for bed, when I heard a noise downstairs...'

He paused, as if suddenly back in the moment.

'I hoped I was imagining things, the mind plays tricks on you when you're alone, but I came down to investigate anyway. I thought perhaps someone might have tried to access the side door... but actually he'd come in through a back window.'

Another short pause, his voice shaking slightly.

'I didn't see him, not at first, though I sensed that something was wrong. Then suddenly he's on top of me, hand over my mouth, forcing me down to the floor. Next thing I know, I'm coming to on the carpet, trussed up like a turkey...'

There was anger in his voice, but distress too, his eyes rheumy and moist.

'I tried to talk to him, asked him what he wanted, but he just shoved a dirty rag in my mouth. Then he went upstairs, took what he could and came back down.'

'And then?'

It was a gentle prompt, Helen sensing that Morton wanted to retreat from the memories of his ordeal.

'Is that when he hurt you, Roger?'

Morton nodded mutely. Helen watched a single tear roll down his cheek.

'Why did he hurt you?'

'I've no idea. I was tied up, entirely at his mercy...'

It was said with such force, such passion that Helen was in no doubt that it was the pointlessness of the attack, as well as its severity, that cut deep. Helen took a moment to register the legacy of the attack – the livid scarring round his temple and cheek, the permanently altered hair line, the incessant tremor in Morton's hands. She had no idea what he had been like before his ordeal, but he seemed cowed now, in full retreat from life.

'He didn't give a reason?'

Morton shook his head vehemently.

'Each time he raised that bloody hammer, I begged him to stop, begged him for mercy, but he couldn't hear me through the gag, or didn't want to hear me...'

'Did you get a proper look at him during the attack?'

'Not really, I was face down on the ground and he kept pushing me back down, this heavy hand on my back.'

'Did he speak to you at all?'

'No, he swore a couple of times, but that was it.'

'So you heard his voice?'

'Very briefly.'

'Was he a local man?'

To her surprise, Morton laughed, long and bitter.

'Far from it. He was foreign. East European, Russian maybe…'

Helen paused, surprised, before replying:

'I see. Did you notice anything else about him?'

'Well, he had tattoos on his forearm, military ones by my reckoning. I wanted to spit out my gag, ask what the hell an ex-soldier was doing attacking a pensioner, but I never got the chance. When I turned to him, he hit me flush on the cheek with the hammer.'

Morton gestured to his ravaged face. Helen winced inwardly, picturing the collision of steel and bone.

'After that, I couldn't speak. Not that it would have mattered if I could have. The guy was possessed, crazed. All I could do was just try to turn away, lessen the blows, see if somehow I could survive. I tried to think of Miriam, of what I'd lose if I gave in, anything to try and keep myself conscious and fighting, but it was no good. His blood was up, his hatred boiling over, I didn't stand a chance. I wanted to live, I really wanted to live…'

He looked up at Helen, his eyes now brimming with tears.

'…but, honestly, I thought I was going to die.'

Chapter 63

If he could have closed his eyes and drifted quietly into oblivion, he would happily have done so. For what possible purpose did life serve now?

Richard Westlake lay on the crisply made bed, his eyes fixed on a small brown stain on the ceiling. He had retreated here on the insistence of his sister, who was clearly fearful he was about to collapse from exhaustion. It was true he hadn't slept a wink since it happened and it felt like he was orbiting a far-off planet, looking down on the unfolding tragedy as if from a distance, but what were the odds that he would find any repose, any peace? He was cast adrift, without his beloved son, without his wife of over twenty years by his side. Even now, Victoria was lying in his sister's guest bedroom, medication dulling her grief and he had crept past without a second glance. He couldn't face being near her right now, saddened by her medicated state and fearful of what might happen when the drugs wore off. They were just at the beginning of this nightmare, that was for sure. The worst was yet to come.

Victoria loved her son with a passion that was sometimes hard to describe. It had been a battle to conceive him, and his birth difficult, but this only seemed to magnify his mother's love. Every comfort was provided, every opportunity given, every modest triumph heralded. The road that Vicky had to go down now was one no mother should have to face and Richard wondered if she would have the strength to make it, or if *he'd* have the strength to help her. Before that, there were more pressing indignities, more painful episodes to come. He'd been told that he'd have to identify the body and that shortly after that, Ethan would be released for funeral. God alone knows how they would get through that.

What could one say in the circumstances that would do justice to him, amidst the horror and confusion of his death? It would be hard enough anyway for a parent to summon the words to give voice to their love, their devotion, in the teeth of an unexpected and premature death. But to do so in the shared knowledge of Ethan's wicked, gruesome end – what could one possibly say that was not despairing, wretched, angry and forlorn?

It was this thought, this image of his poor boy lying bound and helpless, that rendered sleep impossible. Resting on the cold, unforgiving bed, Richard wondered if he would ever sleep again, whether he would ever be able to shut his eyes and not picture that terrible scene. His only son, confused and terrified, writhing on the floor, panicked and in tears, as his pitiless killer raised the axe above his head.

He clapped a hand to his open mouth, stifling the scream that seemed to pour from him. It was a hideous, constipated noise of hopeless agony and it provided no relief, no respite. There would be no coming back from this, no road forward that made any sense. Richard could only look back, wishing things were different, wishing that he could have taken the blows to spare his son. If he could swap places with his boy, he would have done so in a heartbeat, happy to lay down his life so that Ethan could embrace his future. But there was no chance of this, of course, no miracle shot at redemption.

All he *could* promise his son was that the person responsible would be brought to justice. That much Richard Westlake was certain of. He and Victoria were well off, if need be they would spend every penny they had, devote every hour of the day, to the hunt for Ethan's killer. Please God, the police would capture him quickly, but if they didn't, he would take matters into his own hands. He would do it for Ethan, for Victoria, but for himself too – his current plight too awful to endure. His son was dead, his only child was lying on a slab in a police mortuary across town, whilst out there somewhere lurked a killer, who even now was plotting to pitch another undeserving family into hell. Well, he would not give the sick bastard any peace. He would devote his life, his fortune, his soul to hunting him down – or die trying.

Chapter 64

He stared down at the evidence table, trying to banish the nausea that gripped him. Japhet Wilson was not a lightweight – he'd endured some harrowing days on the job – but there was something about the neatly tied knot that unnerved him. As a piece of evidence, it was unremarkable, a short length of elasticated cable that you might pick up in any home store, but it was the use that it had been put to that chilled his blood. What had Ethan been thinking as he lay on the floor, bound and helpless, as death circled above? Had he been conscious, aware, fearful? Wilson hoped not, but if DS Brooks' theory was correct – if sadism and terror lay at the heart of these crimes – then he feared that the first blow had been just the beginning of the poor boy's ordeal.

'Curious little piece, isn't it?'

Wilson looked up to see the chief forensics officer approaching, a smile playing on Meredith Walker's lips. In all honesty, he wasn't sure where her levity came from, given the circumstances, but perhaps that was just her nature – some folk were like that, naturally immune to the horrors of their job. Perhaps in time, when he knew her a little better, he would understand.

'Looks fairly bog standard to me,' he replied, in a downbeat mood.

'The provenance is not of any real interest, you could never pin it down for sure...'

'I suppose it's too much to ask for any DNA, a partial print, hair...?'

He tailed off, for Meredith was already shaking her head.

'Or deposits at all? The cloth that was used to gag Martha White had some kind of engine oil on it.'

'Clean as a whistle, I'm afraid. I'm presuming it's fresh out the packet.'

Wilson took this on board, still curious as to what her perky demeanour presaged.

'No, it's the configuration, that's interesting,' Meredith continued, gesturing at the evidence on the bench.

'Because it's a different knot to the one used on Martha White, you mean?'

'Exactly. A standard figure of eight was used on her wrists. This is a little more elaborate, and consequently more secure. It's called a thief knot.'

Wilson raised an eyebrow, the title of the ligature strangely appropriate.

'So... maybe the perpetrator thought Ethan posed more of a physical threat than Martha White, was more likely to break free, so he used a different knot?'

'Could be.'

'Is it complicated to tie?'

'Not if you know what you're doing, which is really my point. It's not obscure – it's a play on your standard reef knot, yet most folk wouldn't know how to do it.'

'Right, so this guy's into boats?'

'Could be, but they also use them in the armed forces and the emergency services, especially the fire service.'

Wilson mulled on this, not entirely comfortable with the drift of Meredith's thoughts.

'It's also possible that someone who regularly needed to secure things – and secure them *properly* – would make use of it. Someone transporting heavy loads, perhaps even removals men ... but for my money this is a bit exotic for them. I'd be looking at navy, army or something a bit closer to home if I were you.'

Thanking her, Wilson headed on his way. It wasn't much, but it was something to offer to his new boss, a small kernel that might yet pay dividends for the team. More importantly, *much more importantly*, it was the first tiny mistake this shadowy killer had made.

Chapter 65

Helen marched back to her bike, deep in thought. Leaving Poole, she had raced along the A31, keen to be back at Southampton Central, driving for over an hour before her light-headedness reminded her that she hadn't eaten or drunk anything in hours. Adrenaline can only get you so far and, as her bladder was also protesting, she pulled off into the Picket Post services. Having wolfed down a sandwich, she now crunched over the gravel towards the bike park, clutching a strong black coffee from Costa. Refreshed, her mind was firing once more, as she continued to mull on Morton's surprising testimony.

It had never occurred to Helen that their perpetrator might be a foreign national. In one sense this was alarming. If they somehow managed to get sight of this pitiless killer – a witness testimony, a CCTV still – would they even be able to identify him? Was it possible he had even come here illegally, slipping beneath their radar? On the other hand, this small clue might yet hold the key. How many East European housebreakers were likely to be operating on the South Coast?

It was a tantalizing thought and Helen longed to be back in the incident room, interrogating this latest lead. But as she scurried across the loose gravel towards her bike, she noticed something. A regular crunch, crunch, crunch, keeping time with her footsteps. It was soft, it was subtle, but it was clear enough to alert her to the danger. She was in a quiet part of the services, heading to the bike park on the fringes and she suddenly realized how vulnerable she was. Raising her coffee as if to drink it, she shot a look at the rear windscreen of the car to her right. Yes, there was no doubt about it, her would-be assassin was back.

She sped up, but so did the footsteps behind her. Her hands were occupied, helmet in one hand, coffee in the other. Should she dump them and haul out her baton? Or should she drop them and run, in the hope of making it to her bike? She hesitated, only for a second, but it was a second too long. The man suddenly lunged forward. In the glinting windscreen, Helen spotted the telltale flash of steel, the sunlight reflecting off the man's blade.

Instinctively, she spun round, the knife just missing her back and cutting a nasty gash in the side of her leathers. Her assailant, hooded and wild-eyed, was almost upon her, his bulk blocking out the sun. Without thinking, Helen hurled her coffee into his face. Crying out in pain, the man stumbled slightly, but then came again, knife outstretched. There was no way back for him now, the element of surprise long gone. It was kill or be killed now.

The point of the knife shot towards Helen, heading inexorably for her heart. Wrenching her left arm up, Helen swung her helmet in front of her, her only means of defence. It knocked the man's arm away, sending the knife off course. Helen longed to hear it skittering away over the surface, but still the man gripped it, coming for her again, slashing wildly at her face. Helen was off balance now, staggering backwards, swinging her helmet in wide loops in a desperate attempt to fend off the blows. But he was coming at her fast, too fast, and surely one lunge would pierce her defences.

Then suddenly her breath was knocked from her, as she collided sharply with a car. Now she was trapped and her assailant seized his chance, closing in for the kill. Again, instinct saved her, her free hand batting the blade away. It veered off sharply, but not before catching the exposed skin between sleeve and glove. Pain seared through her, as the razor-sharp blade tore her flesh, but she never took her eyes off her attacker, swinging her helmet round with all her might.

Finally she got lucky, the heavy helmet catching her attacker on the back of the head. He stumbled forwards, colliding with another car, before spinning once more to face her. Helen looked her attacker square in the face – unshaven, curly blond hair beneath the shadowy hood, there was no doubt it was the man who'd gained access to her building two nights earlier. But there was barely time to register this before the man took a step towards her again. This time, Helen reacted sharply, stepping back herself whilst drawing her baton. This seemed to give her assailant pause for thought, his eyes flitting to her baton, then beyond her to a frightened family who were rooted to the spot, alarmed by the conflict playing out in front of them.

That seemed to decide it for him and, turning tail, he ran. Helen reacted quickly, but he still had a head start on her, haring away as if his life depended on it. He was making for the main body of the car park, but raising her speed, she sprinted after him, determined to bring this deadly game to an end. He was fast, but she was a born athlete, slowly narrowing the distance between them. There was still a chance that he might escape, however, so Helen upped her pace, skidding over one bonnet, then another, to bring herself directly behind him.

Sensing the danger, the man sped up, but Helen felt certain

there would be only one winner now. This guy was an amateur and though she would have to be careful, she was confident she could disarm him. Reaching out an arm, she grabbed at his sleeve, just missing him. He burst forward again, terrified of capture, but Helen refused to be beaten, lurching at him once more. As she did so, however, a savage blast rang out, an articulated lorry appearing from nowhere, bearing directly down on her. Helen had only a second to react, the driver's horrified face shockingly visible, and she jerked violently backwards. Miraculously, the HGV missed her by a whisker, the side wing battering Helen's face, pushing her backwards, even as the truck skidded to a halt.

Helen stood there for a moment, shocked and breathless, before coming to her senses. Her attacker must have been hit, killed even. Dropping to her knees, she peered under the body of the vehicle, expecting to see a crumpled mass of blood, bone and sinew. But there was nothing there.

'Shit.'

Straightening up, Helen rounded the vehicle. The driver was getting out, gesturing and shouting, but she ignored him, pushing round to the far side of the truck. Desperately she scanned the busy car park, but there was no sign of her attacker, just row on row of parked cars.

'What the hell?'

She stalked forward, ducking down to check under the parked vehicles, changing rows suddenly, doing everything she could to pick up his scent. But it was no good. She had been so close to catching him, so close to bringing this ordeal to an end, but against the odds he had eluded her once more, vanishing into thin air.

Chapter 66

His body was in revolt, craving fresh oxygen, but still he held his breath. If he made even the tiniest noise now, she would surely hear.

His heart continued to thunder in his chest, as fear gripped him. He had come close to capture, but even nearer to death, the cab of the lorry glancing him as it roared past, sending him spinning away onto the tarmac. He had hit it hard, grazing his face nastily, even as he lost hold of the knife, the blade skittering away from him. Shocked, dazed, he hadn't bothered to look for it. His only thought now was to get away.

But how? His car was parked some way off and how could he get there without giving his position away, bobbing up and down between the parked cars. For one desperate, hopeful second, he wondered if Grace had been flattened by the truck, but then he heard her scrambling footsteps, saw her round the HGV, searching for her prey. He had immediately ducked down, flattening himself next to a Ford Kuga, praying it would provide him with enough cover. But Grace was not to be denied, her footsteps crunching ever closer.

Unbidden, he now felt tears prick his eyes. Was this how it would end? Arrest, disgrace, imprisonment? Would he tell all in the hope of leniency? Or would he keep his mouth shut, taking what was coming to him without revealing his weakness and depravity? In spite of himself, he wanted to howl, to cry, to berate Blythe and the whole hideous mess he had got himself into . . .

Crunch. Crunch. Crunch.

Still Grace came on, now just a few yards away on the other side of the car. Part of him was tempted to call out, to bring this terrible chase to an end, but instead he remained quiet, his body stilled, the quarry praying for deliverance. And now to his utter astonishment, he heard her footsteps heading away, marching back in the direction of her bike.

He could have laughed, could have cried out in shocked triumph, but he bit his tongue, barely believing his good fortune. Against all the odds, he had survived. He had been spared.

And he would live to fight another day.

Chapter 67

'Jesus, Helen, are you OK?'

Charlie hovered over her friend, visibly shocked by the nasty cut on Helen's wrist, which Helen dabbed at aggressively, trying to remove the caked blood.

'Looks worse than it is, it's just a flesh wound.'

'You should go to A&E.'

'It's really not that bad.'

'At least let me have a go, do it properly...'

Without waiting for an answer, Charlie took over. They were closeted away in Southampton Central's first-aid room, a shabby space no bigger than a cupboard. Helen watched her friend gratefully, as methodically, patiently, she wiped the blood away, before slathering on the disinfectant, causing Helen to wince sharply.

'Did you get a good look at him?' Charlie asked, ignoring her discomfort.

Helen nodded.

'And?'

'Didn't recognize him.'

'But you saw enough to piece together an accurate picture of him? Something to run through the system?'

'Sure, but it won't do any good. The guy was new to this, wild and amateurish, I'd be surprised if he's ever done this before.'

'So who is he?'

'Just one of Blythe's proxies. Someone with a stain on his conscience. With a job, or wife or family to lose...'

Charlie seemed depressed by the thought; as to be truthful so did Helen. She knew she should detest her assassin, but actually she felt nothing for him, except disgust and perhaps even a little pity. It was Blythe that Helen reserved her hatred for.

'So what now?'

Helen hesitated long enough for a severe frown to settle on Charlie's features.

'You *are* going to report this?'

Helen remained silent, not wanting, or needing, Charlie's censure.

'I know he'll be long gone from the scene now, but there'll be CCTV, witnesses...'

'I already checked that,' Helen countered. 'There was no CCTV near the bike park and there's no telling which of the hundreds of cars that passed through the general area was his...'

'Someone just tried to kill you, Helen,' Charlie insisted, as if she was speaking to a recalcitrant child. 'The team need to be aware of that, the unit hunting Blythe needs to be aware of that—'

'It won't do any good and it'll just distract our guys from the job in hand. We have a double murderer to apprehend and—'

'You can't seriously expect to keep this a secret? What did the guys on front desk say?'

'Told them I came off my bike. They loved that, of course.'

Helen's attempt at humour cut no ice with Charlie.

'This is madness.'

'You have to trust me to handle this—'

'And see you end up on the slab, no thank you.'

'You're being overdramatic.'

'At least tell Peters—'

'No!'

The word shot out, harsh and decisive.

'That's the last thing I'm going to do,' Helen added firmly.

'OK, conceal it from the team if you must, but he's your boss.'

'A boss who is determined to get rid of me.'

'And hiding this from him is going to *help* your case?' Charlie countered.

'This is exactly what he wants,' Helen insisted. 'A confession that I'm vulnerable, distracted, running scared. I'd be on sick leave before the hour was out and it'd be a fair chance I'd never set foot in this station again…'

She had raised her voice against her old friend, but couldn't help herself.

'Not a word of this. To anyone. Understood?'

Charlie looked like she wanted to continue the fight, to argue for a sensible approach to this tricky situation, but wisely she backed down.

'OK, but I'm not happy about it.'

'And your concern is noted,' Helen said softening, laying a hand on arm. 'Now let's get to it. We've got work to do.'

Chapter 68

'Nikolai Davidoff.'

DC Jennings lingered over the name, enjoying the many syllables and the slight Slavic lilt he afforded them.

'Tell me more.'

Helen was back at the helm, the team gathered around her. In spite of her unpleasant encounter earlier, she was determined to make progress, now they had fresh evidence.

'Originally from Romania, part of a gang based in Streatham. Done two stretches for breaking and entering, one for ABH.'

'Where were these offences committed?' Helen demanded.

'London mostly, but he did stray into Sussex and Kent.'

'Recently?'

'Released six months ago, is suspected of being involved in the failed burglary of a commercial premises in Streatham. Gave the security guard a right pasting, left a lot of DNA behind.'

'Keep on it, but I'm not sure our man would be so careless,' Helen cautioned. 'Who else?'

'I think I might have something, guv,' DC Malik offered. 'Alexander Zychenko, ex-army, came here illegally in 2010, we think. Been arrested multiple times, always offering a different identity and charges have been hard to make stick, his victims often too traumatized to speak up.'

'How so?'

'Well, in addition to theft and burglary, he enjoys humiliating his victims. Sexual assault, urinating on his victim, he even tried to cut off one of his victim's ears on one occasion.'

'Interesting. Last offence?'

'Two years ago,' Malik conceded. 'That we know of. He might have been active, but just hasn't shown up on the radar.'

'Possibly,' Helen said thoughtfully. 'Anyone else?'

Now DC Reid stepped in.

'Andrey Shilov. Boxer, brawler, but also itinerant worker. Travels round the country with a rag-and-bone outfit. Narcotics think it's probably a cover for selling drugs, but he also likes assault, battery, burglary.'

'This is good. Currently active?'

'Whereabouts unknown but they're certain he pulled a nasty aggravated burglary in Salisbury six weeks ago.'

'And before that?'

'Last certified offence was nine months ago, property in the Wirral, got off on a technicality.'

'And before that?'

'Manchester. Eighteen months ago.'

'It doesn't fit the pattern.'

Heads turned now in Charlie's direction, surprised by the firmness of her tone.

'These are all interesting suspects, but the more you look at this, the more you see there is a clear pattern. A flurry of attacks – two, three, even four in a fortnight – then nothing. Four months later, the same thing. Three months, later the same. Always bunched together and always in and around Southampton. Sometimes he strays to Bournemouth or Chichester, but I think he's based here.'

'Perhaps he's committing offences elsewhere in the interim?' offered DC McAndrew.

'I've spoken to Greater Manchester, Northumbria, the Met, Devon and Cornwall, I can't find any similar offences in their jurisdiction during the period he's quiet down here. Plus, he'd have to be incredibly prolific to keep that pace up all year. No, I think he seizes his opportunities when they come, then disappears from view.'

'Could he be inside? Perhaps for a lesser offence?' DC Wilson queried. 'Perhaps he can't offend because he's behind bars.'

'Maybe, but I'm sure someone like that would have shown up in our initial sweep, especially if we're right in thinking he's a foreign national. But I like the idea that there's some reason why he can't act, that stops his spree,' Charlie continued, energized. 'Because of his job, or family set-up—'

'What if he's not in the country during those periods?'

Now heads pivoted towards Helen, her voice cutting through.

'What if his work takes him away for periods, then brings him back? Perhaps it's contract work, or he's on leave.'

'Could be in the army,' DC Jennings suggested. 'Roger Morton said he had military tattoos.'

'That would work if he was in the *British* Army,' Helen countered, 'but not if he's a foreign national. We can also rule out any link to the Royal Navy in Portsmouth on that basis, but if he worked on a *different* type of ship.'

'And was on shore leave when these offences took place,' Charlie added.

'That would certainly fit with the thief knot,' Wilson added, pleased to be able to offer something. 'It is, basically, a nautical knot.'

'What are you thinking?' Charlie continued, picking up the baton. 'One of the big cruise ships? A private charter?'

'I can't see our man working on one of those, unless perhaps in security,' Helen replied thoughtfully. 'No, I was thinking one of the big cargo ships. It's hard, unremitting work, attracts rough types, often people with a criminal record.'

'Plus they dock for a week or two at a time every few months,' Jennings added, 'so the timings fit.'

'You know, perhaps we've been thinking about this all *wrong*.'

All eyes were now glued to Helen.

'Perhaps the reason none of the stolen items have turned up in the UK is not because the perpetrator's hoarding them, not because they're trophies, but simply because he is selling them abroad. It's kind of brilliant if you think about it. You commit a series of violent, aggravated burglaries—'

'Then sail away with your ill-gotten gains,' Charlie added, completing Helen's thought. 'Perhaps this guy is doing this all round the world, in Trieste, Istanbul, Cape Town, Shanghai. Imagine the charge he must get from it, knowing he's going to get away scot-free every time, well out of jurisdiction before the investigation gets going.'

'It would certainly explain the increasing violence,' McAndrew overlapped, showing her experience once more. 'He obviously enjoys the violation, the fear, the sadism and if he now feels untouchable, beyond the scope of the law, then what's to stop him going further, satisfying his darkest fantasies?'

It was a sobering thought, but one which struck home.

'OK, drop whatever you're doing,' Helen demanded. 'Let's focus all our energies on this. I want us to interrogate the records of the NCA, Interpol, FBI, every international justice agency that'll talk to us, let's see if they have a perpetrator who fits the bill. Also I want the shipping records of the major cargo companies pulled – I want to know if there's a vessel out there whose docking pattern matches the timings of this crime.'

The team were still staring at her, so rising, Helen urged them to work.

'Well, let's get to it, then…'

Now they were standing to attention.

'Let's find this guy.'

Chapter 69

Fear stalks Southampton, second home targeted by vicious killer.

It wasn't a witty or memorable headline, but that wasn't the point. It was effective. Raising her eyes from the newspaper, Emilia could see it was having the desired effect on Sam, his countenance sombre and thoughtful.

'Read the article,' she urged, directing his attention to the copy below.

This was the real prize. The sub-editors mangled, often rewrote the headlines, but they seldom altered her prose. Not if they knew what was good for them.

'The front page isn't bad, but it's the spread in the middle that'll really tickle you.'

She was impatient for Sam to get to the good stuff, practically turning the pages for him, wanting him to see her photo of Greg White, the cruel irony of Richard Westlake's bold declaration: *We'll build the perfect home for you.* She still found that darkly funny, though she was at pains to hide it.

'It's one of my best ones, I think. In terms of a major piece, I mean...'

She was blatantly fishing now, frustrated by his continued silence. They were tucked away in Cosa Nostra, one of Sam's favourites, the perfect setting for Emilia to showcase her work, to get her new lover's approval and she suddenly realized how much she wanted it. She had been unnerved by her feelings at the breakfast table and now at dinner was once more thrown off kilter. She really cared what he thought. Did that mean she was developing feelings – proper feelings – for Sam?

'So, go on? Tell me what you think?'

She sat back in her chair, awaiting his verdict. The marine engineer thought for a moment, then replied:

'Well, it's certainly very striking.'

'Striking?'

His words had landed with a dull thud and Emilia couldn't help pick him up on it.

'I mean, you don't pull any punches, that's for sure,' he continued, his eyes lowered. 'And you're certainly clear about your version of events.'

'I'm just establishing the facts, painting a picture for the reader.'

'Which you do very well.'

His tone was oddly pointed with a ring of finality about it.

'Now, how about we order? I could eat a horse...'

'What's up, Sam?' Emilia enquired, ignoring his clumsy attempt to end the conversation.

'Nothing, I just want to eat, that's all.'

'Look at me.'

Somewhat reluctantly, Sam raised his gaze. Immediately, Emilia clocked the tension, the forced jollity in his expression. This young man was many things – a good conversationalist, a loyal friend, a passionate lover – but he was a terrible actor, totally failing to disguise his deep discomfort.

'What's wrong?'

'Nothing, nothing at all,' he insisted. 'I've said I like it, so let's move on.'

'What exactly do you like about it?'

'Please don't be like that, Emilia. I don't want to get into an argument.'

'Why would we argue about it?'

Her blood was up now, fired by hurt and disappointment.
'*Why?*'

There was a long, heavy pause, then Sam finally answered:

'Look, Emilia, I know you have a job to do. And I know you're very good at it. But don't you ever think that all this is a bit… I don't know… cruel?'

Emilia felt like she'd been slapped. Despite his stumbling words, he sounded so confident of his opinion, his judgement, as if it was self-evident.

'I mean, these guys are suffering, suffering like you wouldn't believe, so this… this kind of intrusion… well it can't be helpful, can it?'

'"This kind of intrusion"?' Emilia parroted, her words ripe with indignation.

'It's almost like you're enjoying it, feeding off their misfortune—'

'All right, enough. Let's order.'

She picked up the menu, unsettled. But to her surprise and distress, she could tell Sam wasn't going to let it go.

'Look, the last thing I want to do is offend or upset you. I like you, you know I do. Which is why I find this difficult…'

'Why do you find this "difficult", Sam?'

'Please don't be sarcastic, Emilia. I'm just being honest. Surely you must see the inherent contradiction in all of this…'

She hated the way he said it, as if her words, the newspaper, were worthless trash.

'Enlighten me.'

'You're a good, warm-hearted person, who cares deeply for others.'

'I don't know where you get that from.'

'Look at how you are with your siblings. The love, devotion, money, time and care you lavish on them. You would do anything to protect them from harm, to keep them secure and happy and yet you willingly twist the knife in other people's wounds and... and it just doesn't make any sense.'

He ground to a halt, aware he had probably said too much already. Emilia stared at him, feeling more shaken than she had in years. Tears were threatening, but she was not going to give him the satisfaction.

'Enjoy your meal, Sam.'

She rose, picking up her bag and phone, trying to conceal her distress. True to form, her new beau *had* turned out to be too good to be true, after all.

'Don't go, Emilia. Not like this.'

'I'm sorry, but I've got *work* to do...'

She stressed the word in a feeble attempt at sarcasm.

'...and besides, I've lost my appetite.'

Chapter 70

Charlie felt sick, but there was no question of backing out. One way or the other, she *had* to know.

Closing the front door quietly behind her, she stood in the hallway, trying to suppress the nausea that threatened to overwhelm her. A large part of her was tempted to run – to take the coward's way out – but what excuse could she dream up for doing so? Steve was home, the girls were asleep, the house was peaceful. If ever there was a time to have *that* conversation, it was now.

Dumping her bag in the hallway, she walked towards the kitchen. The door was closed, but light crept underneath and the radio was playing. As she neared the moment of truth, Charlie's brain went into overdrive. How should she play it? Should she launch straight in? Or should she build up to her question – her *accusation* – softening her attack by admitting to her own part in their growing separation? How were you supposed to *do* this?

Pressing the handle down firmly, she stepped into the room. Her heart was in her mouth, she was finding it hard to breathe … yet to her surprise the room was empty. The washing up had been done, her dinner was warming in the oven, it was a picture of domestic peace, but Steve was nowhere to be seen. Unnerved,

Charlie walked slowly towards the sink, her emotions swinging violently from relief to fear. And now as she reached the countertop, she spotted him. Steve was in the darkened garden, drawing on a cigarette, chatting happily on his mobile.

The sight angered her. Here she was, going out of her mind, whilst he appeared relaxed, content, a smile spread across his face. It was grossly unfair, wrong even, and fired by a sudden desire to get the thing done, Charlie tugged the window open. She was about to call out, to summon her partner inside for the reckoning, but something made her pause. She could hear him talking, talking in a way that unsettled her. It was not so much what he said, she couldn't really make this out, it was his tone that undid her. Soft, secretive and intimate.

Charlie paused, should she shut the window and walk away? Should she call out to him? Or should she stay and listen? He hadn't noticed her yet, was unaware she was listening. She made to shut the window – the idea of spying on Steve was crazy – but instinct stayed her hand. She had to know.

Leaning forward, she strained to hear, the words slowly coming into focus.

'I'm good for tomorrow night,' Steve intoned. 'Eight o'clock OK?'

Charlie's heart sank, a deep sadness stealing over her. Oblivious, Steve chuckled at the response, happy and carefree, before adding:

'I love you.'

Charlie pulled the window shut, unable to listen to any more. Immediately, Steve looked up, his face a picture of alarm. Waving awkwardly, he turned away, lowering his voice and talking urgently into the phone. Seconds later, he finished the call and turned once more towards the kitchen window, an innocent smile spread across his face.

But Charlie was already turning away, unwilling to let Steve see the tears running down her cheeks. There was no point in confronting him now, no point in talking.

She had her answer.

Chapter 71

Questions, questions, questions.

Helen paced the smooth wooden floor, back and forth, back and forth. She was safely back in her flat now, the door bolted, the windows secure, but still she found it impossible to settle, her mind obsessively turning on the events of the day. Who was this hooded assassin? What had he *done* to be driven to such a desperate act? And crucially, would he give up now, retreat to his ordered, ordinary life? Or would he return for the kill?

Her eyes strayed to the knife on her desk. She had bagged it after his escape, waiting until she was home to dust it for prints. It was no surprise that it was clean as a whistle, not a mark of any kind on it. Her would-be killer was obviously an amateur, but he was not an idiot. So where did that leave her? The snatched glimpse of his face was enough for her to recognize his mug shot, but an hour's search on their database had turned up nothing. She could go further, issuing an appeal for witnesses, alerting the press, but to do so she'd have to go through the official channels, which would inevitably alert Peters, something Helen wouldn't, *couldn't*, countenance.

Tugging her cigarettes from her pocket, Helen lit up. She never usually smoked in the flat, but she needed the nicotine hit. She had never felt so besieged as she did tonight. Every area of her life was in revolt, subtly joining forces in a concerted conspiracy to destroy her. An assassin dogging her heels, a boss who wanted her head, a vicious killer who continued to elude their clutches, ghosting in and out of people's homes with practised ease. Yes, they had made progress tonight, but were they actually any closer to identifying the suspect? Helen knew she was being overly negative, her anxiety, her fears making the situation seem blacker than it was, but suddenly a resolution to this difficult case seemed a long way off.

How she regretted her isolation now. As Charlie had shown, relationships were not plain sailing, or trust a fragile commodity. But at least she had someone to talk to, someone to go home to. Other people seemed to manage these things, even new boy Wilson had a lovely fiancée in tow, so why couldn't she? Why was she forever left to face life alone? It made things twice, three times as bad, having no one to confide in, no one to lean on in times of crisis. Yet maybe this was her lot – every time she *did* try and connect with someone it went badly wrong, ending in bitterness and recrimination, or tragedy and bloodshed. Suddenly her head was flooded with images of Mark Fuller, an officer she'd had feelings for a long time ago, before his untimely, gruesome death, but she pushed these demons away. That way madness lay.

Stubbing out her cigarette, Helen crossed back to the sofa, which was now covered in shipping schedules and port documents. Despite her personal problems, the many dangers and uncertainties swirling around her, she had to focus on the job in hand. There was a killer at large and it was her duty to hunt him down, whatever the cost to herself. Applying herself to the task, Helen ran her finger down endless columns of names. But the words seemed to dance in front of her, merging with each other, rendering them meaningless and opaque. Angered with herself, Helen dug her fingers into the wound on her forearm, reacting sharply to the searing pain.

'Come on, Helen, focus...'

She tried to interrogate the transcripts again and this time she made some sense of them, slowly, but patiently logging the comings and goings from Southampton's busy cargo port. It was incredible really, the volume of trade, the sheer number of ships that visited the city. They came from every corner of the globe – South America, South Africa, China, Japan – and all had exotic names. The *Algoma Compass, American Courage, Estelle Maersk, Federal Yukon*. She enjoyed turning the words over in her mouth, even as she plotted their structured, repetitive journeys to and fro. Every now and again, she'd be gripped by a sudden excitement, a ship's docking pattern appearing to match a spate of burglaries, but this exhilaration repeatedly turned to disappointment, as the pattern suddenly disintegrated, the ship on the other side of the world when the latest outrages took place. Was it possible their perpetrator had changed jobs? Changed ships? If so, how would they ever find him?

Pushing that worrying thought to the back of her mind, Helen pressed on with her enquiries, determined not to be downcast. And now finally she got a break. The *Spirit of Enterprise*, an eighteen-thousand-ton cargo ship, registered in Panama, but active in Europe, had docked in Southampton a year ago, then again seven months later, then three months after that, then again just a fortnight ago. A perfect mirror of their suspect's sprees of violence and burglary.

Snatching up her phone, she dialled quickly.

'Port Authority...'

The man on the other end sounded beleaguered, but Helen ignored this, swiftly establishing her credentials and impressing upon him the urgency of her enquiry.

'What was the name again?' the official droned, seemingly uninterested.

'The *Spirit of Enterprise*,' Helen repeated, crisp and clear.

There was a long pause, as he typed. Helen realized she was on her feet again, nervously pacing back and forth as she waited for his response.

'Yes, the ship's still in port...'

Helen exhaled, tension flooding from her, but her relief was short-lived.

'But you'll have to be quick,' the official added pointedly. 'It's due to set sail for Trieste in the morning.'

Day Five

Chapter 72

The vans slid past the barrier, heading speedily on their way. Nestled in the passenger seat, Helen glimpsed the curious expression of the security guard and wondered what he thought they were here for. Illegal immigrants? Drug smuggling? Gun running? He would learn in time that it was nothing so mundane.

The van bucked as it mounted a speed bump, causing an audible groan from the occupants to the rear. Helen glanced in their direction. Jennings, Wilson and McAndrew were visible amongst the clutch of anonymous uniformed officers, the latter nodding purposefully back at her boss, determined, focused, full of anticipation for what was to come. Once again, Helen was reminded of the value of experience – DC McAndrew would keep a cool head if, when, things kicked off.

'Everyone OK?'

Nods from the panorama of faces.

'Good. Because we'll be on in two minutes. ID clearly visible, please, and game faces on.'

As the team fussed with their lanyards, Helen returned her attention to the scene in front of her, peering through the windscreen at the majesty of Southampton Docks. It was one of the busiest ports in Europe, a ceaseless hive of activity and endeavour. Vast warehouses reared up one side, on the other a metallic mountain of stacked containers. In their shadow, one felt tiny and insignificant, but they were positively minuscule next to the awesome bulk of the cargo ships themselves. As they rounded the final corner, emerging onto the docks, the *Spirit of Enterprise* finally came into view, impressive and intimidating.

It seemed to cast a shadow over everything, blotting out the soft winter sun, arrogant in its size and stature. Looking at it from this lowly vantage point, it seemed miraculous to Helen that such a vast beast could ever be shifted, that there were engines powerful enough to propel this metal hulk across the sea. But travel it had, across the Atlantic, the South China Sea, round the Cape of Good Hope and more besides. It didn't look new or attractive, but it was battle-hardened, a wily veteran that had faced down adversity many times and come out on top.

Towering above the vast ship was a crane, at the very top of which perched the pilot, carefully picking and depositing the final containers onto the busy deck. Helen shuddered inwardly – couldn't think of anything worse than being alone up there – then returned her gaze to the boat itself. It was alive with tiny figures, port officials and crew completing the final checks, signing off the paperwork, preparing the *Enterprise* for her imminent departure. They had arrived not a moment too soon.

Clicking the button on her radio mic, Helen spoke crisply: 'Right, this is it. Everyone ready?'

There were two other vans, following dutifully in their wake.

'All ready here,' Charlie responded.

'Ready and raring to go,' DC Reid added happily, overplaying his hand as usual.

'OK, then,' Helen replied. 'We do this quickly, we do this cleanly, but, please, be on your guard. If we can identify a potential suspect, he is to be approached with extreme caution. He's a highly dangerous, highly motivated individual who's unlikely to come quietly.'

No one spoke, Helen's words focusing minds.

'You know the drill. Team C will secure the dock, Teams A and B to board the vessel. I will direct operations throughout, so please keep your comms open. Anything suspicious, anything of note, you radio it in *immediately*. I want maximum eyes and ears on this one, as it's a vast search area.'

The van slowed to a halt, just shy of the main gangplank. This was it then, the moment of truth. A couple of crew members looked up, intrigued, so Helen didn't hesitate. Pulling the search warrant from her pocket, she checked her pepper spray and baton were to hand, then flung open the door, marching purposefully towards the ship.

Chapter 73

He pressed his face to the glass, his eyes riveted to the activity below. His bunk mate, a slovenly Estonian, blathered on, but he had stopped listening ages ago, his attention consumed by the alarming sight. Plain-clothed police officers swarmed up the gangplank, warrant cards held out in front of them like some kind of lucky charm, followed by a small unit of armed police. His eyes came to rest on them briefly, clocking the Glock submachine guns they cradled, remembering the pleasing resistance of the trigger in happier days, before returning his gaze to the lead officer.

She was lithe and athletic, her face a picture of concentration and determination. She clearly meant business, but looked tense, as if expecting resistance, hostility, even danger. Attractive in a severe, powerful sort of way, he felt oddly pleased. Was this impressive figure to be his nemesis?

He had known this moment would come. That one day his endeavours would be suddenly checked, his carnival of crime and bloodshed brought to an end. But now that it was here, he wanted to push it away, to reject this sudden and unwelcome intrusion. He wasn't ready to finish yet, not when there was still so much fun to be had. What right had *they* to tell him that the party was over?

There was no question in his mind that they were here for him. You didn't descend in such force for non-payment of port fees or an irregularity in the paperwork. No, they had come to clap him in handcuffs, to drag him away in disgrace, to parade him in front of a grateful public. They were only just in time, the *Enterprise* due to depart in a matter of hours, but perhaps this had been done on purpose, ensuring that the ship's full crew would be present and correct. Had they turned up last night, they would have found him missing, but today they had their man trapped like an angry wasp in a bottle.

The question was what to do now. He would never give himself up, for an ex-soldier surrender was unthinkable. What mercy would he receive from *them*, after all? What mercy had the world ever shown him? No, he would shrug off their pathetic attempts to contain him, but how? Should he hide? Should he run?

Or should he fight?

Chapter 74

'You must be out of your mind.'

Captain David Wetherall, a six-foot-four mountain of teak skin and muscle, could hardly contain his outrage.

'There is no question of delaying this vessel's departure. We have perishable goods on board that are due in Trieste in less than a week's time, not to mention two thousand tons of other cargo—'

'I'm *perfectly* within my rights to delay departure, under the terms of this warrant,' Helen fired back, brandishing the paperwork. 'And I expect your co-operation. The port authorities are fully aware of our operation – indeed we couldn't have proceeded without their express permission, though of course you're welcome to ring them to check...'

Wetherall thought about it, then demurred.

'It is still *my* ship. And as its captain, I retain—'

'Not anymore,' Helen interrupted, cutting off his pompous rant. 'This ship is now officially impounded and will remain in dock until *I* say it can leave.'

The experienced mariner looked aghast. Whether this was at the thought of his vessel being impounded or having to take orders from a woman, Helen wasn't sure.

'I'd suggest it's in everyone's interests that we proceed without delay,' she continued. 'First thing first, I'll need you to instruct the crew to return to their berths and remain there until given the all-clear to leave.'

Wetherall swallowed an expletive, but Helen was relieved to see that he was prepared to play ball, nodding his permission to the first mate. The latter disappeared and seconds later, his voice boomed from the public address system, issuing Helen's instructions.

'Next, I need the ship's manifest. I'm particularly interested in the personnel on board, so if you could direct me to the crew list. I want their names, obviously, but also nationality, age, length of service on the *Enterprise*...'

With evident reluctance, Wetherall opened the safe and retrieved the weighty document, tossing it onto the desk.

'Crew details start on page twenty-six, but if you tell me what this is about, perhaps we can speed things up a little?'

Helen suppressed a smile – Wetherall's desire to get rid of her might make all their lives easier.

'I'm looking for a male crew member, probably around six foot or so, East European or Russian probably...'

'You're going to have be more specific than that, we have over three hundred people working on this ship.'

'He will have been a crew member for at least a year, docking several times at Southampton during that period. We also think he might have been in the army, prior to joining the merchant navy.'

'OK, that narrows it down a bit,' the captain replied thoughtfully. 'But there's still upwards of fifteen names I could give you – many of the guys on this ship have some kind of military background. What sort of crime are you investigating? What's this person supposed to have done?'

'Murder.'

A single word that silenced the experienced seaman.

'Two counts of murder, in fact,' Helen continued. 'In addition to aggravated burglary, false imprisonment, breaking and entering, plus a host of other charges. Has any member of your crew ever been suspected of these sorts of serious crimes before?'

Wetherall had gone white as a sheet.

'Well?' Helen demanded.

'So I wouldn't want to damn a man in absentia, but... but Marko Dordevic *might* fit the bill. He was in the Serbian Special Forces before joining us and we have had some... some problems in the past, with the law enforcement agencies in Manila and Shanghai. Nothing was ever proven, mind...'

'What sort of offences?'

'Theft, ABH and, in one instance, false imprisonment and... assault with a deadly weapon. He was accused of beating a homeowner half to death, though no charges were ever brought.'

'And you still employ this animal?'

'Like I said, he was never charged and good crew are hard to find. Dordevic is tough, experienced, knows the idiosyncrasies of the ship—'

'And would you say he's capable of these crimes, then? Could he kill?'

Once more, Wetherall lapsed into silence, but his face said it all. He was in no doubt that this ex-Special Forces operative was capable of *anything*.

'Right, I need his berth location and I need it now. I think we've found our man.'

Chapter 75

They scurried over the surface of the ship like disturbed ants, scuttling along walkways and up stairwells, before withdrawing into the nest.

Charlie had remained portside with her team, keeping a watchful eye on the unfolding drama. Armed officers stood ready nearby, but front and centre were Charlie and her fellow officers, binoculars raised, searching for signs of suspicious activity. Moments earlier, the team had heard the public address message, signalling the official start of the search. And now, on cue, Charlie's radio crackled into life, Helen's voice ringing out.

'The suspect is Marko Dordevic, repeat Marko Dordevic. Serbian national, six-foot-two, short black hair, tattoos on his forearms and his neck. Commencing search now, over.'

'Roger that, over,' Charlie radioed back quickly.

They had a name. Finally, they had a name to put to the shadowy killer who had haunted the nightmares of homeowners all across Southampton.

'Right, look alive, people...'

Slowly but surely, the decks were clearing, as the crew members returned to their bunks, no doubt wondering what on earth was going on. As each little dot disappeared, Charlie wondered if the departing figure was Dordevic, retreating inside the forbidding metallic hulk. Was he even now plotting his escape? Preparing for one last stand?

Her binoculars strafed the ship's walkways, but they were deserted now, the crew scrabbling back to quarters with impressive efficiency. If only her own team were so well drilled, she thought to herself, as she continued her patient search.

'Come on, Marko. Where are you?'

She whispered the words, as if casting a spell. But there was no response, no movement in front of her, the *Enterprise* appearing more like a ghost ship than an ocean-bound vessel. Was it possible that he would escape? On paper, their mission seemed easy – board the boat, identify and capture the suspect – but looking up at the vast vessel now, Charlie was riven with doubt. The search area was huge, with myriad cubby holes and hiding places. Dordevic had home advantage and would presumably put it to good use, either by making good his escape or sitting it out in some ingenious hiding place, until his pursuers tired of their search.

A lot would depend on whether he knew they were coming for him. It was possible that he'd assume the police presence on board was unrelated to him, as he'd never yet appeared on British police's radar. If so, he might be surprised and taken easily, trapped in some cooped-up berth. But how likely was this? Surely this seasoned criminal would read the runes correctly, guessing that such a show of force meant that the British police had finally picked up his scent? And if so, surely he would attempt to escape?

Charlie once more scanned the top of the boat, letting her gaze drift over the tops of the multicoloured containers. Finding nothing, she lowered her binoculars to the access stairwells, then lower still to the main deck. Now she slowed, taking her time to inch along its vast length, but still she found nothing. The ship was ... dead.

Lowering her binoculars, Charlie exhaled slowly. She was out on her feet, exhausted after a sleepless night, during which she'd vacillated endlessly between waking Steve to challenge him about his infidelity or ducking the confrontation, in a vain attempt to protect herself and the girls from the inevitable fallout, eventually opting for the latter. Riven with doubt, anger and self-recrimination, what Charlie really wanted to do was to run away – from her job, from Steve, from her life – but there was no question of that, given the importance of their current operation, so instead she turned to DC Jennings, wearily commenting:

'Well, I don't know about you, but—'

'There.'

Charlie turned to the voice, which belonged to a uniformed officer, who was pointing towards the boat. Restoring her binoculars, Charlie scanned the ship once more, her eyes scanned over the walkways, but she could see nothing of note.

'I can't see anything.'

'At the top, on the containers ...'

'I've just checked th—'

But Charlie's words petered out, as she spotted movement. There *was* someone up there, a tiny figure who seemed to be moving steadily forwards over the stacked containers, jumping from block to block. It was presumably a highly dangerous manoeuvre, especially as the wind was strong; one Charlie suspected you wouldn't even attempt unless you were desperate, unless you needed to get *away*.

Clicking her radio mic, Charlie rasped:

'Suspect spotted moving east on top of ship's containers.'

Chapter 76

'Repeat – suspect spotted moving east on top of ship's containers.'

Charlie's voice bounced off the walls of the tiny cabin. The Estonian sailor who had been trying to answer Helen's questions looked startled, but Helen felt flooded with relief. Busting a gut, she had raced to Dordevic's cabin, only to find that their prime suspect had fled minutes earlier. His bunk mate denied all knowledge of his whereabouts or intentions, but his blustering denials didn't matter now.

'How certain are you?' Helen radioed back.

'Can't be from this distance, I'm afraid, but it's hard to imagine who else would risk such a crazy stunt. If he falls onto the deck from there, he's a goner.'

'OK, keep your eyes on him, I want to know where he is at all times. I'm heading up there.'

Clicking off, she turned back to the Estonian sailor, whose expression was a mix of curiosity and fear.

'How do I get on top of the containers?' she barked.

'You can't, it's not permitted…'

'Forget the protocols, if I wanted to get up there, how would I do it?'

'It's impossible,' the flustered sailor insisted. 'The access stairwell gets you level with the second container, but there are three more stacked on top of them, so unless you climbed up—'

'Where's the nearest access stairwell?'

'A deck. If you go out of here, turn left, then—'

But Helen cut him off, grabbing him by the collar and hauling him towards the door.

'Show me.'

Chapter 77

He teetered on the edge, staring into the abyss. He was a fit man, battle-hardened and athletic, but suddenly he felt as if he couldn't take another step. His muscles ached, his lungs burned, his head was pounding. Back in Serbia, he had hunted with his father, enjoying the thrill of the chase, but now he understood what it felt like to be the quarry.

They were combing the ship for him. He'd had a lucky escape, ducking into the food store, as two officers raced down the corridor towards his berth. As they ran past, he'd heard their radios crackle into life, heard his name fill the air, the British officer mangling his birthright with her terrible pronunciation. In that moment, his worst fears were confirmed. This was the end of the line.

Unless ... he could escape. His decision to abandon his berth had proved a wise one – it was probably already crawling with police officers – now he had to make good on this stroke of luck. His initial plan had been to head to the main deck, see if he could make his way to the prow of the ship undetected, but the deck was already well populated, so he'd had no choice but to duck under the cover of the containers themselves. Mounting the stairwell, he'd put some small distance between himself and his pursuers, but from there he had only one option. Straight up.

It had been agony. Just working out a potential route up was hard enough, but pulling it off was purgatory. The locks, clasps and bolts provided some sturdy footholds, but often he was confronted by a vast sheet of smooth, corrugated steel to scale, at which point his only option was to make use of the proximity of the containers, pushing his back hard against one, whilst pressing his feet against its neighbour, sliding slowly upwards as his legs burned and his muscles protested. Any mistake, any loss of pressure in his stance, would have been fatal – he would plunge down onto the unforgiving metal floor below. Holding his breath, furious at his predicament, he moved upwards inch by inch, until finally, miraculously, he made it to the top.

This successful ascent did not lessen the danger, however. As soon as he clambered onto the highest container, the wind had ripped over him, knocking him off his feet. Feeling himself falling, he clawed at the surface, just about saving himself from disaster. Staggering to his feet, pressing his bulk into the biting wind, he had moved purposefully forwards, heading east. His plan was simple. If he could make it to the prow of the ship, he hoped to descend unseen and from there make his escape, using the ship's anchor chain to descend to the water. If he was spotted, he'd drop, hoping not to break his neck or legs in the process. If not, he'd shimmy down the chain until he could gain access to one of the tugs below. From there he'd either clamber onto dry land or commandeer the vessel and drive off, outwitting his leaden-footed pursuers.

But there was still work to do. The prow of the ship was two hundred feet away and the gaps between containers seemed to be getting larger. Or was he just more tired, unable to spring forward with the same alacrity as at the start of his flight? Either way the chasm in front of him suddenly appeared very daunting.

Any misstep now would result in death, so he hovered on the edge, willing himself to move, but fearful of taking the plunge.

But events now took the decision out of his hands. To his shock and dismay, he heard someone calling his name. How could that be? There's no way he'd be able to hear someone shouting at him up here, in the teeth of the howling wind, unless... unless they were up here *with him*.

Spinning, Marko Dordevic was stunned to see the lead police officer clambering on top of one of the containers. She was a hundred feet away, but even now she was moving forward fast, calling to him, holding up her identity card. Swearing viciously, he turned away from this awful vision and leaped across the chasm.

Chapter 78

He had misjudged it. He was going to fall.

Helen's heart was in her mouth as she watched the fugitive's desperate leap, convinced he had just signed his own death warrant. But to her surprise, he made it, cresting the other container, before scrambling to his feet and racing away.

Helen couldn't believe it. She was utterly spent from her reckless ascent to the summit of the ship's containers. Drenched in sweat, gasping for oxygen, she had nearly killed herself several times, sliding back down the metal walls towards her terrified Estonian guide, yet somehow, she had made it to the top. Scrambling up, she'd spotted the fleeing Dordevic and called out to him, hopeful that discovery might encourage surrender. But it was not going to be that easy, the Serbian turning tail. The chase was on.

Cursing her luck, Helen urged herself forwards. The wind was roaring past, slapping her in the face, pushing her weary body backwards, but she had to battle on. Exhaustion was stealing over her, rendering her legs leaden and heavy, but somehow she found reserves of energy to drag herself forward. She reached the first gap and leaped, landing safely on the other side. The second was not so easy, a sudden increase in wind speed seeming to stop her in mid-air. Arms wheeling, neck craning forward, she just reached the opposite lip, scrambling gratefully on top of the giant metal box. Still she kept going, driven on by the sight of the fleeing figure in front of her.

She was gaining on him. Dordevic had slowed, progress proving more difficult now, so there was only fifty feet between them. Helen's spirits rose, her body suffused with new energy and she surged forward, hurdling the next chasm. She was picking up speed, shrugging off the wind, sprinting for all she was worth, now only thirty feet from the suspect.

Dordevic sensed her approach, turning and clocking her advance. Helen watched on now as he leaped another gap, landing safely on the other side. There were only a couple of containers left before he'd reach the front of the ship, and who knew where he would head from there? Upping her pace, Helen saw a much larger gap open up in front of her, but didn't hesitate, hurling herself across the divide.

She flew through the air, arms cartwheeling, feeling oddly weightless. But then gravity took hold, as the wind pushed her body back and she felt herself falling down, down, down.

She had misjudged the distance, she wasn't going to make it. There was no doubt about that now, the lip of the container seeming to rise above her. Flinging her arms forward, first one elbow, then the other caught the unforgiving surface. Pain ripped through her, arrowing up her spine into her teeth, but in spite of the agony, she held firm, propping herself up on the edge of the container. In her fear, her discomfort, she had closed her eyes, but now snapped them open, wanting to convince herself that she was really still alive.

What she saw chilled her blood. Dordevic was now heading directly towards her. Seeing how perilous her position was, he was determined to end their pursuit once and for all.

Helen scrambled to gain purchase on the metal container. But her hands kept slipping, she was going backwards rather than forwards. She felt the container rattle as Dordevic landed on it and watched in horror as he raced towards her. Twenty feet from her, now ten, now five, even as her legs swung hopelessly beneath. Suddenly he was upon her, raising his boot to kick out her arms.

But now Helen's own foot found a foothold and, with all her might, Helen pushed up. She launched her body onto the container, grasping the arm of the surprised Dordevic and dragging herself to safety. She collapsed onto the dirty metal, still clasping the fleeing Serb, but the impact knocked the wind from her lungs, loosening her grip. Now Dordevic wriggled free, booting her hard in the ribs before fleeing once more.

Gasping, Helen pushed herself up and, finding her feet, hurried after him. Her elbows were on fire, her legs battered and bruised, but she pressed on, leaping the remaining gaps without hesitation, hoping that God, fate or karma were on her side. Cresting the final gap, she was pleased to see that Dordevic had stopped and was now desperately scanning the container wall for a safe passage down.

Slowing, Helen clicked on her radio mic.

'Suspect now at the eastern end of the ship. All officers to the prow of the ship to affect arrest...'

Her words were audible to Dordevic, who span to face her, an expression of naked fury on his face. He was clearly not used to being pursued. And he was certainly not accustomed to being trapped. Desperate, he started marching towards her, eyes blazing.

'Easy now, Marko,' Helen urged, carefully extending her baton. 'Think about it. There's no way out and if you come quietly, things will go better for you—'

She didn't get to finish her sentence, the huge figure hurling himself towards her. A meaty fist swung at her, brushing her nose, as Helen jerked her head backwards. If one of those giant paws connected, the fight would be over. He swung again, but this time Helen was ready, ducking the blow before swinging her baton into his midriff. Dordevic grunted, staggering backwards, but Helen now felt herself flying through the air, propelled towards him. Dordevic had grabbed hold of the end of the baton, yanking his pursuer in his direction.

Helen stumbled, before regaining her footing, but it was too late. They were now locked in close combat, Dordevic landing two hefty punches to her stomach, before launching his forehead at her nose. Instinctively, Helen pivoted away, but not fast enough. Dordevic's forehead smashed into the side of her head, sending her tumbling back onto the roof of the container.

For a moment, Helen didn't know which way was up, her head spinning, her ears ringing. She expected Dordevic to close in on her, to hurl her over the side of the container, but now as her vision stabilized, she saw that the contact had also left her attacker dazed. He swayed back and forth, appearing drunk and disoriented. Spying her opportunity, Helen clambered to her feet, holding up her hand.

'Please, Marko. You're totally surrounded, so please, give yourself up...'

The dazed fugitive peered over the side of the container, the hopelessness of his position finally making itself felt. Helen eased her cuffs from her belt in readiness.

'If you surrender to me now, we can get off this thing safely. Nobody needs to get hurt.'

The Serbian scanned below, searching fruitlessly for some method of escape, but there was none. Finally, he turned back to Helen, his sweaty face pale with anger and despair.

'Come on, Marko. Let's bring this thing to an end...'

Immediately, Helen saw she'd miscalculated. The fire seemed to return to Dordevic's eyes, his glance alighting on the metal cuffs. Yelling out his fury, he chose death before dishonour, lowering his head and charging directly at her.

Chapter 79

For a moment, it was as if time stood still.

From her vantage point portside, Charlie had watched the struggle on the containers with increasing dread. She had hardly dared to breathe as Helen leaped from one giant metal box to the next, convinced on one occasion that she hadn't made it, only to see her suddenly pop up into view again. Once she had seen her old friend catch up with Dordevic on the final container, Charlie had felt sure that the pursuit would be peacefully resolved, the hopelessness of the fugitive's plight evident. To her dismay, however, he had opted to fight, hoping for some kind of salvation in spite of the overwhelming odds against him.

Charlie's heart had been in her mouth as she'd watched the pair trade blows. Helen was a natural athlete and a born fighter, but her adversary was ex-Special Forces, a trained killer with no qualms about shedding blood. Charlie watched on, helpless, as first Helen seized the initiative, then Dordevic struck back, knocking Helen to the ground. She was pleased to see Helen scramble to her feet and even more pleased when there was a sudden lull in the conflict, Helen presumably appealing to the desperate suspect to see sense.

But then it happened. Dordevic burst forward, throwing himself at Helen. Perhaps he caught her off guard, perhaps she didn't have sufficient time to avoid his desperate lunge, for now the battling pair pitched forwards and off the side of the boat, plummeting downwards. They were locked together in a grim embrace, even as they plunged towards the unforgiving surface of the water below.

Charlie cried out in horror, but there was nothing she could do to stop the pair's dizzying descent. Down, down, down, they sped, whistling through the air, before hitting the water hard, the sound of the dreadful impact echoing across the harbour towards her. Charlie gasped audibly, as tears filled her eyes.

There would be no coming back from that. This was the end.

Chapter 80

Slowly, but inexorably, the two bodies sank towards the seabed. The dull sunlight above them was fast receding, sucked ever deeper into the silty depths. These murky waters had claimed many lives over the centuries – today they would claim two more.

The couple looked as though they were sleeping, eyes closed, bodies limp, as their saturated clothes tugged at them, pulling them further under. Darkness was closing around them, before long they would be lost from view, there to rest, until the search team found them. *If* the search team found them.

The heavier of the two led the way, the woman slightly above, but keeping pace with the leader. The pair seemed joined together in catastrophe, as they continued their inevitable descent. Enemies in life, they would be companions in death, sharing the same fate. For one, death at sea had always been a danger, for the other this end was as surprising as it was tragic.

Darkness. Inky black darkness. Surrounding her, enveloping her.

Helen's right eye crept open, but she could see nothing. Where was she? Her other eye now opened, but her confusion remained total. Then suddenly a flash of silver, something scaly darted past her face, brushing against her. And immediately Helen knew where she was, how dire her predicament was.

She was sinking, dropping ever deeper below the surface of the water, now barely visible above. Panic gripped her, bubbles tumbling from her mouth, as she emitted a silent scream. She needed to swim up, to claw her way out of this hell, but her body wouldn't respond. Had she broken her arms, her legs, her neck even? Was this how she would die, body limp and useless, but her mind sickeningly, terrifyingly alert?

The sun had disappeared. It was all but impossible to see down here, but Helen knew which direction she needed to head in. And now, suddenly, surprisingly, she felt a tingle in her fingertips, as if her body was finally coming back to life, shaking off the shock at her point of greatest need. Relieved, she tried to claw her way upwards, but to her horror her arm still refused to respond, even as pins and needles seared up and down her useless limb.

Come on. Please, come on... Helen thought, willing herself to remain calm.

Her body *was* coming back to life, the sensation in her arm ebbing and flowing now, as the pins and needles wore off. Gritting her teeth, trying to suppress a desperate desire to open her mouth and breathe in, she raised her left hand, then her right, pulling hard down on the water. Joyously, she now started moving, her leaden body rising a couple of inches. But as she did so, her foot touched something beneath her and she remembered.

Dordevic. He had entered the water with her, was presumably still close. Turning slowly in the water, she glimpsed the sole of his shoe pointing up at her, but the man himself was obscured below. He was four to five feet beneath her and darting a look up in the direction of the surface, still shadowy and obscure, Helen knew it was hopeless. There was no way she could tend to him *and* survive herself. Summoning her courage, Helen prepared for her desperate ascent.

She couldn't leave him. It was crazy, it was beyond reckless, but he was only just beneath her. Maybe she could still save him – if he had survived the fall, that is. Turning once more in the water, Helen drove downwards, ever further from salvation. It was impossible to see now, the darkness at this depth total, and her hand swept the water hopelessly, finding no purchase. He had been just there, surely she can't have lost him? It would be cruelly ironic indeed if she lost her life trying to save the elusive corpse of their suspect.

Her hand had hit something hard and slippery. His boot. Clawing at it, she delved further down, finding his ankle. Immediately the extra weight told, pulling her still deeper, but summoning her last reserves of strength, she tugged for all she was worth, clawing at his trouser leg, then his belt, then his jacket. Now he was by her side, facing the right way, but still unconscious. Tearing at the water, Helen tried to pull them both up, but instead they started sinking again. Helen's lungs were exploding now, there was no way she could carry on, she would have to sacrifice him.

No, not whilst there was still life in her body, she would not give up. Redoubling her efforts, she clawed frantically and now they did start to rise. Slowly, very slowly, but they were heading in the right direction. Up, up, up, the surface now a distant prize above, shimmering hints of sunlight seeming to offer redemption. But with each surge Helen was getting weaker, the effects of their terrifying impact on the still waters of the dock starting to take effect as the shock wore off. They were only thirty feet from the surface, but their progress had stalled; Helen's energy, her strength, finally exhausted. So close, but so far.

Then suddenly, to her surprise, Helen found that she was rising again. Confused, she turned to her companion to see his eyes were open wide. His face was white as a sheet, his features contorted, but there was determination in his expression and he tore at the water, pulling them both upwards. Helen responded, renewing her efforts, and seconds later they broke the surface, thrashing in the water as they gratefully sucked in the cold morning air.

Chapter 81

'Can I help you? Are you OK?'

Richard Westlake turned sharply, to find the earnest face of their family liaison officer looking back at him. Nikki Crowther had been ever present in their lives since that grim night, offering warmth, comfort and support, whilst guiding them through the process of a murder investigation. He had been giving her a hard time, constantly demanding to know what progress was being made in the hunt for Ethan's killer, losing his temper when there appeared to be *none* – yet she had never once reacted to his provocation, always patient and kind. And she stood in the hallway of their family home now, offering a helping hand, trying to will him through the door by the force of her goodness alone.

But still he hesitated, hovering on the threshold. He had walked this path hundreds of times, yet this morning his feet refused to move.

'Just give me a minute, it's harder than I thought it would be.'

'No problem, love. Take your time.'

He'd known that returning home would be traumatic, but the reality was far, far worse. He felt totally debilitated, his gaze, his thoughts constantly straying to the front room where his beloved boy...

He swayed in the doorway, reaching out a hand to support himself, suddenly dizzy and unstable. It was madness. He knew he had to be here – he'd need his laptop and card reader if he wanted to access funds to help catch his son's killer – but now he felt utterly incapable of moving, as if the simple act of stepping over the threshold might break him.

'If you like, we could come back another time ...'

It was sorely tempting, but wouldn't that just be putting off the inevitable? All he had to do was walk up to his office, gather what he needed, then get the hell out of here.

'I ... I ...'

Was he losing the power of speech too?

'I'm not sure I can. Would ... would you do it for me?'

'Of course,' his companion replied cheerily.

'My office is at the top of the stairs on the left. I'll need my laptop and charger and in the main desk drawer, you'll find my card reader. Is that OK?'

'Sure, no worries. I'll be back in a jiffy.'

'I'm sorry.'

The apology spilled from him, his voice thick with emotion.

'You've nothing to apologise for. Why don't you get some air and I'll be back in a tick?'

Squeezing his arm, she stepped inside, removing her shoes, before hurrying up the stairs. Richard remained where he was, undone by her kindness. He could feel the sadness, the anguish, rising inside him, robbing him of breath and bringing tears to his eyes. Her generosity, her warmth was such a tonic, so necessary, yet it only served to underline the awful loss they had suffered. His beloved Ethan, so kind, so mild, so harmless ...

His feet sprang to life, propelling him back down the drive, away from the house. He wanted to be clear of the hallway, the cheery front door, the neatly tiled porch. They belonged to a different life and the mere sight of them mocked him, reminding him of a time when happiness was possible. He didn't want any part of it, couldn't be near it, stumbling thirty yards before coming to rest by one of their apple trees. Leaning on it, he cast an accusing look back at the house. It had taken him years to build, years of blood, sweat and tears and until today he'd been enormously proud of it.

But now he hated it with every fibre of his being.

Chapter 82

The sudden movement made her look up.

Emilia had been standing quietly by the locked gates, casting an eye over the swathes of floral tributes outside the Westlake property, snapping photos of some of the more touching messages. But then the sound of footsteps on the gravel drive had caught her attention and, peering through the forbidding metal railings of the security gate, she clocked Richard Westlake. He seemed distressed and unstable, half walking, half stumbling, before eventually coming to a halt by some fruit trees.

Straining, Emilia tried to make out what he was up to, as he loitered by the trees. Was he hiding? Had he spotted her? No, his gaze seemed to be drawn back to the house, his expression fearful and haunted. Had something happened? Some new outrage? Or was it just his reaction to being at the family home again? Whatever, his predicament now afforded her an opportunity.

Emilia Garanita knew Nikki Crowther well and had come to dislike her heartily. People said she was sensitive, thoughtful and always professional, but to the journalist she had always been an annoyance, a barrier, sticking to her charges like glue. Crowther was used to the press trying to access the bereaved and had become adept at shielding these families from the likes of Emilia. But for once Crowther had let her guard down, disappearing into the house and leaving Westlake alone.

It was now or never. Emilia knew she would be breaking the law, trespassing on Westlake's property, but fortune favours the brave, so slinging her camera bag onto her shoulder, she mounted the gate, scrambling up and over the top, before dropping deftly down on the other side. Her boots made a satisfying crunch on the gravel and then she was on her way, trotting determinedly towards her prize.

Distracted, Westlake didn't notice her approach, only looking up when she was virtually upon him. At first, he appeared completely stymied, as if Emilia was some supernatural apparition whose appearance defied reason. Then, as a dim recognition stole over him, he found his voice.

'What the hell are you doing here? This is private property.'

'I appreciate that and I'm so sorry to intrude, but I've been desperate to talk to you. My name is Emilia Gara—'

'I know who you are.'

His bitterness, his anger, was unmistakable.

'Trust me, I haven't come here to upset you or make your life any harder than it already is, but you're the only one that can help me.'

He said nothing, surprised by her warm, earnest tone.

'The police are telling us nothing. And if there *is* someone out there who is a danger to the community, I think people have the right to know.'

'I can't talk about that.'

'But they must have told you what they're thinking, who they believe might be responsible for this terrible tragedy. Perhaps you already know who—'

'I'm telling you nothing.'

'Come on, Richard. This isn't going to go away. Talk to me

now, tell me what you know, and I promise I will leave you and your family alone. You have my wo—'

The mere mention of the word 'family' seemed to have an immediate effect on Westlake. It was as if he'd crumpled inside, collapsing in on himself.

'Go.'

He could barely say the word, grief choking him. Emilia knew this interview was slipping away from her, but there was no guarantee she would get another shot.

'Do the police have *any* lead as to the motive? Was it a personal thing? Or was Ethan just very unlucky?'

She hoped her persistence might break the vulnerable man's resistance, as it had many times before, but instead of weakness she now saw horror in his expression.

'How dare you come here, to *my* home, questioning me about what happened to our son ...'

'I'm just doing my job, Mr Westlake ...'

'Bullshit. You're a fucking parasite, feeding off other people's unhappiness, their loss ...'

He choked on the final word, a sob rising into his throat unbidden. With each utterance, he seemed to be growing smaller, as if each utterance cost him some strength, and he steadied himself on one of the trees. His breathing was rapid and shallow, as if he was on the brink of a panic attack and Emilia reached out a hand to support him, but he batted it away angrily.

'Get off my drive or I will have you arrested, you stupid bi—'

He couldn't complete the sentence. He began to sob, deep guttural moans of anguish, oblivious now to her presence. She was lost to him and, frustrated, Emilia stepped away, preparing to make her retreat. But as she did so, she slipped her camera bag from her shoulder, extracting her Nikon and readying it for action. Steadying herself, she made sure her target was dead centre in the viewfinder, framed nicely by the leafless trees, teasing the button down halfway to ensure the photo was properly focused. As she did so, Richard Westlake raised his head, staring directly down the camera lens. He looked hollow, broken, yet there was still a flash of anger, of defiance there, as if lambasting her for her intrusion on his grief.

To her surprise, Emilia hesitated, her finger resting on the button. Was it the hostility in his expression that made her pause? Or was it the legacy of her distressing conversation with Sam? Either way, there could be no question of ducking this moment, of losing this powerful shot of grief and desolation. So summoning her courage, Emilia pressed down hard on the button. Click, click, click.

Nobody was going to tell her how to live her life.

Chapter 83

'No way. Absolutely not.'

Charlie was looking at Helen as if she was absolutely mad, but the latter persisted nevertheless.

'I've told you, I'm *fine*.'

'Helen, you've just fallen the best part of a hundred feet into the water, sustained significant injuries whilst bringing a suspect into custody *and* half drowned in the process.'

It was true, Helen *did* look a state, battered, bruised and swathed in a paramedic's blanket, her clothes lying in a sodden heap on the floor. The pair were sitting in a security guard's cabin, hidden away from the prying eyes of passing dock workers.

'You need to get to hospital,' her deputy insisted. 'Get some scans, make sure you're *properly* checked out.'

'The paramedics have *done* that,' Helen retorted. 'My vision is fine, my hearing too. They've checked my blood pressure, *twice*. I'm not in danger of a sudden heart attack or brain haemorrhage—'

'You can't know that for sure and, besides, you're obviously concussed.'

'Maybe a little bit...'

Charlie pulled a face, unimpressed. It was true that the impact of hitting the water had affected Helen – she was nauseous and unsteady on her feet – but it was no worse than she'd felt after a dozen similar encounters. And she hadn't run crying to A&E then.

'It'll only take a couple of hours and Dordevic is going to have to get checked out anyway—' Charlie insisted.

'Doesn't matter. I want to get back to the station, make sure we're properly prepped for the interview. In the meantime, I want him fast-tracked and back at Southampton Central within the hour.'

'I don't know why you're being so pig-headed. It's common sense to get yourself checked out after a major shock like that.'

'And have a load of strangers poking and prodding me, whilst Peters rubs his hands together back at the station? No, thank you. I will not show weakness in front of him, or the team—'

'It's not weakness, Helen. It's standard practice. You *know* that.'

Charlie's tone was impassioned, exasperated, her emotion almost appearing to overwhelm her, but Helen was not for turning.

'No, it's taken us far too long to get to this point, far too long to bring this guy to book. Please don't fight me on this, Charlie.'

Her old friend stared back at her, saying nothing. What could she say? Too much blood *had* been shed, too many lives shattered, to think of easing up now.

'All I need is some dry clothes, a hot coffee and your presence in the interview suite. Marko Dordevic has some serious questions to answer...'

Helen's hand shook slightly as she held it out to Charlie, beseeching her support.

'...so, please, let's get to it.'

Chapter 84

Japhet Wilson tore into his work, driven by adrenaline and the heady prospect of a swift conviction. He had never experienced a morning like it – the nervous anticipation, the sudden explosion into action, Grace's terrifying plunge into the water and the sudden, unexpected triumph at the end of it all. It was the stuff that a police officer's dreams are made of and he was still pinching himself, scarcely believing what he'd just witnessed.

There was no time for anyone to rest on their laurels, however, to mentally replay the drama of Dordevic's capture. Despite clearly being in shock, DI Grace had nevertheless taken command of the situation, ordering him to search the suspect's cabin, even as she stumbled onto the dockside, dripping wet and unsteady on her feet. Wilson had hesitated, not wanting to tread on Meredith Walker's toes, but the look Grace gave him sent him on his way. The forensics officers would pore over Dordevic's cabin when they arrived, but his superior was hungry for hard evidence now, to bring this investigation to a timely conclusion.

Having slipped on shoe coverings and latex gloves, he began his investigation of the cabin Dordevic shared with Jevgeni Kaasik, his Estonian crewmate. Wilson marvelled that two blokes could share such a confined space for long periods without killing each other, as there was barely room to swing a cat in the claustrophobic berth. There were two bunks, a sink unit and a built-in wardrobe-cum-chest of drawers. That was it, the pair's main recreation space for weeks on end. If anyone knew the suspect well, it was Kaasik, hence why DC McAndrew was quizzing him dockside. Hopefully that would throw up some answers, but Wilson nevertheless felt the pressure to deliver himself, having personally been given this task by DI Grace.

So far, he had found nothing, however. He had interrogated the sink unit, testing the interior for loose panels, before moving onto the plumbing, unscrewing the U-bend to ensure that nothing had been disposed of in the waste system. Coming up empty-handed, he'd moved onto the wardrobe, emptying the drawers, searching the overalls that hung inside, before poring over every inch of the interior. But it had not been tampered with or customized in any way and with a heavy heart he'd replaced the suspect's clothing. He'd entered the cabin intent on unearthing something significant, but already he felt the chances of making a meaningful contribution slipping away from him.

Now only the beds remained. Perching on the lip of the lower bunk, he pulled himself up, examining the narrow bed above. He brushed his hands over the sheet, checking for bumps in the surface, but found nothing, save for a novel written in a Cyrillic script that he couldn't read. The pillowcase contained some cash and Kaasik's passport, but little else of interest. Lifting the mattress, Wilson found only dust and an old copy of the *Sun*, so he turned his attention to Dordevic's bunk instead.

This was similarly bare. The crew's service rota was pinned to the wall, just above a couple of dodgy magazines, which appeared well thumbed. Otherwise, there was nothing of any interest, despite his rigorous search of the bedding – these men clearly travelled light. With a heavy heart, he now heaved up the mattress, but yet again he was disappointed. What had he been expecting? A blood-caked axe? A signed confession? Whatever he'd expected, there was nothing hidden beneath the tired mattress, save for the dust and body hair of many previous inhabitants.

'Bloody hell...'

Sighing, Wilson made to drop the mattress, mentally rehearsing how he would dress up his failure to his new boss, when he noticed something. The interior of the bunk was very dusty indeed – save for a small spot in the nearside corner, which seemed oddly clean. Lifting up the mattress, he peered at the adjacent corner. This too seemed brighter and cleaner, the dust having been dispersed in that area.

Tugging the mattress onto the floor, he examined the other two corners. There were signs here, too, that the dust had been recently disturbed. More intriguingly still, in the back right-hand corner, there was a small hole. Perfectly round and smooth, it was not the result of accidental damage, it had been drilled into the wood deliberately. Intrigued, Wilson probed it, his finger fitting neatly through the fabricated gap. Sensing a breakthrough, Wilson tugged hard at the wood. At first it refused to yield, then suddenly it came away from the frame. Gripping the edge, Wilson lifted it up and away, depositing it carefully on the floor behind him.

Turning back to the carcass of the bed, he stopped in his tracks. Dordevic had been clever, but his subterfuge had not been good enough. Hidden within the secret compartment, he had fashioned a treasure trove of ill-gotten gains. Maps of Southampton, with addresses ringed in pen, a battered mobile phone, a pair of leather gloves and next to them clear sandwich bags containing numerous items of value. Picking up the uppermost one, he drank in the contents. A Rolex. An engraved lighter. A clutch of war medals. And a large haul of ladies' jewellery. Wilson felt his heart skip a beat as he cupped the valuable items reverently. They felt heavy in his hands, but their weight would be most felt by Dordevic himself. He had led them a merry dance so far, spreading terror and bloodshed in his wake, but here was final proof that they had their man.

His reign of terror was over.

Chapter 85

'How sure are you?'

The answer came back quickly, but her sub-editor's voice was drowned out by the roar of the car's engine. Easing off the accelerator, Emilia punched up the volume on her phone.

'Say again...'

'It was *definitely* Grace. She and her team turned up at the docks first thing this morning, raided the *Spirit of Enterprise*.'

'And she went off the front of the boat?' Emilia continued, scarcely crediting the latest reports from the newsroom.

'Her and the suspect, I believe. One of the guys who works at the docks rang us straightaway, as the pair of them were being fished out of the drink.'

It was incredible, but as usual where Helen Grace was concerned, it was true.

'Were they hurt?'

'They managed to walk to the ambulance apparently, so I'm guessing it's nothing too serious.'

'And he's back in custody now?'

'Arrived ten minutes ago, fresh from being given the all-clear from the hospital. Grace has probably got the thumb screws on him as we speak.'

Emilia smiled at the image, before replying:

'Who is he?'

'Crew member, I think. Our source has seen the guy around the docks, but has no idea what his name is.'

'And we're certain this is to do with the current spate of murders?'

'Has to be,' her experienced colleague replied. 'The whole of the MIT was down there, plus uniform and tactical support. It was a big show of strength.'

'Fair enough,' Emilia conceded.

'So how do you want to play it?'

'Send Banyard down to Southampton Central, see if he can get media liaison to confirm that they've arrested a suspect in connection with the White and Westlake murders. I'll head to the docks straightaway, see if I can dig up a name. Call you in an hour?'

'I'll look forward to it,' came the excited reply.

Ringing off, Emilia shook her head, smiling to herself. You had to hand it to her nemesis – whenever you thought Helen Grace was on the canvas, she had a way of springing back to life, snatching victory from the jaws of defeat. On the one hand, this was annoying – Emilia enjoyed goading Grace and the longer the suspect remained at large, the more scared the general population would be. On the other hand, it might play well for them. If the perpetrator turned out to be some rough crewman, with violence in his blood and fire in his soul, then that would work too. Imagine waking up to find some vast hairy brute looming over your bed, a dirty great axe in his hand? Emilia felt a shiver even as she thought it – it was an image that would shake the citizens of Southampton to their very souls.

But that was for later; the priority now was to get to the

docks before the rest of the press. So, dropping her trusty Corsa into second gear, Emilia spun the wheel, executing a perfectly illegal U-turn, ignoring the blaring horns of the oncoming traffic, before speeding away in the direction of the docks.

Chapter 86

He remained perfectly still, his gaze locked onto hers. In spite of herself, Helen was almost impressed by Dordevic's refusal to be intimidated, his preternatural calm. Once in the interview suite, suspects either recede into themselves or lash out in anger, as the hopelessness of their predicament sinks in. But the Serbian veteran had so far refused to show any weakness, staring right back at Helen, as if challenging her. Had he had interrogation training in the army? Had he been captured? Faced similar situations before? If so, then this might yet prove to be a gruelling encounter.

'How long have you been employed on the *Spirit of Enterprise*, Marko?' Helen asked, in a deliberately conversational tone.

The burly crewman shrugged, before eventually answering:

'Three years, maybe more. I'm a good worker, so they keep me on...'

A smile tugged at his lips.

'How much do they pay you?'

'Not enough, given the shit we have to do.'

'Is that why you have your little sideline?'

The smile was slowly replaced with a frown.

'I don't understand. My English is not very good...'

'You understand perfectly well, so don't play dumb. You know you're here because you are suspected of several counts of burg-lary, false imprisonment, assault and murder ...'

Dordevic exhaled dismissively, studying his hands, as if sud-denly bored by the process.

'...offences which, if proved, will land you in prison for the rest of your life. So I would suggest you take this conversation seriously, Marko.'

In response, he raised his eyes to hers, but offered nothing more.

'When did you start house-breaking? Was it in this country or abroad?'

Silence filled the room, the three occupants staring at each other, as the digital recorder blinked between them.

'I have to say I admire your professionalism, it was a very slick operation. In and out the country in two weeks, taking your booty with you to sell in Hong Kong or Yokohama, never around to carry the can when the local authorities finally pick up a scent. Must have been a real money-spinner, but that wasn't really why you did it, was it? You *enjoyed* it.'

A slight reaction from Dordevic. Helen took him in, the strong, unshaven jaw, the small, coal black eyes, the heavy tat-tooing on his neck and forearms. He would be a terrifying sight to encounter in the dead of night.

'You enjoyed the feeling of terror you inspired, the control you had over your victims. Did you enjoy the violence too?'

'I have never used violence in that way, only to defend myself in battle.'

'Except that's not true, is it? There were the charges levelled at you in Manila and Shanghai, not to mention the crimes you committed on our soil. Do you remember this man?'

She slid a series of photographs across the table towards him. They were all of Roger Morton, taken shortly after the attack, revealing the horrific injuries he'd sustained. A broken cheek, nose and jaw, two fractured ribs, hideous bruising and swelling all over the elderly man's body. Dordevic didn't want to look at them, but had no choice. He tried to disguise his reaction, but his discomfort was clear, the ex-soldier shifting uneasily in his seat.

'You broke several bones that day, Marko,' Charlie added, stepping into the fray. 'But more than that, you broke his spirit. Is that what you get off on? Knowing that your visits leave scars that last a lifetime?'

'I don't know this man.'

'That's funny because he remembers you. He's in the station right now and I'm confident he's going to pick you out when we conduct an identity parade later.'

This was a lie, but had the required effect. For the first time, Dordevic appeared rattled.

'I don't *know* him,' he insisted angrily, but his protests were waved away dismissively by Helen.

'Look, let's not play that game. You are an experienced house-breaker, with a very lucrative, very destructive line in aggravated burglary. That's not in question. What I am curious about is how you select your victims?'

Dordevic dropped his eyes to the table, keen to avoid Helen's penetrating gaze.

'Over the year or so that you've been active here, you have been very cautious, very precise, very professional. We have clear evidence now of a spate of burglaries all carried out when you were on shore leave from the *Spirit*, all targeting high-net-worth individuals in the more exclusive parts of the city – Shirley, St Denys, Freemantle.'

'Many of these individuals,' Charlie said, overlapping, 'were happy to advertise their good fortune on Facebook and

Instagram – Roger Morton, for example, was keen to show off his new Omega watch, which he'd been given for his seventieth birthday. A watch which was taken from him during an aggravated burglary on the twenty-sixth of October 2021. Alison Pierce did likewise with a new diamond necklace, a few days before *she* was targeted at her garden flat in Ocean Village in late October. Now we've had look at your phone, Marko, and for a man who doesn't have any friends or family, you spend a lot of time on social media. This is more than casual interest. This is cyber stalking…'

A curt shake of the head, but Helen could see that the pressure was growing. A thin film of sweat clung to Dordevic's forehead, his enjoyment of this 'game' over.

'Is that how you did it? Or was it more the geography that influenced you? You definitely know the layout of Southampton – the better neighbourhoods, places where'd you'd find large, easily accessible houses. Was that the most important criteria for you? Why you kept going back to the same areas, drawing from the same well?'

Still the suspect maintained his silence, licking his lips nervously. Helen watched his large pink tongue slide over them with distaste.

'The question that really interests me is how you know *when* to strike? How diligent, how patient was your surveillance? Did you hack their phones, their computers? How did you know that your victims would be home alone when you broke in?'

There was no subterfuge here on Helen's part. She was extremely keen to work out their suspect's MO, how deeply he had climbed into his victims' lives. So far, they had no evidence of any physical surveillance or stalking.

'Look, lady,' he replied, scratching at his stubble. 'You got the wrong man. I'm just a sailor, right—'

'You're an ex-Special Forces operative,' Charlie interrupted. 'Trained to penetrate, disarm and kill, someone who would be more than capable of sophisticated surveillance, discreet entry and extreme violence.'

'That's all in the past. What I did, I did to protect my country, nothing more.'

Contrary to his earlier assertions, Dordevic's English was extremely good. Helen wondered how far this bright, articulate man had risen in the army before he eventually retired from active duty.

'You say I'm *this*, you say I'm *that*, but no. I'm just a simple guy trying to make a living—'

'No, you are a liar, a thief and a killer,' Helen replied tersely, swatting him down. 'And as such I would seriously suggest you co-operate with us. Given the gravity of your crimes, any privileges you might receive, any possibility of later parole, is entirely dependent on your co-operation now. Which is why we need details? How, when, why?'

But Dordevic waved the questions away.

'You have nothing on me, no proof—'

'On the contrary.'

'You can't place me there.'

'Is that so?'

Helen's tone was amused, knowing, which clearly alarmed Dordevic.

'I'll admit you've been cautious, clever. Always operating at night, wearing gloves, choosing your moments carefully. Your phone is unregistered, the SIM constantly changed, but we can trace its most recent movements—'

'Maybe I lost it, maybe someone stole it from *me*.'

'And we are currently scouring St Denys and Freemantle, interrogating every CCTV feed, every traffic camera, talking to everyone with home security systems, dash cams, bike cams. We will be able to place you there and when we do, you can be assured you will be charged with two counts of murder, with a recommendation that you never be release—'

'I don't know these places, you're talking rubbish.'

'Then how do you explain this?'

Helen slid the map that Wilson had recovered across the table towards him.

'This was recovered from a secret compartment underneath your bunk earlier this morning.'

The suspect stared at the map, the blood draining from his face.

'Along with a considerable quantity of watches, jewellery, medals and cash, all of which we're confident we'll be able to link to previous offences committed by *you*.'

The net was closing fast – Dordevic stared at the map, dumbfounded.

'You'll see that there are various markings on the map. A handful of properties have been ringed in black pen, two of which – on Hayling Road and Granton Terrace – were burgled last week. But it's these two markings which intrigue me most...'

She stabbed the map on the table.

'Two black crosses. One at an address in St Denys. And one at an address in Freemantle. The White home and the Westlake home. Now I'm assuming the black cross denotes the fact that the occupants were murdered, rather than simply assaulted and robbed, but what I'd like to know is whether you made the crosses before or after the attack?'

Dordevic stared at her, caught in Helen's tractor beam.

'Did you specifically set out to murder the inhabitants or was it something that happened in the moment?'

Dordevic's eyes were wild, his mouth locked in an unpleasant grimace. Helen was suddenly aware of the strong smell of sweat in the room, the heat emanating from the cornered man.

'Tell me, Marko,' she barked, her voice suddenly loud and commanding. 'Why did you do it? Why did you kill those innocent people?'

There was a moment's silence, the calm before the storm. Then with a savage roar, Dordevic threw back his chair and lunged across the table, wrapping his hands around Helen's throat.

Chapter 87

'I hope they lock him up and throw away the key.'

'Go on...' Emilia purred. 'Why do you say that?'

'There was something evil about him, something that made your skin crawl.'

Emilia scribbled down 'evil' underlining it twice. It had taken her a couple of hours to track down the *Spirit*'s crew, most of whom were holed up in the back room of the Mermaid awaiting orders and longer still to get Jevgeni Kaasik, Dordevic's berth mate, to talk to her. But a couple of pints to the good, the Estonian was finally beginning to express himself.

'How so? What did he do to make you feel—'

'It was the way he looked at you, the way he approached you. Always angry, always violent. Like he wanted you to challenge him, wanted a fight.'

'Why was that? Because of his childhood? His time in the army?'

'I've no idea what happened to him in the Yugoslav war, he never spoke about it. But he was happy to talk about the things he'd done in the army, even though it was classified. The killings, the torture, the rapes...'

Kaasik hesitated, as if wary of offending her, but she waved away his concern.

'Don't worry about me, I'm a tough cookie.'

'I can give you details if you want, but those experiences changed him. Made him angry, restless, hostile...'

'Did he cause trouble on the ship?'

'Of course, but he was never disciplined. Either there were no witnesses or they were too afraid to speak up. I think even the captain was scared of him.'

'What did he do?'

'Everything, anything. He emptied his bowels onto my bed after one argument.'

Emilia winced, but Kaasik continued:

'Urinated on me whilst I slept another time. He threatened to kill me numerous times, but I was one of the lucky ones. He beat the cook half to death with a wrench. Would have been arrested if anyone had seen it. But we all knew it was him.'

'And have the police spoken to you about this?'

He nodded, but didn't look happy.

'I told them what I know. They say they have to speak to me again.'

Casting an eye over the sea of weathered faces around them, Emilia noticed that the majority of the crew seemed similarly disgruntled. Due to the ongoing investigation, they were likely to be stuck here for some time, wasting time and losing money.

'And if we were to print your testimony, would you be happy to be named?'

'No, no way.'

'If you're worried about Dordevic, I wouldn't be. He's not getting out any time soon—'

'No names,' Kaasik responded firmly.

'You're the boss,' she trilled back happily.

Was he really scared of Dordevic? Or was he nervous of suddenly being in the spotlight? Was it possible that he himself was of interest to the authorities abroad and didn't want his name appearing in any media outlet? It was intriguing to know, but Emilia had what she needed, so slipping him a crisp £20 note, she rose swiftly.

'Have a couple on me, sounds like you've earned it.'

Thirty seconds later, she was pushing through the doors of the grimy pub, glad to leave the airless den behind. The Mermaid had long been a dive of the first order, a place to drink cheap beer whilst purchasing hooky goods. It was certainly not Emilia's natural milieu – she was a woman who favoured more sophisticated venues.

Walking back to her car, her thoughts turned to the wine bars and gastropubs she'd frequented of late, to her dates with Sam. She had been chewing on their disagreement since it happened, replaying their dispute repeatedly, attempting to analyse where things had gone wrong, to apportion blame, to make herself feel better. Yet despite her best efforts, she couldn't. Putting aside the rights and wrongs of the debate – she really didn't want to go *there* – the truth was that she missed him. Missed his easy confidence, his warmth, his laugh. She'd assumed that he would be in touch, to make up, or if she was really lucky, apologize. But there had been no contact of any kind, just a persistent, hurtful, silence. Tugging her phone from her pocket, Emilia checked her messages, her gmail, her voicemail . . . but there was nothing.

Emilia couldn't deny that this hurt. Normally so armour-plated, so inured to life's slings and arrows, this was one disappointment she couldn't shake off. So successful in every other field of her life, her failure to land Sam struck home, tinged as it was with a powerful sense of shame at his evident disapproval of her job, her character, her soul.

Leaning against her car, a tiny silhouette against the vast hulk of the cargo ship beyond, Emilia suddenly felt very alone.

Chapter 88

She stood before him, her emotions in riot.

'It's a simple question, Helen. Can we make it stick?'

'Yes, I'm fine, sir. Thank you for asking.'

It was petulant, insubordinate, but Helen couldn't resist, such was her outrage. It had taken her, Charlie and two uniformed officers several minutes to subdue the desperate suspect and Dordevic had used this time profitably, landing two good punches to Helen's ribs in addition to locking her in a couple of very unpleasant choke holds. Even now, Helen could feel her neck beginning to swell, livid bruising staining her skin, but Peters seemed uninterested in her welfare, his mind squarely on their chances of a conviction.

'I'd expect nothing less,' her superior responded. 'You seem to be strangely indestructible.'

Helen didn't care for his tone, which was laced with regret.

'It's a good thing I am or we wouldn't have a suspect in custody,' she countered.

'Which leads me back to my earlier question,' Peters replied. 'Do we have enough to bring charges against him?'

His eyes were boring into her, challenging her to react, but Helen kept her cool.

'It's on a knife edge, sir. We can certainly link him to a string of recent burglaries, no question about that, so we've enough to hold him. We also have very strong circumstantial evidence linking him to the White and Westlake properties, but nothing more concrete than that. Ideally I'd like us to unearth some of the items taken from those houses or better still to be able to place Dordevic in the vicinity on the nights in question.'

'What's the latest on that?'

'I've scrambled the whole team to St Denys and Freemantle, this is their sole focus now. We need witness or CCTV footage for the nights of the ninth and eleventh, but we're also after evidence that he was watching the properties prior to that, that he *knew* his victim would be home alone before he struck.'

'But so far we've got nothing, right?'

'The search has only just begun.'

'But as of this moment, we are not in a position to recommend charges relating to the recent murders?'

'Not yet.'

'Then I won't keep you. All of your efforts, every waking hour must be dedicated to finding the evidence required to charge Dordevic. You wouldn't believe the heat we're getting on this one – it's as if the whole city, and its elected officials, have gone mad.'

He flicked open his agenda, running his finger down his list of commitments. Helen, however, remained stock-still, flabbergasted by his tone, his manner, the crushing lack of respect.

'Is that all you've got to say to me?'

He raised his eyes to hers, annoyed.

'Is that really the *best* you can do?'

'Careful, Helen, you're skating on thin ice as it is. Don't make a bad situation—'

'How dare you. How dare you speak to me like that, after

everything I've done for this station, everything I've done for you...'

Peters flinched, unnerved by this personal attack. It was time to retreat, to shut up, but Helen was too far gone to back down now.

'And what exactly have you done for me, Helen?' he replied witheringly.

'I've made you look good, I've made this station look good. If it wasn't for me our clear-up rates would be in the toilet. We would have lost control of the city and this station would, frankly, be in Special Measures.'

'Because I can't run Southampton Central?' Peters spat back.

'Oh, you can shuffle papers with the best of them,' Helen laughed ruefully, 'but when it comes to police work – when it comes to the actual business of keeping the citizens of this city safe – there's only one senior officer doing the business here.'

Enraged, Peters was about to respond, but Helen didn't want to hear it.

'Now if you'll excuse me, I've got a job to do.'

With that, Helen turned and marched purposefully from his office, not quite believing what she'd just done.

Chapter 89

'Are you serious?'

She hadn't meant to sound critical, but her tone had an unpleasant, accusing ring to it.

'You want to offer *money*?' Victoria Westlake continued, trying not to make it sound like a dirty word.

'Not money, a *reward*. There's a difference.'

'Is there?'

Richard Westlake looked up sharply at his wife, clearly angered by her insistence on questioning everything he said. But what choice did she have when he kept coming out with such strange things. First, he'd wanted to drive the streets himself looking for Ethan's killer. Then he'd wanted to hire a private detective. Now he wanted to offer a huge sum of money for information leading to the capture of their son's killer. She knew where this came from, how his frustration, his anger, his guilt, was driving him slowly insane, but surely it wasn't *their* job to unmask the perpetrator of this dreadful crime?

'I just think we'd be setting ourselves up for a fall,' she said, in a more emollient tone. 'I want justice, just as much as you do, but if you bring money into the equation we'll get all sorts of chancers trying their luck, offering up a score of dead-end leads which could hinder the police investigation, rather than help it.'

'You don't know that. It's helped before, in other situations.'

'Has it? When?'

She didn't want to be so aggressive, so challenging, but she was convinced this was madness. Richard turned away from her, barely bothering to conceal a scowl. He was a man who liked to be in control, who had taken the lead with the police when she was too broken, too distraught to utter a word and she was grateful to him for that. But she was annoyed now by his evident irritation that she had finally found her voice again.

'I don't understand why we can't just let the police do their job.'

'What have they done so far?' he retorted, witheringly. 'They arrested the wrong guy, had to let him go. Since then we've been left totally in the dark. The only contact we've had was from that bloody journalist and she only wanted to wallow in our misery...'

Privately, Vicky wondered whether *this* was the root cause of her husband's erratic behaviour. He had been left raging by Garanita's earlier intrusion at the family home, threatening to sue the journalist *and* the paper. She too had been livid – would have torn Garanita limb from limb if she'd encountered her subsequently – but she had the distinct feeling that their clash had pushed Richard over the edge. He'd hardly slept, hardly eaten and was becoming harder and harder to reach.

'Look, I know you're upset and you've every right to be. But this isn't our job.'

'Isn't it? We failed to protect our son, the least we can do is help to find his... his killer.'

His words near enough broke her heart, not only for the truth contained in his accusation, but because of the crushing guilt that infused every word. Richard had been absent when their son was attacked, they *both* had, a fact that would haunt them for the rest of their lives. But whilst she was destroyed by her guilt, he was tormented by it, his apparent 'failure' goading him night and day. Crossing to him, she put an arm around his shoulders, pulling him to her.

'None of this is our fault. So don't go feeling that we need to make things right, even if such a thing were possible. They said on the radio that the police had raided a ship at the docks, that an arrest was made—'

'It'll come to nothing, then we'll be back to square one. You mark my words...'

She was shocked by his certainty, his cynicism. Did he trust no one anymore?

'Which is why I'm actually trying to *do* something. Anything's better than sitting round here day after day, wallowing in it...'

A clear dig at her, but she refused to take the bait.

'Look, I'm not sure we're going to agree on this now, so why don't we sleep on it? Then, in the morning, if you still feel like it's a good—'

'Don't treat me like a child, Victoria. I know my own mind. And I know when we're being soft-soaped, lied to. We have resources, we have a voice, let's use that to make a difference.'

'Richard, you know what I think about this—'

'Don't I just?' he said, pulling away from her. 'You can't wait to put me down, to find fault with what I want to do. Jesus Christ, it's like you don't *want* to find out who did this to our boy!'

She stared at him, dumbfounded. How could he say something so cruel, so unwarranted to his own wife? What had *she* done to deserve such treatment?

'Shame on you, Richard. Shame on you for saying something so ... so vile.'

He was about to respond, visibly shocked by her response, in spite of his anger. But she wasn't going to hang around for his apologies. He'd made his feelings clear, accusing her of being weak, spineless and uncaring and now she just wanted to put some space between them. Half marching, half stumbling up the stairs, she made it to the sanctuary of their bedroom, slamming the door behind her, before crumpling down on the bed in tears.

She didn't want to cry, but she couldn't help herself, assailed suddenly by an unstoppable wave of despair. How had it come to this? A few days ago they were a happy loving family, now it felt like they had been cast onto the rocks, bereft, broken and helpless. She knew the death of a child could have a devastating effect on those left behind – would it scupper their marriage now? Previously, she'd never have believed it, would have stood four square behind her belief in the strength and resilience of their union.

But now she wasn't so sure.

Chapter 90

She was staring down the barrel this time. There was no doubt about that.

Helen scaled the stairs to her flat, replaying her bitter clash with Peters. Why had she been so reckless, so rash? Calling her superior out for his lack of compassion was bad enough, but accusing him of being a desk jockey, whilst casting herself as the saviour of the station was beyond stupid. It wasn't true for one thing, overlooking Peters' track record, not to mention the dedication and skill of her team. Nor did it truthfully reflect her feelings – her career at Southampton Central had never been about *her*. But today her judgement had been clouded by righteous anger, the accusations spewing from her unrehearsed, and this lack of self-control might yet cost her her job.

How was such a thing possible? How had she managed to back herself into this corner? Over the past ten years, she had worked tirelessly to protect the weak and bring the guilty to justice, making countless personal sacrifices to get the job done. Her dedication had cost her emotionally, psychologically and physically, something that was all too obvious today as she limped towards the top floor, her body battered and broken, after another encounter that had almost finished her.

It wasn't right, it wasn't *fair*. She had given everything, but it still wasn't enough, the top brass forever gunning for her.

Whittaker, Harwood, Gardam – her previous bosses had all tried to sink her, but perhaps it would fall to Peters, the ultimate politician and time-server, to deliver the coup de grace. None of them had been able to tame her, to control her, constantly angered by her impulsiveness, her recklessness and, truth be told, her success. She had always been able to fight them off, to carry the day, but as she gripped the bannister and tugged herself upwards, Helen acknowledged that she had never felt more like an injured bull in the ring, unable to escape her tormentors, forever waiting for the blade to fall.

Would Peters ring her tonight? Summon her back to the office for a formal charge of misconduct? Or would he get one of his stooges in HR to do it, lacking the courage to do the deed himself? This seemed more likely and only served to anger her further. Why should it be that it is always those who do nothing, who keep their hands scrupulously clean, that eventually carry the day? Where was the justice in *that*?

Fuming, Helen crested the top landing of her building, her ordeal nearly at an end. She was utterly spent, weighed down by self-recrimination and despair – all that was left to do now was to retreat. Perhaps after a night spent licking her wounds, she would find the strength to fight again. To see off Peters. Why not? She had done it before...

She sensed it before she saw it. A tiny movement, a noise behind her, alerting her to the danger she was in. Crazily, recklessly, she had failed to carry out her usual security checks, distracted by her interview with Peters and her aching body. For a second, she had let her guard down and her nemesis had not hesitated to strike. Footsteps hurried up fast behind and then his hand shot towards her, fast and deadly.

This was it then. She had made a mistake – one simple, unforgiveable mistake. And now she would pay the price.

Chapter 91

He grabbed her shoulder, pulling her roughly towards him. Instinctively, she swung out an arm to defend herself, but it met thin air, and she tumbled backwards into his clutches. She was off balance, defenceless. Any minute now she would feel the cold steel of his blade sliding between her ribs, robbing her of her fight, her strength, her life.

Falling backwards towards destruction, she acted on instinct, risking one last throw of the dice. Jerking her neck savagely, she threw her head backwards. She half expected to crash to the floor in a heap, but instead her head cannoned into her attacker's face, crunching bone, causing him to cry out in pain. Immediately, his grip relented and now Helen *did* fall, crashing down onto the cold, hard floor.

Shocked, breathless, she scrambled to her feet. Her attacker was bent double, cradling his nose, groaning, so Helen sprang forwards. She raced towards him, determined to disarm him before he could regain his momentum, but her assailant now straightened to resume his attack. She'd been too slow, there was no way she could grasp his arm in time, so acting on instinct she jumped into the air, raising her foot in front of her. Surprisingly the man now froze, as if this was the very last manoeuvre he'd been expecting. And his hesitation cost him dear, Helen planting her heavy boot squarely in the middle of his chest.

She collided heavily with him, before crashing down to earth with a bump. But her nemesis fared even less well. Unprepared and off balance, he flew backwards under the weight of her assault, powerless to arrest his sudden retreat. Helen felt a shiver of excitement, of release, hoping now that he would crash to the ground, winded and stunned, unable to resist her, as she fell upon him. But instantly hope turned to horror, the shadowy figure crashing hard into the bannister, before flipping up and over the barrier, carried inexorably backwards by his momentum.

Helen cried out, but it was too late, her distress drowned out by a blood-curdling scream as the man plunged down, down, down. Seconds later a horrible thud echoed up the central stairwell, then all was quiet once more.

'Bloody hell...'

Helen gasped the words as she scrabbled to her feet. What had she just done? Shaking off her pain, she tore down the stairs, leaping whole flights at a time, desperate to see what had become of her would-be assassin. Sweating, desperate, she hit the ground floor hard, turning to face him, hoping against hope for any signs of life.

Once more, however, fate was against her, the man's broken body hideous to behold, his limbs jutting out at the most unnatural angles. Already a pool of blood was forming around him, but ignoring this, Helen hurried over. Was it really impossible that somehow he might have survived? Surely she'd be able to do something for him?

Hauling the man over, she reached forward, cupping his face and turning it to hers. As she did so, she gasped in agony, barely believing what she was seeing. For the dead man in her arms was *not* her murderous attacker from the bike park.

It was DS Joseph Hudson.

Day Six

Chapter 92

Charlie stared at him open-mouthed, before eventually finding her voice.

'Hudson?' she eventually stammered in response. 'Are you *sure?*'

'I identified him myself,' Chief Superintendent Peters replied grimly. 'Not that I needed to, Jim Grieves knew perfectly well who he was.'

Charlie collapsed into her seat. Normally she would have asked for permission to do so, but her legs refused to hold her. She hadn't liked Hudson, had perhaps even hated him at times, but ... dead? It didn't make any sense. Then again, nothing that had happened in the last couple of days made sense – it was as if Charlie was stuck in an ever-deepening nightmare.

'Do we ... do we know what happened?'

'Well, we have DI Grace's account, though obviously we have to take that with a pinch of salt, as she appears to have been the aggressor here.'

'I don't follow.'

'She claims DS Hudson ambushed her last night, when she returned home. According to her, there was a scuffle, during which he went over the bannisters, falling to his death.'

Charlie felt a wave of nausea sweep over her, as an image

of Hudson hitting the cold stone floor forced its way into her thoughts.

'Dear God...' she whispered. 'Where's Helen now?'

'She's in custody. She called the incident in, handed herself in. She's due to be interviewed in half an hour and I'd like you to be in the room.'

Once again, Charlie couldn't believe what she was hearing.

'But surely we'll get an outside Force in to investigate this?'

'Are you mad?' Peters snapped back. 'I have no intention of letting a rival Force destroy the reputation of this station. I'm sure they would love to stick their beaks in, rummage through our dirty laundry, but there's no question of anyone but our own people dealing with this.'

Charlie raged at this predictable, cotton-headed response – with Peters' reputation came above all things. But wisely she hid her anger, keeping her temper in check.

'Then let Professional Standards do it. We can't be involved.'

'They will have a role to play, of course, but we will lead the interrogation.'

Charlie felt sick, the idea of having to quiz Helen was horrific, insane.

'But we have history with her, we know her.'

'Which should save us time. I'm sure you'll agree this needs to be dealt with swiftly and efficiently.'

'And *fairly*,' Charlie insisted. 'With respect, sir, you have had numerous run-ins with her—'

'That's not relevant.'

'And I'm her... I'm her closest friend, for God's sake. She's my mentor, my boss, godmother to my children—'

'You are also now the acting head of the Major Incident Team.'

This was news to Charlie, who was silenced by Peters' well-timed bombshell.

'DI Grace has been suspended, pending investigation, which means *you* are in charge now. She has not yet been formally disciplined or dismissed from the Force, however, so she is still technically a member of your team. As such, you need to be in on the interview, as do I.'

'If the process is to be honest and impartial, we should *not* be in the room. I feel very strongly about that, sir.'

She had never spoken to Peters in this manner before, never stood her ground so defiantly. If she was hoping it would carry the day and free her from this terrible obligation, she was disappointed, however, Peters glaring at her with ill-disguised irritation.

'It's a simple choice, DI Brooks. Either you accept your temporary promotion, join me in the interview and thereafter run the team to the best of your ability. Or you step aside from the process, refuse your promotion and effectively write your own resignation letter.'

His cold eyes settled on hers.

'Which is it going to be?'

Chapter 93

'Where is it?'

Manoeuvring her youngest sibling out of the way, Emilia Garanita scanned the living room, desperate to locate the source of the sound.

'Whoa there, where's the fire?' Marcia complained, angry at being manhandled.

'Shhh,' Emilia hissed, pulling the cushions off the sofa. 'I'm trying to find my phone. It's in here somewhere...'

'Is that all?' her sister replied dismissively. 'Expecting some breaking news, are you? Or perhaps it's lover boy, calling to whisper sweet nothings in your ear...'

Ignoring her sister's laughter, Emilia renewed her efforts. Although she'd never admit it, that was precisely what she was hoping for. She had sent Sam a couple of messages last night, apologizing for her behaviour and suggesting they meet up. This had come at some personal cost – Emilia never apologized and wasn't sure it was warranted – but if it had paid off, it would have been worth it.

'Aha!'

She was down on her hands and knees, but had finally located the trilling phone, easing it from its hiding place under the sofa. Snatching it up, she was disappointed to see it was just her

Southampton Central mole Jack Sumner calling. Answering, she turned away from her sister, walking towards the window. If anyone knew Sumner was giving her privileged information, it would cost him his job.

'Morning. What can I do for you?'

'I hope you've got your wallet open,' the young man crowed in response. 'Because this is going to cost you.'

'If it's about the Dordevic arrest, don't bother. I know all about—'

'No, it's much better than that. An officer's been killed.'

Emilia was surprised by the excitement in his voice. Normally the police community took the death of one of their own exceptionally hard.

'Well, an ex-officer, anyway. DS Joseph Hudson.'

For a minute, Emilia was speechless. What the hell?

'Are you certain?'

'No question about it, he's already been identified. He's at the police mortuary now.'

'What happened?'

'Fell to his death apparently, during a fight.'

Emilia digested this, scarcely believing this sudden and unexpected twist of fate.

'Who on earth was he fighting? Presumably not a criminal, as he'd had his wings clipped.'

'Not a criminal, no,' Sumner teased.

'A family member?'

'Nope.'

'A member of the public then? Was he pissed-up?'

'Wrong again.'

'Then, who, for God's sake?'

'He was killed by a fellow officer.'

Emilia felt a shiver of excitement ripple down her spine. Already she had a suspicion where this was heading, but nevertheless her world was rocked on its axis, as Sumner confirmed.

'DI Grace.'

Chapter 94

Helen sat at the table, staring straight ahead. She did not want to look at Peters, she did not want to look at Charlie, fixing her gaze instead on the opposite wall. This situation was beyond grotesque – deliberately so, Helen suspected – but she was not going to play ball, nor be undone by their presence in the room.

'I'd like to establish from the start,' her union rep stated, 'that DI Grace has fully co-operated with this investigation from the off, never trying to conceal her part in this terrible accident.'

She stressed the last word, eyeing Peters as she spoke.

'She called in the incident herself and is more than willing to accept her portion of blame for the unwitting part she played in DS Hudson's tragic death. Indeed, she would like to put on record both her shock and her profound sadness at his passing.'

How bald, how formal the words sounded, how inadequate they were to express the gut-wrenching torment, the over-whelming guilt Helen felt. She still couldn't quite believe it, yet there was no arguing with the facts. Her rampant paranoia, her frantic attempts to save herself from a perceived assassin, had resulted in the death of an innocent man, robbing the world of a troubled but talented police officer and a little boy of his father. It made Helen sick to the stomach, but remorse, recrimination and atonement would have to wait, as it was clear from Peters' hostile expression that Helen had a battle on her hands if she wanted to somehow salvage her career.

'Noted,' Peters responded drily. 'Now, can we begin?'

He was deliberately trying to belittle her, Helen's companion shifting uneasily in her seat.

'I'd like to establish why Joseph Hudson was at your flat last night, DI Grace?'

'He wasn't at my flat,' Helen replied quickly. 'He had concealed himself on the top landing and approached me – no, ambushed me – when I returned home.'

'I presume the front door to the flats is generally locked, so he'd have to be buzzed in?'

'I assume he gained entry when another resident entered or left the building.'

'Do you have any evidence to support that?'

Helen stared at Peters for a moment, before answering. She'd assumed he'd give her a rough ride, but hadn't expected such overt suspicion from the start.

'No, of course not. But I'm sure if you canvass my neighbours, they'll be able to shed some light on things.'

'I see. So this wasn't a pre-arranged meeting?'

'Absolutely not. I haven't seen him in months.'

'And are you happy for us to check your phone, your computer, to verify that no such arrangements were made?'

This came from Charlie, who appeared keen to clean up this mess and be out of the room as soon as possible. She held Helen's gaze, wanting to appear professional and impartial, but the strain was clear.

'Of course. I should say that he *did* try to contact me during the last few days, hoping to get me to withdraw from the criminal proceedings against him, but as of a couple of days ago I had severed all contact with him.'

'I see,' Peters replied meaningfully, scribbling a note.

'I can only hazard a guess as to why he was at my flat last night, but I suspect he had come to reason with me in person, to beg me perhaps to...'

She was about to say 'save his skin' but swallowed the words.

'But he had been to your flat previously. Several times in fact...' Peters countered.

'DS Hudson and I were briefly romantically involved,' Helen conceded. 'And during that period he visited my flat a few times, staying over on the odd occasion.'

Helen was aware of her rep's interest in this confession, but ignoring her prurient gaze, she continued.

'But that was over four months ago. He hadn't been in my flat recently and I certainly didn't invite him over yesterday.'

'That's still to be established. Can you walk us through the events of last night?' Peters continued, effortlessly dismissing her claims of innocence. 'Step by step, please.'

'As I said before,' Helen replied, trying to contain her anger, 'I climbed the stairs to my flat and was about to open my door, when I heard someone coming for me.'

'Coming for you?'

'Approaching me swiftly from behind. Given the overt threat to my life as a result of my involvement in the Alex Blythe case, I assumed that I was about to be attacked and I responded accordingly.'

'Why did you think you were being attacked?' Peters challenged her. 'Did you see a weapon of any kind? Was anything said or done by DS Hudson to suggest your life was in danger?'

'No, it all happened too fast for anything like that. I just felt someone rush up behind me and grab my shoulder.'

'And that was enough to prompt your attack?'

'I didn't attack DS Hudson,' Helen protested. 'I defended

myself. I ... I have felt for some days now that my life was in danger. In fact, two days ago, someone attacked me at the Picket Post services. A guy in a hoodie came at me with a knife.'

Peters seemed perplexed, though whether this was genuine or feigned, Helen couldn't tell.

'There's no record of any such attack in our files. Did you report it to anyone?'

His scepticism, his doubt, couldn't have been clearer.

'I mentioned it to DS Brooks, but only in a personal capacity. And I asked her not to say anything.'

'Is this true, DS Brooks?'

'Yes, sir,' Charlie replied, looking ever more awkward. 'And I must put on record that I believed her.'

'Well, we'll clearly have to look into this. Were there any witnesses to this "attack"?'

'Yes, for sure, though obviously I can't give you any names.'

'I see. So either this crime is fictitious, a conveniently timed invention to explain away your attack on DS Hudson—'

'Now hold on a minute,' Helen exploded, but she was cut off before she could continue.

'Or a crime was committed, a crime which two serving officers knew about, but decided to conceal from the authorities. Can I ask why you might have asked DS Brooks to keep her counsel on this matter?'

Another trap had been set, but Helen wasn't going to walk into it, not going to accuse Peters of looking for a reason to relieve her of her post. They were way beyond that now, so instead she simply stated:

'I wanted to keep the team's focus on the current investigation, didn't want to distract them from their duties.'

'Very noble, I'm sure. So, to return to the incident last night—'

'Look, I've told you what happened,' Helen butted in. 'He

grabbed me, so I threw my head back, catching him in the face. Thereafter I had a split second to decide what to do and I launched myself at him, kicking him in the chest. He stumbled backwards, went over the rail and that was that. He was already dead when I got to the bottom of the stairs, but I still called the paramedics. And that's it. That's what happened. I really, really wish things had turned out differently, but they didn't. And I'm going to have to live with that.'

Helen came to a halt, emotional and breathless. But the attack on her resumed without hesitation.

'Were there any witnesses to this fight?'

'Not that I'm aware of.'

'And how was it that you didn't see Joseph Hudson when you crested the landing? I presume there are no obvious hiding places?'

'The landing light went a day or so ago, so it's very dark up there. I assume he had positioned himself in the adjacent doorway, so he'd be hard to spot. Besides, I was just focused on getting in my front door, so I wasn't looking that way.'

'Right...'

'Look, if you don't believe me,' Helen continued angrily, 'check out the door-cam footage from my flat. It'll show you exactly what happ—'

'We've already done that,' Peters interrupted. 'But I'm afraid it's far from conclusive.'

Helen stared at him in disbelief. Surely the footage would exonerate her?

'The footage shows you shrugging him off, before going on the offensive, landing two heavy blows on him before his fatal fall. But because it's only activated by movement, it can't show us what preceded your attack on him—'

'I didn't attack him.'

327

'And that's a real pity,' Peters continued, ignoring her, 'because the context of this struggle seems paramount to me. Was he there last night at your behest? Did a conversation, an argument, precede this violent encounter? What was the nature of your relationship, your feelings for him in the moments preceding his death?'

And there it was, Peters' intended angle of attack, laid out for all to see. Helen could scarcely credit it, but her own boss was going for her jugular. She knew he wanted her out of the Force, that much had been obvious for some time, but actually his ambitions were far greater than that, extending potentially to criminal charges. With a shudder Helen realized the full extent of the peril she was now in. Peters didn't just want to take away her badge.

He intended to take away her liberty too.

Chapter 95

All eyes were on her, the assembled faces waiting for her to speak.

'Thank you all for coming in so early. I appreciate this can't be easy for any of you. We're all in shock following the events of last night, and I'm sure you have many questions, but the important thing now is keeping our focus on the matter in hand.'

Her voice had shaken a little at first, but McAndrew was finding her stride. Stepping to one side, she gestured to the murder board. Photos of Martha White and Ethan Westlake stared out at the team, their happy smiles tragically at odds with their fate.

'We have two murders to solve. It is imperative that we do so efficiently and professionally. DS Brooks will be taking the lead in due course, but for the moment you're stuck with me as acting SIO, so let's pool what we've got.'

'I interviewed Roger Morton again last night,' DC Jennings offered, bravely trying to contain his shock at his superior's sudden fall from grace. 'He positively identified Dordevic as his attacker and would be prepared to ID him in person if required.'

'How sure was he?'

'One hundred per cent. Recognized the distinctive tattoos on his arms.'

'Good, get that booked in. What else?'

DC Reid raised his hand.

'Similar story from Alison Hughes. She didn't see her attacker's face because he was wearing a ski mask. But she also recognized the tattoos and confirms that the intruder had a thick East European accent. Her property was one of the ones ringed on Dordevic's map.'

'Good work. Have we accounted for all the addresses that were circled on the map?'

'Not yet,' DC Malik answered. 'DC Wilson and I are going to head out this morning, see what we can find out. There appear to be two addresses ringed by Dordevic that he didn't manage to target. No crimes have been reported, there's no record of officers attending these properties, so …'

'OK, quick as you can, please. The more we know about his MO, his movements, the better. Anything from the search team?'

This time DC Wilson answered. It was as if all officers present were all keen to chip in, to show that they were ready and willing to step up during this unprecedented crisis.

'They're tearing the ship apart. It's possible Dordevic had other hiding places for his booty, but nothing new to report as yet. Meredith Walker has all his clothing and is currently analysing them for any forensic link to the crime scenes. We should know more shortly.'

McAndrew scribbled down a note, reminding her to chase up Meredith, before turning to address the team once more.

'OK, let's redouble our efforts on this one. Things will go much easier with a confession, but to get that we'll need more leverage, something that absolutely ties our suspect to those murders, those properties. Tell your partners, friends, family that you won't be home until late, because I want no stone left unturned, right?'

Nods from the assembled faces.

'Despite everything that's gone on over the last twenty-four hours, we still have a job to do. Let's exercise our duties professionally, staying in contact at all times. I want no gossiping, no speculation and absolutely no talking to the press. We keep our focus on the investigation, on getting justice for Martha White and Ethan Westlake. If we do that, if we acquit ourselves well, then we will have done our duty. These are strange times, but all we can do is put our best foot forward, so let's go to it.'

The team rose and hurried off to begin their investigations. Relieved, but exhausted, McAndrew watched them go. She had played her part well enough, keeping the investigation on course, but she hadn't enjoyed it for a single second. She had never wanted to be a leader and felt profoundly odd telling her colleagues what to do. She hoped she'd given them the appropriate steer, but was riddled with doubt, feeling the absence of DS Brooks and DI Grace. The latter had been her boss for many years and, though McAndrew had learned much from her in that time, there was no replacing Helen – her presence, her energy, her inspiration. There was nothing they could do, except carry on and hope for the best, but in truth McAndrew was deeply concerned about the team, the investigation and the future. The MIT had been at the top of its game for years, but she sensed troubled waters lay ahead now. She prayed otherwise, but in her heart she knew that it would be hard to keep the ship off the rocks, now that their captain had been thrown overboard.

Chapter 96

'Sorry, who is this? What do you want?'

The Mancunian accent was unmistakable, raising Emilia's hopes.

'Is that Karen?'

'Yes, who are you?' the hairdresser snapped down the phone.

'My name's Emilia Garanita, I'm the Chief Crime Correspondent of the *Southampton Evening News*. I was wondering if I could have two minutes of your time?'

A small, but distinct sigh on the other end.

'Look, if this is about Joseph's trial, I've said all I have to say. What Joseph did or didn't do is none of my business – we've been divorced for some time now. So if you'll excuse me, I've got a client wait—'

'It's not about the trial, it's much more serious than that.'

Now she had her attention. Emilia could sense Karen processing this response, trying to work out what could be worse than the prospect of disgrace and prison time.

'I have some very bad news,' Emilia continued, seizing the nettle. 'I'm sorry to have to tell you that Joseph is dead.'

Stunned silence at the other end. In the background, the chatter and clatter of the salon could be heard, but no sound came from Karen Price.

'It happened last night. I wasn't sure if the police had contacted you or not, but I thought you ought to know.'

There was a gasp, a stifled sob and then finally Hudson's ex-wife found her voice.

'Was it ... was it at his own hand?'

'Oh, God, no, it was nothing like that. He was determined to contest the charges against him, to clear his name,' Emilia replied quickly, putting as positive a spin on things as she could.

'What then?'

'I'm afraid he was killed during a fight with a fellow officer.'

'But ... why? Who would do such a thing?'

'His old boss, DI Grace.'

Another sharp intake of breath, then Karen continued:

'But what were they even doing together? I know they had been in a relationship, but I assume that she hated him now.'

'You knew about them?' Emilia queried, surprised.

'Yeah, she called me about a year or so ago, pretty much asked for a character reference – and didn't like what I told her.'

'I see.'

'Still, she seemed sound, though, sensible enough ...' Hudson's ex continued, disbelief colouring her every word. 'Why on earth would she ... would she kill him?'

'That's what we're endeavouring to find out, but in the meantime, tell me about your time with Joseph, what kind of guy he was ...'

Karen Hudson continued to talk, her client long forgotten. She was tearful, shocked, but appeared keen to talk out her distress. Emilia encouraged her, keen to get as much juice as she could before she turned her attention to her article. It would be a blinder. In fact, it might very well prove to be the most important piece she'd ever written.

The final chapter in the Helen Grace story.

Chapter 97

'So are you going to charge me? Because if not, we're done here.'

The words sounded so strange coming out of Helen's mouth. Many times she'd heard them uttered in this close, confessional space, by angry suspects struggling to escape an ever-tightening net. But now it was *her* using them.

'I would remind you, DI Grace, that you don't call the shots in this room. I will decide when this interview is over.'

Helen noted that Charlie was not referenced. This was Peters' show, pure and simple.

'What more is there to say?' she hit back. 'I've told you what happened, step by step, second by second. Now, if you have concrete evidence that contradicts that narrative, that conclusively proves I'm lying, then charge me. If not, I'd suggest you let me go.'

'Just like that?'

'In case it had escaped your notice, there is a double murder investigation in progress, an investigation that DS Brooks—'

'DI Brooks,' Peters corrected.

'That DI Brooks should be leading,' Helen replied carefully. 'Every second spent pursuing this witch hunt against me is time that could be better used bringing Dordevic to book.'

'You're changing the subject, DI Grace.'

'I'm reminding you of your priorities. Now what's it to be? Are you going to charge me or can I leave?'

Helen stared at him, refusing to show any sign of weakness or fear. In truth, her nerves were jangling, but a show of force was vital now.

'What do you think, DI Brooks?' Peters said, turning to Helen's old friend. 'Do you think we have enough for now?'

'More than enough.'

Charlie clearly just wanted to leave, unable to meet Peters' or Helen's gaze.

'In that case, DI Grace, you are free to go – for now.'

Helen rose, pushing her chair back sharply, the metal legs scraping across the battered floor.

'You know the drill. Stay local, keep your phone on. No doubt we will have further questions for you in due course.'

Helen glared at her boss. Incredibly, he seemed to be enjoying himself.

'I would hope that in a matter of days we'll be in a position to tell you whether we intend to press criminal charges...'

How Helen longed to slap him – he really was milking this.

'In the meantime, you are suspended from your post, with DI Brooks taking over with immediate effect as head of the MIT.'

Helen chanced a look at her deputy, but Charlie's gaze remained rooted to the ground.

'We will, of course, require your warrant card before you leave.'

The corners of his mouth twitched, but Peters managed to suppress a smile. Even he was aware of the magnitude, the importance of this moment. Helen said nothing in response, a wave of nausea, of sadness sweeping over her. Her whole identity was wrapped up in this job, her whole reason for being, now she was being asked to willingly give it up.

She reached into her pocket, tugging out her warrant card

and slapping it down on the table. Stepping forward, Peters scooped it up quickly, before leaning into Helen. She flinched as his face came to rest next to hers, his soft whisper inaudible to the recording device.

'And don't count on getting it back any time soon, Helen...'

He couldn't resist injecting a note of triumph into his voice, as he concluded:

'You're done here.'

Chapter 98

He stabbed the button angrily, but it was no use. The doorbell was broken, a pointless decoration on the smart detached house. Irritated, DC Wilson knocked on the door, but there was no movement inside, so he stepped away, heading for the side gate instead. It had been a frustrating morning and he was determined not to leave empty-handed.

Clutching a photocopy of Dordevic's map, he tugged at the iron gate that led to the side access. The large property in Lordswood had been circled by the housebreaker and seemed a promising target – one elderly resident living alone, whose affluence was trumpeted by the trio of classic cars displayed on the front drive. Yet no attempted break-in had been reported, which seemed odd to Wilson, given the Serbian's efficiency in targeting the other properties on his list, before the *Enterprise*'s scheduled departure date. He was keen to talk to the owner, a Mr Edward Grey, but as yet there was no sign of the retired car dealer.

The side gate had a padlock on it, but it wasn't secured, so Wilson teased it off. Stepping into the side passage, he called out:

'Mr Grey?'

His voice echoed down the narrow passage, but elicited no response.

'Hello?'

Pressing on down the passageway, he spotted empty flower pots and an open bag of compost ahead, a pile of which was scattered on the paving stones. Picking his way carefully over the mess, he scanned the expansive garden. The lawn was beautifully maintained, the beds neatly planted; this was clearly the owner's pride and joy. Taking it in, Wilson became aware of noises emanating from the shed at the rear. Smiling, he strode quickly down the flagstone path. He had found his quarry.

'Mr Grey?'

There was movement within the neat wooden shed, but no response, so Japhet Wilson teased open the door and, offering another greeting, stepped inside. Immediately, he ground to a halt. A blade flashed towards him and he jerked his head back to avoid being hit. As he did so, he realized that there were in fact *three* sharp points arrowing towards him and now the situation became clear. His attacker was the property's elderly owner, who seemed intent on skewering his visitor with a garden fork.

Backing out of the shed, Wilson retrieved his warrant card.

'Easy there, sir. I'm a police officer. DC Japhet Wilson from Southampton Central.'

'Toss it here.'

Clearly Mr Grey was not going to take anything on trust, despite Wilson's neat appearance and polite manner. The latter did as he was asked, and after a moment's close inspection, the pensioner handed it back.

'What do you think you're doing, creeping up on me like that?'

'I did knock several times *and* call out to you. Perhaps you didn't hear me?'

'Been out here all morning, and my hearing's not what it was,' Grey replied truculently, tapping the hearing aid in his right ear.

'No problem. I'm sorry to have startled you.'

'Typical, though, isn't it? Never around when you're needed, always present when you're not.'

'I'm sorry?'

'Could have done with you the other night, but where were you then?'

'Can I ask what happened?' Wilson replied, suddenly interested in the old man's complaints.

'Bloody great brute tried to come in the back door. He had the lock half off by the time I caught him.'

'Did you confront him?'

'Of course, I bloody did. This is my property and I've seen off bigger than him in my time. Came at him with a poker – he didn't like that I can tell you.'

'Did you fight with this man?'

'Not really. He didn't see me coming, did he? It was late at night, perhaps he thought I was asleep. Anyhow, I came down to get a glass of water, saw what was happening and caught him on the side of his neck. Followed up with another to his ribs and he just turned and ran.'

'I see. And can you describe this man?'

'Six foot and a bit more, tattoos on his forearms.'

'Was he English?'

'Oh no, Russian maybe. Swore like a trooper in some such language as he legged it. Not made of the same stuff as us, are they?'

There was a glint in his eye, clearly pleased with his successful defence of the homestead.

'We don't seem to have any record of this incident on our system. Did you call it in?'

'What's the point? He wasn't coming back and it would have been a lot of fuss and paperwork for no good reason. I could live without it.'

Wilson was very tempted to lecture him about the importance of community policing – of reporting such incidents – but he decided to let it go as there were more pressing matters at hand. Tugging a photo of Marko Dordevic from his file, he handed it to Grey.

'Was this the guy?'

The pensioner studied the photo, running a finger over the tattoos, before replying:

'Yes, I'd say that was the fella.'

'And can I ask when this occurred?'

'It was a couple of nights ago. Thursday night.'

'And you say it was late in the evening?'

'Around quarter past ten.'

Wilson felt his heart sink, but he persisted nevertheless.

'How can you be sure of that timing?'

'I'd listened to the first two or three stories on the ten o'clock news – I like to have the radio on before bed – but then I got thirsty. It was definitely quarter past, give or take.'

Wilson smiled, but his hopes were dashed, the investigation having hit the buffers once more. If the old man was telling the truth, if Dordevic had tried to break in at that time, on that day, then there was no way he could have killed Ethan Westlake.

Chapter 99

The door slammed shut behind her, causing several startled drinkers to look up. Helen ignored them, walking straight to the bar. Leaning against it, she surveyed the glinting selection of optics, as the landlady of the Parrot and Two Chairmen approached.

'Lunch break, is it, Helen? What can I get you? Tonic, ice and a slice?'

Helen didn't look at her, didn't return her smile, as she said: 'Double vodka, please.'

There was a pregnant pause. Sally Rutherford had never seen Helen order an alcoholic drink in all the years she'd been coming here, for team-bonding sessions and send-offs.

'No ice,' Helen added, keen to get this over with.

'Whatever you say,' Sally responded, the warning note all too evident.

Helen ignored this, didn't need to be judged by her, on top of everything else. Taking the drink, she slipped a twenty-pound note onto the counter and headed off, without waiting for the change. Odds on, she would use up that credit in the hours to come.

Seeking out a discreet table at the back of the pub, Helen sat down, turning away from the other drinkers. She wanted to blot out the world, pretend it didn't exist. She didn't want people staring at her, gossiping about her and she certainly didn't need witnesses for what she was about to do. She hadn't touched a drop of alcohol in over twenty-five years, had seen what it had done to her parents, her sister, how it had driven them to become their darkest selves. But she needed the hit now and on instinct she had returned to the poison that she had first tasted when she was eleven. Clear, pure and punishingly strong, vodka had always been her route to oblivion.

Raising the glass to her lips, she took her first sip. The alcohol scorched her tongue, then slid down her throat with a slow burn. It didn't taste nice, but it jolted her system, her brain firing wildly as the liquor entered her bloodstream. It wasn't a pleasant feeling but it was what was required. She took another sip, then another and before long the glass was empty.

She'd hoped it would transport her away from her disgrace, from the regret, sadness and guilt that threatened to overwhelm her, but it provided no such release. Terrible visions kept dancing through her mind – Hudson's blood-smeared face, Peters' wolfish grin, Charlie's refusal to meet her gaze. Each was as bad as the other, her horror at Hudson's grim face matched by her anger towards Peters, who had finally claimed his catch. Oddly, though, it was Charlie's refusal to stand up for her, or at least her willingness to take over at the helm of MIT that cut the deepest. This was crazy, Helen knew that, this minor betrayal an irrelevance compared to the death of a man, but Helen couldn't deny that it hurt. Even though it was logical for Charlie to take her seat, it didn't seem right. After all they had been through together, the many times Helen had propped her old friend up, pulling her back from the brink, wasn't she due some loyalty? If Helen's career was over at Southampton Central – as seemed undeniable now – would her former deputy just slot seamlessly into her position, taking the extra kudos, responsibility and salary that came with the position, without once looking back? Try as she might, Helen couldn't conceal her anger, her disappointment, wondering what it meant for their friendship. Helen had often been a guest at their house for Christmas, birthdays and more, but how could she go there now?

Helen felt utterly adrift in the world. She had lost her badge, her purpose and looked set to lose the one friendship that had ever meant anything to her. She was alone, utterly alone, with only the ashes of her defeat for company. Clutching the glass, Helen turned her gaze towards the bar, determined to secure another shot. But as she did so, she found Sally staring right back at her, a concerned look on her face.

Helen dropped her eyes, not in anger but shame. Sally wasn't judging her, she was *worried* about her. Slamming down the glass, Helen rose. How stupid she was to have come here, how self-pitying her desire to dive into a vodka well. She had broken two and a half decades of sobriety and for what? The chance to blot everything out, to forget? There was precious little chance of her forgetting anything that had happened over the last twenty-four hours, so marching quickly to the door, she nodded curtly at Sally before taking her leave.

The answer was never to be found at the bottom of bottle. Even at the tender age of eleven, Helen had known that.

Chapter 100

Helen hurried down the street, wanting to put as much distance between herself and the pub as possible. The disasters that had befallen her had up until this point been the product of bad luck, bad faith and bad timing, none of the blame for which could be laid at her door. But this, this foolish moment of weakness, was hers to own.

Annoyed with herself, she strode on. Whatever indignities lay in store, she must not bow her head, she must not give in. She had been a police officer for more years than she cared to remember and had always fulfilled her duties efficiently, effectively and with pride. This realization, this memory, seemed to give her renewed strength. Yes, her paranoia, her fearfulness, may have made her rash, even reckless, but over the years she had proved what an honest, upstanding, trustworthy public servant she was. She must remember that as the blows landed over the coming days and weeks, keeping her head held high, apologizing for nothing, defending herself and her record with all her might.

This was easier said than done, of course. Despite her bluster, her concerted rearguard action, guilt hovered just beneath the surface. Not for Hudson per se, who had in many ways invited his eventual oblivion, but for those who were left behind. Hudson played little part in the lives of his ex-wife Karen and son Kieran, Helen knew that, but they still loved him. His passing would affect them deeply, the little boy especially, and there would be no denying Helen's part in this tragedy. It was *this* ultimately that would keep Helen awake at night. Should she call them? Reach out to them? And if so, what on earth would she say?

Helen was still pondering this when she became aware of something. Footsteps behind her, mirroring her pace. In an instant, she knew that it was him – her assassin had returned.

It didn't seem possible, but once more she had stumbled into danger. Her bike was parked a fair distance from the station, in a multi-storey car park. Could she make it there before he set upon her? Probably not. Could she dart back to Southampton Central? Again no, not without turning in his direction. No, she would have to find another way out of this.

He was gaining on her, just ten paces or so behind. Helen's eyes darted left and right, searching for some means of salvation, but there was nothing, no escape route, no weapon to hand. In the reflection of a shop window, she saw the shadowy figure bearing down on her. Panicking, she wondered if she should dart into one of the stores that lined the street, but would that save her? If this guy was desperate enough to attack her in broad daylight at a service station, who was to say he wouldn't do so in there, stabbing her in front of the horrified shoppers? No, there was no question of exposing members of the public to that danger; Helen would have to deal with this herself.

Up ahead, she spotted an alleyway, a cut-through linking this street to the next. Perhaps she could make to walk past it, then change direction, sprinting away to safety? It wasn't much of a plan but it was the best she could come up with and readied herself for the challenge. The mouth of the alleyway was soon upon her, and, taking her chance, she dived down it. Only to find her route blocked.

A lorry was stationed in the passageway, its rear doors open, crates of beer bottles clogging the path, as a delivery was made. Helen hesitated for a second, but it was a second too long. The footsteps sped up, he was almost upon her now. She had only an instant to react.

Lurching forwards, she grabbed a crate, hauling it up and over her shoulder in his direction. A dull thud, a groan and then an ear-splitting crash, but still he kept coming. This time, however, Helen was ready, taking advantage of his momentary distraction, to swing an arcing leg along the ground. Her heavy boot crashed into his ankles, sweeping them from the floor and for a second he was airborne, before coming to the ground with a savage thump. Now Helen pressed home her advantage, pulling a beer bottle from a nearby crate and smashing it, sticky, bubbly lager cannoning up into the air. Her attacker was trying to get to his feet, but Helen fell upon him, pressing the jagged edge to his neck.

'You move an inch and you're a dead man,' she hissed, meaning every word of it.

Her assailant, the man who'd already tried to kill her twice before, held up his arms in surrender.

'Please, I don't mean you any harm.'

'Are you serious? You tried to stab me, you crazy bastard.'

'I know and I'm so sorry. I should never have listened to him.'

Helen kept the bottle pressed to his neck, but eased off the pressure a little, intrigued by this tacit mention of Alex Blythe. But her captive clearly still felt in peril, his shrill voice insisting:

'Please, Helen. I didn't come here today to hurt you. I want to *help* you.'

Chapter *101*

'Start talking.'

The glass bottle was still pressed to his neck and Helen wasn't minded to release it. Nearby, the delivery man was eyeing the confrontation, talking anxiously to the bar owner, but Helen ignored them, her focus riveted on the powerless stalker who lay in her clutches.

'Name?'

He said nothing, squirming a little in her grip, before giving up the fight.

'Nicholas Martin,' he whispered, his shame clear.

'Did Alex Blythe put you onto me?'

'Yes.'

It was a gasp; part confession, part release. Helen had the sense this tortured figure had been living with his dark secret for some time now.

'Because he had compromising information on you?'

The man lowered his eyes, but nodded. Helen felt the jagged edge of the bottle press into his soft flesh and now removed it. The man seemed to sag in her arms, flooded with relief that she was not going to make good on her threat.

'I'm so ... I'm so sorry, Helen. I have nothing against you personally, I never wanted to harm you, I ...'

'You just couldn't see another way out,' Helen added, finishing the thought for him. 'Look, Nicholas, I'm not interested in what you've done, what he's got on you. Maybe I should be, but I suspect you won't go there again after this, that you'll seek the help you need...'

Martin nodded purposefully and Helen believed him.

'I'm only interested in Blythe. Tell me how he contacted you?'

'He phoned me. He has my mobile number and he rang me three weeks ago.'

'Landline? Mobile?'

'I'm not sure. Number withheld.'

'What did he say?'

'Just that he would tell my family, my friends, my colleagues everything, unless I agreed... agreed to kill you.'

He could barely say the words, as if disbelieving that he could ever have contemplated something so reckless.

'Of course, I told him to piss off. But he called again three days later, then three days after that. In that third conversation, I asked for details. I thought I wasn't committing, that I could find a fault in his plan, dissuade him even. But I was just kidding myself. He had it all worked out – told me where you lived, worked, who your friends are, how to do it... And I... I allowed myself to believe that I could do such a thing.'

He looked pitiful, bereft, a man caught between arrest and disgrace.

'When was your last call with him?'

'Two days ago. He gave me my final warning.'

'Which is when you confronted me at the service station.'

Another nod.

'Do you think he'll call again?'

'I'd imagine so. If he doesn't hear that you're dead, he'll ring to challenge me. He's desperate... desperate to hurt you, but I sense he doesn't have anyone else who's ... stupid enough to play ball. Otherwise, he would have dumped me days ago; I'm hardly cut out for this sort of thing.'

Helen felt cheered by this. Perhaps Blythe wasn't the bogeyman she'd built him up to be; perhaps his exposure and flight from justice had weakened his power over his charges.

'Maybe we can use the present situation to our advantage ...'

Helen couldn't believe she was saying this, as if Hudson's death and her disgrace could somehow be a positive thing.

'... you can buy yourself some time by saying that I was in custody, that you couldn't get to me. But when he calls you, you're going to have to say exactly what I tell you, in exactly the way I tell you to say it. Can you do that for me?'

'Yes, yes. I want to help you, really I do. Whatever happens to me now, I don't want Blythe to win.'

He seemed sincere, desperate even, to make amends for his attempted assassination. And for the first time in days, Helen felt a shiver of excitement pass through her. Her life was over – friendships broken and her career at Southampton Central finished – but maybe, if things went to plan, she might be able to take Dr Alex Blythe down with her.

Chapter 102

It was wrong. It was all just plain wrong.

Charlie stood in Helen's office, as she had countless times before, but now she was on the business side of the desk. No longer the supplicant, the loyal deputy. Now she was in charge.

In other circumstances, she might have been exhilarated by this sudden elevation, but in truth she felt sick. She was still in shock, the events of the last forty-eight hours having barely sunk in. Each disaster, each setback, seemed to be followed by something worse. Steve's betrayal, Hudson's sudden death, Helen's arrest, then that hideous interrogation this morning, Peters seeming to take great delight in torturing both Helen and Charlie during that awful dance in the interview suite.

Charlie's black mood had not been improved by the team's reaction as she took the helm, shortly after Helen's release. She had tried to front it out, concealing her nausea and distress by pitching her elevation as the natural and obvious course of events. And of course it *was*, but that didn't stop people looking at her oddly, as if she was clambering over her friend's body to get to the top. Did they really think so little of her? Surely they knew that she was hating every minute of it?

Raising her eyes from the desk, she glanced out into the incident room. Several heads were down, chasing up leads, but now she met DC Ellie McAndrew's gaze. The experienced officer immediately broke eye contact, turning away from her and moments later was on the move, making her way to the exit as fast as she could, clutching phone, coat and bag. Charlie felt as if she'd been punched, as if her colleague was bailing on her, a rat scurrying from a sinking ship. Another small, but significant betrayal.

'Come on, Charlie. You can do this...'

She wanted to convince herself, but the idea of concluding a major investigation without Helen's guidance felt all wrong. They had fought shoulder-to-shoulder for years, how would she cope alone? A long, difficult future seemed to spread out in front of Charlie. The next few weeks would test her resolve, expertise and professionalism as never before, even as her personal life unravelled, and she suddenly felt completely unprepared for the challenge.

Rising, she snatched up her phone. Her nerves were on edge, her confidence shot, but she knew it would be better to be outside – corralling the team and driving the investigation forward – than locked away in Helen's tiny office, letting fear and anxiety overwhelm her.

Pushing through the door, she was surprised to see DC Wilson hurrying towards her.

'Got a minute...'

He was clearly about to say 'DS Brooks', but changed his mind at the last minute, adding 'guv' to the end of his question.

'Fire away.'

'So I tracked down Edward Grey. He owns one of the properties that Dordevic was planning to target?'

'And?'

'Well, Dordevic *did* go there, but the old boy saw him off.'

'I see,' Charlie replied, suddenly interested. 'When was this?'

Wilson paused, his face falling, as he replied:

'Thursday night, around 10.15 p.m. And before you ask, he's one hundred per cent sure of the identification and the timing.'

Charlie stared at him, speechless.

'On the way back here, I've been tying myself in knots, trying to work out if there's any way he could have attacked Ethan Westlake and still made it to Grey's house by quarter past, but Ethan's gaming stopped suddenly at 10.08 p.m. and, given the distances between the properties, I just don't think it's possible, which means...'

Charlie didn't let him finish, applying the coup de grace herself.

'That we're back to square one.'

Chapter 103

He stood stock-still on the doormat, overwhelmed by the crushing silence. Greg White had been building up to this moment, convincing himself that this was their home, their *family* home, and that a swift visit to gather some fresh clothes shouldn't be beyond him. He didn't need to hang around, could be in and out in thirty seconds. But the spirit of Martha's killer seemed to linger in the sepulchral quiet, poisoning the atmosphere. He was tempted to turn and run, but something – a sliver of pride, defiance? – stemmed his panic. It was madness to be run out of his own home by a feeling, by his own rioting emotions. How complete did he want her killer's victory to be?

He found himself moving, marching up the stairs. Battening down his emotions, he made swift progress, cresting the landing and hurrying into Bailey's room, scooping up great piles of clothes and toys, stuffing them into his bag. Each childish bauble, each item of clothing threatened to undo him, as they had all been carefully selected with love by Martha, but he persisted and was soon padding across the landing to the master bedroom.

His hand shook as he grasped the handle. For a moment, he was back there on that awful night, pushing into the room, finding his beautiful wife spread-eagled on the bed...

'Please, God, no...'

He screwed up his eyes, trying to banish this nightmarish image, then pushed down on the handle. The door opened and he stepped inside. He left the light off and kept his gaze away from the bed, which he knew was now stripped and naked, the mattress and bedding having been carted off to the police laboratory. He tugged open the wardrobe, threw more clothes in at random, then hurried over to the chest of drawers to complete his mission. This also looked odd – Martha's jewellery boxes having been removed – and he paused now as he noticed a covering of white powder on the surface, where the police had dusted for prints. He stared at this residue, horrified by the idea of a brutish, sweaty murderer laying his hands all over their things, dark thoughts once more crowding in on him.

A sudden sound made him jump, snapping him out of his hideous daydream. His phone was buzzing violently in his pocket, playing the *Succession* ring tone that he'd bought a few days ago when trivial fun still seemed possible. Greg located it quickly, fearful that it would be his mother reporting some fresh problem with Bailey, and was relieved to see that it was Southampton Central calling. He hesitated, his finger hovering over the answer button – it could be an important development in the case, but was more likely DC Wilson chasing him about that bloody Fitbit – then ended the call. The thought of having a long conversation, here of all places, was too much for him to bear.

Pocketing his phone, Greg pulled open the middle drawer, scooping up his clothes and dumping them in his holdall. Now he was tugging the zip closed – suddenly his nerve, his composure, had deserted him and he wanted be away from this place. Shutting the drawer, he snatched up the bag and hurried from the room. Crossing the landing, he took the stairs two at a time, desperate to be outside in the fresh air, as if this alone could somehow banish his dark thoughts. As he reached the ground floor, however, he slowed, clocking something. An envelope lying on the doormat.

Momentarily, he was thrown. The envelope hadn't been there when he arrived moments earlier, so must have just been delivered. Its arrival was not in itself surprising – dozens of sympathy cards had been delivered in the past few days – but it was odd that he hadn't heard the letterbox, whose rusty hinges always squeaked. Putting his bag down, Greg moved forward to scoop it up. He found these cards painful to read, but they did on occasion provide some comfort, if only because they showed that people cared, that they too loved Martha and were desperate to help. It was generally best to get these things over with, so he tore open the envelope eagerly.

As he did so, he was surprised to realize that there was no card inside, that the envelope was floppy and light. For a moment, he thought it might be empty, a hoax even, but now he became aware that there *was* something inside. It felt small and heavy, like a two-pound coin, as if someone had made a donation to him. This was clearly ridiculous, a comic notion, so he tugged open the envelope, curious as to its contents.

Immediately, he gasped, unable to believe his eyes. It couldn't be ... but it was. Sickened, horrified, he wrenched open the front door and ran outside, his holdall redundant and forgotten on the polished wooden floor.

Chapter 104

He tore down the pathway, his feet pounding the smooth stone. As he did so, Greg's eyes scanned the street, desperately seeking the fleeing figure. Seeing no one, he hauled open the front gate, spilling out onto the pavement. Now he clocked movement to his right... but it was just a local mum pushing a pram, clearly startled by his sudden appearance.

Turning away, he stepped between the parked cars and ran out into the road. He fully expected to see a man haring away and was fully primed to give chase. In fact, he would have run a marathon, would have run until his feet were blistered and bloody to catch this bastard, but incredibly he was nowhere to be seen. How much of a head start had he had?

His hands were shaking, sweat was running down the crease in his back and he felt dangerously light-headed, but he mounted the opposite pavement, scanning along the line of parked cars to see if his quarry was hiding here. But there were no signs of life, no movement of any kind. It defied belief, yet another moment of exquisite torture in a brutal, brutal week. Her killer – Martha's killer – had been right here, walking these pavements, marching up their garden path bold as brass and now he had vanished into thin air. How was that possible? What kind of phantom was this guy that he could ghost up to their house, deliver his little gift, adding outrage to outrage, then just... evaporate?

Greg was moving along the line of cars, tugging at the handles, convinced that Martha's attacker had secreted himself in one of the vehicles. At the fourth attempt, the car's alarm sprang into life, wailing loudly, but Greg ignored it, working his way steadily up the line, before crossing the road to try the other side.

He had to be here, he *had* to be. How Greg would enjoy throwing him to the ground, stamping on him, punching him, letting him feel the full force of his rage and grief. If he went to prison for it subsequently, so be it. His blood was up, his fury at this man's depravity red hot. But as he reached the last car in the line, it became clear that his tormentor was not in any of the cars, or indeed anywhere on the street. Greg emitted a low, anguished moan, which was saturated in despair and disappointment.

Where the hell was he?

Chapter 105

Where was she?

Emilia glanced at her watch, frustrated and annoyed. Having been turned away from Southampton Central, she had journeyed to Helen's apartment block, hopeful of snagging her prize there. She'd heard that she'd been released pending further investigation, so surely she would return home to her sanctuary, to hole up and consider her next moves? Yet two hours on from Emilia's arrival, there was no sign of her. Where had she gone?

A loud screech made Emilia look up and her heart lifted as the metal grille began its slow mechanical rise. She had driven underneath it herself, taking advantage of one of the other flat owners' exits, just sneaking her Corsa below the descending barrier. She had congratulated herself on her speed of thought and cunning, convinced she would now secure her prize. But once more her optimism gave way to annoyance, as she spotted a BMW saloon enter the underground car park, driven cautiously by an elderly man.

Picking up her phone from the dashboard, she pressed redial. But once more she heard her adversary's measured tones:

'This is Helen Grace, please leave a message.'

She hung up, tossing the phone onto the seat next to her, but now she heard something that made her heart leap. The throaty roar of a motorbike. Right on cue, Grace's Kawasaki came into view, swinging round a concrete pillar and pulling up sharply in the bike park. Emilia's door was already open and she was nearly upon her when Grace turned to face her, her expression one of simmering rage.

'Helen, we meet again...'

'You're trespassing.'

'Only technically. And I would love a quick w—'

'This is private property, you have five seconds to leave.'

'Or you'll what? Call the police?'

Emilia knew it was naughty, but she couldn't resist.

'I'm not sure they're taking your calls anymore, are they? Not after the unfortunate incident with Joseph Hudson. Could I ask you a couple of questions about that?'

Simmering anger now seemed to turn to rage, Helen Grace's eyes narrowing as she advanced towards the journalist.

'Did he attack you? Is that what happened?'

Still she marched towards her.

'Was it suicide? An accident?'

Helen had now stopped directly in front of her, eyeing Emilia with evident disgust.

'Please, Helen. I can't leave my readers in the dark over this. You've got to give me something to print...'

And now something seemed to change in Helen's countenance, her face relaxing, as an expression of bitter triumph stole across her features.

'Print this.'

And so saying, Helen Grace stepped forward and punched Emilia squarely in the face.

Chapter 106

She slammed the door shut behind her, moving fast towards the kitchen. Grabbing a glass from the rack, Helen filled it with cold, crisp water, drinking it down in one go. It was refreshing, revitalizing, but did nothing to stem the raging torrent of recrimination swirling inside. What the hell was she doing? What was *wrong* with her?

Biking home, she had initially been buoyed by her encounter with Nicholas Martin, hoping now that she might be able to resolve at least one aspect of her current crisis. But as each minute passed, her optimism had started to dissipate. Would Blythe really allow himself to be trapped? Would a spineless worm like Nicholas Martin really prove to be the instrument of her liberation? Suddenly it seemed a preposterous notion and Helen found herself in a troubled, fitful mood as she returned to her flat. Just the wrong frame of mind in which to be ambushed by Emilia Garanita.

Her response to meeting the veteran journalist was inexcusable, but somehow in that moment, years of antagonism and hostility had come together, Garanita's evident enjoyment of her predicament, her casual indifference to Joseph Hudson's death, enraging Helen beyond measure. She had been assailed by red mist, by frustration, by an overwhelming sense of how

360

catastrophically her life had imploded and for a brief second it appeared as if there was nothing holding her back, as if she couldn't fall any lower, so she had lashed out, knocking her long-term adversary onto her backside.

It was an image which gave Helen fleeting pleasure, but her overriding emotions now were shame and frustration. Emilia was already set to enjoy Helen's downfall and Helen had handed her extra ammunition. She would eviscerate Helen's character in the *Evening News*, portraying her as unhinged, out of control, a killer – all of which was hard to deny. She could even seek to press charges, dragging Helen back to Southampton Central in cuffs. How her nemesis would enjoy that.

Helen had contrived to shoot herself in the foot and padding into the quiet living room, she was suddenly crushed by a feeling of desolation. She had been so caught up in the horror of Hudson's death and the subsequent torture of her arrest and interrogation, that she hadn't had a moment to consider what lay ahead for her. But now, isolated and rudderless, a bleak vision of hopelessness, of impotence, spread out before her. She had spent many hours in this space, pacing the floor, trying to solve any number of baffling cases. It had been her special place, a place where the various pieces of the jigsaw seemed to fit together better, where the guilty parties presented themselves to her, but what would she do here now without that urgent impetus? How would she fill the long, blank days ahead?

Standing alone in the silent room, Helen was confronted by the most pressing question she'd ever faced. Without family, without a job and without purpose, what was she *for*?

Chapter 107

She knew it was time to ask the question, to confront Steve with his wrongdoing, but still she hesitated. Did she really want to do this?

Charlie watched her partner as he carefully hung out the last of the clothes on the rack. Having heard what was going down at Southampton Central, he'd rushed home to field the kids and knock up dinner, even promising to stay home tonight, rather than working late as per usual. The dishwasher was burbling away, the girls were reading happily upstairs and Steve was finishing off the chores of the day. This, then, was Charlie's opportunity. But could she get the words out?

'Charlie?'

She'd zoned out, lost in her own thoughts.

'Sorry, I was miles away.'

'I said, do you want a hot drink?'

She shook her head gently.

'OK, well, I might go and check on the girls, then. If you're sure you're OK, that is...?'

They had talked over dinner about Helen and the awful predicament Charlie found herself in and Steve had been sympathetic and supportive, but still she didn't feel any better.

'Yes, I'm fine,' she lied.

'Good, well, I'll be back in a jiff—'

'Actually, I'm not fine...'

Steve stopped, surprised.

'...and I need to ask you something,' Charlie continued quickly.

'Go on,' Steve replied cautiously, unnerved by her tone.

'I don't want you to soft-soap me or bullshit me or do anything other than be completely honest.'

'OK...'

'Are you having an affair?'

She got the words out just before emotion ambushed, choking her voice.

'I'm sorry?' he replied, ashen.

'You heard me. Are you having an affair?'

Steve stared at his partner with ill-concealed horror.

'No, no. I never *would*. What on earth...?'

He seemed genuinely astonished, but could she trust him? She'd known many men lie to their girlfriends – swear blind that white was black – before being eventually caught out.

'Why would you think that, Charlie?'

Now he seemed hurt, even angry, so Charlie continued quickly:

'We hardly see other anymore. When we *are* both here, it's like you're not interested in me, finding any excuse to get out of the house.'

'That's not true.'

'So why have you worked late every night this week? And the one before that? You never want to spend time with me anymore. Who's out there who's so much more interesting than me?'

'No one, I swear.'

'Then who were you talking to in the garden the other night? You arranged to meet them, told them you loved them and half jumped out of your skin when you clocked me...'

And now Steve's face fell, crumpling up in discomfort and embarrassment.

'Oh God, Charlie, what a mess.'

Charlie braced herself for what was coming next.

'The last thing I ever meant to do was hurt you...'

'What?' Charlie demanded.

'I'm only staying out late at night because of you...'

'Because of *me*?' Charlie shot back tersely.

'I mean *for* you, *for* us...'

'Look, stop speaking in riddles, Steve. You told me you had to work late, but when I went down to the garage, it was clear you haven't been there after hours in months.'

'Because I was at the lock-up, there's where I've been most nights.'

Now Charlie was more confused than ever. Steve had a lock-up near the train station, but he'd never made much use of it, more a dumping ground than a workshop.

'I don't understand...'

'Look, I didn't want you to know until our anniversary, but I've got you a little present. It's old and needed an awful lot of TLC, but it's nearly there.'

He picked up his phone, opened the photo app and handed it to her.

'I know you've always wanted one and I couldn't resist.'

Charlie stared at the picture. The workshop was dimly illuminated by a naked bulb, but plum in the middle of the scruffy space was a bright yellow Mustang.

'That's where I've been. That's the other lady in my life...'

'But... but who were you talking to in the garden? Why did you say those things?'

Instead of answering her, Steve bent down, opening one of the low storage cupboards. Pulling out a number of Tupperware boxes, he removed a long strip of shiny paper that had been secreted behind the containers.

'This was going to be the icing on the cake, draped over the bonnet for the grand unveiling,' Steve said, as he unfurled the silver banner. 'You must have heard me ordering it from Janice the other night.'

Looking down at the banner, Charlie took in the message: I LOVE YOU spelled out in baby blue letters. She let out a gulp of laughter, even as tears filled her eyes. She had been so worried, so sure Steve had lost interest in her, that her relief now was overwhelming. But this feeling of release soon gave way to other more powerful emotions – embarrassment and shame.

'Oh, Steve, I'm so sorry...'

'You've nothing to apologize for, sweetheart. I know you're under crazy pressure, that all this stuff is messing with your head. But please know that you can trust me, that I'll never cheat on you, because *I really love you.*'

'Even when I look like this,' Charlie replied, gesturing dismissively at herself.

'Especially when you look like that,' he said crossing to her, putting his arms around her. 'You're the most gorgeous girl in the world. I would never look at another woman, unless, of course, she was a vintage American automobile...'

She punched him playfully, then snuggled into his arms. He continued to reassure her, stroking her hair, kissing her forehead, but she was barely listening anymore, just losing herself in his embrace. For the first time in ages, she felt relaxed, wanted, at peace, chiding herself now for being so foolish. She had feared the worst, imagining a loveless future full of conflict and complications, riven with problems and pain, when in reality there had been no betrayal, no infidelity.

She had made the whole thing up.

Chapter 108

Was she imagining it? Or had she really heard a noise downstairs?

Kay Sheffield stood at the top of the stairs, peering down into the darkness below. She was exhausted, ready to collapse into bed, but she felt certain she'd heard a muffled bang. She was not prone to paranoia, would normally have dismissed the idea that there was an intruder in the house, but given that there was a violent prowler on the loose, it was understandable that all sorts of unpleasant images now swirled round her mind.

Should she call James at the shop? Call the police? No, that seemed ridiculous, completely over the top. No, best to go downstairs, reassure herself that nothing was amiss, then hit the hay as she'd originally planned. Flicking on the lights, she hurried down the stairs, pausing at the bottom to retrieve James's old hockey stick from the hall cupboard. Her husband didn't use it anymore, said he was too old for contact sports, but it still had its uses and she enjoyed its weight in her hand. It wouldn't help her much if there *was* a homicidal maniac in the kitchen, but she could at least give him something to think about.

Amused by this thought, she marched into the nearby living room, completing a quick circuit of it, before continuing on to the kitchen. This too was empty, but still she paused for a moment to look out into the night. How she loathed January, she thought to herself, how she hankered for spring. For light, warmth, comfort and life. Turning, she continued her tour, checking out the utility room and downstairs bathroom, before returning to the hall, confident now that she was jumping at shadows. Replacing the hockey stick in the cupboard, she turned her attention to the small keypad on the wall. She'd warned James that she was going to activate the alarm on the ground floor when she went to bed – until this maniac was caught, at least. She just hoped her husband remembered to disable it before he opened the front door.

The alarm bleeped loudly, signalling that it had been activated. Satisfied, Kay climbed the stairs, chiding herself for having delayed her retreat to bed. She had been looking forward to this all day, having tossed and turned all night, and entered her bedroom with a broad grin spread across her face.

Tonight she would enjoy the sleep of angels.

Chapter 109

He watched her bedroom light blink out. The moment was close at hand now and once more he felt his heart thump in his chest.

He was wound tight tonight, his nerves fraught, his head pulsing. On more than one occasion already, he'd considered giving up, retreating to safety, convinced he was about to be discovered. Firstly, when he'd accidentally knocked one of their wheelie bins against the side door, then shortly afterwards when the lights had suddenly clicked on downstairs. Moments later, Kay Sheffield had appeared in the kitchen, staring out into the night. Part of him expected her to throw open the doors and race to confront him on the shadowy lawn, but thankfully she had eventually turned away. Moments later, he heard the dull bleep of the alarm activating, before his prey rose to the first floor, entering the master bedroom.

Their room looked out onto the large garden and though the curtains were closed, he could still make out her shadowy form, undressing, and visiting the bathroom, before heading to bed. She was a woman of habit and at ten thirty the bedroom light was once again extinguished, plunging the upper floor into darkness. Now was the time for him to focus, to make his preparations, and checking his kit, he slid on his leather gloves, building himself up for what was to come. He remained crouched in the darkness for a further fifteen minutes, then, reassured that all was quiet, he padded out of his hiding place, towards the wheelie bins concealed behind the adjoining garage.

In moving them earlier, he had made a mistake, a moment's clumsiness that could have cost him dear. Now he was more deliberate, more cautious, easing himself up onto the brown waste bin, before slowly straightening up. Now he let his gloved fingers play over the brickwork until they reached the lip of the flat garage roof. Testing his grip, he pushed off the bin, pulling hard with his hands whilst his feet bounced up the brickwork. Moments later, he was standing on top of the flat roof. As this was the most conspicuous point of his journey, he didn't linger, padding across the roof to the window of the family bathroom.

Kay never used this room. It appeared to be reserved for her husband, whilst she monopolized the master bedroom. He suspected James Sheffield used it to perch on the toilet whilst reading arcane magazines about furniture restoration. It was a comic image, but he pushed it from his mind now. His business here was deadly serious.

The window was a wide, double-glazed affair, with a smaller ventilation window at the top. This was almost never closed, allowing a free flow of air at all times, and sliding a knee onto the windowsill, he reached up to the guttering and rose swiftly, slipping an arm in through the opening. Feeling around, he quickly located the handle for the larger pane, and pushing in the little key, turned it. The window sighed gently as it opened and he paused once more to listen. But there was no movement inside, nothing to hinder his progress.

Holding tight to the window frame, he lowered one foot into the bath, then another, sliding his rangy form inside the room. Then, turning, he shut the window, locking out the night. Satisfied, he stepped lightly onto the tiled floor, before teasing open the bathroom door. Once again he paused, wondering if he would be able to hear any movement above the thumping in his chest, but mercifully the house was at peace. Reaching inside his coat, he pulled out the hatchet and taking care to tread as lightly as possible, padded swiftly across the plush carpet towards the master bedroom.

Chapter 110

'Are you sure you want to do this? It's not too late to back out.'

Victoria Westlake peered through the gap in the curtains, taking in the crowd of journalists who'd gathered in their front garden. Alerted by her husband, they had come eagerly and in force, intrigued by his mysterious summons.

'We don't have a choice. I spoke to the FLO, like you asked, and she confirmed that they're going to have to release the guy they've got in custody.'

'You didn't tell me.'

'I've only just got off the phone to her and, besides, I wasn't sure you wanted to talk to me. You seem so... so angry all the time.'

'I'm not angry with you, of course I'm not,' Victoria insisted. 'I just don't want what... what happened to Ethan to become part of some circus.'

She gestured to the throng of reporters below.

'Once we let the genie out the bottle, I'm not sure we'll ever get it back in. You'll be pulled into their "story", they'll feel they have carte blanche to contact us at any time of the day or night. Whereas at the moment, we can use the police as a shield to keep them away from us.'

'And what good has that done? Are they any closer to catching this guy?'

'I don't know. You're the one that's had all the conversations with them.'

He turned away from her, angered by her jibe.

'I just don't think it's our job,' she persisted, 'to play detective. To bribe people into giving us information.'

'We've been through this. It's not a bribe...'

'What's to stop people leading us on a dozen wild goose chases just because they spot an opportunity to make a fast buck? Why would we let people profit from... from Ethan's death?'

'Look, Victoria,' Richard replied, his manner formal and cold. 'I understand your concerns, but I want to do this. Someone out there...'

He stabbed a finger at the window, gesturing to the dark night beyond the curtains.

'...knows what happened to our son. Knows why he died, knows why that bastard came to this house. I need to know that and I need to know it soon. I think I'll go mad if I don't...'

And now his grief pushed through, his anguish clear to see. Victoria wanted to hug him, to draw him to her, but she could see he didn't want comfort tonight. He wanted to act.

'Well, if you feel you must do it, then I can't stop you. But honestly, I think this will only make things worse for us. It'll antagonize the police for starters—'

'They can go to hell.'

'And I don't think it'll get us any further on.'

'Well, I guess we'll have to agree to disagree.'

Victoria felt a stab of sorrow, of despair in her soul. It was said with such hissed vehemence, such force, that she couldn't help but feel the fissure in their love.

'I'm doing this, Victoria. Obviously, I'd like your blessing, but either way it's going to happen. I can't sit here and do nothing, whilst the killer's out there. I just can't.'

Having said his piece, he walked out, shutting the door firmly behind him. The noise reverberated through the house, breaking Victoria's heart in two, sounding every inch like the death knell of their marriage.

Chapter *III*

He stared at her, gripping the hatchet in his hand.

Kay Sheffield was face down on the bed, moaning quietly, her hands tightly bound. She had been the easiest of the lot to subdue, comatose to the world when he eased open her bedroom door and crept inside. She had been lying on her side already and needed just a gentle nudge to roll onto her front. She'd complained gently when he pulled her wrists behind her back, but remained utterly unaware of the danger she was in, even as he tugged the elasticated cord tight. It was only when he stuffed the rag into her mouth that she finally came alive – but by then it was too late.

She had thrashed and cried, but a solid punch to the back of her head had silenced her. After that, she had lain totally still, groaning pitifully and emitting the occasional stifled sob, whilst he removed her wedding rings and emptied her jewellery rack. Satisfied with his haul, he'd then returned to the bed.

Kay turned her head slightly at his approach. As she did so, one eye crept open, looking up at him in fright, as if realizing for the first time what was happening. She groaned, deep, despairing, as her pupils grew wide.

'Please…'

She mumbled the word, the rag in her mouth rendering it dull and indistinct.

'Please, don't hurt m—'

He brought the axe down, slamming it into the back of her skull. Once, twice, three times. Now he was slashing at her back, her shoulders, her arms, in a frenzy of anger and anguish. On and on he went, before shuddering to a halt, exhausted and breathless. Looking down at his victim, he was both awed and sickened by what he'd done. The terrified woman, who'd been living and breathing thirty seconds ago, was now a wretched, bloody mess.

Turning away from the scene of the butchery, he was alarmed to see that he looked little better. Catching sight of himself in the wardrobe mirror, he realized that his face, neck and coat were covered in her blood. What the hell was he thinking? How could he have been so reckless, so self-indulgent? Furious, he hurried from the room. He had been so careful up until now, so cautious, why had he lost control at this late stage?

Gathering his wits, he told himself to remain calm. Everything would be all right if he could keep his cool, remember the plan. He had toyed with climbing out the bathroom window, retracing his steps, but Kay's husband was not due home for another hour and it would be simpler to slip out the back door. If he could get to the end of the garden and away, then he would have the chance to clean himself up, then quietly, discreetly resume his place in the fabric of this brooding city. He just had to hold his nerve.

He hurried across the landing, grabbing the post at the top of the stairs as he threw himself down. Reaching the turn, he swung around to descend to the hallway and as he did so, he noticed three things. The temperature was icily cold down here, the front was door wide open and standing in the hallway, his face a mask of shock and terror, was James Sheffield.

Chapter *112*

She couldn't keep her eyes off him, her gaze riveted to the small screen.

'Which is why I'm announcing today that we are offering £50,000 to anyone who brings forward concrete information that leads to the arrest of our son's killer.'

Helen leaned forward, thunderstruck. What Richard Westlake was proposing was madness, would set the investigation back days, perhaps even weeks, flooding the incident with all manner of half-baked theories and spurious leads. Not that the assembled press seemed to mind, drinking in the drama of the moment, flashlights popping in the night sky as the newspaper reporters jockeyed for position with the TV crews.

'We believe this is the best way to bring our son's killer to book and keep Southampton safe. We'd urge anyone with information about this terrible crime to come forward.'

He was polished, in command, as if this whole circus was normal. He seemed to be implying that Hampshire Police had endorsed this unexpected twist in the tale, but surely Charlie hadn't signed off on this? It would be reckless in the extreme. But there was no way of knowing for sure; Helen was on the outside looking in and didn't think the new boss of the MIT would welcome her call. In all probability, though, she was just as shocked as Helen.

Initially, Helen had decided to hide herself away. Drop the blinds, turn on the TV and tune out, pretending the world outside didn't exist. But when she'd stumbled onto the local BBC news and heard the newscaster say that Richard Westlake was holding an impromptu press conference, Helen hadn't been able to resist tuning in. Old habits die hard.

'I'd like to put on record my gratitude to my family and friends, and of course the local community, who have been an enormous source of comfort during these dark times.'

Helen noted how he scrupulously avoided thanking the police. Had there been some falling out? Some kind of problem? Was this *her* fault for not having spent enough time reassuring the bereaved parents? Speaking of which, where was Victoria Westlake? Was she absent simply because she didn't want to face the cameras? Or was she against her husband's decision to monetize the hunt for Ethan's murderer?

'I have nothing more to say now...'

A volley of questions flew at him, the hacks scared he was about to retreat into the house, but to his credit, Westlake pressed on, ignoring them.

'...except that... that we were and remain very proud of our beautiful boy. Ethan was loving, kind, a constant ray of sunshine in our lives. He will be terribly, terribly missed by all who knew him and I...'

He paused for a moment, emotion almost overwhelming him, before concluding:

'...and I am so devastated, so ashamed that we weren't there to protect him when he needed us most.'

Now his composure *did* desert him, tears coursing down his face. Turning, he hurried back inside, pursued by journalists' questions, but his job was done. He'd made the appeal, he'd shared his pain and the result would be a frenzy of interest from the local and national press. It was a very heartfelt appeal, but, sadly, a deeply unhelpful intervention.

Turning the TV off, Helen stalked over to the balcony, throwing the window open. Freezing air ripped over her face, her exposed shoulders, but it didn't refresh her in the slightest. She felt hot, flustered and annoyed, powerless to influence events and tormented by her ignorance. McAndrew had given her a two-sentence summary of where they were at – Dordevic would be charged with several counts of aggravated burglary, but Edward Grey's testimony had put him in the clear for the Westlake and White murders, the thinking now being that the black crosses on the Serbian's map were there to remind him to avoid these areas of concerted police activity – then had rushed off to do her bidding, leaving Helen in the dark. If the Serbian thug really was innocent, then who on earth was responsible for these vicious murders?

How she longed to be back in the incident room, poring over the files, searching for evidence, a tiny break in the case. But she was excluded now, an ex-officer, washed up and redundant. Perhaps this then would be Blythe's ultimate triumph, sweeter even than her death. Instead of a moment's savage violence, she would instead endure a lifetime of patient, pointless suffering, forever wondering 'what if'. What if she'd caught Blythe first time round? What if she'd been more cautious that fateful night? What if Hudson hadn't toppled over the edge? What if, if, if...

It was exquisite torture, a way to drive herself mad, and she wondered if Blythe would settle for this, even *prefer* it? Better a long, slow death, than a short, merciful one. Her thoughts now strayed back to Richard Westlake and his stuttering, grief-laden appeal. Ethan had suffered terribly, the victim of a hideous attack, but his ordeal had been brief. It was his parents, Victoria and Richard, who would suffer now, year on year on year, robbed of their only son, their loving family. The same was true of Greg White, robbed of his sweet wife, his life forever overshadowed by unexpected tragedy. Who was to say who would suffer more, the victims or those left behind? Helen seriously suspected it would be the latter.

Her mind was now drawn back to a previous case, to Marianne's dreadful crime spree, in which the agony of the survivors had proved to be the whole point of a vicious string of murders. It had seemed impossibly wicked at the time – a unique crime in Southampton's history of bloodshed – yet now for the first time Helen wondered whether there might be an echo in their *current* investigation. So far they had been unable to find any reason why a vicious killer might target his victims, especially in the case of Ethan Westlake, who appeared to be an unremarkable, slightly gormless teenager, who'd made no enemies or indeed much of a mark on the world. The same could probably also be said of Martha White, who – with the odd exception of Andrew Berman – was universally liked. Given that it seemed unlikely that robbery was the real motive, given the meagre amount of jewellery taken and the exceptional levels of violence, was it *possible* then that the real target of this killer was those who were left behind? It was, after all, they who'd discovered the bodies, walking in on a gut-wrenching scene of bloody carnage? Was Richard and Victoria Westlake's anguish the point of all this? Was Greg White's crushing grief the prize?

It was an electrifying thought, even though the precise connection between the bereaved families lay well beyond Helen's grasp. *Could* there be a connection? A motive that somehow linked these two families? It seemed improbable, a flight of fancy perhaps, and yet in the absence of all other credible theories, surely it had to be considered?

Helen's eye was now drawn to the latest edition of the *Southampton Evening News*, on the front cover of which sat a beaming family photo of the Westlakes in happier times, a cruelly ironic image given their current plight. It was an image of domestic bliss that intrigued Helen, seeming somehow to lend weight to the theory now forming in her mind. Normally, Helen would have taken herself in hand at this point, telling herself not to fantasize about resolving the case, of reminding everyone at Southampton Central of her true worth, but as her mind continued to turn on possible motives for these horrific attacks, one thing kept nagging away at her.

Why, when talking about his absence that fateful night, had Richard Westlake chosen to use the word 'ashamed'?

Chapter 113

He pressed his car door firmly shut, before turning to survey the street. It was past eleven now and gratifyingly the gloomy road was deserted. He had chosen it carefully, three streets from his, with minimal street lighting and no cameras, and he was glad of his foresight. Here he could come and go undetected.

Locking the car door, he hurried away, pulling his cap down to conceal his face. He was clean now, having washed off the blood, changed his clothes and stowed the gear, and he cut an unremarkable figure, just a man hurrying home after a long day, but in truth his emotions were in riot. Things had gone wrong tonight, very badly wrong, and he burned to know why.

Part of his problems stemmed from his own weakness, spending too long slashing his supine victim, when he should have just finished her off. Even so, that shouldn't have brought him into contact with James Sheffield, who normally didn't return until just before midnight. What had precipitated his sudden return to the family home? Was it just a chance encounter? Or had he *known* something was wrong?

Cursing his luck, he hurried on down the street. Every part of him ached and he was sure there would be telltale bruises on his arms, face, body. His tussle with Kay's outraged husband had been brief but vicious, a wretched breathless scuffle on the hall floor. He'd tried to make a break for it, taking advantage of Sheffield's stupor and shock, but the large man had tackled him, sending him tumbling to the ground. It had knocked the wind out of him and for a moment he had faced the horrifying prospect of capture. But his desperation, his fear, had galvanized him and he fought back, punching, kicking, bucking, before eventually escaping from the desperate man's embrace. Again, he'd come at him, but this time he was ready, catching his attacker on the jaw with the heel of his axe. Sheffield had gone down like a sack of potatoes, hitting his head on the floor. His assailant was now stunned, floundering, and he hadn't hesitated, abandoning his best-laid plans by flinging the front door open and running for his life.

It had been a close-run thing. Even as he sprinted along the road, he was aware of lights coming on, of raised voices behind him. He half expected to see a lynch mob pursuing him and he didn't stop running until he was well past the train station, a couple of miles at least from the Sheffield house. Aware that someone – or worse still, some camera – could have clocked his breathless pursuit, he then took care to double back on himself, seeking out side alleys and back streets as he made his way to his parked car. His hand was still shaking when he slid the key into the ignition, but at least he was safe, for now.

Teasing open his garden gate, he hurried up the path, making sure to pad lightly over the stones as he did so. The benefit of living in such a geriatric, suburban location was that no one was awake at this time, allowing him to slip into his home unnoticed. Turning the key into the lock, he disappeared inside, pushing the door shut behind him. Leaning against it, he breathed out heavily, exhaustion now tempering his relief. How close he'd come to disaster tonight, how near he'd come to ruin. Dragging his body into the kitchen, he pulled open the cupboard and tugged out the bottle of Dalwhinnie. He poured himself a generous measure, then another, the fiery dark liquid seeming to revive his protesting body. Perhaps, at last, after the most difficult of nights, he could finally relax.

Suddenly the kitchen lights flicked out, blinding him. Shocked, disoriented, he turned to find Alicia leaning against the sink. She had been there all along, watching him.

'What the hell are you doing?' he demanded, trying to mask his fear with outrage.

'I might ask you the same question, you fucking animal...'

There was fire in his wife's eyes, but more than that, there was horror. She knew. It was impossible, he had been so careful, yet there was no doubt about it. She *knew*.

'It was *you*. All this bloodshed, all this agony, it was you, you little shit...'

'I don't know what you're talking about,' he blustered, but his protest lacked conviction.

'How could you? How could you do that to those poor people?'

And now he understood why James Sheffield had returned home early. *She* had worked it out, *she* had warned him of the impending danger.

'They had done nothing to you and yet you butchered them...' she continued, venom dripping from every word.

'You can't prove anything.'

'Oh no? Look at yourself, would you? You're covered in scratches and bruises, you're a fucking mess. Which is odd, really, as you were supposed to be at home tonight. Do you really think it's going to take the police long to put two and two together?'

The mere mention of the authorities sent a shiver down his spine. He was tempted to beg her for mercy, but she wasn't finished yet.

'I knew you were a worm, a coward. But I never had you down as a criminal. A common-or-garden murderer.'

She spat the word at him, her revulsion clear.

'It's not like that, you *know* it isn't...' he hissed back furiously.

'Oh, save it for the police. I don't want to hear it.'

Turning away, she picked up her phone and started dialling. He stared at her, transfixed. Was this how it was going to end?

'Police, please...' she intoned, her voice urgent and focused.

There was no hesitation at all – she was going to turn him over to the authorities without a second thought. It was unjust, unfair, just plain wrong. How could she *do* this to him?

'Come on, come on...'

She was tapping her foot impatiently, waiting for the operator to connect. He had a split second to act and he didn't hesitate. Picking up the griddle pan from the draining board, he stepped forward decisively, slamming it into the side of her head.

Day Seven

Chapter 114

He was a mess, battered on the outside, hollow on the inside.

James Sheffield couldn't meet Charlie's eye, partly because the right side of his face was viciously swollen, but mostly because he didn't want to engage with her, because that would mean facing up to the awful tragedy that had suddenly befallen him. The antiques dealer had protested at her arrival, arguing forcibly with the doctors that he wasn't feeling up to it, but Charlie had refused to leave. She needed answers and she needed them now.

'I know this is tough for you, James. I know you're suffering, grieving, but you are our only link to this guy. You're the only one who's *seen* him.'

Her officers were busy scouring the streets of Highfield and its environs, had been there since Kay Sheffield's gruesome murder was reported late last night and she sincerely hoped they would turn up a concrete witness sighting or CCTV grab. But this patient, this bereaved, beaten widower had actually encountered their killer, grappling with him in the hallway of his home. They had already whisked his clothes away for analysis, taken samples from underneath his fingernails, but Charlie wanted his eyewitness report.

'I don't know if I'm up to it,' he protested. 'My ribs are on fire, I can hardly breathe...'

'Just five minutes of your time. That's all I ask. If you won't do it for me, or the other families, do it for Kay.'

A groan escaped his lips, one so rich in despair that Charlie felt the emotion rise in her own chest.

'I know it's difficult,' she continued. 'But we have to bring this man in before he hurts anyone else. Can you tell me what happened last night?'

'So I finished a stock take at the shop around ten o'clock – I run an antiques dealership on Newton Street...'

Charlie nodded, encouraging him to keep talking.

'Got back home about fifteen minutes after that. And... and I'd barely set foot in the door, when this guy comes charging down the stairs. I was so startled, he was on me before I had a chance to react.'

'Are you able to describe him to me?'

'I didn't see much,' Sheffield wheezed, clutching his ribs. 'It was all a blur.'

'Anything at all? Height, weight, ethnicity...'

'Well, he was white, for sure. And he was old.'

'Old?' Charlie parroted, unable to contain her surprise.

'Yeah. Sixty at least, maybe more.'

'But athletic? Strong?'

Sheffield nodded dully, before replying:

'I tried to pin him down, to stop him, but he just shook me off.'

'Anything else you noticed about him? Facial features? Eyes? Any marks or tattoos on him?'

'No, his face was normal. Large, prominent nose, small eyes, but nothing odd. He was wearing dark clothes, a jacket and black jeans maybe, but that's all I can tell you for sure.'

'You're doing well, James. Thank you.'

Her compliment seemed to go unremarked, the widower staring blankly ahead.

'And can I ask what happened after you shook him off?'

'He hit me.'

'With a fist? With an axe?'

'The axe,' he confirmed grimly, pointing to the swollen bruising on the side of his face. 'I hit the deck, by the foot of the stairs. Didn't really know which way was up.'

'And then?'

'And then nothing.'

'He didn't attempt to attack you further? Even though you were at his mercy?'

The thought seemed to land with Sheffield, who suddenly looked unnerved and confused.

'I suppose he could have... could have killed me,' he replied, fear creeping into his voice now. 'But, no, he... he just stared at me for a minute and then ran. And that was it.'

Charlie continued to probe, asking standard questions about his movements, past conflicts or potential enemies, but her mind continued to turn on Sheffield's description of his attacker's departure. Was the fact that the killer had spared his victim significant? Did it suggest that this was *not* violence for violence's sake? Or even that he was uninterested in Sheffield, intent only on murdering his wife?

It was possible he'd been tempted to kill his prone victim, but with the door open and people on the street passing by, had simply thought better of it. Yet, it was also undeniable that he'd had a clear opportunity to kill and had spurned it. Was this an act of mercy? Because this murderer only killed when he had a specific purpose in mind?

Or was James Sheffield's survival somehow important?

Chapter 115

Helen pressed the doorbell for a second time, hopping impatiently from one foot to the other. This was partly out of nervous excitement and partly because she wanted to be hidden away, out of sight. A disgraced copper had no right to be here.

Thankfully, she now heard footsteps and seconds later the smart front door swung open. There was a flicker of recognition on Margaret Westlake's wrinkled face, but Helen wasn't taking any chances, moving quickly to reassure her.

'Mrs Westlake. It's DI Grace, I'm running the investigation into Ethan's death,' Helen lied confidently.

'I know who you are, my dear. I'm not a total imbecile. I expect you'd like to come in?'

Thanking her lucky stars, Helen stepped inside, shutting the door behind her.

Five minutes later, they were ensconced in Mrs Westlake's lounge.

'You've a lovely place here,' Helen offered, feeling more relaxed now.

'A present from my Richard. He thought it would suit me better than the old place. And there's no denying it's a step up in quality.'

Helen took in the interior, with its fashionable colour scheme, double-glazed windows and luxurious carpeting. Westlake's advertising boasted about creating perfect family homes and Helen could see why. It was well done, with real attention to detail, and in truth was far too big for a single woman living alone.

'It's rather too large and fancy, of course,' the old lady opined, seeming to read Helen's mind. 'But I couldn't say no really. He seemed so *keen* to have me here. It's only five minutes from his house, you see, and he's often here for work, so...'

Her words drifted off, the old lady smiling as she studied her tea.

'How many of the units has he sold?' Helen enquired.

'I've no idea, though there's not too many folk about, so I suppose only a handful. But he has buyers lined up for the rest, I think, which is why he was keen to bag this one for me. He's a good, thoughtful boy, really.'

Helen nodded, smiling, but Margaret's evident pride in her son didn't make her task any easier. Biting the bullet, she decided to cut to the chase.

'Could I ask you about the night Ethan died?'

Immediately, Margaret's face crumpled, the pain of her loss making itself felt once more.

'I don't mean to upset you and this won't take long. I just need to double check the timings of that night.'

'Well, I'll do my best, but I don't think I was much help when I spoke to your colleague the other day. I get confused so easily.'

'That's no problem, just do what you can. You said that Richard popped round at roughly 7 p.m. that night?'

'That's right. He *always* turns up around seven, when I've got the news on. He gets my dinner ready in time for *EastEnders*.'

'I see. Do I take it from that that he didn't eat with you?'

The old lady hesitated, before answering:

'I don't think so, he doesn't usually.'

'But he still cooks for you?'

'Well, if you can call heating up a microwave meal cooking.'

There was the tiniest hint of judgement in her voice.

'So he heats it up for you and then you watch TV together?'

And now Helen saw it in the old woman's expression. Uncertainty and unease.

'Mrs Westlake?' she prompted.

'Well, no, not really. At least I don't think so. He was here for a while – always stays to chat for a bit – but then he had to nip out.'

Helen leaned forward, intrigued.

'And how long did he nip out for?'

'I couldn't say that, not for sure. He did come back later to make me some Horlicks and bid me goodnight.'

'This was an hour later? Two?'

The woman shrugged, ill at ease.

'Can you remember what you were watching when he made you your Horlicks?'

'I think... I think it was the local news.'

'The late bulletin?'

Margaret Westlake nodded briefly.

'I believe so.'

'So he was gone for most of the evening, really?'

'It's possible, but you don't really want to go listening to me, love. I lose track of time so easily. I'm afraid I'm not what I was upstairs, if you know what I mean...'

She tapped her head ruefully. In other circumstances, Helen might have assumed this was evasion, but actually she believed the old lady.

'Did he drive off? Go somewhere else?'

'Oh no, he always leaves his car here. I can see it out the window when I'm watching the TV. Great big Mercedes.'

'And you've no idea where he goes?'

'No,' she replied uncertainly. 'He just pops out the back and returns when he's done. I assumed it was work, showing people round – a sales pitch – though in truth it did seem a bit late in the day for all that. That said, he's always been a hard worker.'

She was trying her best to cover for her son, sensing some anomaly, yet trying to put the best face on it. Helen suspected she didn't want to go there, didn't want to ask questions she might not like the answer to, but she had to press her nevertheless.

'So just to be clear, Mrs Westlake, to the best of your recollection, on the night of Ethan's death, Richard popped in to see you around 7 p.m., stayed for half an hour or so, then popped out for two hours or more, before returning to make you a hot drink?'

'That's about right, dear. But look he's not in any trouble, is he?'

'Absolutely not,' Helen reassured her. 'And there's certainly no suspicion regarding him in relation to Ethan's death. But it is crucial that we're clear on this point. Can I ask whether this is the usual pattern of his visits to you? Does he generally pop out?'

The old lady screwed up her mouth, as if displeased by the question, but her answer, when it came, was what Helen had been expecting.

'Yes, to be honest, it is. It's lovely that he pops in every week to see his old mum, but he doesn't want to sit here watching TV all night. He's a busy man, a successful man ...'

'And if it's not an indelicate question, can I ask whether ... whether you think he knows that his presence is missed. Is it possible he believes you might not notice his absence?'

It was not a pleasant question and Margaret Westlake seemed

discomfited by the implication, toying anxiously with her wedding ring as she replied:

'Well, I suppose it's a possibility. I *do* get confused, about days and times, and my memory is shot, so perhaps he thinks he can sneak out without my noticing. But if he does, he's mistaken. I may be dotty, dear...'

She raised her eyes, locking onto Helen's gaze, as she concluded:

'...but I'm not completely gone.'

Chapter 116

Helen hurried away from the house, her mobile phone clamped to her ear. Margaret Westlake lingered in the doorway, watching her, a look of concern on her face, but Helen's sole focus was on her next steps, on finally bringing some clarity to what had been a bewildering and disquieting case.

The call took a moment to connect, but after a few seconds, she heard DC Japhet Wilson's voice. He sounded surprised, even a little unnerved.

'DI Grace, is that you?'

'Right first time, Japhet. Can you talk?'

'Hold on a minute...'

She heard urgent footsteps, then a door opening and closing. From the sound of the burbling toilets in the background, she suspected he'd hidden himself away in the gents.

'Should I be talking to you?'

'Not really,' Helen replied honestly. 'And if you want to hang up on me, that's fine.'

He didn't, so she continued.

'I may not be part of the team currently and I am well aware that I have no right to ask you to do anything, but I can't take this to DI Brooks or Chief Superintendent Peters. I need someone discreet, someone loyal, someone who knows what to do with a good lead.'

Silence on the other end, but Helen sensed she had his interest.

'I've got some important information, plus a potential new line of enquiry. It involves Greg White – are you still in contact with him?'

'Well, I'm supposed to be liaising with him, following up on some things, but in all honesty, he's been quite hard to pin down.'

'OK, well, I need you to flush him out, ask him some questions. Go round there if you have to, but we need to talk to him.'

'OK…'

'It goes without saying that if anything comes of this, the credit goes to you, I don't need to be involved at all. But I'll need you to trust me and do exactly as I say. Do we have a deal?'

There was a long pause, the soft gurgling of water audible in the background, before Japhet Wilson replied:

'What do you want me to do?'

Chapter 117

Should she stick the knife in? Or should she be merciful?

Emilia stared at her reflection in the mirror, as she turned this vital question over and over in her mind. Initially the sight of her face had driven all other considerations from her mind, the dull, historic scarring down one side of her face now complemented by a livid black eye on the other. Overnight it had mushroomed into an explosion of aubergine purple, fringed with a hint of rancid butter yellow. It really did make her quite a sight, one no amount of concealer could ... conceal.

There was no question Helen Grace had overstepped the mark this time. Normally their skirmishes had been impassioned, occasionally even vitriolic, but they had never included physical violence before. It had been the last thing she was expecting, caught entirely off balance, as she crumpled to a heap on the dirty car park floor. She must have sat there for a full five minutes, processing what had just happened and running a hand over her cheek to see if the bone was broken. She'd only snapped out of her stupor when the elderly driver who'd witnessed the attack suddenly appeared, helping her to her feet, whilst offering to talk to the police, should he be required to back up her version of events. When Emilia had informed him that the person who'd just knocked her onto her ass *was* the police, he'd appeared less keen, but she was confident he could be leaned on to add credence to her claims, should she decide to press charges.

But would she? There was no denying it was tempting, Helen Grace having had fun at Emilia's expense on numerous occasions over the years. It would be amusing to see Helen squirm on the hook for once and, who knows, she might even seek compensation or, better still, an apology. How sweet that would taste.

Even so, Emilia hesitated to pick up the phone. Part of her wondered if it was worth it, occasioning a lot of hassle on her part, when Grace was already facing manslaughter charges, which trumped the relative minor misdemeanour of common assault. Would it even make it to court if Emilia pressed charges, or would the CPS throw it out, concentrating their focus on the more serious charge? Even if she could get Helen Grace in the witness box – tempting, tempting – was it the right thing to do?

This was Sam's doing – Emilia knew that. In days gone by, she wouldn't have given it a moment's thought, pulling the trigger without hesitation or regret. But even in the short time she'd known him, Sam had affected her thinking. Emilia's actions did have consequences and perhaps nowhere more pertinently than in the case of Joseph Hudson and Helen Grace. Emilia had spotted Hudson's weakness, exploited that to make him her mole within the MIT, then tossed him to the wolves when her own liberty was threatened. As a result, his career had been ruined and he found himself on the scrap heap whilst still a relatively young man. How desperate he must have been, how scared, facing the prospect of ending up behind bars with people he'd help put away. No wonder he had sought out Helen Grace, though whether this was to beg for mercy or confront his former flame, Emilia would never know.

Was it fair to say, then, that Emilia had unwittingly had a hand in his tragic death, laying him low, before Grace delivered the final blow? That she had to accept her share of the blame? If so, was it fair now to hang Helen Grace out to dry on the front cover of the *Southampton Evening News*?

Yet if she didn't, what was she *for*? Her tussle with Grace was the stuff of legend. What would her colleagues, her boss, make of it, if she pulled her punches? Would they accuse her of going soft? That was something she couldn't countenance; she had always been a street fighter, fearing no one and nothing. But how to square the circle now when her instinct demanded one course of action and her conscience another?

Emilia continued to stare at herself, wrestling with this most difficult dilemma. Should she spare Helen Grace? Or should she bury her?

Chapter 118

'I could destroy you, Nicholas. It would be as easy as clicking my fingers.'

Alex Blythe's voice insinuated its way down the phone line, cold and pitiless.

'I'm trying my best, OK?' Nicholas Martin protested. 'Grace has been arrested, she's in custody.'

'She *was* in custody. Don't lie to me or you'll make me angry...'

'Well, that's good news, right?' Martin bluffed. 'If she's out, if she's been kicked off the Force, then she's got nowhere to go. I can lie in wait, do as you asked...'

'Except you won't, will you?' the psychiatrist snapped.

'I made a promise, didn't I? I'll do anything to avoid my wife fin—'

'Face it, Nicholas,' Blythe interrupted. 'You are a failure and a coward. I asked you to do one thing, one simple thing—'

'I wouldn't call cold-blooded murder a simple—'

'And you messed it up. Despite my very clear warnings about the consequences of failure.'

His words were laced with frustration and anger.

'How about if I pay you?' Nicholas responded suddenly.

There was a stunned silence, then laughter.

'*You* pay *me?*'

Blythe sounded incredulous, amused.

'Look, you must need funds, right? You're a wanted man. I can wire money to a bank or an account, whatever you want. I've got savings, plus I could remortgage the house.'

'You really are a worm, aren't you?' Blythe replied. 'Do you honestly think that I can be bribed into sparing you? The destruction of your life is part of the *fun*.'

He stressed the last word, prompting anger to flare in Nicholas Martin. How he wanted to slip his hands round the neck of this sadistic bastard and squeeze, squeeze, squeeze. But he kept his cool, responding with vigour.

'Name your price, Blythe. However much you need, I'll get it. I want this thing gone, I want my life back.'

'Then do what you promised. Kill Grace – or face the consequences.'

Before his victim could respond, the psychiatrist abruptly hung up. Nicholas Martin breathed out heavily, wiping the sweat from his brow, before turning to DC Ellie McAndrew.

'Was that long enough?'

Chapter 119

'And what time was that again?'

Richard Westlake's face was a picture of exasperation, but Helen wondered if another emotion lay behind his apparent outrage.

'Do we really have to do this again, Inspector? I've already given my statement.'

'Humour me.'

Westlake didn't look in the mood to do any such thing, shifting uneasily from foot to foot on the springy turf. As he maintained his stony silence, Helen angled a glance back to the house, where Victoria Westlake stood sentry by the French doors, her unease, her suspicion, clear. Helen turned away – she had taken a big risk coming here, when she had no authority to do so. The Westlakes would be well within their rights to turf her out, call the authorities, but news of her suspension had not broken yet, leaving her a short window to work in.

'You arrived just after 7 p.m.?'

'Yes.'

'Then you made your mother dinner and you both watched *EastEnders*?'

'Like I said.'

'Did you both eat?'

'Yes,' came the razor-sharp response.

'What did you eat?'

'Er... just a ready meal, I think. A curry. I'm not much of a cook, I'm afraid.'

'I see. And what did you watch?'

'I'm sorry?'

'What did you watch on the TV? You were there from seven until just before eleven, so what did you watch?'

There was a pause, then Westlake said:

'I honestly don't remember. I think we turned it off shortly after *EastEnders* and had a chat.'

'That's funny because your mum said she watched TV all night.'

'She must be getting it confused with another night.'

'No, she gave me a very detailed report of your evening together. Even told me what happened at the end of *Silent Witness*. No need for me to watch it now, I guess...'

Helen pulled a funny face and finally Westlake seemed to relax.

'You're right, of course. We did watch that. I'm sorry, in all the confusion and upset, I just forgot.'

'Can *you* remember what it was about?'

'Oh, the usual, you know. Every episode's the same, right?'

Helen stared at him, letting the silence do its work.

'Sorry, I'm having a bit of mind blank...'

'*Silent Witness* wasn't on that night, Richard. So please stop lying to me.'

Westlake looked stunned, suddenly realizing the extent of Helen's duplicity, the trap he'd been led into.

'I'm *not*, I swear,' he blustered, his eyes flicking back towards the house.

'Yes, you are. Your mother may get confused at times

– something I suspect you were banking on – but she is very clear about that night. You made her dinner, settled her down in front of *EastEnders*, then left via the back entrance. You were gone nearly two hours.'

'That's not true.'

'Apparently, this is not unusual,' Helen continued, ignoring his protests. 'In fact, she says you do this every Thursday, when you visit. She's prepared to confirm as much in a written statement.'

This was a lie, but it seemed to have the desired effect. Westlake swallowed an expletive, as his pacing increased in tempo, sweat forming on his brow.

'Look, Richard, I'm not here to make you suffer or cause you any domestic problems, but I do need you to tell me the truth. So, either you refuse to co-operate and I arrest you or you tell me what I need to know and I head quietly on my way.'

The bereaved father appeared pained, suspecting perhaps that either path would eventually lead to his exposure. But Helen needed concrete information, so she upped the pressure.

'Either you tell me where you *really* were that night or I drag you from this house in cuffs. Which is it to be, Richard?'

Chapter 120

'What the hell were you thinking? Have you gone completely mad?'

DC Wilson had never seen Charlie Brooks so exercised before, taken aback by her fury.

'DI Grace is suspended from this Force, she is not a serving officer,' his superior continued. 'She has absolutely no right to ask you to do anything and I'm staggered that you would even consider obeying her.'

Wilson could see the strain Brooks was under, having to lead the team, whilst casting her old friend out into the cold and he knew he had to tread carefully. She was fit to blow.

'She was very insistent – was *sure* she had an important new lead.'

'And that makes it OK, does it? You blatantly disregarded the chain of command, lying to me, to your colleagues, despite having been here a matter of days…'

'It wasn't like that, I never lied to anyone.'

'Betrayed, then. Does that sound better?'

'Look, I'm here now, aren't I?' he protested, feeling the sweat prickle on his neck. 'I could have kept this to myself, but I didn't. I thought you ought to know.'

It was a weak rearguard action, but he had no choice. He'd

been hoping Brooks' longstanding affection for Grace might make her more receptive, but now he realized he'd seriously misjudged the situation. She seemed determined to toe the party line, come what may.

'You know, I *should* take this straight to Peters,' Brooks continued tersely. 'Get *you* chucked out of Southampton Central as well.'

'There's no need to do that,' Wilson countered quickly. 'What I did, I did with the best of intentions.'

'And then what? You got scared, decided to come clean to save your own skin.'

'No, it's nothing like that,' Wilson retorted, frustration rising in him now. 'I came to tell you that I think DI Grace might be *right*. I think she's onto something.'

Brooks stared at him, wrong-footed. Wilson seized the moment, carrying on quickly.

'You know I've been trying to get hold of Greg White, doing a bit of belt-and-braces on his alibi for the night Martha was killed?'

Brooks said nothing, but made no move to cut him off.

'I've been calling him for a few days now. Usually, he ignores the calls and on the odd occasion he has picked up, he's been incredibly evasive. At first, I thought he was distracted by family stuff, the investigation, the other murders and so on, but after my chat with DI Grace, I got suspicious, decided to go round there.'

'This better be good, Wilson,' Charlie warned, clearly unimpressed that he'd interviewed one of the victims without her say so.

'Hear me out. Back when this all started, DI Grace asked me to see if he had Strava, or a Fitbit or other device, to confirm his movements that night. Turns out he *has*, which is presumably why he's been avoiding my calls. This morning he reluctantly handed over his Fitbit to me and, having examined the data, I can see why he wasn't keen.'

'Spit it out, Wilson.'

'Well, he said he trains three times a week. That's true, but here's the thing. On Sunday and Friday, he regularly covers twenty-six miles as he previously stated, but on Tuesday night – the night Martha White died – he only covered one mile.'

'Which is what?' Charlie asked, doing the mental maths. 'To the Common and back?'

'Exactly. I think he ran there, stayed there for two to three hours, then came home.'

'You've checked the location of his Fitbit?'

'Yup, he never moved from the Common in all that time.'

'But it would have been freezing. And nothing's open at that time on the Common, so ... he must have been meeting someone. In one of the car parks perhaps?'

'I can't say for sure, but I guess that's what DI Grace is thinking.'

'Well, there's no point speculating,' Brooks said, snatching up her bag. 'Why don't we go ask her?'

Chapter 121

Helen's footsteps echoed through the drab NCP car park, as she made her way towards her colleagues. DC Wilson and Charlie leaned against their car, darting nervous looks around them, as if fearful of discovery. As Helen approached, however, Charlie turned to face her, her expression unreadable.

For a moment, the two women stared at each other, tense, wary. Then Charlie broke the silence.

'This conversation never happened, OK? If news gets out that DC Wilson or I have been in direct contact with you—'

'Then you'll be out on your ear. You don't need to spell out the consequences to me, Charlie.'

Her words sounded brittle and harsh. Helen hadn't wanted emotion to colour this conversation, but it was hard to keep her frustration at bay. Casting her eye around the tired car park, Helen gathered herself, trying to suppress her churning emotions, before continuing in a more emollient tone.

'But thank you for reaching out to me. It's appreciated.'

Charlie looked awkward, clearly uncomfortable with the formal nature of this meeting.

'OK, I think we can skip the pleasantries,' the acting DI continued briskly, casting around, 'we're all taking a massive risk here, so—'

'Can we get on with it?'

Charlie nodded, clearly keen to be away as soon as possible.

'So here are the facts,' Helen continued swiftly. 'Both Greg White and Richard Westlake lied about their whereabouts on the night their houses were targeted. They deliberately misled the investigation to save their own skins.'

'You think they're in on this?' Wilson queried, incredulous. 'That they had a hand in these deaths?'

'Not in the way you mean. They didn't strike the blow themselves, nor were they responsible in any way for the planning or execution of these murders. But their involvement is crucial.'

'I don't follow...' Wilson persisted.

'Well, it was a previous conversation with Charlie that put me onto it. We'd been talking about... about infidelity and the idea of someone having an affair kind of stuck in my mind,' Helen said quickly, avoiding Charlie's eye. 'Anyway, I spoke to Richard Westlake earlier and under duress, he confessed to me that he's been cheating on his wife for the past six weeks with a woman he met online. A woman calling herself Amanda Abingdon, though he suspects that's not her real name. Like Westlake, she'd signed up to Sweetmeets, a website that connects married people who want to have discreet, casual encounters, without endangering their marriage. Every Thursday he'd visit his mother, telling his wife he'd be there all evening, but actually, having set up his mother with her dinner, he'd slip out the back to rendezvous with his lover in the show home.'

'What a bloody rat,' Charlie responded, venomously.

'I suppose he reasoned that if his wife ever raised any suspicions – if there were ever any anomalies about his whereabouts – he could always blame his mother's faulty memory.'

'Jesus Christ...' Wilson breathed, as sickened as his companions.

'And you think Greg White was also having an affair, with the same woman?'

'I think it's worth asking the question,' Helen returned meaningfully. 'Because if he *was*, then it gives someone a very good motive for murder.'

'But why wouldn't our killer just target the men themselves? Or his own wife?'

'I'm sure he was tempted to, but perhaps he wanted his revenge to be more twisted, more devastating than that. These men betrayed their wives, their families, took them for granted. Well, they'll have plenty of time to rue their casual betrayal of their marriage vows now, won't they?'

A hushed silence filled the car. It was brilliant, and terrible.

'So …' Charlie finally responded, her brain spinning. 'If that's the case, the fact that the victims were home alone isn't relevant.'

'Precisely,' Helen replied. 'Remember Victoria Westlake was supposed to be home that night, it was only by chance that she wasn't. I think our perpetrator intended to kill both Ethan and Victoria Westlake, take out the whole family.'

'The key thing, then,' Wilson overlapped, 'was that the husband was away from the house, unable to intervene to save his family, giving the perpetrator a free run.'

'While the cat's away …' Helen murmured by way of response.

'And if these men *were* with the same woman – this Abingdon person – then not only would they be well out of the way, but the killer's wife would also be indisposed, meaning he could slip out of his house and return undetected.'

Charlie paused, energized now, as the pieces of the jigsaw started to slot into place.

'Who is Amanda Abingdon?' she asked.

'There's no one of that name registered in the Southampton

area,' Helen replied quickly. 'Sorry, I've still got my access codes for Holmes, so I ran a quick check...'

Charlie waved away her indiscretion.

'She's clearly using a false name, wants to protect her marriage. So your best bet now is to talk to Greg White, find out if we're right, and if so, get a description.'

'Where do you think I'm heading?' Charlie replied, firing up the engine.

As Wilson opened the rear door to get out, Helen did likewise from the passenger side.

'Oh and Helen...'

Helen turned back to Charlie, even as the latter broke into a smile.

'Thank you.'

Chapter 122

'Did you ever really love me?'

The question hung in the air, charged and angry.

'I loved *you*, loved you with all my heart. You brought me back to life, I'm man enough to admit that. Might have thrown in the towel if I hadn't met you.'

He was surprised to feel tears on his cheeks, his emotions still near the surface despite of – *because of* – everything that had happened.

'Funny then, how things worked out, isn't it? That instead of saving me, you destroyed me.'

He rose unsteadily, walked towards her.

'But I suppose it hasn't been without consequences for you either, has it?'

He turned to his wife, who sat upright in the kitchen chair, her head lolling backwards. He ran his hand down the side of her cheek, which was cool to the touch, avoiding the sticky mass of congealed blood on her temple.

'I'm sorry it had to be like this. I had other plans, if I'm honest. But... but I couldn't let you turn me in, not while I still have work to do.'

He looked to her for a response, but she continued to stare dully at the ceiling, her eyes wide open. It was a close confessional space – with the curtains tightly shut so no one could penetrate the cosy atmosphere of their little kitchen – but of course *she* had never intended to reveal her wrongdoing. She was a woman with deceit at her very core.

'Perhaps this is for the best. I wouldn't have taken any pleasure in your death, despite what you've done. I guess I'm just a foolish old man, right?'

He leaned down, kissing the top of her cold head, then moved away.

'I wouldn't say I enjoyed the others either, to be honest,' he continued, talking to thin air. 'But I did enjoy what came after. The horror, the desolation, the grief. Those men will suffer, my, how they will suffer.'

He paused, crouching down to look at his dead wife directly.

'And who could say it wasn't their due? In fact, if you want my opinion, my love...'

He hissed the final word.

'...I think they got exactly what they deserved.'

Chapter 123

Greg White stared at Charlie, distraught.

'I never thought I'd be the type; to be unfaithful, I mean. That was for weak men, cowards…'

Charlie didn't disagree, but didn't press the point. The widower was on the edge.

'But somehow things changed. Martha's pregnancy was difficult, the birth even more so, and I guess we lost the intimacy, the spontaneity that we used to have.'

He didn't dare look up at Charlie, knowing full well that these were tired, familiar excuses. Instead, he stared at his hands, picking at a scab. The pair were hidden away in his parents' bedroom, talking in hushed tones, aware that Gerald and Anne White were just downstairs, tending to Bailey.

'I tried to talk to Martha a couple of times about it, but she said I was being insensitive and hurtful. Said I had no idea what it was like to be her, to have had your body changed by childbirth, to be exhausted to the very core of your bones. So I kept quiet after that.'

'When did the affair begin?' Charlie prompted, cutting to the chase.

'Couple of months ago. There's a website called Sweetmeets,

which is aimed at local professionals. It's kind of an Ashley Madison clone, you can chat to people, arrange hook-ups...'

He winced as he said the word, knowing full well how grubby it sounded.

'And that's how you met Amanda?'

'That's not her name,' Greg replied quickly. 'She called herself Sarah Keynes.'

'I see. Can you describe her to me?'

'About five foot ten, long blonde hair, hazel eyes, slender figure.'

Charlie nodded, reassured. His description was a perfect match for the woman calling herself Amanda Abingdon, as described to Helen by Richard Westlake.

'And you saw her every Tuesday night?'

He nodded, shamefaced.

'I'd run to the Common, then we'd spend a couple of hours in her car. It was a bit reckless, I suppose, we could have been caught, but she seemed to... to get off on that.'

Pushing that image aside, Charlie continued:

'Did she ever mention anything about her home life? Where she lived? Who her husband was?'

'No, that was strictly off limits. That's the whole point.'

'Nothing at all, no hints of any kind?'

'She mentioned once that he was significantly older than her, but...'

He petered out, finally looking up at Charlie.

'Is that why this is happening? Is this *him*?'

'We believe it's a possibility.'

'So those other men – the husbands, I mean – they were also...'

'Richard Westlake was definitely seeing the same woman and it's probable James Sheffield was too...'

'Jesus...'

He rose quickly and for a moment Charlie thought he was going to punch the wall.

'So this is all because of me, because of what *I've* done?'

Charlie shrugged a 'yes', not wanting to increase his anguish, but a direct accusation would have had the same effect, his expression horrible to behold.

'Dear God...'

'Greg, I need you to stay focused—'

'So this was *him?*' he fired back. 'Her husband, he did this to Martha...'

'It looks that way.'

'He wants to hurt me, to torture me.'

'It's possible.'

'No, I know he does,' the bereaved husband insisted angrily, marching over to the dresser. 'He was here yesterday.'

Now it was Charlie's turn to be rocked back on her heels.

'He came *here?*'

'I didn't see him. He was gone before I realized what was happening, but he left this.'

He handed her a pristine envelope. Flicking it open, she saw a ring nestled inside.

'It's Martha's wedding band, the one he took. He posted it through the door yesterday. Wanted to make a point, I suppose, to rub my bloody nose in it.'

Charlie stared into the envelope, the implications of this unexpected development leaving her reeling. Helen's first instinct had been right – the removal of Martha White's wedding ring *was* important, these attacks *were* personal.

'And you didn't think to tell us?' Charlie replied, aghast.

'I was going to,' White protested weakly. 'I just wanted to find the right time.'

'Or maybe you were planning to keep quiet about it because deep down you sensed what this was about? You knew we were sniffing around your alibi, that your deception might be exposed at some point—'

'Look, what was I supposed to say?' White demanded angrily. 'That I was out having sex with another woman whilst a madman killed my wife, threatened my child. I couldn't do it, I just couldn't do it. I'd be a bloody outcast.'

'So you're more interested in your own reputation than securing justice for Martha?'

He turned away, shame drowning his anger.

'If you'd come to us yesterday, we could have swept the neighbourhood for witnesses. But, no, you let him get away. Better that, than have to own up to what you did, what you really are...'

She had gone too far, but couldn't help herself. Her blood was boiling at his selfishness. But she had no need to judge him, he would do that all by himself, crumpling now to the floor and dropping his face to his hands. The perpetrator of these terrible crimes had set out to destroy these perfidious, unfaithful men and there was no question he had succeeded.

Looking down at the broken, sobbing heap in front of her, Charlie knew that Greg White would be haunted by his actions for the rest of his life.

Chapter 124

'I think I might have something.'

Wilson looked up from his desk, excited by the urgency in DC Malik's voice. Hurrying over to her, he leaned down to look at her monitor. On it was a grainy CCTV still, showing a white BMW parked by a smart, double-fronted house.

'I had a look at the CCTV from the Grange Park estate,' Malik continued breathlessly. 'Richard Westlake's car always remained parked outside his mother's home for the duration of his Thursday night visits, so I reasoned that his lover must come to *him* – walking, driving, cycling to the show home. Well, this BMW 5 Series turns up every Thursday at around eight o'clock, parking towards the rear of the estate, a few minutes' walk from the show home.'

'Very cautious, very discreet,' Wilson agreed.

'I cross-referenced it with last week's traffic cam footage on Winchester Road and, look, the same BMW enters the Common on the ninth of January at around 7.30 p.m. and doesn't leave until 11.45 p.m.'

'Who does it belong to?'

'According to the DVLA, it was bought two years ago by Alicia Stoneman. DC Jennings did a little digging on the name – she lives at an address on the edge of Ocean Village with her husband, Michael. And this is a picture of her from her Facebook profile.'

Japhet Wilson leaned in closer, as Malik pulled up the picture. The attractive, smiling face was framed by long blonde hair, her hazel eyes sparkling in the summer sunshine.

'That's her,' Wilson breathed out, exultant. 'That's our woman.'

Chapter 125

'Michael Stoneman, retired businessman, living in Ocean Village with his second wife.'

Helen was hunched over her laptop in her kitchen, talking fast into her speaker phone, as she scrolled through Stoneman's Facebook page.

'What happened to the first Mrs Stoneman?' Charlie's disembodied voice asked, a note of anxiety in her tone.

'Rosemary Stoneman died of breast cancer in 2018,' Helen replied. 'Lots of historic posts about that. They had been together for over thirty years and by the looks of these photos were very much in love. I'd say he was virtually destroyed when she died.'

'No hint of foul play? Violence?'

'I'd say not. There's lot of supportive messages bemoaning her death, railing against cancer, offers of charitable contributions and so on, plus it's clear that they had plans for the future. He's a shipbuilder by trade, or was at least, and five years ago, he built himself a boat, planned to go around the world with his wife after he'd retired. Even named it after her, called it the *Lady Rosemary*...'

'But then life – or cancer – intervened.'

'Exactly,' Helen replied, feeling oddly moved for the couple, in spite of her growing suspicions about Stoneman.

'When did he marry Alicia?'

'Christmas 2020. Doesn't say how they met, but the wedding photos seem happy enough. Decent crowd in attendance and Stoneman looks, well, he looks pleased as punch.'

'She's a pretty girl, right? Younger than him, full of energy, vigour.'

'He posted frequently on the website, saying how she'd brought him back to life, taught him how to love again. And they look happy enough, to start with at least.'

'Let me guess,' Charlie replied, the noise of the incident room punching through behind her. 'The posts tail off more recently.'

'Yes, this last year they were sporadic, and about five months ago he stopped posting altogether. No mention of his wife, or their life together, despite the fact that they are still married, still living together.'

'Love's young dream had turned sour?'

'Certainly looks that way. I don't know if he loved her, hated her or was indifferent to her, but he certainly didn't want to talk about her.'

'But you think his feelings for her, at the start at least, were genuine? It wasn't just sex?'

'Impossible to say,' Helen responded. 'But he never mentions her looks, despite the fact that she's obviously gorgeous. He talks about her warm heart, her optimistic outlook, her kindness.'

'Which might suggest he's not a very good judge of character. I wonder when he found out she was playing away?'

'No idea, but it would have been pretty crushing for him. It's not as if she had even fallen in love with someone else. She was just after a bit of fun, a bit of youth elsewhere and doing it pretty regularly too.'

'So Stoneman was just a meal ticket for her?'

'Could be. What do we know about her?'

'Not a lot. Brought up by a single father, local hood and minor criminal. He went inside when she was fifteen and after that she kind of goes off the radar. We do know she worked at one of the casinos as a waitress and there's a suggestion she may have done some adult modelling work.'

'Surviving by her wits,' Helen replied, thoughtfully.

'Exactly. Anyway, we're scrambling units to their house now. I'll ring you once we have him in custody, but if you find out anything in the meantime, snapchat me, OK? I think it's safer that way.'

Helen agreed, ringing off. Privately it seemed absurd to her that she would have to send covert messages to Charlie to further the investigation, but she knew her old friend was right to be cautious. It wasn't just Helen's career on the line here.

Returning her attention to the screen, she drank in Michael Stoneman's rugged features once more. He was a tough, practical man, whose weathered face spoke of a lifetime spent on the water. Jarringly, in these pictures, many of them from his recent wedding to Alicia, he appeared joyous, even carefree. Helen suspected the reality was rather different and that what she was in fact looking at was a bitter, vengeful man, who'd been deceived by his new wife and meted out a depraved revenge on the men he held responsible.

Chapter 126

'What are you telling me, Richard? What are you *saying?*'

It was worse than he could have possibly expected. Victoria was wild with anguish and distress, as realization slowly dawned.

'I never meant to hurt you and, please believe me, it didn't mean anything. It was just a mistake, a stupid, stupid mistake.'

He turned to his wife, hoping that his words would cut through. But he saw only revulsion in her expression.

'Who was she?' his wife demanded, anger colouring her cheeks.

'Someone I met online, I never knew her real name...'

'Dear God.'

With each passing second, his humiliation increased.

'Please, Vicky. I know you've every right to hate me, but believe me when I say that I love you, always have, always will. This was just... just a moment of madness.'

He moved towards her, but she pulled away from him.

'Why?'

It was an impossible question to answer, but he was about to respond, when she continued:

'Why would you tell me this now? After everything that's happened to us, why would you do that to me?'

Her words chilled his soul. How to explain his part in this hideous nightmare?

'I wanted to be honest with you. It's been eating me up.'

'Bullshit, you don't know the meaning of the word. Tell me now or I swear to God...'

She was advancing upon him, but he held up his hand in surrender, arresting her progress.

'Look, I – I don't how to say this, Vick, but the police...'

His voice shook, but he pressed on.

'...the police think her husband may have had something to do with...'

He couldn't finish, but he didn't need to, his wife's face collapsing.

'Ethan?' she whispered.

Richard Westlake nodded dully.

'*You* did this?' she demanded, sickened.

'No, I – I...'

The words wouldn't come. But what was there to say?

'I didn't know that... that he—'

But she had heard enough, stepping forward and slapping him hard across the face. His head rocked back, but still she fell upon him, slapping, beating, punching him for all she was worth.

'He was my boy, you piece of shit. He was my beautiful boy...'

Suddenly she relented, pulling away from him, as if infected by his touch. He stared up at her, expecting another attack, but instead she hissed:

'I will never forgive you. For as long as I live, I will *never* forgive.'

In tears, she fled the room, thundering down the stairs. Seconds later, Richard Westlake heard the door slam shut, the final full stop to what had once been a happy marriage.

Chapter 127

'Are we ready?'

A phalanx of police cars surrounded the quiet family home, whilst uniformed officers guarded front and back. Charlie stood by a small unit of armed officers, tense but focused.

'Ready when you are,' Sergeant Miller confirmed.

'Let's do it then.'

Stepping aside, Charlie gestured to Miller to deploy his unit. Moving swiftly, they took up their positions to the side of the door, then nodded to the uniformed officer to proceed. Marching forward, he gathered himself, then hurled the barrel charge forward. It connected sharply with the door, smashing it off its hinges. The violent noise echoed around the quiet terraced street, but was drowned out by the sound of boots pounding down the hallway.

Charlie held her breath, expecting shouts, gunfire, a scuffle. But the first twenty seconds elicited no drama and, as the boots thundered up the stairs to the first floor, Charlie ducked inside the neat suburban home.

'DB in there,' one of the officers said as he hurried past, nodding towards the kitchen, which lay just off the hallway.

With a sinking feeling, Charlie made her way towards the kitchen. Stepping inside, she was depressed, but not surprised to see a woman sitting stock-still on one of the kitchen chairs. Sliding on shoe coverings and latex gloves, she moved towards her, pausing as she clocked the nasty wound to the side of her head. Her face was pale and Charlie felt solid resistance from the woman's arm, as she squeezed it. Rigor mortis was well established, the woman had been dead for some time.

There were more shouts of 'Clear' from upstairs, then the sound of boots descending. Seconds later, a concerned Sergeant Miller joined Charlie in the kitchen.

'No sign of him. We'll do a sweep of the garden, but honestly I think uniform would have spotted him if he was hiding out there.'

'Best to be sure, eh? Radio in if you spot anything.'

Nodding, the armed officer retreated, leaving Charlie alone. They had been too late, too slow in their investigations, and now another life had been lost. Charlie stared at Alicia's hard, beautiful face, wondering how her last minutes had played out. Did she know what her husband had been doing? Or had he surprised her before she could work it out?

It made no difference, Stoneman had evaded them – that was the takeaway from this failed intervention. He was out there right now – but was he running or had he more bloodshed in mind? They had no idea of his whereabouts, his intentions, or indeed his state of mind. Even as she thought this, however, Charlie spotted something. A crisp white envelope propped up against the salt cellar on the kitchen table. Picking it up, she took in the front of the envelope on which, in neat, spidery handwriting, were written five simple words:

To whom it may concern.

Chapter 128

'Have you gone completely mad?'

Emilia held the phone away from her to spare her the full impact of her sub-editor's explosion.

'This is the biggest story that's dropped into our lap for years and you want to bury it?'

His voice seemed to echo round the white walls of the hospital atrium, causing a couple of heads to turn. Moving away from the waiting area, Emilia moved fast to appease him.

'I'm not saying we won't run the story, it's just a question of timing.'

'Are you feeling all right, Emilia? You've been after Grace for years and now you've got her on a spit. Why aren't you turning the handle?'

'Because it'll muddy the water, confuse people. We have a very clear, very scary narrative. A madman has killed three times and is primed to strike again. Focusing on the threat of home invasion is the best way to boost sales, trust me.'

'But the head of the MIT has been booted off the investigation, suspended for killing another officer. Putting aside that it's a fucking sensational scoop, it doesn't take a genius to work out how to stitch it into the wider story. Phantom killer, incompetent cops, you've written it a hundred times…'

Never a truer word, but today this didn't make Emilia feel proud.

'Look, Paul, I'm not saying we don't mention the goings on at Southampton Central, but I don't want to get into a whole Helen Grace retrospective, when it's the perpetrator that's the real star here. Besides, I think there's an argument to be made for waiting to see how things pan out with Grace, whether they are going to charge her or not.'

'I'm sorry, I just can't see why we would sit on this one. If you don't want to write it, fine. There are lots of others who cou—'

'No.'

Her refusal shot out, harsh and percussive, raising more heads.

'Helen Grace is *my* specialist subject,' she continued tersely. 'And I will deal with her, when the time is right. For now we keep our focus on the Sheffield attack. Everything else will have to wait. Are we agreed?'

Emilia fully expected him to tell her to go to hell, despite her bold posturing, but to her surprise she heard her colleague sigh, as he replied:

'Have it your own way, Emilia. But if another outlet gets this before us, I will hold you personally responsible.'

'They won't, I promise you,' she responded quickly.

'You know you really are a pain in the arse, Emilia. If I had a penny for ev—'

'That's very sweet of you, Paul,' she cut in, 'but I've got to go now, speak later.'

She hung up, diverting her attention to the downcast man shuffling across the atrium towards the exit. He had a cap on and stared fixedly at the ground, but there was no mistaking that it was James Sheffield. He was limping slightly and had heavy bruising on his face and neck, but otherwise seemed in decent shape. How he felt on the inside was a different matter, Emilia sensing that those scars would take a *long* time to heal.

Slipping her camera from her case, she padded silently towards him, her pumps sliding over the polished floor. She had a couple of questions about the incident itself, whether he saw the attacker, whether he had any clue as to motive, then she would take the obligatory snap. Flicking the camera on, she scanned the atrium for nurses or porters who might attempt to intervene and as she did so, she spotted movement to her left. A middle-aged woman had entered the hospital and was running towards Sheffield.

Emilia slowed, watching the scene play out. Sheffield raised his gaze, recognized the woman – sister? friend? – then promptly fell into her arms. They clung to each other, propping each other up, the middle-aged man sobbing uncontrollably as he rested his head on her shoulder. It was as surprising as it was affecting, a scene of utter emotional devastation.

Instinctively, Emilia raised the camera to take in the sad couple... but then paused. Something wasn't right. Was it that the shot wouldn't look right? That they were too far away, that she couldn't see their faces? Or was it that – for perhaps the first time in her life – Emilia felt like she was intruding?

A lump in her throat, Emilia lowered the camera, sighing heavily. Then, taking one last, lingering look at the tragic pair, she slowly retreated.

Chapter 129

Michael Stoneman walked fast along the road, keeping to the shadows. Night had fallen, the all-pervading gloom encompassing him, and he felt beset by powerful, contradictory emotions. There was excitement, exhilaration even, that the final act was close at end, but regret too that his victory would not be complete. During the weeks of careful planning, he had climbed inside the lives of all his victims, knowing their routines and movements intimately – and he had planned accordingly. It was simply bad luck that Mrs Westlake hadn't been in the house that night – he'd ached to murder that faithless fuck's *entire* family. Part of him was tempted to return to Victoria Westlake now, to mete out his revenge in full, but he knew this was just a pipe dream, a sure-fire way to get arrested. No, he had to remain disciplined, if he was to ensure that *everyone* was punished. Westlake would suffer enough as it was – people always say you never truly got over the death of a child.

Cutting down Marsham Street, he crossed the road, sliding in between parked cars, before continuing his steady progress along the pavement. He noticed he had quickened his pace, adrenaline and anticipation driving him forward. It almost felt as if he was about to break into a run, so he slowed now, deliberately dropping his pace. There was no point in drawing attention to himself when he was so close to his prize.

Approaching the Portsmouth Road, he came to a halt at the pedestrian crossing. Eagerly he scanned the traffic, praying it would slow, so he could proceed. As he did so, he caught the eye of a young girl, clutching her father's hand. Looking up, she smiled warmly at him. Taken aback, he surprised himself by smiling back. He had many regrets in life, but the one that really hurt was the fact that Rosemary and he had never had kids. They had tried, God they had tried, but always to no avail. It was a pity, she would have been a wonderful mother and it would have been nice for him to have a daughter to spoil.

The girl's smile had faded now, disturbed perhaps by the way he was staring at her, so he moved on, hurrying across the pedestrian crossing, as the cars pulled up at the stop line. Striding purposefully, he gobbled up Alma Street, before cutting down Cottonmill Lane. Moments later, he found himself by the back wall of 24 Havelock Road.

There was no one about, as he'd anticipated, the only life in the street a ginger tom who eyed him curiously from across the street. Ignoring this surveillance, he seized the bin that had been strategically placed here for those retreating from the park and heaved it over to the wall. Balancing one knee on the rim, then another, he clawed at the wall until he was fully upright. Then, gripping the top, he hauled himself up, scrambling over the brickwork, until he gained the summit. Now he dropped down into the foliage on the other side, landing silently on the soft soil.

Moving forward stealthily, he reached the fringe of this natural cover. Pausing, he surveyed the impressive property. Three storeys high with an ageing conservatory – whose back door would not hinder him for more than a minute – and a single light burning in the upstairs window. Justin Brown was still out, meaning Anna was home alone, readying herself for bed. She was a creature of habit, who loved her beauty sleep and right on cue now, the light went out, plunging the house into darkness.

A shiver of excitement wriggled down his spine, even as his hand sought out the axe in his pocket. He wouldn't rush, he wouldn't hurry, but the moment had come. It was time for the final act.

Chapter 130

She raced across the dirty floor, eating up the yards to her bike. Helen had been locked away in her flat, turning over the pieces of this troubling case, climbing inside the head of a merciless killer, but the time for reflection was over. She had to act.

This investigation had been one of the most difficult of her career, their best endeavours stymied at every turn by a ruthless and elusive adversary, but Helen knew that they were now approaching the endgame. She had heard from Charlie that their raid had yielded nothing, save for another body and a mea culpa from Michael Stoneman, confessing to the murders. Perhaps there would be more blood spilled, perhaps he had more scores to settle and she prayed that Charlie and the team would intervene – even now they were opening up Alicia Stoneman's computer, desperate to see if she had any *other* married men on the go – but whatever happened in the next few hours, Stoneman would flee. His house had been raided, his confession found and photos of him would soon be circulating in the press, the face of the phantom revealed at last.

He wouldn't give himself up, but nor – Helen suspected – would he be easy to catch. So far, his planning, his execution of his murderous scheme had been flawless and she felt sure he would have made preparations for his eventual flight. The letter left behind by Stoneman only served to reinforce Helen's conviction that the perpetrator was determined that the final act should unfold exactly as he had envisaged. He had an escape route in mind, she felt sure of that – the question was how he would avoid detection, when the authorities at ports, airports and train stations were alerted to his identity and possible flight risk. Would he simply disappear, surfacing elsewhere in the UK under a new identity, or would he attempt to escape abroad? If so, how would he slip under their radar, when the world was looking for him?

Helen had an inkling, running the last few yards to her Kawasaki. Retrieving her helmet, she mounted her ride and fired up the ignition. Suddenly she felt powerful, back in control. The team would be busy scrambling to save other potential victims from harm, whilst running the rule over Stoneman's local haunts. They would have their hands full, whilst Helen was a solo agent, unfettered by protocol or responsibility. Lacking any jurisdiction to get involved, she still felt she had a part to play in Stoneman's capture, that her intervention might yet prove crucial. She would do it alone and unprotected, but she would do it nevertheless.

Finally, the shocking events of the last few days made sense to her. They had imagined all sorts of wicked possibilities, but the truth was simple and all the more shocking for it. A lonely, troubled man seeking comfort and love, who'd been betrayed by his younger wife. A man who would have liked to have had kids, a family, but never did. Was that why he had spared Bailey White? Was there still a semblance of decency, of humanity, in Stoneman? There was no way Helen could count on that, as he was clearly a fit, powerful man and no stranger to violence. A shipbuilder all his life, the knots he used to subdue his victims, even the weapon he used – a common-or-garden sailor's hatchet – all made perfect sense to her now. They had the why, the how, the who – now all they needed was the man himself, cuffed and in custody at Southampton Central.

Teasing the throttle, Helen inched her bike forward, picking up speed gradually as the barrier slowly rose before her. Reaching the ramp, she sped up and away, roaring down the darkened city street. She had been running scared for so long, jumping at her own shadow, but tonight, shorn of her badge, but not her vocation, she felt powerful and alive.

Chapter 131

'I want her brought in.'

Charlie stared at Peters in disbelief, silence filling Helen's office.

'I can't spare a single soul,' she protested. 'Pretty much everyone we've got is deployed in the search for Stoneman.'

'Then bring her in yourself.'

Another slap in the face.

'On what grounds?'

'Don't pretend you don't know what she's been up to,' Peters shot back. 'She visited Margaret Westlake this morning at Grange Park, then hared straight round to see Richard Westlake, despite the fact that she has no bloody right to.'

'That's news to me, but obviously I can tal—'

'Don't bullshit me, Brooks. There's no question of her doing this without your say so.'

'That's totally untrue and I resent the insinuation.'

'Resent it all you like, but I want her brought in, arrested and charged with interfering with an active investigation. Perhaps a few nights in the cells will cool her ardour.'

'But I can't leave the incident room, I'm the SIO on a major man hunt.'

'McAndrew can run things in your absence, she's got more experience than you.'

Ignoring the jibe, Charlie pushed back.

'Look, if you really want her brought in, I'll send uniform round to—'

'They won't have the balls to do it, it has to be you. So either do as I ask and help me bring the curtain down on Helen Grace once and for all, or give me *your* badge.'

Fixing her with a baleful glare, Peters held her gaze for a moment, then turned and stalked out, almost barrelling into DC Jennings as he did so. The junior officer leaped out the way, waiting until Peters was well clear of them, before entering.

'Sorry to disturb you, boss...'

He was looking at Charlie warily, aware that some bombshell had just landed.

'But you need to see this.'

Charlie snapped out of her introspection, hurrying over to her colleague.

'We've managed to access Alicia Stoneman's message history on the Sweetmeets website. Three of her current lovers have already been targeted, but there's another guy she's been seeing whose family hasn't been attacked yet – Justin Brown. He lives with his wife, Anna, in Bitterne Park, just off Drover's Way...'

Charlie was already on the move, ushering Jennings out of her office. Whatever Peters might say, her priority now was to save lives and bring Stoneman in. So she would trust her instincts, be the police officer she knew she could be – and hang the consequences.

Chapter 132

'Just pick up the phone, you little shit...'

Anna muttered angrily to herself, her mobile pressed to her ear. This was the third time she'd tried to contact her husband tonight and still he refused to pick up the phone. She'd made a personal vow to herself that if he didn't pick up this time, she would throw his belongings into a suitcase and toss it out on the street.

It rang and rang, before eventually, predictably, clicking to voicemail.

'Hi, this is Justin Brown. I'm not available right now, so—'

But why wasn't he available? That was the question. He'd told her he'd be at the Crown Plaza, doing the wedding photos for a young Asian couple, but when she'd called the hotel earlier, pretending to be a guest needing directions, they had confirmed that no such event was taking place. He had lied to her – again.

The message bleeped, prompting her to speak. She paused, thought about hanging up, then went for it anyway:

'Hi, Justin. This is your wife. Remember me? I was just calling to say don't bother coming home tonight. I'll put your things at the end of the drive for you to collect, but don't leave it too long, it's bin day tomorrow, so...'

She hung up but felt no triumph, just bone-crushing sadness.

She had been lying in the darkness for what seemed like an age, willing sleep to come, wanting to forget about her faithless husband. But she couldn't drive the dark thoughts from her brain, images of him even now panting on top of some impressionable young woman. So she'd snatched up her phone and called him, before tossing the phone onto the bed as if scalded, the desolation of her marriage now clear.

She'd known he was unreliable when she married him, that he was prone to moments of weakness. But if she'd known then what she knew now, she would've run a mile. He seemed incapable of resisting a good-looking woman and as a local photographer regularly came into contact with potential conquests at graduations, birthday parties, wedding celebrations and even baby showers. The more inappropriate the conquest, the more he seemed driven to pursue it – she knew for a fact that on one occasion he'd bedded a bride-to-be whilst her fiancé was downstairs planning his stag do. When news of that dalliance broke, she'd very nearly thrown him out, the humiliation of it almost unbearable. But he'd begged and pleaded, promised to change, and silly cow that she was, she'd relented.

But not this time. She had no interest in the identity of his latest squeeze; no, the only person that mattered to her now was herself. She'd endured too much, suffered too many indignities, but she was still young, she could start over, find a better life. First thing in the morning, she would change the locks, then call a lawyer. The fightback had begun.

Giving up on the idea of sleep, she rose, heading out of the bedroom and towards the stairs. She needed water, a large glass of ice-cold water to wash down a couple of Nurofen. She had a splitting headache and desperately needed some relief from the insistent, low-level pounding. Padding down the stairs, she slid into the kitchen, hurrying over to the fridge and pulling the door open. Bright yellow light suddenly illuminated the room and she eagerly sought out the bottle of mineral water. Tugging it out, she raised the neck to her lips and drank greedily. God, it felt good, the icy-cold trail sliding down her throat. Suddenly she felt vital, energized and alive – ready for anything.

Grasping the bottle, she shut the fridge door with a slam. As she did so, the bottle fell from her grasp, shattering on the tiled floor, as she cried out in shock. Standing in front of her, clutching a hatchet, was a muscular man with murder in his eyes.

Chapter 133

For a second, nobody moved, the intruder appearing just as shocked as she was. Then, gathering herself, Anna screamed. The sound had barely left her lips, however, before a gloved hand clamped onto her mouth cutting off the noise at source. Desperate, she flailed at him, tugging her body away, as she stumbled backwards. But his grip remained firm, his heavy boots crunching on the broken glass as he moved with her. Still she struggled, but now he yanked her towards him, raising the axe above his head. She could see the blade clearly, knew that any second now it would descend upon her, crushing her skull and rendering any struggle redundant.

Without thinking, she threw herself towards him, unbalancing him slightly, causing him to hesitate. A second's delay was all she needed and she drove her knee into his groin. Gasping, he stumbled backwards, losing his grip on her. Now Anna turned and ran, sprinting towards the front door. She'd put both deadlocks on tonight, given recent events in the city, and cursed her caution now. Her sweaty fingers slid off the key as she tried to affect her release, costing her valuable seconds, time she didn't have.

'Come on, come on…'

The bottom bolt slid across and tugging out the key, she jammed it into the top lock. As she did so, however, something heavy cannoned into her, snapping her head against the hard wood door. For a minute she thought she might faint but something – some will to survive – kept her conscious. She was seeing stars, however, and her attacker was on her again, gripping her shoulder tightly, as he raised the dreadful axe once more.

She went for his eyes, but he turned away, evading her attack, so she raked her long nails down his face instead. Another swallowed howl of pain and she was free, shaking off his grip and haring towards the stairs. Now finally she had the advantage. This was her house, she knew its shape, its idiosyncrasies, having climbed these stairs hundreds of times. She raced over the soft carpet, swinging round the post at the top and sprinting towards her bedroom. She could hear his heavy tread behind, her attacker thundering up the stairs. Could she make it in time?

Bursting into the bedroom, she ran towards the bed, snatching up her phone. This cost her further precious seconds and looking up she was horrified to see her attacker in the doorway. Crying out, she lunged away from him, feeling his hand tug at her pyjamas. Wrenching herself free, she tore towards the bathroom, covering the short distance in a second, sprinting inside. He was almost upon her now, so slamming the door, she slid the lock across.

Her assailant crashed into it, but the door held. He tried to shoulder charge it, but still it didn't yield, so Anna turned her attention to her phone, feverishly dialling 999. But even as the call connected, a noise made her look up, a noise that chilled her blood.

The sound of his axe smashing into the wooden door.

Chapter 134

She killed the engine and slid off her bike. Raising her visor, Helen turned to look at the desolate space in front of her. The dockyard was dark and deserted, lifeless save for the insistent sound of the rigging rattling in the breeze, but Helen felt sure this unprepossessing spot might yet be important.

The yard had not been easy to find. It was a private dock twenty minutes down the coast from Southampton's main harbour. It was owned by a local businessman who'd had several brushes with the law over the years and the authorities had long had their doubts about what kind of sailor might use it. Smuggling – both of people and drugs – was suspected and on one occasion the police had had to impound a boat whose owner had made a fraudulent claim on it, insisting it had gone down at sea. Helen herself had never visited this lonely spot before and, as it didn't register on Google Maps, she'd had to follow the garbled instructions of a duty officer from the narcotics team, doubling back twice on reaching dead ends, before she'd finally alighted on this deserted outpost.

Wheeling her bike into the bushes at side of the road, Helen stowed her helmet, then approached the chain-link fence. It was certainly tall, but with no razor wire on top, presented few difficulties. Helen suspected they didn't get many unsolicited visitors down here, and she was glad of it, scaling the fence easily before dropping down on the other side. Straightening up, Helen scanned the bobbing boats now tethered along various jetties. It was time for her search to begin.

The idea had struck her when she was searching Stoneman's Facebook page. He and his first wife had planned to sail the world following his retirement and in preparation Stoneman had built a thirty-footer from scratch, naming it *Lady Rosemary*. He had posted many photos of it during their later years, but after his first wife's untimely death these posts had tailed off and after his second marriage there was no mention of it all.

It wasn't hard to understand why. The ghost of the sainted Rosemary must have loomed large over Alicia's union with Michael, the boat he'd built a testament to his fervent love for his first wife. No wonder he had hidden it away, but it was telling that he hadn't got rid of it. Perhaps it was just too precious to him, or perhaps he sensed that one day he might need it, to run from this life to a brave new world. Whatever the reason for keeping it, Helen knew she had to locate it, eventually running it to ground thanks to a standing order for a mooring fee, paid promptly every month, from Stoneman's current account.

The wind was growing in strength, sails flapping and rigging snapping in the air, as if crying out in alarm at her approach. Ignoring the butterflies in her stomach, Helen pressed on, her footsteps making a dull thud as she paced down the first jetty. Her eyes were keen, her pace swift, but she came up empty-handed. Urgently she pressed on to the next jetty and, on finding nothing there, moved on to the final one. As she passed each boat, her anxiety rose. Surely he hadn't fled already?

Desolate, Helen was about to turn back to her bike when she spotted an isolated mooring at the edge of the yard, hidden away behind the office building. Intrigued, she hurried over to it, rounding the wooden shack to find a smart yacht rising and falling on the swell.

It was unmanned, the lights extinguished in the cabin, and was altogether unremarkable, but Helen felt a surge of adrenaline course through her, for etched neatly in black paint on the hull of the sturdy yacht was a name.

Lady Rosemary.

Chapter 135

'My name is Anna Brown...'

As she spoke, another blow landed, the blade splintering the wood.

'I'm at 24 Havelock Road. A man's forced his way into my house and is trying to attack me...'

The hatchet was wrenched from the door, the wood squealing in agony.

'Please come quickly. I need your help...'

Once more the door shook, the axe punching a hole in one of the panels this time.

'Units have already been dispatched to your address. Keep the door locked, barricade yourself in—'

'What do you mean, they've already been dispatch—'

'They're on their way to you now,' the operator insisted, urgently. 'Just try and sit tight, they should be there in minutes.'

Anna's head was spinning. Why were the police already on their way? Did they *know* this man was coming here?

Looking up, Anna now realized the hammering had stopped. For one glorious moment, she thought he'd given up, but then a gloved hand thrust its way through the hole in the door, feeling for the lock. Terrified, Anna raced forward, but her attacker's leather fingers found purchase and he turned the lock, flinging the door open. Anna came to a desperate, sliding halt and immediately started retreating, even as the intruder entered the room, clutching his hideous axe. Desperately, she staggered backwards, but collided with the toilet and – off balance – tumbled backwards, crashing to the floor. Her head connected sharply with the tiles, even as the breath was punched from her.

She lay there, helpless and defeated, as the old man loomed over her. He looked wild – hair unkempt, livid scratches down his face – and there was real rage in his expression. Sweating, resolved, he lifted the axe above his head. Anna knew this was the end, but still held up her hands in a desperate attempt to defend herself, hoping for a miracle. And now, as the man was about to let loose his weapon, something strange happened. He hesitated, the axe frozen in the air, as if he was having second thoughts.

And now Anna heard them. Sirens.

It was now or never, the sound of the approaching police cars getting louder all the time. Sensing the urgency, her attacker returned his attention to his prone victim, a look of grim determination on his face.

Chapter 136

The car skidded across the gravel drive, Charlie flinging open the passenger door before the vehicle had stopped. She leaped out, racing up the path, DCs McAndrew and Wilson just behind her. Without hesitation, she hurled herself at the front door, which shook violently under the assault. Pain seared through her shoulder, but recovering, she aimed a heavy boot at the lock. Once, twice, three times, then the door burst open.

'You check out the ground floor,' she barked at McAndrew. 'Wilson, come with me.'

She flew up the stairs, barely touching the carpet as she bounced from step to step. Skidding onto the landing, she tried to get her bearings, but even as she did so, a blood-curdling scream rang out nearby. Following the sound, Charlie raced towards the bedroom door, hurrying inside. As she did so, her heart skipped a beat – even in the gloom she could see the splintered bathroom door. Pulling her baton from her belt, she raced across the room, kicking the door open. She raised her arm, ready to strike... but the bathroom was empty, save for a terrified young woman, who was cowering next to the toilet, screaming for all she was worth.

'Anna Brown?'

The woman nodded.

'Are you OK?'

Anna stared at Charlie mutely.

'Are you hurt?'

The woman slowly shook her head.

'Good. And the man who attacked you, where's he?'

Anna lifted a hand, pointing to the rear of the house.

'Wilson...'

Charlie gestured to her colleague to tend to the terrified woman, as she turned and fled. Rushing into the bedroom, she hurdled the bed, flinging the window open. Beneath her, she could make out McAndrew standing in the shadowy garden.

'Anything?'

McAndrew shook her head.

'Downstairs is clear and I've done a quick tour of the garden, but...'

Charlie swore, angrily slapping the windowsill with her hand. Thankfully they had saved Anna Brown, but the perpetrator had slipped through their fingers yet again. Had they been minutes earlier it might have been a different matter, but that was academic now.

They had been close, but not close enough.

Chapter 137

His feet slapped the pavement as he hurried down the quiet street, casting anxious looks behind him. He was furious, frustrated, but also scared. For the first time since this started, he was the hunted not the hunter.

He had evaded capture by the skin of his teeth. Had he stayed to finish the job, burying his blade in Anna Brown's skull, he would have been apprehended for sure. As it was, he had only just escaped, managing to stay one step ahead of his pursuers, by scrambling onto the conservatory roof and then away down the garden to the back wall.

Some helpful citizen had replaced the bin to its correct position, so he'd had to jump, twisting his ankle badly as he landed. The injured joint throbbed hideously, his foot feeling heavy and ungainly as the swelling increased. Still, there was no question of stopping, he had to get away. Hobbling along Daventry Street, he could hear the police activity in the background and even now a squad car swung around the corner, roaring along the street towards him. Throwing himself to the ground, he sought the cover of a parked car, and mercifully the vehicle kept going, racing on towards the scene of the crime.

Exhausted, desperate, he clambered to his feet and continued his loping flight. Conflicting emotions gripped him; relief and joy at his escape tainted by disappointment and anger. He had been so close to completing his revenge, paying back those sex-obsessed dogs who'd circled his faithless wife like flies round shit, but at the very last Justin Brown had escaped punishment. He was probably the worst of the lot – a man who literally couldn't keep it in his trousers – and it burned to think that his sins would remain unpunished. Perhaps he could return to finish the job one day? Settle the score with this amoral chancer?

Even as he thought this, he knew it was pure fantasy. He would never return to Southampton, never return to this happy hunting ground. Brown was free and clear and, though that hurt, he at least had the satisfaction of knowing that White, Westlake and Sheffield had been repaid in full. They were in the darkest pit of despair now and Stoneman hoped they would remain there for a very, very long time.

If he was to evade his own form of hell, he would have to move swiftly. The police had arrived fast – too fast – meaning they must already have discovered Alicia, have worked out who was responsible for the terror that had gripped Southampton. The name Michael Stoneman would soon be infamous, his picture circulated in the media, with Border Force – the eyes of the world would be on him now. He would only get one shot at salvation.

Hurrying down Riggot Street, his heart leaped as he saw the battered Ford Ka he'd bought four weeks ago. He had left the door unlocked and wrenched it open now, climbing inside. Moments later, he was on the move, driving quickly but sensibly to the junction at the end of the road. As he did so, he heard more sirens and, looking up, saw a police van speed across the junction. He watched it go, happy that he was hidden away in his modest little hatchback, then, as it receded swiftly into the distance, he indicated right and carefully set off in the opposite direction.

Chapter 138

There was no time to waste. What Helen was doing was impulsive, illegal and potentially hazardous, as there was no telling how often Stoneman came to the boat. If she wanted to unearth final proof that it was the retired shipbuilder who was behind the recent orgy of bloodshed, she would have to do it now and she would have to do it quickly.

Her reasoning was simple. Stoneman's secret boat might well be a useful means of escape, but could also be used as a bolthole, an HQ, from which to plot and execute his grim season of revenge. According to Charlie, Alicia Stoneman had not been dead long, meaning that her husband must have carried out the first two to three murders without exciting her suspicion. She must have had her doubts, of course, given the identities of the victims, but news of the arrests they had made – first of Berman and Dordevic – would have softened or even quelled her doubts. How rash, how stumbling their investigation seemed now – by directing public attention to Martha White's stalker and later the Serbian housebreaker, had they unwittingly played a role in Alicia's murder? It would still have been a massive leap for her to think that her elderly, law-abiding husband was responsible for these awful crimes, but might she have come to that conclusion *earlier*, had they not trumpeted other suspects so loudly?

They would never know, of course, and there was no point dwelling on this now. Angry, annoyed, Helen flung open cupboards and rooted through cardboard boxes, searching for the evidence that would confirm Stoneman's evil and bring this troubling investigation to an end. To avoid suspicion, Stoneman must have prepared for each attack away from the family home and potentially even cleaned up afterwards too, each murder blood-soaked and gory. What better place than here, a haven that his wife and the wider world were oblivious to? Yet, try as she might, Helen could find nothing. She tore apart the tiny bathroom, pored over every inch of the galley kitchen, lifted the mattress in the bedroom, examined every book on the shelf, but there was nothing. The place was clean.

Marching back into the living area, Helen tugged the cushions off the sofa, revealing a storage unit underneath. Seizing the handle, she flung it open, expectant. But the interior revealed an old pair of deck shoes and a coil of rope. Straightening, Helen sighed, her body sagging with disappointment. She had raced here, full of optimism and intent, sure the final pieces of the jigsaw would fall into place on the lonely boat, but now it appeared she had trespassed for no reason, her latest misdemeanour just another wrong step.

Standing alone in the cramped galley, she scanned the interior once more, hoping for some sudden burst of inspiration. And it was as she was standing there, stewing in disappointment, that a memory came back to her, fleeting at first, then suddenly vivid. The drugs bust at the port. It was only a few days back, but seemed like a lifetime ago. Even so, the details of it flooded back and in a flash she was marching to the rear of the cabin. The smugglers they had arrested were experienced sailors, who knew every inch of their craft. As such, they had worked hard to create the most ingenious hiding place for their ill-gotten cargo, hollowing out a secret compartment in the transom, just in front of the propeller.

Making her way there now, Helen felt along the joins of what appeared to be a flat wall. To Helen's joy, it rattled slightly when touched. Teasing her fingers along the bottom lip, she now found purchase and with a heavy tug, teased the board away from the wall.

Laying it down, she peered inside the hollow and instantly her heart leaped. Inside were maps of Southampton, elasticated cord, a pair of gloves and crucially assorted jewellery scattered over the floor. Reaching in, Helen picked up an engagement ring – a gold band with three small, distinct diamonds standing upright, demanding attention. There was no doubt in Helen's mind that this was Martha White's engagement ring and, there, tossed casually on the floor next to it, was a chunky platinum necklace that she was sure belonged to Kay Sheffield. This was it – Michael Stoneman's grim hoard.

Had these baubles, these jewels, ever been important to him? Or were they, as Helen now heavily suspected, taken simply to cloud the real motive for the killings? Pointing the police towards the aggravated burglary angle, when in reality these murders were motivated by cold-hearted revenge?

Helen remained where she was, clutching the ring. It was horrible to think of the circumstances in which it had been taken, but there was some satisfaction in knowing that the perpetrator of these terrible crimes had finally been unmasked. Putting the ring back with the rest of the haul, Helen replaced the false wall. There could be no question of her calling this in, she would have to alert Charlie or McAndrew and let *them* discover it. By which point she would be long gone.

Turning, Helen was about to head for the stairs, when a loud thump above stopped her in her tracks. Frozen, she listened with growing horror as she heard footsteps pounding the deck. She had come too late, stayed too long and now she would pay the price.

Michael Stoneman had returned.

Chapter 139

'Have we heard anything from Border Force?'

Charlie was marching back to her car, DC McAndrew by her side.

'Nothing yet. No sign of Stoneman at local ports or airports. We've run his name through passengers lists for the ferries and cruise ships, but have hit a blank.'

'What about the transport police?'

'Nothing from the major train or bus stations. I also checked out car hire, but...'

She didn't need to say more, her frustration clear.

'OK, ask Jennings to hurry up with the CCTV trawl near Havelock Road. I'm guessing Stoneman must be using a car – if we can trace his vehicle, then we should be able to get a read on where he's heading, what he's planning. In the meantime, make sure Anna Brown gets the medical treatment she needs, but get a full statement off her – her eyewitness testimony will be *crucial*.'

'Sure thing.'

'When you've done that, meet me back at the incident room. I'm going there now to coordinate the search.'

Breaking away, Charlie hurried to her car, zapping it open. As she did so, her phone pinged loudly. Curious, Charlie opened the message, coming to an abrupt halt as she did so. Helen's message was short and sweet, but changed everything:

At Frampton End mooring on Lady Rosemary. *Stoneman here. Send backup ASAP.*

Chapter 140

The footsteps were growing louder. Any second now, Stoneman would throw open the cabin door and descend upon her. Desperately, Helen searched for somewhere to hide. Dare she make a break for the bathroom? Even if she did, what good would it do? It would take the police backup ten minutes, maybe more, to get to this isolated spot, by which point the fight would be over. No, the situation was hopeless. In this cramped cabin, she could run but she couldn't hide.

Stoneman had reached the cabin door, but to Helen's immense surprise, his footsteps carried on past, buying her a moment's respite. Now she came alive, padding quietly across the wooden boards, frantically scanning the surfaces for something to defend herself with when the reckoning came. She had her baton with her, but surely that wouldn't be sufficient in the circumstances? As the axe was not in Stoneman's hidey hole, it was safe to assume he had it on him, skewing the battle in his favour. It had already been used to kill four people and it seemed odds on that there would be more bloodshed tonight.

Finding nothing in the cupboards, she hurried to the kitchen. Perhaps there would be a kitchen knife, something that would give Stoneman pause for thought. But there was nothing here, save for some old cutlery and a tin opener. Rueing her luck,

Helen turned to resume her search, but was now distracted by an unpleasant mechanical noise emanating from the front of the boat. For a moment, she was confused, wondering what on earth could be making such an unholy racket, but now the boat appeared to wobble and suddenly Helen realized what was happening. Stoneman was hauling anchor.

Seconds later, the noise ceased, only to be replaced by the dull throb of the engine. Now the boat lurched more violently, Helen stumbling sideways onto the sofa. As she saved herself, straightening up despite the movement of the boat, she saw the jetty through the window, receding now as the boat pulled away. It wasn't possible, it was like some ever darkening nightmare, but it was true.

Helen was alone on the high seas with a vicious killer.

Chapter 141

He kept his hand firmly on the wheel as the boat cut through the water, moving further and further from land. The wind was high tonight, the water pitching and swelling – hardly optimal conditions for sailing, yet he couldn't have been happier this evening. The breeze whipped his face, the spray fell relentlessly on him, but still he had a broad grin on his face. After all the excitement, adrenaline and surprises of the last few hours, he could finally relax. He had made it, he had got away.

He cast a look over his shoulder, one last view of the Hampshire coast. Southampton had been his home for over thirty years and he had many happy memories, from the early years especially. But that life was irrevocably tainted now and he was pleased to be leaving behind a city synonymous for him with hurt, despair and violence. It was time to turn over a new page now – to start over – and returning his gaze to the horizon, he scanned the inky blackness ahead.

Many would have been perturbed by the view – the darkness seemed impenetrable and sailing at night was always hard. But to him it was thrilling. Right now the police were scouring Southampton for him, even as Border Force officials scanned every face that passed, searching for a killer, but he had outwitted them. He would disappear into the moonless night, vanishing from their radar for good.

How ironic it was that he was setting out on this journey, on this boat, after everything that had happened. He had been destabilized by Rosemary's death; no, he had been capsized by it. Floundering, wretched, achingly lonely, he had been desperate for company, for a woman's touch. This weakness on his part had driven him into the arms of a rapacious, cold-hearted harpy, who pretended to love him, but wanted only the security and money he provided. Friends had warned him, counselled him not to marry in haste, but he had ignored them and repented at leisure. He had been so excited by her company, by her humour, her lithe, responsive body. But almost as soon as the ink on the marriage certificate was dry, she had changed.

Now she didn't want to spend time with him, certainly wasn't interested in anything physical, married to him only in name. She'd had a tough life, abandoned by her mother, brought up by a low-life father – he could see why she'd seek a safe, practical marriage. But the callous way she treated him, the way she made little attempt to hide her infidelity, was unconscionable. It was not just the betrayal, it was the way it all meant so little to her, to the men she took to bed. To them, these sessions in cars, show homes, in the back room of an antiques shop, for God's sake, were just moments of leisure, something enjoyable to pass the time. When he made love to Rosemary, it was exactly that – a loving, tender act. But not to this lot – to them it was just a 'hook-up'. How he hated their modernity, their twisted words, their empty souls. Many was the time he longed to send them to hell, and now he had done just that.

This was never how it was supposed to be. This boat, which he had built for his one true love, was supposed to have been his future, *their* future. He and Rosemary had grand plans to sail around the world, visiting Bali, Indonesia, Australia. Exotic, faraway places full of adventure and mystery. But then her disease had intervened, with the result that the ship had never left the coast. Ironically, this was its maiden voyage. But it would not be its last.

No, he would make many journeys on *Lady Rosemary*. Of course he would have to change her name and appearance as soon as possible, get new documents for her, but after that he would be free and clear, moving around the world, changing his own name whenever necessary, always keeping one step ahead of the authorities. It wasn't an ideal lifestyle; he imagined it would be trying, expensive and perhaps lonely. But he could live with that – he'd his fill of the human race.

This was his future, a fugitive on the run, finding solace where he could. The old man and the sea. Many would have run from such a fate, but he would willingly embrace it, which is why, even though the sharp wind tore into him, Michael Stoneman continued to smile.

Chapter 142

Slamming her foot on the accelerator, Charlie urged the car on. The chain-link gate seemed to race towards them and she clung to the wheel as they crashed through the barrier, sending it barrelling up into the sky. Even as it returned to earth, Charlie slammed on the brakes, bringing the vehicle to a skidding stop. Flinging open the door, she leaped out.

'Helen?'

On the way over, she had debated whether to employ speed or stealth, opting for the former. Yes, her explosive arrival might alert Stoneman to her presence, allowing him to flee, but his capture was secondary now to Helen's safety. Anything she could do to alert the killer to the police presence would be worthwhile, might even make the difference between Helen's survival or her death at his hands.

'Helen?'

She roared her name a second time, but no response was audible over the rattling of the rigging. The following cars were pulling up behind now, providing strength in numbers, so Charlie set off, hurrying towards the line of boats on the first jetty.

'Helen, it's me. Can you hear me?'

The rigging continued to rattle and wail, slapping the masts,

465

beating out an incessant rhythm. The sound set Charlie's nerves on edge, the tension that gripped her rising with each passing second and she upped her speed, sprinting the length of the first jetty. But the *Lady Rosemary* was nowhere to be seen, so turning she retraced her steps, reaching the head of the jetty, just as Jennings emerged from the second, shaking his head.

Charlie tore past him, gobbling up the third jetty, before returning empty-handed to the site office. Just beyond the shabby building she spotted a vacant mooring and raced over to it, her eyes drawn to the sea water that stained the aged boards, a vivid contrast to the bone-dry jetties. Someone had cast off here recently, but not recently enough for Charlie's liking. Screwing up her eyes to penetrate the darkness – to cut through the fog that even now was starting to descend – she looked out to sea, but could make out no lights, no sails, nor even the silhouette of a boat. They were too late.

Tugging out her phone, Charlie dialled feverishly. But her disappointment was not long in coming.

'Hi, this is DI Helen Grace, please leave me a mess—'

She rang off, despondent. Helen was out of reach, cut off from her colleagues, isolated and vulnerable. Where was Stoneman heading? Was there any chance Helen could overpower him? Even if she could, would she able to pilot the boat to safety? Charlie stared out to sea, searching for answers, but the darkness was total, the night refusing to give up its secrets.

Chapter 143

She only had one shot at this and she had to get it right.

Standing alone in the poky cabin, as the boat pitched and tossed on the waves, Helen weighed up her options. A full-frontal assault on the fugitive would be extremely dangerous, despite the element of surprise. Stoneman was old, but also strong, athletic and a seasoned killer. Concealment wasn't an option either; at some point her adversary would repair to the cabin to shower, eat or rest, and there would be no hiding then. Which left the third option. If she could somehow let the authorities know where she was, perhaps they could ride to the rescue.

Helen knew that every seaworthy vessel had to have a marine radio, so she'd set about her hunt with energy and urgency, swiftly locating the VHF set in a purpose-built unit. Picking up the receiver in her hand, she examined the controls carefully. She'd never used one of these before and was wary of creating unnecessary noise, despite the cover provided by the howling wind and slapping waves.

The volume button was obvious enough and Helen eased this down to a low setting, before hitting the 'on' switch. The machine sprang into life, emitting a low crackle. It was set to channel one and tentatively she held down the button on the receiver.

'This is DI Helen Grace aboard the *Lady Rosemary*. Are you receiving, over?'

Nothing, just the same lifeless crackle. Flicking it to channel two, she tried again.

'This is DI Helen Grace, can you hear me?'

Nothing. Sweat crawled down her back as she tried channels three, four and five, with no response of any kind. Was there really no one out there?

Keeping her voice low, she tried each channel in turn – six, seven, eight, nine, ten. With each failure, her heart sank lower. What the hell would she do if she couldn't reach anyone? Still she tried – thirteen, fourteen, fifteen, sixteen.

'This is the *Lady Rosemary*. Do you read me, over?'

More crackling and Helen was about to move on, when suddenly she heard a voice.

'This is the UK coastguard, please switch to channel sixty-seven, over.'

'No, you don't understand—'

'We need to keep this channel clear. Switch to sixty-seven, over.'

He clicked off. Swearing quietly, Helen pumped the button feverishly until she found the requisite channel.

'Please state your position, over.'

'I don't know my position,' Helen replied sharply. 'My name is Detective Inspector Helen Grace. I'm on the *Lady Rosemary*, with Michael Stoneman who is currently wanted by Hampshire Police on suspicion of murder. I'm requesting a coastguard intercept, over.'

'Have you any idea of your position?'

'Not really, we left Frampton End mooring half an hour ago, and...'

She peered out of the porthole at the moon, which was threatening to peek from behind the dark clouds.

'…and I think we're heading in a south-easterly direction, over.'

'Can you a see a red flap near the bottom right-hand corner of your radio, over?'

'Yes, over.'

'Lift it up. Your distress button is underneath that flap. If you press and hold that for three seconds, we should be able to get a handle on your location.'

Helen obliged. She held it down and three seconds later a loud beep signalled that the coordinates had been sent. Letting go, she picked up the receiver once more. She squeezed the button down, but as she did so, a brief squawk of feedback rang out. Immediately, she released the button, stepping further away from the machine, before trying again. This time she connected cleanly.

'Distress signal sent, over.'

'Roger that,' the coastguard replied. 'Just sit tight now and we will—'

But then there was a loud bang from the deck above and the line went dead.

Chapter 144

Gripping the handle, Stoneman tugged the axe free. He had swung his weapon so fiercely that the blade had embedded itself deep into the wood, which splintered now as he retrieved it, but no matter – the cable to the radio antennae had been cut neatly in two and there would be no more communication from the *Lady Rosemary*.

The wind was getting stronger, the waves higher, the yacht rolling and pitching viciously, but Michael Stoneman was an experienced sailor, moving with speed now along the slippery deck towards the cabin door. His face was set, his determination unwavering, but still shock, anger and confusion pulsed through him. It seemed utterly impossible ... but someone was on board. Someone who was determined to give away his position, drawing the coastguard onto him. He hadn't believed his ears at first, yet in his heart he knew he'd heard it – the sharp, metallic beep of the dynamic position system, sending out the boat's coordinates. He'd fought against this notion – it was crazy – but then a sharp blast of feedback had confirmed his worst fears. Without thinking, he had cut the cable, instinct telling him that every second counted. His aim was true, the blow clean, but this was the easy part of the job. The next part, dealing with this unwelcome intruder, would be significantly more difficult.

It had to be her. It had to be Grace. But how had she done it? How on earth had she managed to get *ahead* of him, anticipating his flight from justice? How long had she known that he was responsible for the killings? He had only written his confession this morning, leaving it neatly propped up on the salt cellar for the cleaner to discover in the days to come. How then was his nemesis here, beneath his feet, intent on bringing him to justice?

Don't get distracted. Don't be thrown off course. Those questions were immaterial now, there would be plenty of time later to chew over the events of the last few days, trying to divine what tiny error had betrayed him. Right now he had to neutralize his adversary.

Reaching the cabin door, he grasped the handle. The important thing was to dispatch her as swiftly and safely as possible, then take evasive action, plotting a new course to steer him clear of any intervention by the coastguard. There was no time to plot, no time to strategize; his only option now was all-out attack.

Turning the handle, he yanked the door open and stepped inside the cabin.

Chapter 145

A sudden, violent roar made her turn. Helen was at the far end of the cabin, engaged once more in a desperate search for a weapon, but the crash of the door and howling wind beyond alerted her to the danger. Spinning, she caught sight of him. Wild and dishevelled, sea water dripping from his lank hair, Michael Stoneman descended the creaking stairs, a hatchet clamped in his hand.

She was trapped. There was no denying it. Helen desperately wanted to run, to escape this claustrophobic coffin, but where could she go? The windows were too narrow to crawl through and, even if she could get out, she would only be embracing certain death at the hands of a thrashing sea. No, her only choice was to stay and fight.

She was clutching a metal tray, the only form of defence she could find. It was pathetic, inadequate, so much so that she now saw a grim smile twist Stoneman's features.

'You shouldn't have come here, Helen.'

'Put the axe down, Michael.'

'I don't think so.'

'It doesn't have to be like this. We can talk about what's happened—'

'I think we're a bit beyond that, don't you?'

He took a step towards her, the boards groaning under his feet.

'I've killed four people.'

It was said without emotion, a cold statement of fact.

'Would have taken another with me, if your lot hadn't intervened. The fish that got away, right?'

'Michael, listen to me, it's not too late—'

'Yes, it is. That old life, that old me has gone. Took me a long time to realize it, but that man died with Rosemary. What's left is something entirely different.'

He took another step forward, his pitiless eyes never once leaving Helen.

'I can't say I care very much for this new me, but I don't intend to spend the rest of my life behind bars. No, it's time for me to disappear, start over. I won't be happy, but at least I'll be free.'

'And you can live with that, can you?' Helen demanded. 'Knowing the hurt, the anguish, the desperate grief you'll leave behind?'

'The suffering was *the whole point,*' Stoneman exploded. 'I want them to suffer, I want those faithless fucks to feel pain every day of their life. Knowing what they took for granted, what they betrayed. I won't be able to see them in the flesh, sadly, not where I'm going, but I will check in on them online, enjoying the funerals, the tributes, the gaping holes in their worthless lives...'

Still he advanced, now only a few feet from Helen.

'Look, I've radioed the coastguard, they know where we are—'

'And by the time they get here,' Stoneman interrupted, 'I'll be long gone. I'm sorry, Helen, it was never meant to end like this, but I really can't have you—'

She hurled the tray at him. Stoneman hadn't been expecting

it, throwing up his arm to protect himself, but too late. The tray bit into his forehead, ripping a large cut in the skin just above his eye. Stumbling backwards, he righted himself, then turned to her, rage gripping his features.

'You stupid bitch,' he rasped, touching his forehead, looking at his sticky red fingertips. 'You'll pay for that...'

Helen had her baton extended now, but Stoneman seemed hardly to notice it, charging towards her. She swung wildly at him, but he checked his progress, avoiding its bite, before hurling himself forwards once more. She swung at him again, but this time he caught the baton with his free hand, wrenching it away from him, and now he raised the axe above his head, ready to split her skull in two.

Both his arms were away from his body and this was what Helen had been waiting for. Her other hand, which had been dangling concealed behind her back, now shot up and gripping the pepper spray firmly, she pressed down hard. The hideous mist shot out, spewing directly towards her assailant's eyes, but at the last moment he jerked away, narrowly avoiding blindness. As it was, however, the mace spread over his face, ears, hair, her assailant crying out in agony, backing away. Helen didn't hesitate, barging past him and racing out of the cabin.

Chapter 146

She scrambled up the stairs onto the deck, skidding to a halt on the slippery surface, scarcely believing what she was seeing. When they had hauled anchor, there had been a few vague signs of mist, thin wisps drifting across the moonless sky, but now the whole boat was enveloped by a thick, cloying blanket. It crawled over Helen, chilling her skin and sapping her morale. How on earth would the coastguard locate them through this, even if they *did* have some inkling of their position? The boat was drifting fast, tossed on the waves, and now the fog obscured them from view, leaving Helen alone with her attacker. It was like something from her worst nightmares.

Hearing movement below, Helen raced to the wheel. The radio antennae was useless, Helen had worked that out already, but perhaps there might be other ways of communicating. Her eyes were instantly drawn to it – the fog horn. It was a sound she loved, having heard it hundreds of times drifting across the Solent, but today she liked it even more. Slamming her hand down, she gave it a long, sharp blast, the deep boom drifting away through the mist, then another, then another.

The last blast ebbed away, then a noise behind her made Helen turn. Stoneman had emerged from the cabin and was once more hurrying towards her. Blood caked his face, his right eyebrow was swollen and distorted, but he was moving freely, rage propelling him forward. He was on her in a flash, swinging his vicious blade at her throat. Throwing herself backwards, Helen cannoned off the wheel, then crashed to the floor, narrowly avoiding Stoneman's desperate lunge. She hit the deck hard, her ribs smacking the unforgiving wood. She howled in pain, but there was no sympathy, no mercy to be found here and Stoneman was upon her again. Scrabbling down the deck, Helen sought any means of escape, her eyes alighting on the mast. Her pursuer was close behind and she threw herself towards it, grasping at the rigging. If she could scale the teetering tower perhaps she could buy herself some time, maybe long enough for the cavalry to arrive.

She grabbed hold of one of cables and planted a foot on the mast, ready to climb. As she did so, however, she heard a deafening cry, as Stoneman launched himself at her. Without thinking, she pushed off hard, propelling herself away from the mast. She was only just in time, the axe blade slamming into the fibreglass with a sickening crunch. Helen now found herself sliding towards the prow of the ship, unable to arrest her progress. Moments later, she came to a sudden halt, her head butting up hard against the metal rail. Dazed, in pain, she clambered to her feet once more, only to find her pursuer moving in for the kill.

Trapped in the pointed prow of the boat, there was nowhere for Helen to run to. Sensing this, Stoneman bore down on her, axed raised. The craft was lurching on the waves, rising and falling violently, and once more Helen slipped, saving herself by clinging onto the safety cable which threaded through the metal rail, the only barrier now between her and the foaming sea. The cable supported Helen, but also trapped her, hemming her in at the prow. Stoneman took full advantage of her predicament, swinging a low blow that caught her by surprise. She swung her legs away, trying to flatten herself against the rail, but too late – the blade tore across her left thigh, cutting a nasty gash in the side of her leathers.

The pain was awful, but she swallowed down a scream, unwilling to give Stoneman the satisfaction. Smiling in triumph, he launched the axe again. Throwing herself backwards, Helen cannoned into the rail, before bouncing back towards the blade. She tried to arrest her momentum, but to no avail, the axe raking across her belly.

For a moment, Helen thought she was going to pass out. Pain ripped through her, agony so intense that it rendered her powerless to move. Raging like the sea that surrounded them, Stoneman raised the hatchet high above his head, then brought it down with all his might. Helen threw herself to the right, the blow missing her by inches, the blade neatly cutting the safety cable, before embedding itself in the metal rail beneath. Cursing wildly, Stoneman tugged the hatchet free. Helen, on her hands and knees amidst the severed cabling, scrambled to a vertical position, aware that there was now nothing but a broken rail between her and the water.

Again Stoneman came, swinging wildly at her head. Helen could picture the carnage as her skull imploded under its weight, and in desperation raised a hand to defend herself. She caught Stoneman just beneath the wrist, gripping his skin tightly and twisting for all she was worth. Surprised, off guard, her assailant howled in pain, releasing his hold on the axe, the weapon hitting the deck before bouncing into the choppy waters below. Stoneman was up close and personal now, Helen could feel his breath on her face, so she didn't hesitate, launching her head forwards, catching Stoneman on the bridge of his nose. Crying out, her assailant staggered backwards, before righting himself,

M.J. ARLIDGE

staring at Helen with hollow-eyed hatred, as blood streamed down his face.

For a moment, the pair stared at each other, the boat pitching wildly as the sea roared. Helen prayed that, robbed of his weapon, Stoneman would see sense, surrender even, but instead he came again, closing in for the kill.

'Give yourself up, Michael. It's over…'

He glowered at her, his mind consumed by fury and violence.

'How right you are…' he hissed back.

His eyes locked onto hers. Helen had hoped to see despair, exhaustion, even regret there. But instead she saw the same burning rage that had assailed Marko Dordevic just before *he* had charged her. Instinctively, Helen crouched down, bracing herself for history to repeat itself, but still it chilled her to the bone when Stoneman breathed:

'Let's finish this together.'

He charged at her, roaring out his anger and frustration. His burly frame cannoned into her and the two bodies crashed through the damaged rail, careering off the boat towards the churning water below. Now the world turned upside down. Disoriented and dizzy, Helen thought for a moment she was flying, plunging to her doom, then suddenly she was yanked sharply backwards, the surprised Stoneman continuing his terrifying descent alone. Pain tore through Helen, bringing tears to her eyes, but looking up, she was pleased to see that the severed safety cable that she'd coiled around her wrist seconds before was holding. Dordevic had made a fool of her, but she wasn't going to fall for the same trick twice.

Below, Stoneman was flailing in the water, hands outstretched. Helen's first instinct was to reach out to him, to draw her attacker back to the boat, but the murderous anger in his eyes made her pause and in that second all was lost, Stoneman disappearing beneath the waves. Helen continued to hang from the front of the boat, her battered body thrown repeatedly against the prow. Her grip on the cable was beginning to loosen, the fight going out of her, but with one last desperate lunge, she brought her spare hand up to the remnants of the broken rail, clasping it firmly.

Screaming in agony, Helen hauled herself up, dragging her carcass back onto the boat, before discarding the cable and collapsing in a bloody, exhausted heap on the deck, clutching her damaged wrist. And it was as she lay there, helpless and broken on the listing ship, that she finally glimpsed the coastguard's prow emerging from the mist.

Epilogue

Chapter 147

He strode purposefully along the corridor, scattering bystanders in his wake. The task that lay ahead would be challenging, distressing even, so there was no point prevaricating – when a limb is infected, the best thing to do is chop it off quickly and cleanly. That's exactly what Chief Superintendent Alan Peters intended to do. It was time to bring the curtain down on Helen Grace's career at Southampton Central.

All eyes turned as he barged into the incident room, several of the junior staff rising from their desks. Scanning the room, Peters swiftly located Charlie Brooks, hidden away in her office with DC McAndrew, gesturing to the pair to join him.

'OK, guys, gather round,' he said in an affable tone, as the two women approached the semi-circle of officers that now surrounded him.

'Something wrong?' Brooks asked, clearly alarmed by his sudden appearance.

'On the contrary,' he replied generously. 'In fact, I came here to congratulate you all. We've had a couple of days now to digest what happened the other night and I must say your quick thinking and bravery not only saved a life, but also helped bring a vicious killer to book.'

This was not strictly true, though no one corrected him.

Michael Stoneman's body had washed up on a beach in Somerset early this morning. His reign of terror was over, but the justice that the White family and Stoneman's other victims craved would be forever denied them.

'The commissioner is very pleased with the result, as am I, so I wanted to thank you in person for a job well done. I also wanted to confirm that there will be changes to the unit, now that the dust has settled. As you know, DI Grace is suspended, pending a full internal investigation, so I'm confirming today that DS Brooks' temporary promotion to Detective Inspector will be made permanent with immediate effect.'

Silence in the room, so Peters continued quickly.

'I'm sure you'll all agree that she deserves it, so can I invite you to put your hands together and congratulate your new team leader?'

There was a smattering of applause, which quickly died out, as the assembled officers clocked Charlie's reaction.

'You can't be serious,' she eventually said, her face ashen.

'There's no need to thank me,' Peters replied, laughing awkwardly. 'As I say it's well deserved and—'

'What about Helen?'

'What about her? She's not part of this unit anymore, so—'

'She *is* this unit.'

Brooks spat the words at him.

'Without her, it would be nothing, *we* would be nothing.'

'You're exaggerating and besid—'

'Do I need to remind you, sir, that it was Helen who intercepted Stoneman, who predicted his attempted escape, who broke this bloody case?'

'You do yourself, and your colleagues, a disservice, DI Brooks.'

'It's DS Brooks. And might I also remind you that she risked her life to bring him to justice.'

'Ignoring the fact that she was suspended from the Force and breaking all protocols.'

'She put her body on the line, as she's done dozens of times over the years, because she cares, because she believes in what we do here, because she is a natural leader.'

Brooks' eyes seem to linger on him, her expression disdainful and hostile.

'This unit, this team, cannot survive without her. I understand there's an internal enquiry that needs to be carried out, but we know what happened, we know that Hudson ambushed her, that she was just defending herself.'

'So she *claims*.'

'The testimony of her neighbours has made that abundantly clear. They heard Helen arrive home *seconds* before the fatal fall. There was no argument on the landing, no "context" to the incident—'

'That's for the enquiry to decide,' Peters replied coldly, surprised by the force of her resistance. 'But whatever happens, one thing is clear. DI Grace has no future at this station.'

'You've decided that already, have you? Without any regard to due process?'

'I would have thought it was self-evident.'

His tone was firm and determined, wanting to put an end to this skirmish.

'Well, I can't accept it,' Brooks replied swiftly. 'I won't.'

'Do I take it from that that you want to *refuse* your promotion? Languish at DS level, as you've done for so many years.'

'No,' Brooks countered, shaking her head vigorously.

Peters smiled inwardly. He'd never known an officer refuse a promotion, whatever their professed scruples might be.

'I don't want your promotion,' Brooks continued. 'In fact, I don't want to be part of this team without Helen at its helm. I resign.'

He stared at her in consternation, not quite believing what he'd just heard. But Brooks quelled any doubts by tossing her warrant card onto the desk in front of him. There was a moment's stunned silence, then Peters heard another voice.

'Me too.'

DC McAndrew stepped forward, throwing *her* warrant card onto the desk.

'And me.'

Now it was DC Reid's turn, adding his card to the growing pile. Peters stared at them, aghast. His three most senior CID officers had just resigned en masse.

'Sorry, sir,' Malik said, as she followed suit, investing the last word with as much derision as she could.

Barely had the words left her lips, than DC Jennings stepped forward, adding his badge. All eyes in the room now turned to DC Japhet Wilson, the newest member of the team.

'What about you, DC Wilson?' Peters asked scornfully. 'Are you going to throw away your career *too*?'

There was a long pause, as the new DC wrestled with his conscience, forced into a position he never thought he'd have to face.

'Guess I'll have to,' he eventually said, discarding his warrant card. 'Helen Grace was the whole reason I came here.'

And now they turned as one to Peters. He stared at them, for once unable to muster a pithy comeback. It was madness, utter madness, but their resolve, their determination, was crystal clear and in that moment Detective Superintendent Alan Peters realized how badly he'd misjudged the situation.

He had come here wanting, *expecting*, to bury DI Helen Grace, but perhaps it was *him* that was finished.

Chapter 148

This was it. They had reached the end.

Alex Blythe hammered the keyboard, his fingers a blur as he typed out Siobhan Martin's email address. He was livid with Nicholas, but just as furious with himself, realizing now how badly he'd misjudged this would-be assassin. He'd needed someone powerful, determined and above all desperate, someone he could strong-arm into destroying Helen Grace. On paper Nicholas Martin seemed the perfect fit, but his selection had proved disastrous – first the teacher had tried to wriggle off the hook, then he'd reluctantly tried and failed to ambush Grace, before attempting to bribe his persecutor into releasing him from his bond. Blythe had obviously put the little voyeur back in his place, reminding Martin of the deal they had struck, expecting him to come to heel instantly... but instead Martin had vanished. There had been no contact at all in the last three days, during which time Helen Grace had gone about her daily business entirely unmolested.

Despite all this – despite Nicholas Martin's failure to make good on his promise – Alex Blythe had held off punishing him. Part of him still hoped the teacher would finally act, because in truth there *was* no one else. The two other candidates Blythe contacted had both called his bluff, challenging him to make good on his threats, preferring disgrace to murder. They had correctly judged that Blythe wouldn't make any communication with the outside world unless it was absolutely necessary, for fear of being traced. Martin, however, had buckled quickly, terrified of losing his family, his position, of finally being exposed as the pathetic pervert he was. But in the end he wasn't made of the right stuff, unable to sacrifice his soul to save his livelihood. And now that Martin's failure was evident, he'd gone to ground, turning his back on his former psychiatrist. Numerous phone calls had gone unanswered, which told Blythe all he needed to know. Was Martin even now confessing to his wife? His colleagues? Attempting to diminish, even explain away his wrongdoing, even though it was both distasteful and criminal. Well, he was damned if that worm was going to get away scot-free. Alex Blythe knew that he would be burning his bridges by exposing the schoolteacher, but his rage precluded any other course. The man *had* to be punished.

The incriminating video clips took a few seconds to upload, Alex Blythe using this time to add Martin's parents' email addresses to the CC line, before finally pressing 'send'. It was with a heavy heart, but at least he would destroy one life in the process. He knew that it was a pyrrhic victory, however, signalling the end his long pursuit of Helen Grace.

Rising, he crossed to the window. Would it be mad to return to England? To pursue Grace himself? It would be insanely risky, but what was the alternative? A life spent skulking in the shadows, moving across the continent from provincial hotel to provincial hotel, whilst she thrived on the South Coast? No, it didn't bear thinking about. But heading back to Southampton? Into the lion's den? Surely he couldn't be that stupid?

Abandoning these idle fantasies, Blythe crossed to his bed. His holdall lay open and he packed quickly now, throwing his few possessions inside. He had planned to stay longer, but Martin's radio silence was making him nervous and in his darker moments he'd convinced himself that the teacher had sided with his enemies to bring him in, allying himself with Grace, rather than destroying her. He was probably being paranoid, but there was no point taking chances.

Returning to the desk, he picked up his laptop, bending down to pull the charger from the plug socket. Straightening up, he was about to cross back to the bed when he spotted something. Movement outside. Hurrying to the window, he peered through the net curtains, a pulse of alarm coursing through him. Three unmarked cars had pulled up outside the hotel, blocking entry or exit. Even now, sober-looking men in suits were climbing out, warrant cards open and ready. It was impossible but true. They had found him.

Moments later, Blythe was pounding down the corridor, his holdall bouncing on his back, as he raced away from his room. He could already hear loud voices downstairs, the French CID officer in charge barking instructions to his team. Reaching the main stairwell, Blythe peered over the bannister, alarmed to see officers already scurrying upwards. His room was only on the second floor, they would be here in seconds, so he didn't hesitate, marching swiftly along the corridor and pushing out through the fire exit.

As the door swung lazily to, Blythe thought he heard an alarm ring out within. Increasing his pace, he skipped down the metal staircase, keeping noise to a minimum. His car was parked at the rear of the building, in a small car park – if he could make it there he might still be OK. Hitting ground level, he kept close to the wall, reaching the rear of the hotel unimpeded.

Now he paused, craning round the side of the building to check for danger. To his relief, there was no one in sight. It was now just a thirty-second trot to his car. Once behind the wheel, he could speed down the side alley and be away before they had even realized he'd gone.

'Not far now, Alex,' he muttered to himself, as he scurried towards his car, trying to calm his nerves.

Two minutes more and it would all be over. He was twenty yards from the car, now ten, now five. This was it, he was free and clear. With a sigh of relief, he pulled at the handle of the door... then suddenly lurched sideways. Confusion and disorientation gripped him, followed shortly afterwards by searing pain, as he hit the ground, a heavy weight pressing down on him. The holdall slid from his shoulder, freeing him, but even as he struggled to regain his footing, he felt a bony knee press into his back, whilst his hands were unceremoniously yanked behind him. He was breathless, in shock, but there was no question now that he had been wrong – the police *had* been monitoring the car park, had been waiting for him, and now they had their prize.

As the handcuffs pinched his wrists, fury and outrage ripped through him, only to be immediately replaced by a crushing sense of hopelessness. For so long all powerful, a sinister puppet master destroying lives on a whim, now it was *he* who was destroyed and defeated. So, even as the arresting officer read him his rights, keeping him pressed to the floor, Alex Blythe neither fought back nor acknowledged the officer's presence, instead lying still on the floor, his face pressed to the dirty tarmac, stonily silent in defeat.

Chapter 149

Helen stared down at the body, feeling no triumph, just an overwhelming sense of sadness. A dog walker had discovered Michael Stoneman early this morning, the fugitive's corpse lying face down in the surf. In life, he had been a powerful, vital man, but now, coated in weed and sand, he seemed pitiful.

Why did some cases affect you more than others? It was hard to say, but Helen couldn't deny the pit in her stomach, a nagging sense of nausea, as she looked down at her attacker. The murders he'd carried out were wicked in their planning and depraved in their execution, yet Helen knew that Stoneman hadn't been born bad. That was why his terrifying death, fighting the waves that fell remorselessly upon him, occasioned only sorrow.

Had life panned out as he'd planned – if his beloved wife Rosemary had beaten cancer – then Stoneman would have seen out his days as a happy, law-abiding citizen. But his life had gone badly awry, the hurt and indignities he'd suffered after her passing, robbing him of his moral compass and ultimately his sanity. His rage, his grief, had been dissipated momentarily by his relationship with Alicia, only to return with double force when he realized how badly he'd tarnished Rosemary's memory by remarrying badly and in haste. How he must have raged at himself – for his impulsiveness, his stupidity, his blindness – his self-hatred gnawing away at the goodness within him, until all that remained was anger, despair and violence.

Helen would never excuse what he'd done – how could she? – but nor would she damn him for his actions, and if she could have reached out a healing hand, restoring him to life so he could face a just punishment, she would have done so. She hadn't wanted it to end like this, despite his murderous attack on her, and it gave her no satisfaction. Just another death on her conscience.

'You all done, ma'am? Forensics would like to get cracking.'

Helen turned to see the eager detective sergeant from Avon and Somerset Police hovering.

'Of course, it's all yours. Thanks again for letting me come down.'

'Least we could do.'

He stepped back, clearing a path for her, his expression one of unconcealed awe. Thanking him, Helen headed on her way, but as she reached the coastal path that led up to the cliff above, she paused to look back at Stoneman's lifeless body. This was a man who had lived, loved and lost. Who felt *too much* perhaps, his grief and anger eventually destroying him. A man who ultimately had been unable to cope with the sharp sting of betrayal.

Something Helen knew a lot about.

Chapter 150

'I fucked up. No other way of putting it. I'm really sorry for the way I behaved. I had no right to treat you in that way...'

The words tumbled from her, the novelty of apologizing rendering her tongue-tied and clumsy. Emilia could feel herself flushing, colour rising to her cheeks as Sam sat opposite her, dispassionate and silent.

'More than that,' she continued. 'You were right. Now, that's not an easy thing for me to say, believe me...'

She smiled at him, attempting humour, but received nothing in return.

'I... I can be cruel and unfeeling. I've intruded upon people's grief – their misery – countless times, without any real thought for the pain I might be causing them. And I know I don't fully weigh up the effect of my actions, my words, either, and I should, because what I write, what we print, has an impact. I can't stop asking those questions, being in those situations, but perhaps I might approach them in a more considered, more mindful way and think more carefully about what I write, *before* I write it.'

This wasn't some half-baked humble pie to appease her date, she *really* meant it. Something *had* changed in her these last few days; she was more circumspect now – so much so that she had effectively pardoned Helen Grace, opting not to report the assault on her and burying any mention of her involvement in the death of a former police officer, which had been widely reported as a tragic accident. This kernel of self-knowledge, this semblance of restraint, was perhaps the true legacy of Emilia's involvement with Joseph Hudson.

'Anyhow, that's my mea culpa, the professional bit, at least. On a personal level...'

Emilia could feel herself turning crimson, but pressed on:

'I miss you. There, I've said it. I don't know what these feelings are – we hardly know each other – but whatever they are, they're strong. So, if you've just come here to accept my apology, then let's shake hands and part as friends. But if you are prepared to forgive me and start again, I'd like us to try and make a go of whatever "this" is. Because... because I would be really sad if we didn't.'

She sat back in her chair, exhausted. Sam watched her for a minute, then replied:

'You know what, Emilia...'

She tensed herself for the blow.

'...that's the nicest thing anyone's ever said to me. So, apology accepted and, yes, let's date the shit out of this thing. I'd be an idiot to let you go because of a stupid argument that was mostly my fault. My sister always says I'm too fond of the view from my high horse...'

Emilia laughed, moved and more relieved than she could say.

'As for you,' Sam continued. 'You may be a hard arse, with a spectacular black eye...'

He reached out, running a finger down her cheek.

'...but guess what? I like the look of you.'

Leaning across the table, he kissed her gently on the lips. Emilia felt her heart lurch, overwhelmed with emotion. She was shocked and surprised.

But more than that, she was happy.

Chapter 151

'Honestly, I wish you'd been there. I've never seen Peters speechless before... and, frankly, I enjoyed it.'

Helen stood with Charlie on the cliff top, stunned by what she was hearing.

'Even so, Charlie, you shouldn't have done it. I can fight my own battles, plus you have your career, your family to think about—'

'No way, I owed you,' Charlie countered forcefully. 'I've been no help to you these past few weeks, far too bound up in my own worries—'

'That's not true.'

'Yes, it is, which is why this morning's little show of force was both necessary and deserved. The MIT can't function without you.'

Helen didn't believe that for a second, but that didn't make it any less enjoyable to hear.

'So what happened after that?' Helen asked, all curiosity.

'He slunk off without another word. Last I heard he was holed up in his office. Licking his wounds, perhaps, or even better writing his resignation letter.'

'One can dream,' Helen said wistfully, breaking into a smile.

'Anyway, I wanted to say sorry. For being distracted, off the pace—'

'You never need to apologize to me, Charlie. You know that.'

'But I've hardly helped, have I? Given everything you had on your plate already.'

Helen shrugged and turned away to admire the view once more.

'What's the latest on Blythe?'

'They traced his last phone call to Martin to a village in Normandy. French police picked him up at a hotel there this morning.'

'And they're *sure* it's him?'

'Absolutely. They've printed *and* swabbed him. Plus, he was threatening everyone he came into contact with, with dire vengeance.'

'That sounds like Blythe,' Helen replied ruefully.

'So I guess that's over then?'

'I hope so. Nicholas Martin was the only one desperate enough to play ball and even he couldn't do it in the end. I think Alex Blythe may have just run out of accomplices.'

'Amen to that.'

The pair stood silent for a moment, the fading sun bathing them in a golden glow, then Charlie spoke once more:

'Well, I'd best be getting back. Give this baby another run out...'

They both turned to take in the sparkling yellow Mustang parked up by the roadside.

'The original girl racer,' Helen replied, laughing.

'You better believe it. I know it's just a car... but I *bloody* love it.'

Charlie didn't need to explain why. Helen was happy and

relieved that things had worked out so well for her, her suspicions about Steve proving way off the mark.

'Well, drive safely...' she added.

'That's rich coming from you.'

'...and thank you, Charlie, I owe you.'

'As if,' Charlie replied, throwing open the driver's door.

Helen watched her friend drive away, more moved than she could say by her unswerving loyalty. As a child, Helen had thought she'd never elicit any affection, sympathy or love and it was still a profound surprise to her that there were people out there who had her back, who would protect her come what may. For the first time in months, Helen felt safe, happy, even optimistic about the future. Stoneman's reign of terror was over, Blythe was safely behind bars and, with the team backing her to the hilt, Helen was determined to fight tooth and nail to get herself reinstated as the head of the MIT at Southampton Central.

Turning once more to drink in the sunset, Helen felt a surge of hope and happiness. Perhaps tomorrow *would* be a better day after all.

Credits

M.J. Arlidge and Orion Fiction would like to thank everyone at Orion who worked on the publication of *Cat and Mouse* in the UK.

Editorial
Emad Akhtar
Celia Killen

Copy editor
Marian Reid

Proof reader
Clare Wallis

Audio
Paul Stark
Amber Bates

Contracts
Anne Goddard
Paul Bulos
Jake Alderson

Design
Debbie Holmes
Joanna Ridley
Nick May

Editorial Management
Charlie Panayiotou
Jane Hughes
Alice Davis

Finance
Jasdip Nandra
Afeera Ahmed
Elizabeth Beaumont
Sue Baker

Marketing
Tom Noble

Publicity
Leanne Oliver

Production
Ruth Sharvell

Operations
Jo Jacobs
Sharon Willis
Lisa Pryde
Lucy Brem

Sales
Jen Wilson
Esther Waters
Victoria Laws
Rachael Hum
Ellie Kyrke-Smith
Frances Doyle
Georgina Cutler